Chronicles of the Medieval Underworld

Vol. 1: Thurmond's Saga

Vol. 2: Castle of the Red Contessa

Available at all major online retailers and

robertjohnmackenzie.com

THE
BATTLE OF
GORGONHOLM

CHRONICLES OF THE MEDIEVAL UNDERWORLD,
VOL. 3

ROBERT JOHN
MACKENZIE

Design and Distribution by Bublish, Inc.

ISBN: 978-1-64704-224-0 (paperback)
ISBN: 978-1-64704-225-7 (eBook)

TO THE MAD RIVER BOYS

THE
BATTLE OF
GORGONHOLM

CONTENTS

Glossary of Characters

Asmodeus: wizard of phenomenal ability

Sir Bartholomew Staynes: mercenary leader and Sarah's half-brother

Bodo: one-legged carpenter

Count Borgo: archfiend specializing in all things military

Sir Brandon Phugg: sheriff of Avincraik

Brodar Eaglebeak: warchief of the Blue Horse People

Cob: Roscoe's man-at-arms

Drax: mercenary in the company of Sir Bartholomew Staynes

Dreego: burner of charcoal and taverns

Fergis mac Brude: Ard Righ of the Keltins

Florio: Roscoe's reeve

Kak: treacherous peasant

Grinder: Blue Horse warrior

Gustavus: Lord Ubo's sergeant-at-arms

Brother Jerome: cellarer of Gray Friar's monastery

Brother Julian: choir master of Gray Friar's monastery

Sir Lorenzo di Prativentosi: adventurous young knight

Malachai: magician of fearsome power

Oengus mac Brude: brother of Fergis

Pons: treacherous Road Guard

Pozi: Bodo's adopted daughter

Earl Ralf Mortimer: Earl of Avincraik

Roscoe Franklin: Thurmond's mentor and Adventurer in good standing

Sarah: Thurmond's closest friend and fledgling Adventurer

Slow Pate: Lord Ubo's serf

Sir Seymour Guff: knight in the service of Earl Ralf

Thurmond: fledgling Adventurer and our hero

Lord Torgul Bonelip XXIII: doughty dwarf and Adventurer in good standing

Tuck: Roscoe's man-at-arms

Lord Ubo Futz: Lord of Skut

Uncle: headman of Skut

Wat: Roscoe's man-at-arms

Wynkyn Whoorm: Earl Ralf's chamberlain

Zeb the Prophet: fanatical blowhard

PART 1

CROSSED
STARS

CHAPTER 1

THE CALL OF THE
BLACK STONE

The stars twinkled merrily overhead, entirely unconcerned with the comings and goings of men, and yet inevitably intertwined with their destinies. Their influence was undeniable.

Consider for a moment the unlikely alignment of three certain stars directly over Skut, a tiny hamlet nestled deep in a forest glen several leagues south of Gorgonholm and a few more to the east. What else could account for the strange events that occurred there?

Skut was so far removed from the other villages of the county of Avincraik that few non-natives were even aware of its existence. Over the generations, the lack of fresh blood had caused its inhabitants to develop certain unique physical characteristics—curiously narrow heads, fishy eyes too far apart, ridiculously long arms, hands with fat, stubby fingers, and a loose-kneed, shuffling gait. Their intelligence was abysmally low, the result of too many cousins marrying cousins.

One such specimen was a woodcutter by the name of Slow Pate. He had never exhibited any traits suggesting ambition, authority, or nimbleness of mind. Yet, when the combined light of those three stars beamed down upon his filthy hovel, he was a man transformed.

On that remarkable night, he awoke from the most compelling dream in which a deep and fearsome voice had commanded him to dig beneath an ancient oak, where he was to find a wonderful treasure. The woodcutter leapt from his bed with uncharacteristic zest. He was out the door in an eyeblink with a shovel in his hand. But his frantic delving revealed not a golden trove only a flat, black stone—square cut, some four feet wide, and three times as long. Immensely heavy. The stone was just the thing a man might set in place to thwart the removal of a buried hoard.

Poor Slow Pate. Lifting the huge stone would demand the strength of many men and require tools he did not possess. Great wealth was almost within reach, but he could think of no way to bring this wonderful treasure into his hand.

Thus, the luckless woodcutter did what he and his neighbors always did when faced with a problem—he sought out Uncle, the headman of Skut. This decision would be costly, for the headman was certain to take a large share of the treasure for himself. But only Uncle could muster the resources to pull the great stone from the earth.

Despite his congenial nickname, Uncle was no blood kin to Slow Pate, nor did he exhibit any of the warm, nurturing qualities one might expect from a close family member. Rather, he was greedy, self-serving, and cruel. His position as headman was secured neither by his sage advice nor mature discernment, but by his immense size and willingness to use fist, club, or knife to enforce his dictates. Uncle was a dangerous fellow.

Slow Pate approached Uncle's cottage just as the sun was climbing above the treetops of the surrounding forest. This was perilous, as Uncle might be suffering the ill-effects of the previous night's drinking. Or he could be taking his pleasure with one of the village women. In any case, he would not be pleased with a visit from a hapless dimwit like Slow Pate.

Before knocking, the frightened woodcutter paused and listened at the door. Loud snoring within confirmed that the headman had not yet risen. Slow Pate hesitated, afraid. Waking Uncle would most surely rouse his ire.

Slow Pate summoned what little courage he had and knocked. When the snores continued uninterrupted, he knocked harder and called out softly. When this failed to elicit a response, he pounded on the door and shouted.

The snoring ceased, and after a few moments, the cottage door swung open. Uncle stood there, naked, hairy, and huge. His scarred face twisted with disgust upon seeing Slow Pate standing at his threshold.

"Whadda you want, you little string of snot? Why'd you wake me up? You better have a damn good reason, or you'll get beat like you never been beat."

Slow Pate stated his purpose as best he could—verbal expression had never been his particular gift. Uncle listened with growing irritation until he at last grasped the meaning of the words. Then his response was explosive! He ran fully nude down the length of Skut's single street, bellowing for the villagers to come forth.

And come they did. The magical word *treasure* filled the normally lethargic serfs with unprecedented enthusiasm. At Uncle's command, they sprinted to fetch spades for digging, ropes for hauling, wooden timbers for bracing, oxen for pulling.

Slow Pate cursed silently, for he now saw that his share of the treasure—*his treasure*—would be woefully small. Uncle would not care that it had been his dream that brought such good fortune. Nay, he would claim all gold for himself and then dole out pitiful handfuls to his favorites. Slow Pate had never been one of those. He might receive nothing at all.

Regretfully, the woodcutter led the entire population of Skut to the site of his discovery. They fell to work at once. By midmorning, the dirt had been removed from all four sides of the stone, revealing a slab about a foot thick. The village carpenter and his sons erected a stout wooden tripod at one end of the excavation. A heavy rope was then passed beneath the stone, run through a block and tackle atop the tripod, and attached to a yoke of oxen.

At Uncle's signal, a plowman gave the beasts a smart blow with a switch, driving them forward. Ever so slowly, the black stone was drawn from the ground until it stood upright, twice the height of a tall man. The exultant villagers jumped in the hole, shovels flying, lusting for the riches that would soon be theirs.

Yet nary a single bronze farthing came to their avaricious fingers. They dug and dug, but nothing did they find. In his disappointment and frustration, Uncle turned on Slow Pate and beat him bloody.

Tired and resentful, the villagers unyoked their oxen, coiled their rope, shouldered their spades, and headed for home. None seemed aware that the great stone, no longer supported by rope and tripod, continued to stand, seemingly of its own volition.

Nor did they note the cold, leering visage in the stone's rough texture—fashioned not by any human hand but formed naturally from the living rock.

That night, another strange thing occurred. Slow Pate's dream voice returned. It was different this time, promising not treasure, but something even more desirable—revenge upon the odious Uncle. Without hesitation, Slow Pate took up his reaping sickle and slipped silently from the door of his hut.

The woodcutter was not the only one to hear voices that night. The diggers, the builders, the plowman—all of whom had lent a hand in the raising of the stone—were roused by a call to cast off the restraints that kept them in want and degradation, to know the bliss of limitless power.

Late that night, drawn by some uncanny instinct, they gathered around the stone. Some brought gifts for their new idol. Slow Pate laid Uncle's severed head reverently at its base.

In his private chamber in Castle Skut, Lord Ubo Futz awoke with a start. Somebody was whispering in his ear, but when he looked about, no one was there. A woman's voice, he was certain. But who would dare to disturb his sleep in such a manner?

Certainly not one of the sluttish servant girls he often pulled into his bed—they knew better. And not his wife, that sorry sack of bones—she was smart enough to keep her distance. *Who then?* No one in his household would be so foolish.

He shouted into the darkness.

"Who's there? Come forward! Show your face!"

When no one appeared, Ubo began to have doubts. Perhaps it had been a dream. Or a ghost—the castle abounded with unquiet spirits, many of whom bore him an abiding grudge. Putting the matter from his mind, Lord Ubo turned over and closed his eyes.

The whispers returned at once. Alarmed, Ubo attempted to rise but found himself pinned, as if something heavy had oozed onto his chest. He tried to shout, to command the unseen presence to be gone, but no sound came from his throat.

Ubo, the dread lord of Futz, began to panic, afraid that this thing—whatever it was—was about to stop his breath. But when his lungs continued to draw air, he gradually regained his composure. The whispering thing, it seemed, did not intend to kill him, but it did to want to be heard. So, he listened, and as he did, he slowly comprehended.

The voice was soft, teasing, seductive—the voice of a beautiful woman. It revealed several stark truths Ubo had never before considered, urging him to rise and act upon this new knowledge without delay. To be the man he was born to be.

He resisted at first, but the whisperer continued to tempt, prompt, and prod until he could stand it no longer. At last, he flung himself from bed, donned his clothes, and strode to the stable. There, he kicked the sleeping groom and bade him saddle his favorite palfrey, a chestnut mare of great speed and agility. Then, he rode into the gloom of the night.

Ubo's arrival at the stone filled the worshipers with trepidation, for he had never been a mild or understanding overlord. Indeed, they expected the most severe of punishments for their forbidden devotions. Idolatry was, after all, a crime against all decency or reason. Heretics were sometimes burned alive by the holy church.

They were surprised and confused, therefore, when Ubo did not drive them back to the village with a whip. Rather, he dismounted and, leading his mount by the reins, approached slowly and quietly until he stood directly beneath the great, looming slab. Then, to the utter astonishment of his tenants, Ubo drew his dagger and slashed the great veins in his mare's neck, spraying blood upon the stone's black surface.

As the beast collapsed, Lord Ubo Futz bent his knee and pledged his faith.

The assembly began a slow, tuneless chant. Hands clasped in supplication, eyes squeezed shut, they repeated it over and over, over and over. And the harder they prayed, the greater the stone's power waxed.

Its call reached deep into the forest, beckoning uncouth, fur-clad woodsmen who emerged from the shadows to join the villagers. Next came a cluster of clannish, reclusive charcoal burners.

At dawn, the call was heard upon the Royal Highway, causing wayfarers to turn from their journeys to seek the source of the summons.

The Gray Friars in their monastery heard it too, and some few forsook their holy vows to answer the stone's more pressing call.

In the village of Grimsgard and in the streets of Gorgonholm, in country lanes and in the mansions of the wealthy, an ancient summons was boring into people's brains.

CHAPTER 2

SOMETHING AMISS

Thurmond was perplexed. Everything was going weird. His every encounter that day had twisted into an unwanted, unpleasant confrontation. His huge black campaign hat signaled his membership in the Brotherhood of Underworld Adventurers. This usually afforded him a certain degree of courtesy as he strode the gritty streets of the city of Gorgonholm. But alas, such was not the case today. Instead, the wide-brimmed chapeau seemed to invoke sullen glowering and surly, half-heard mutterings. Street urchins hooted rudely behind his back. He was bumped and elbowed as he made his way through the narrow, crowded lanes and byways. And now this!

The ragged figure standing before him was short and lean, runtish even. His black hair hung long and stringy, and a large, purple birthmark embellished his cheek. The knife in his left hand was held low, aimed at Thurmond's vitals. Lunacy shone brightly in the small, round eyes.

This was just too much.

"Who are you? What do you want from me?"

No response.

"I don't even know you. By God's great belly, why are you doing this?"

This question provoked a twisted grin as the ragged man crouched low and began to sidle toward him, knife foremost. Thurmond kept his eyes riveted on that weapon—curved, narrow, and single-edged. It looked sharp and evil.

Knives made Thurmond nervous. He was well-skilled with the sword, spear, and bow, but he had never mastered close-in knife work. His mentor Roscoe had always stressed the necessity of keeping one's opponents at a distance. In a knife fight, he always maintained, everybody bleeds.

The young man glanced about, seeking a way out, some avenue of escape, but he had foolishly allowed himself to be wedged into an alcove formed by a projection in the city wall. The normally bustling city streets were strangely deserted. He was on his own.

Thurmond drew his own dagger, cursing himself for neglecting to strap on his sword before coming to town.

"All right, you raggedy-arsed bastard, come on! Let's see what you've got."

This was, in sooth, almost entirely bluster. He had no desire to fight this character and was not at all confident that he could best him.

Thurmond was taller and more heavily muscled, but the tattered man was quick as a snake. His knife was a grey blur as it darted at Thurmond's belly and then slashed at his eyes. Deceived by the feint, the young Adventurer could offer no proper counterstrike, could only jerk his head away from the lethal edge that severed a lock of his shoulder-length hair.

Instinctively, he kicked at the smaller man's groin. He missed, but the blow caught him square in his stomach and knocked him off his feet. Yet, the fellow was unfazed by the blow. He seemed to actually bounce from the ground, regaining his feet and instantly resuming his attack.

The small man jinked, ducked low, then closed and seized Thurmond's right wrist, immobilizing his weapon. His hands were small, delicate even, but the fingers possessed an uncanny strength. He grinned again and jerked hard, sending Thurmond into a pirouette that left his back and side fully exposed.

The young man gasped through clenched teeth, fully anticipating the blade sliding into his liver. But instead of pain, there came a soft, musical *thunk*—perhaps the sound of a hollow log struck by a stout stick. Then a familiar voice.

"Well, boyo, if I'd knowed you was plannin' to take dancin' lessons, I would have hired a minstrel to play a jaunty tune."

The young Adventurer found himself face to face with Roscoe, the man who had trained him as a fighter. He was a formidable individual—very tall, large of bone, and heavily muscled. Well advanced into middle age, his chestnut hair and beard were streaked with gray. He held a length of tree branch in one beefy fist.

The tattered man lay insensible at his feet. He looked even smaller now, rather like a child fallen into a deep sleep. Roscoe grinned and prodded him with a toe.

"This laddie seemed right vexed with you, so he did. How did you manage to offend him so grievously?"

Thurmond could only shake his head.

"I don't know—I truly don't. I never saw him before—never spoke to him. He has to be crazed. His eyes were all moony."

Roscoe stooped to retrieve the man's curved knife. He offered it to Thurmond, who declined. Thrusting the weapon into his own belt, he gave his young friend a concerned look.

"Then I hope I didna hit him too hard. They say it's terrible ill fortune to kill a madman."

The younger man shook his head in bewilderment.

"Who could he be?"

The man's identity was readily apparent to Roscoe. Black dust permeated his torn garb and swarthy skin.

"Charcoal burner."

They were an itinerant people who lived in their own closed and secretive society. Inhabiting the deep woods, they generally shunned contact with sedentary townsmen, who they disparagingly referred to as *squanch*. It was unusual to find a burner alone in the city.

Another question suddenly occurred to Thurmond.

"Say, Roscoe, how did you come to be here? I didn't know you were behind me."

"Well, it's like this, see—I was strollin' down the street, havin', for all the world, nothin' but joyous thoughts, when I sees you up ahead. But then, this here devil ..."

The old Adventurer gave the recumbent form another poke with his boot.

"... this devil starts slinkin' up behind you, obviously intent on some mischief. Well, says I, I'd just better follow along and see what that poxy dog is up to. So I picked up this tree branch and that's what I did."

"I'm mighty glad you came along—many thanks, old friend."

"Happy to be of service—you'd do no less for me."

The tattered man groaned and began to raise himself on elbows and knees. Almost gently, Roscoe gave him another crack to the side of the head that sent him back to the ground, silent and insentient.

Thurmond took a deep breath as if inhaling the weirdness in the air.

"The day is definitely out of joint. Nobody's acting right."

"You noticed that, did you? Aye, things have gone a mite cockeyed, so they have. Did you hear 'bout the riot on the docks this morning?"

"Nay, tell me."

"Well now, seems that a bunch of apprentice tanners got into it with some of the offal haulers. Nothin' unusual, just feet and fists. Happens all the time. But then some of the blacksmiths' lads started helpin' the tanners, and before you could spit, a pack of hog bleeders come runnin' up and threw in with the haulers."

Now Thurmond was confused.

"But the blacksmiths despise the tanners. Why would they want to help them?"

Roscoe continued.

"And the hog bleeders ain't exactly friends with the offal haulers, neither. All them groups is bitter enemies. Strange indeed, but then things got even stranger, 'cause the dockers come chargin' in too, and the boatmen, not wantin' to miss the fun, all started comin' ashore. Even the merchants come outta their shops and stalls, and soon everybody was fightin' everybody."

"The merchants joined in? They hate street brawls. Their stalls always get wrecked."

"Maybe so, laddie, but they were right eager to join in this one. It grew into a full-on battle with hammers and knives and gaff hooks and swords—and people killed."

"What were they fighting about?"

Roscoe raised his hands in a gesture of resignation.

"About nothin'—nothin' at all—just seems like the whole dockside was spoilin' for a scrap."

"Maybe the stars are crossed—I've always heard that crossed stars will sour your humors."

"Aye—could be. Or maybe a miasma from the stinkin' mud along the river was turnin' their brains. Whatever it was, we best get home—this burner's likely to have some friends somewhere about."

"I guess you're right. Maybe you should hang onto that tree branch."

Things were indeed going awry in and around the city of Gorgonholm. Odd tales began to circulate throughout the countryside. Green fruit, it was said, rotted on the bough and fell to the ground, milk curdled in the udders of goats and cows, sows ate their farrow. The craws of butchered poultry were filled with disgusting black worms. A woman gave birth to a baby with the head of a dog.

In city and country, fires sprang up with no apparent cause. Horses kicked and bolted, dogs snapped at their masters. Citizens of the mildest temperament grew quarrelsome, while more aggressive spirits unsheathed their weapons and sought the blood of their neighbors. Wives poisoned their husbands.

If Roscoe expected to find all things normal in Grimsgard, the freehold he held in fee from the local earl, he was to be disappointed. That very morning, the village well was clogged with the drowned carcasses of cats, rabbits, and puppies.

Next, the rotting remains of an unknown water creature were found floating in an eddy of nearby Snake Creek. Huge and hideous, it was immediately identified as a bringer of bad luck. Almost at once, a cow bloated and died, and then a young child had a traumatic experience while alone in the privy.

The villagers, frightened witless by any unusual occurrence, immediately abandoned their daily chores and ran to their lord's towerhouse, screaming for protection. Their cries, however, went unheard. Roscoe and Thurmond were off in the city, and their companions in the tower had problems of their own.

Sarah lay writhing on her bed, her stomach knotted in sharp, excruciating cramps. Her spell of invocation had successfully summoned a tiny non-corporeal entity known as a fay. But unfortunately, the necessary binding spell had failed completely, and the fay, in its panic to escape, had inadvertently flown straight down her throat and into her belly—fays have never been renowned for their intelligence. Now that normally inoffensive entity, resentful at its imprisonment in the young witch's bowels, was demonstrating its displeasure.

Torgul and Florio, usually as cordial toward one another as a dwarf and an elf can be expected to be, were in a heated dispute. The former had awakened that morn to find his beard—the very pride of his existence—snarled in a plethora of tiny, inextricable tangles often referred to as elflocks. He had immediately placed the blame on the Florio—the fief's only elf.

Florio was entirely innocent—he would not have dreamed of involving himself in the dwarf's grooming. To be honest, he found the dwarf's excessive facial hair unnerving. Still worse, food morsels invariably lodged there during meals.

The elf was having his own bad day and was in no mood to listen to Torgul's irrational nonsense. He took great professional pride in his cookery, and it always upset him when meals did not proceed perfectly. This was one of those times.

Eight-year-old Rollo, the son of Bodo the village carpenter, had been sent by his mother to deliver a basket of duck eggs to the kitchen. Always an awkward child, he managed to drop his burden on the flagstones of the kitchen floor. Fearing Florio's wrath—the elf was a veritable devil in the kitchen—the lad fled without wiping up the resulting mess.

This had taken place at the very moment when Florio came bustling through the kitchen with Roscoe's breakfast held high on a silver platter. It was a magnificent repast—fat blood sausages enlivened with cinnamon, cloves, and spicy red peppers, goat testes poached in mare's milk, and lightly sautéed blackadder mushrooms, which produced a delightful buzz. A grand way to start the day.

Unfortunately, these fine viands would never make it to his lordship's table. Slipping in the slimy, eggy mess, Florio's feet shot skyward. The platter went sailing from his hands, and as the back of his head smacked hard against the flagstones, a deluge of sausages, shrooms, and steaming nads rained down upon his face. Thus, he was somewhat less than sympathetic when a moment later Torgul stormed in to accuse him of desecrating his beard.

When the mob of distraught villagers arrived, their wailing was drowned by the vehement verbal exchange between elf and dwarf. Frightened and frustrated, the villagers began to punch, kick, and bite each other.

The most distressing event, in a day replete with distressing events, was still a carefully guarded secret. The cathedral's most sacred relic, the hand of Saint Aphazia de Weez, was missing.

It was at first assumed that the artifact had been pilfered, for its glass display case was smashed into tiny bits. But closer examination suggested otherwise. Its hand-shaped reliquary had indisputably burst from the inside, sending long curling shards of bronze across the floor of the nave. There could be no doubt that the blessed relic had broken free from its container and escaped.

To be honest, the hand in question had no actual association with the Saint Aphazia or any other holy figure. Two Yuletides past, a horrible hand had crawled out of the Mad River, gray and bloated. The flopping, twitching appendage—much too large to have belonged to a human—had terrorized the citizenry until driven into a cesspit and captured.

It was then carried to the cathedral and given over to the care of the Blue Friars who endeavored to determine its origins. Unsuccessful in their efforts, they proclaimed it to be an official Yuletide Miracle, had it encased in a heavy hand-shaped reliquary, and put it on display among the other holy artifacts— the mummified nose of Saint Inquisitus, the red petticoat of Saint Hortense the Unclothed, and a set of ivory dice once belonging to Saint Dissimulo, patron of gamblers and liars.

Even locked in its reliquary, the hand stubbornly refused to settle down.

It continued to flutter and jerk, sometimes rattling the glass of its display case. This caused it to become the cathedral's most popular—and therefore most profitable—relic. Eager pilgrims would pay goodly sums to clasp the reliquary between their own hands while seeking its counsel in their personal affairs. The subsequent vellications would then be interpreted by a priest especially gifted in such matters.

After several months, Bishop Boniface, the city's spiritual leader, experienced what he termed a *divine revelation*—the hand was that of Saint Aphazia of Weez, an obscure and probably spurious martyr whose hand, according to legend, had been severed by some long-forgotten tyrant. This positive identification was well received, and the number of generous answer-seekers increased dramatically. No one seemed concerned that the appendage was the wrong size for a human female.

But now the hand, the Blue Friar's foremost money-maker, was gone. It had broken loose and fled the cathedral's sacred confines, apparently of its own volition. This was serious indeed, and an emergency conclave of ranking churchmen immediately convened to determine the optimum course of action.

CHAPTER 3
MORE TROUBLE AT HOME

"Drat the luck! This ain't no proper supper for a man—why there's hardly enough here to fill a child's belly!"

Roscoe was accustomed to a long and leisurely evening meal with a number of elegant dishes served in several removes. Florio was a most excellent cook, and his enjoyment in preparing such feasts was almost as great as the old Adventurer's delight in consuming them.

But the dinner was sparse this day—nothing more than cold odds and ends that he and Thurmond had scavenged from the kitchen larder. A couple of lark and heron pies, a half dozen pasties stuffed with fish giblets, a chunk of stinky, blue-veined cheese, a crockery jar of pickled sheep tongues, some leftover pottage, a miscellany of dried fruits, and an assortment of sugared nuts.

He continued to grouse, his mouth stuffed with pie.

"No sir, not satisfyin'—not at all. First my breakfast goes on the kitchen floor, and now this meager dinner."

Roscoe's rancor was odd. Jovial by nature, he typically endured life's little frustrations without protest. But tonight, everything was pissing him off.

He bit hugely into an oblong pastry that resembled an éclair, chewed three times, scowled in disapproval, and spat out a wad of slimy green goo.

"Ghaaa—what villainy is this? This thing has brought a numbness to my lips and tongue."

The item in question was in fact an elvish delicacy that Florio had prepared for his personal consumption. Finishing his dinner, Roscoe blew his nose into one of the elf's fine, linen napkins. The evil pastry had caused both eyes and nose to run a torrent.

"Where is Florio? I thought you were going to fetch him."

Thurmond only shrugged—he, too, was feeling grouchy.

"In his chamber—having a snit and refusing to come out. When he didn't answer my knock, I stuck my head through the door. He threw a tankard at me."

Roscoe cleared his palate with a swig of ale and shook his head in disbelief.

"Did he really? How did you reply?"

Thurmond again shrugged.

"I wanted to pull off his pointy ears, but instead I walked away. I've dined on enough madness and confusion for one day. I didn't need an additional helping from a deranged elf."

Indeed, both of them had had their fill of bizarre behaviors. Their journey home from the city—a mere couple of leagues—had brought more misadventure. At one point, the Royal Highway had been blocked by an abandoned and overturned wagon, the oxen that had drawn it lying dead in their traces, the vegetables it had carried strewn up and down the roadbed.

Arriving at Grimsgard, they were greeted by additional mishaps. Roscoe's sheep and cows had escaped their fold and were happily consuming his barley crop. Two of the village cottages were smoldering ruins, their thatch having been set alight. The usually docile villagers were not at work, but stood in a brooding, reproachful throng, their faces marked by scratches, bite-marks, and broken teeth. Luckily, no one had been seriously injured during their brawl.

But most puzzling of all was Florio's uncharacteristic behavior. Roscoe took another draught of ale and pushed himself to his feet.

"Mighty strange, so it is. He's usually so mild-mannered. I think I'll go have a chat with the little fella. I doubt he'd be so ill advised as to be flingin' things in my direction."

The old Adventurer was indeed an imposing man. In addition to the sheer size of him and his great skill with weapons, he was the *de facto* lord of the manor. Although a commoner, he had been granted the freehold of Grimsgard by Ralf, the Earl of Avincraik. Landholders of common birth were known as franklins. Thus, he now styled himself Roscoe Franklin.

Florio was much more than a mere cook. His primary role was that of reeve, and as such he was essential. He managed all the estate's affairs and oversaw its workers. His keen financial acumen had rescued the property after Roscoe's ineptitude with handling money had brought it to the teetering edge of ruin. Florio only cooked because he wanted to.

Roscoe headed off to confront the elf, leaving Thurmond in a thoroughly foul mood. The world, it seemed, was conspiring to annoy him. His skin itched. His head ached. His clothes were uncomfortable. He bumped awkwardly into things as he made his way through the towerhouse.

Hoping Sarah might cheer him up, he entered her chamber without knocking. The young witch was still abed. Though the swallowed fay had by now passed completely through her intestinal tract, she yet suffered from the lingering discomforts of its earlier presence. Her chamber reeked of sickness. She was in no mood for company.

"Get out! God's bloody bones! Thurmond, let me die in peace! Go!"

He closed her door without a word and went in search of the dwarf. He found him on the bank of Snake Creek, face and arms smeared with cool mud in an attempt to alleviate the pain of myriad bee stings. After his shouting match with the elf, he had sought solace with his bees. Torgul loved the industrious little creatures, from whose honey he brewed a most wonderful mead.

Yet those same bees, the darlings of his heart, had, for no discernable reason, ruthlessly turned on their doting keeper, stinging him again and again as he fled as quickly as his short legs would carry him. Not until he had plunged beneath the murky surface of Snake Creek did the attack cease. Now his nose, forehead, hands, and arms were red and swollen from dozens of stings. Fortunately, his thick beard had protected most of his face.

It had certainly been a strange day, and everyone went to bed that night hoping to find things returned to normalcy upon the morrow. Their hopes, however, were to be dashed. The strangeness had found the accommodations to its liking, settled in, made itself comfortable. It would stay a while.

After dark, the human population, having slaked its thirst for violence—at least for the time being—seemed to settle down. Husbands and wives still bickered, siblings exchanged the usual threats, but the peace was not disturbed by actual tumult. The mysterious volatility, instead, descended on the village livestock. Throughout the night, bulls bellowed and gored, rams bleated and butted, the geese stretched their necks and attacked the ducks. Roscoe's great black stallion kicked his stall in frustrated rage.

The next morning was bright and clear. Meadowlarks sang as they always did. The farm animals were finally quiet after their restive night. Torgul and Florio reconciled, the elf offering the dwarf a jar of soothing balm that greatly reduced the swellings on his head and arms. Sarah was pale and drawn but finally on her feet. She apologized to Thurmond for her rudeness the previous evening, and he begged her pardon for forgetting to knock. Florio looked positively mortified as he did the same for the thrown tankard.

All was going well, and it was looking like the troublesome influence had passed, but then the two adolescent scullery girls, in the midst of setting the board for breakfast, suddenly fell into a furious bout of hair-pulling.

The shrieks brought the companions running from the tower's various chambers. They assumed, from the sound of things, that they were under assault by a troop of hysterical fiends. Florio emerged from the kitchen with a large iron toasting fork—his weapon of choice. When the girls were pulled apart and calmed with small glasses of Florio's addleberry wine, neither could recall the cause of their dispute. They were soon best friends again.

The girls may have resolved their issues, but Roscoe was far from appeased. Something weird was going on, and he wanted to get to the bottom of it.

"All of you—sit yourselves down. We're goin' to talk about whatever it is that's causin' such bad blood. You too, Florio—I see you tryin' to sneak back to the kitchen. Sit your elvish butt down in that chair. I want to hear what you have to say."

None of the others—and certainly not the elf—was enthusiastic about a discussion that might well lead to hard feelings, but all obeyed Roscoe's command.

The old Adventurer cleared his throat as he always did when addressing a formal meeting, yet there was something different in his voice today. His friendly, jocular tone had a decidedly hard edge.

"I've been thinkin' all along of the foul, stinkin' mud that lies along the riverbank where the knackers drop the blood and offal and the tanners dump their foul scrapin's. That stuff smells worse than a troll's arse, so it does. I'm thinkin' maybe that stench has caused a sickliness in people's brains, just like a miasma oozin' from a fetid swamp. I'm thinkin' people are bein' poisoned 'cause them buggers won't take proper care of the mess they make and that we oughta go put a stop to it."

Torgul, who was usually more bellicose than Roscoe, was quick to intervene.

"Hold on, brother Roscoe. You're right about all the blood and shit stinkin' up the riverbank, but let's not go pickin' no fight unless we're sure. I don't know what's the matter here, but I ain't ready to put blame on anybody in particular."

Roscoe shot the dwarf an inquisitive look, prompting him to continue.

"Seems to me that you humans are just bein' yourselves. Us dwarves bicker all the time—you put two of us together and we'll start arguin' about who has the most illustrious ancestors, but neither one will be lookin' to kill the other."

"Humans are different. When you ain't got no reason to kill each other, you'll just make somethin' up and let on like it matters. I think people are just bein' true to their natures. Ain't nothin' to be done about it. You humans— you're just bein' yourselves."

Roscoe scowled, obviously displeased by his friend's assessment.

"Come now, brother Torgul—us people ain't really so bad as all that, are we?"

The dwarf only grunted. He was of contrary opinion but declined to dispute the point. His failure to take up the challenge caused the old Adventurer to wheel on Florio.

"What say you, Master Elf? Are humans really as despicable as the dwarf would have us believe?"

Florio shifted uneasily in his chair—he did not want to answer the question, but Roscoe would not let it go. When he spoke, his tone was sharp.

"Come on, Florio—speak up. Tell us your mind and be quick about it."

The elf heaved a great sigh—the lord of the manor had commanded him, and he must do as bidden. He drew himself up and, assuming a serious expression, chose his words carefully.

"There is a blight on this land—on your people, your crops, and your livestock. You will never prosper as long as it continues."

The others erupted with one voice.

"A blight? What blight? How could there be a blight? What do you mean, *blight*?"

Despite the uproar, Florio remained calm.

"Something has interrupted the natural balance."

"What do you think we should do?"

"I'm sorry, milord. I have no idea."

Roscoe glowered, angry at the elf. He had serious problem to solve, and his reeve was refusing to help him. Thurmond saw his dire expression and knew that once again every minor annoyance was beyond endurance.

He must distract Roscoe before he vented his ire on the unfortunate Florio.

"Like I told you before, Roscoe, I think the stars are crossed. Everybody knows that the stars and planets affect all our comings and goings. What else could it be?"

Before the old Adventurer could respond, Sarah chimed in, also eager to relieve the rising tension.

"Thurmond's probably right. Last night, I consulted my horoscopes— Odi and Necros are in conjunction with Surt. Those first two stars are bad enough, but Surt's a demon world. That makes their alignment very dangerous. This has to be the evil influence we've all been feeling."

"And I don't think Torgul's wrong—humans do have a savage streak. The joining of these three malignant stars is bringing it out."

Bodo burst into the room, forestalling further discussion. He had served as Roscoe's man-at-arms until a stroke from a sword had cost him his left leg. These days, he was the village carpenter and stumped about on a magnificently carved peg leg.

CHAPTER 4

FOLK MOOT

"Milord, there's trouble. You'd better come see to it."
Roscoe's voice was choked with frustration.

"What now, Bodo?"

"It's the villagers, sir—they're angry. They've taken up rakes and scythes and shovels. It looks like they mean to revolt."

This was too much! Roscoe rose from his seat, his huge hands gripping the edge of the table as if he might flip it over. His eyes burned with a black fire.

"Rise in revolt? Against me? I'll show them ungrateful buggers...."

Then a remarkable thing occurred. Suddenly and inexplicably, the burning rage that had been steadily building in the old Adventurer drained away, leaving him limp and weary. He looked at Bodo with tired eyes.

"What's rilin' them up, Bodo?"

"Can't rightly say, sir. I doubt they know themselves. Yesterday they was all at each other. Today, they're all mad at you."

Roscoe threw up his hands.

"Well, I can't be havin' an armed revolt—indeed I can't—but I won't start killin' my own people neither. So what do I do?"

Thurmond's eyes lit up—he had an idea.

"Hold a folk moot. Call all the villagers together and each of them have a say. Hear them out—that will make them feel better. They know something bad is happening, and they're scared, confused. Let them tell you what they're feeling, and then reassure them that you'll keep them safe."

Roscoe was only half listening to this advice. He more concerned with what had been happening to him. Unreasoning anger had surged through his veins like poisoned blood. He felt as if some unseen devil had reached into his soul and given it a twist.

When he finally responded to Thurmond's suggestion, his tone was doubtful.

"How can I keep 'em safe, laddie, when I don't even know what's happenin' to me?"

"That doesn't matter. Just sound strong and confident—that'll be enough. If they're mad at you, it's because they don't feel like you're protecting them. They need to know you'll take care of things."

As his mind cleared, Roscoe was struck by the wisdom of the young man's advice.

"You're sayin' I should go out and act like a proper franklin?"

"Aye—that's exactly what I'm saying."

Roscoe sent Bodo to summon Grimsgard's leading citizens for a folk moot. This included himself, of course, as well as Florio, Thurmond, Sarah, and Torgul. Also, Bodo, his wife Bess, and their adopted daughter Pozi.

Big Tam the blacksmith was called, as was Fat Annie the alewife and other assorted artisans. The lesser villagers, simple farm laborers and their families, looked on from a respectful distance. This was a singular event—no one had ever before asked to hear their opinions on any subject.

Roscoe ordered a trestle table to be set up on the village common. He wanted everyone in a good humor, and the best way to invoke that mood was, in his experience, with a good feeding. Florio arrived with an armload of fresh-baked loaves while the scullery girls set out jugs of ale and thick slices of cheese.

The old Adventurer waited patiently while his people ate and drank, then got their attention by banging his tankard on the tabletop.

"Alrighty now—we've started this moot out in proper fashion with a morsel of food and a drop of ale, but now it's time for business. There's somethin' in the air that's settin' folk right brainsickly, so there is. Thurmond and I saw some strange doin's in the city yesterday, and we all had a taste of it right here in our own little village. I want you all to speak up and tell me what you think it might ...."

Big Tam did not wait for him to finish. His face was blanched.

"I seen it with my own eyes—there's a hell-demon down to the creek. It's waitin' 'til we slay each other so it can come ashore and eat us ...."

Roscoe raised his hand and shook his head.

"Nay, Tam—that ain't no demon. Torgul and Thurmond was down at the creek and had a look at it. Ain't nothin' more than some strange fish with great long whiskers, though he's a terrible ugly one to be sure. Stinks to hell, I'll give you that, but he's dead and ain't doin' no harm to nobody."

Fat Annie burst in next, her voice loud and tremulous.

"I says there be somebody's puttin' the eye on us. There are them what can strike you down with a look. I says someone be castin' the eye on us, makin' us do stuff."

Roscoe turned to Sarah, his voice gentle and reassuring.

"What do you think, lass? Could someone be castin' the devil-eye, like Annie says?"

Sarah shook her head, not at all happy with the alewife's suggestion. These people were in the grip of irrational fear and were eager for someone to blame for their own misdeeds. Next thing, they might start accusing her, she being Grimsgard's only spellcaster. So she lied.

"Curses are very powerful magic. Only a most advanced sorcerer could lay a curse on an entire village. And nobody's power is strong enough to curse the city of Gorgonholm. Nay, we're not being cursed."

But Annie remained adamant in her assertion.

"I still say it's the eye, and I knows who's doin' it. Remember that fortune-teller what come through here last week? Remember them bright blue eyes of his? Them kinda eyes ain't natural. He's out there somewheres right now, watchin' us and havin' himself a laugh."

Roscoe did not credit Annie's theory, but he saw a chance to distract his villagers from their fears. He would give them something to do.

"Thurmond, you and Torgul need to take some of these people and search the woods. Make sure there ain't no renegade fortune-teller castin' looks in our direction. Will you do that?"

Before he could answer, a ploughman pushed forward from the group of less important villagers. A man of such lowly station had, according to custom, no right to be heard, but the depth of his feelings compelled him to assert himself.

"That ain't enuff. Ever'body knows ya cain't see a warlock or a nighthag weth jist yer eyes. They's got special powers to hide 'em, so they kin be anywhires. We gotta sarch 'em out with fire and iron. Them be clean things. Nuthin' else'll do."

The crowd of villagers behind him growled in angry approval. Some carried the hoes and pitchforks they used in their everyday chores. They now began to brandish these in threatening gestures, their normal passivity giving way to belligerence. Their voices got louder, angrier. The moot was taking an unexpected and dangerous turn.

Thurmond felt the shift. Unbelievable as it was, it did seem as if Roscoe's tenants were on the verge of armed revolt. It was madness. They must know that peasant uprisings were always put down with the utmost savagery. On those rare occasions when the lower classes dared to protest their unhappy lot in life, the nobility quickly descended to crush them. The Quality were not about to risk their privileges.

And why would the villagers turn on Roscoe? He was an extremely kind and giving master—generous to the point of foolishness. Only Florio's astute management had kept the estate solvent after Roscoe had nearly beggared himself in his efforts to better the lot of his people. And yet, these same people were now raising their pitchforks against him.

Luckily, the old Adventurer was an experienced leader. He read the fear in their faces and knew he had to settle things down as quickly as he could. He raised a commanding hand in a gesture for silence.

"I am your franklin, so I am, and it's my duty to keep you safe. I have heard your fears, and I give you my pledge—if anyone—wizard or warrior— is fool enough to assail my people, I will hunt him down and kill him, no matter where he tries to hide. And Sarah, our very own witch-girl, will use all her powers to send his spells back upon him. She'll keep you safe from the devil-eye. You have my word!"

Roscoe's promise, however empty it might be, appeared to reassure his anxious tenants. They were simple-minded souls, accustomed to looking to their betters for answers. Their lord had told them exactly what they needed to hear. The shouting ceased, and the pitchforks were lowered.

Sensing their acquiescence, Roscoe continued.

"Return to your work! It is your lot to labor, and mine to defend. By God's shaggy shoulders, we will not let some unseen spook disrupt the natural order of things. This moot is at an end. Go now to your appointed tasks."

The villagers hesitated, uncertain, unmoving. Then Florio stepped forward and gave them a glowering look. They were unused to taking orders directly from their franklin, but the reeve dictated their comings and goings on a daily basis. They immediately trotted off to attend to their usual chores.

Thurmond let out a long breath—he had not even noticed that he had been holding it.

Lord Ubo Futz had never loved another person. He had no reason to, for no one had ever loved him. His mother had died during his birth. His father, Lord Fugar, had made him well-aware that his presence was an inconvenience he tolerated only because he needed an heir.

His situation worsened with the coming of his father's second wife and the spawning of three much younger half-brothers. The new stepmother became his mortal enemy, for Ubo stood to inherit Fugar's title and estate, leaving her and her children at his mercy. Naturally, she took measures to see that the eldest son should predecease his sire.

The stepmother first hired a poisoner, then a cut-throat, and finally a renegade sorcerer to remove Ubo from the line of succession. Unfortunately for her, the troublesome stepson was highly skilled at managing family relationships. She and her brood now resided in the Futz family cemetery, and Ubo was the undisputed lord of the manor.

The Futz burial ground received many bodies. Ubo's first wife, a pimply girl of fourteen, had lasted but eight months before succumbing to some wasting disease. His current wife, a spindly beldam named Ethel, was looking sickly. She would not live out the year.

Her demise would be welcome because there were always wealthy commoners willing to pay large dowries to wed their spinster daughters to a Futz. Marriage, for Lord Ubo, was strictly a means of generating revenue.

Actually, Lord Ubo was a very insignificant noble, his fief being small, isolated, and meager in resources. But his family was of ancient gentility, and social-climbing merchants were ever eager for any opportunity to worm their way into the upper classes.

Ubo had never harbored any particular ambition to increase his holdings, being content to reign as absolute overlord of the tiny hamlet of Skut. He enjoyed the excellent hunting of his woodland demesne and took great pleasure in terrorizing his tenants. The women of Skut, he had to admit, were a homely lot with fishy eyes. But he had never been a man with a keen appreciation of beauty, so they served his needs adequately.

All that, however, was in the past. Lord Ubo had finally awakened, as if from a dream, to his true destiny. Skut was not enough, not nearly enough. Why should he, a Futz, a man of antique lineage, be content with such a dreadful little shitpile? Why should he, Lord Ubo, a man of daring and skill, not reach his hand to take what he wanted from the world?

He had no army, nor the means to raise and equip one. But he had the Black Stone, and with that, all things became possible.

CHAPTER 5

ENTER ASMODEUS

Thurmond looked on from horseback as a score of villagers searched the woods on the outskirts of Roscoe's property. As he expected, they had found nothing. There was no evil spellcaster lurking in the trees.

To the east, he could see the Royal Highway. This was the main road to the city, so there should have been a steady stream of riders, vehicles, and pedestrians, but today the normally busy track was deserted. More troubling, a column of dark smoke was rising from the direction of the Gray Friars' monastery. What could that portend?

He touched his heels to his mount, a sturdy-legged cob named Millie. Torgul was still off beating the bushes with the villagers, so no one would miss him if he went to see what was causing the smoke. A small, grassy hillock lay just before him—from that vantage point, he should be able to see the monastery.

Thurmond did not like the greedy friars. They held a royal warrant allowing them the exclusive privilege of grinding all grain from the neighboring estates. This enterprise had made them so wealthy that they had relinquished the saving of souls for the counting of coins. Thurmond would not have cared if the whole monastery went up in flames.

Cresting the hilltop, he confirmed that the fire was indeed at the Gray Friars, though a screen of trees kept him from seeing which specific edifice was ablaze—perhaps a barn or granary. The major buildings, including the mill, were all massive stone affairs, so he doubted they would be burning.

The hillock also gave him a good view of the Royal Highway, and it was down this fabled avenue that a most unlikely conveyance suddenly hove into view—a sedan chair.

These were popular in the city, where they saved the shoes of the wealthy from the muddy, dung-covered streets. But they were a most unlikely choice for long distances. Chair-carriers moved slowly and wore out quickly. A swift palfrey or horse-drawn carriages were far more expedient options for the open road.

Yet, this sedan was coming fast, its four carriers running tirelessly, keeping a smooth, even pace in spite of the burden they bore. Intrigued, the young Adventurer rode toward the road for a closer look.

Drawing abreast of him, the chair came to an abrupt halt. The curtains were thrust back, and a voice called to him. A man's voice, though high-pitched and squeaky. Obviously belonging to someone accustomed to obedience.

"You! Boy! Come hither!"

Curious, Thurmond rode closer to the edge of the road. Here was something one did not see every day. The sedan's occupant remained invisible behind the curtains. The voice came again.

"I would speak to a fellow known as Roscoe—Roscoe Appleman. Are you his man?"

Thurmond was a bit offended by the question.

"I am no one's man, sir. But Roscoe Franklin is my boon companion. He styles himself Appleman no longer."

The voice came again—fussy, imperious, entirely oblivious to the distinctions Thurmond had tried to make clear.

"You will take me to him at once. Ride on—my bearers will follow."

Thurmond had half a mind to turn and ride away, to leave this pompous buffoon sitting in the middle of the road. But he was intrigued. With such strange doings in the wind, perhaps this outlandish man was worth tolerating. He turned Millie down the Royal Highway and then took the narrower track leading off toward Grimsgard.

As they approached the village outskirts, Torgul appeared and nudged his horse next to Thurmond. The dwarf was likewise curious.

"I'm wonderin' about this thing behind us."

"Aye—as am I. He called to me from the road—says he has business with Roscoe. Mighty prideful he is, too. Didn't bother to tell me his name."

Torgul scowled.

"Not surprisin'. Didja have a good look at them creatures carryin' the chair?"

"They just looked like servants to me. Must be strong, though, to be running like ...."

"They ain't human, boy. There's some magic on 'em to make 'em look man-like, but underneath, they ain't nothin' more than bones. Them are skeleton-men carryin' that chair."

Thurmond was thunderstruck.

"How do you know that?"

"Grandma's gift."

Torgul claimed to have inherited a bit of the second-sight from his maternal grandmother. It had served them well on prior occasions when he had descried non-corporeal entities invisible to his companions.

Thurmond considered riding ahead to warn Roscoe of their visitor's peculiar method of transportation—he needed to know what was coming at him. Necromancy was a deadly sin, so the use of animated skeletons as chair-carriers was an abomination most foul. No human being with the slightest pretension of decency would even consider such an outrage.

But he was too late. Roscoe was exercising his stallion in the fallow field next to the village. Spotting the approaching sedan, he spurred to the tower, dismounted, and tied his steed to an adjacent hitching post. He struck a commanding pose by the front door, hands on hips, chin raised, shoulders square. Every bit an Adventure Captain.

Thurmond and Torgul arrived within moments but kept their mounts. The sedan followed close behind, and as soon as it was lowered to the ground, a fantastic creature emerged—extremely rotund, with legs concealed beneath the skirts of a long velvet robe of the deepest purple. Arms and hands were hidden in voluminous sleeves. Thurmond thought he looked like a grape.

Only the shiny bald head and fat round face were bare. Cheeks and lips were puffy and pink, childlike.

"Roscoe Appleman?"

Roscoe granted his guest a slight nod. When he spoke, his voice was aloof and wary.

"I was once known by that name. These days I prefer Roscoe Franklin."

The stranger's lips quivered slightly as if he were trying to suppress a giggle.

"So I've been told. Well, that is of no consequence. What matters is that you are known as a man of skill, but more importantly, as a man of discretion."

Flattered, Roscoe allowed himself a restrained smile.

"Well, if those aren't pleasin' words to hear. And who might have been sayin' such lovely things about my humble self?"

The stranger offered no answer, only a single falsetto snigger such as a naughty girl-child might make. Roscoe's smiled faded.

"Did I say something amusin'?"

Instead of answering, the stranger spread his arms wide and smiled broadly.

"Do you have the slightest inkling who I am, fellow?"

Roscoe was growing peeved. He did not like being addressed as *fellow*, especially on his own doorstep.

"Nay—can't say that I do. Now suppose you explain why you've come callin' here today."

The stranger's tone became serious.

"I've come because I have need of someone like yourself—someone brave, resourceful, skilled at battle, experienced. I need something … acquired."

Roscoe's eyes squinted in distrust.

"Then I'd like to know who I'm negotiatin' with, sir."

The small man's voice came as a menacing whisper.

"You may call me Asmodeus."

This caused everyone present—with the exception of the skeleton-men—to freeze and blanch. Everyone knew that name. Asmodeus was the most powerful sorcerer in Gorgonholm. An almost total recluse, he seldom ventured beyond the gates of his great mansion, so few could vouch what he looked like. But the mere mention of his name could scare the unruliest child into submission.

In one oft told tale, Asmodeus was said to have encountered an arrogant young squire who refused to step aside on a crowded street. Offended, the wizard turned him into a ginger biscuit and bit off his head. In another, he caused a saucy servant girl to be snatched through the ceiling of her sleeping chamber by two gigantic, night-black phantoms.

At this moment, Sarah emerged from the towerhouse. Having heard the voices outside, she wanted to see who had just arrived. The small pink man was unfamiliar—she had not heard him say his name—but she was immediately struck by the enormity of his psychic emanations. The magnitude of his power filled her with cold terror. It was far greater than any wizard's she had met before. He seemed not so much a man as an adolescent godling.

Hearing the name, Roscoe's demeanor at once took a different turn.

"I beg your pardon, milord—there was no way I could know who ...."

The sorcerer waved a dismissive hand. He was familiar with every imaginable excuse. His next remark was not a question.

"You are the Roscoe who recovered the Mortimer heirloom gems."

Roscoe and the others were stuck dumb. This was a most carefully guarded secret.

The nasty giggle was back, accompanied by an equally threatening smirk.

"You're wondering how I came to know that. Well, it's my business to know great secrets that are hidden from lesser men."

The sorcerer paused to dab at his lips with an embroidered handkerchief. Finally, he continued.

"As I was saying—I want to make an acquisition, and you are best qualified to fetch the item for me. Here—take this!"

A pudgy, ring-bedecked hand extended from one of his sleeves and thrust a large leather wallet toward Roscoe. The old Adventurer flinched away from it, taking a half-step back.

"Nay, Master Asmodeus—I can accept no payment from you until we've struck a proper bargain—a mutually satisfactory arrangement of conditions, as it were."

Asmodeus raised his eyebrows in feigned surprise.

"Your reticence disappoints me. I would have expected the promise of so much gold to whet your appetite for adventure."

He unbuckled the wallet's flap and held it open for all to see. It held a fortune in bright golden sovereigns.

Thurmond disliked and distrusted the arrogant little twerp and doubted that the gold was real. He had been fooled once before by enchanted river rocks made to appear as gold coins and figured that Asmodeus was tying the same trick. He had to warn Roscoe, but he was too afraid of the Grape to blurt out his suspicions.

Many glamour spells could be disrupted by simply disbelieving them. Staring at the horde of gold, he chanted silently—*I disbelieve, I disbelieve, I disbelieve.* Despite his effort, nothing changed.

Roscoe cleared his throat and spoke in a most respectful tone.

"Master Asmodeus, you must appreciate my situation. That sack of gold is temptin', in sooth it is, but you've yet to tell me what it is your seekin' or where it might be found. Such particulars are critical, so they are."

The sorcerer rolled his eyes as if Roscoe were an imbecile.

"Very well, *Master Appleman* ..."

His tone was dripping with condescension.

"... I seek a hand. A living, crawling hand that the Blue Friars called the hand of Saint Aphazia. It wasn't her hand, of course, but it made them a lot of money, so they named it such and kept it in their cathedral. It has escaped, and I want it. As to where it might be—it is somewhere in the Catacombs."

These words hit Thurmond like a fist driven into his stomach. He knew exactly what that hand really was. But no one—not even his boon companions, not even Sarah—knew that it had been himself who had brought the vile thing into the city in the first place. Unless—Oh! God's holy toes! Nay!— unless the Grape knew.

Roscoe took a deep breath and let it out slowly. He was in a very delicate situation. If he declined the offer, he risked offending a magic user renowned for his capricious, vindictive temperament. If he accepted, he might draw down the ire of the Holy Church, which regarded the hand as its rightful property.

Had he been desperately broke, he might have considered taking the job.

But his coffers still contained coin from his last adventure. He took another deep breath.

"Master Asmodeus, I am honored that you would come to my humble self with your proposal. And the gold is generous—very generous. But I must regretfully decline. My estate, you see, like all the country hereabouts, is sufferin' from some malady that's turnin' the minds of men and beasts. I cannot go off when things is in such straits. I am sorry."

He tensed, expecting Asmodeus to wax wroth, to perhaps fling a lightning bolt in his face, but instead, he gave another of his irritating giggles.

"Quite all right, quite all right—though not what I expected from a man of such reputation. You've put the adventuring life behind you, it seems. You've become a country gentleman."

These words were meant to rankle, and they hit their mark.

"I'm no gentleman, sir. Just a humble franklin tryin' to do the best he can."

Again, the giggle.

"To be sure, to be sure—but perhaps you've not lost all taste for excitement. Even country gentlemen are allowed to enjoy a bit of sport, are they not?"

"Aye, sir, there's many that enjoy huntin', cock fightin' …"

"Horse racing?"

"Aye—that's a most popular pastime, so it is."

"That's a fine-looking stallion you have over there. I saw you on him as we approached. Is he fleet of foot?"

"Aye, sir—fast as the wind, as they say."

"Well then, Master Appleman, let us make a wager. I will pit my sedan chair and its four bearers against your stallion for a distance of, say, two furlongs. If you win, you may keep the wallet of gold without further obligation. If I win, you will still keep the gold but will also undertake my quest."

Roscoe smelled an ambush. Something was wrong about the proposal.

"Where will you be while the race is run?"

"Why, in my chair, of course. Just as you will be on your steed's back. Oh—if you're worried—I promise to cast no spells or use any of my powers to boost the strength or endurance of my bearers, or to interfere with you in any way."

Roscoe was mightily tempted. How could he lose? No human could outrun even a second-rate horse over that distance, let alone humans carrying a heavy chair with a fat man inside. The gold was beckoning, calling for him to accept the wager. So was his bruised pride.

Thurmond read the look on his friend's face, knew that he was about to agree to the magician's suggestion. He opened his mouth to warn him, to reveal the truth about the chair-carriers, but no sound came. He had been struck dumb.

He shot a glance at Torgul, who, like himself, stood silent with a gaping mouth. And then it was too late. Roscoe replied.

"All right, Master Asmodeus, I accept your wager."

Once those words were spoken, there could be no backing out. Lady Fortune would bring dire sorrow to any who reneged on a wager. Everybody knew that.

The race was over before it was well begun. The proper distance had been laid out on the Royal Highway, and both chair and stallion had taken their appointed place at the start line. At Sarah's signal, the stallion shot forward like a bolt from a ballista, while the chairmen moved at an almost leisurely fashion as they lifted their burden and proceeded down the road.

Roscoe had a substantial lead before they took their first step. With such a short course, there could be no doubt as to the race's outcome.

But then something extraordinary occurred. The sedan began to pick up speed, the legs of its bearers pumping up and down, up and down, faster and faster, blurring now, but with no strain visible on their expressionless faces.

The chair soon pulled abreast of the thundering stallion, then slowed sufficiently to keep pace with it. Roscoe looked on in astonishment as the curtains were drawn back to reveal the laughing, mocking face of Asmodeus. He gave the old Adventurer a waggle of his fingers as the chair sped on to victory.

When Roscoe reached the end of the course, the sorcerer was waiting for him. His stallion was lathered and panting, but the chairmen were entirely unfazed by their efforts. They had not even worked up a sweat. Asmodeus tossed the wallet of gold onto the ground, calling back as the sedan began to move away.

"I will return with instructions. Be ready to depart at once!"

And with that, he was gone.

CHAPTER 6

BLOOD AND FIRE

Gorgonholm continued to be torn by civil strife. That same afternoon, a group of charcoal burners arrived in the city, thirsting to avenge Dreego, the young burner who had accosted Thurmond earlier that day. He had been, he claimed, savagely beaten by a gang of men in gigantic black hats. Those drunken bravos had, without cause, without the slightest provocation, thrown him to the ground and battered him senseless with cudgels.

Dreego's word was naturally accepted without question. He was, after all, the son of the charcoal burners' headman. He would never tell a lie. The insult had to be washed away with blood.

Fourscore burners had therefore descended upon the infamous tavern called The Old Traitor's Head. Its signboard depicted a freshly severed head, blood dripping from the stump of its neck with the hand of an executioner holding it aloft by its hair. The establishment's customers most often abbreviated the name to The Severed Head or even simply The Head.

The Head was the unofficial headquarters of The Brotherhood of Underworld Adventurers, Gorgonholm Chapter. This was a band of intrepid warriors who dedicated their lives to winning treasure through the eradication of the traditional enemies of mankind—goblins, trolls, ogres, specters, even the occasional vampyre.

It made no difference that Dreego could not identify the particular Black Hats who had accosted him. The burners ascribed to the ancient ethic that each tribesman is accountable for the deeds of all his fellows. One Black Hat was as good as another.

The charcoal burners had delivered enough of their product to the city to know where Adventurers were to be found. Armed with the crude tools of their trade, they stood in a group before The Head's main door and summoned the Adventurers to come out and fight. No thought was given to stratagems or tactics.

The half dozen Adventurers inside, being more circumspect, declined the invitation, barred the entrances, and commenced shooting crossbows from the windows of the upper floors. This provoked the burners into a reckless charge at the inn's front door, which the vastly outnumbered Adventurers defended with great zeal.

The battle might have ended in a standoff had not the clever Dreego thought to toss flaming brands onto the building's thatched roof. Soon the venerable edifice was engulfed in flame, forcing the Adventurers to abandon their positions and seek escape through the cellars. The innkeeper, along with his family and hirelings, had done so at the very outset of the commotion.

Fire was a terrible thing to a city like Gorgonholm, where most of the buildings were timber-framed and thatched with reeds. Anyone starting a conflagration was likely to be torn asunder by the enraged populace. No sooner had the burning torches left Dreego's hand, than the cry went up— *Bills and Bows! Bills and Bows!*

This was the ancient rallying cry that required all citizens to come to the defense of their city. And come they did, with whatever weapons they had at hand—barrel staves, frying pans, splitting mauls, and brickbats. A few bore actual weapons—spears, swords, and long daggers. Hussies drew hidden stilettos from their bosoms, apprentices swung homemade leather coshes filled with sand.

They attacked the charcoal burners with great gusto—no one liked them under any circumstance, but today they seemed especially contemptible. The burners, being greatly outnumbered, were forced to flee, but not before the street was littered with fallen bodies.

But that was not the end of trouble, for two additional riots took place in the city that day.

In Old Shambles—the city's most impoverished and crime-ridden quarter—the rivalry between the numerous gangs of corner boys had erupted into open warfare. These were pubescent street hooligans who vied for control of territory and strove to garner respect through the most wanton acts of mayhem. Corner boys who managed to live to adulthood might be selected to join the Brethren, the city's powerful crime cult.

These young thugs specialized in being fast and sneaky. They preferred to murder their foes from behind rather than face-to-face and hand-to-hand. Today, however, all that changed. The multifarious crews—including many that had butchered each other for generations—had inexplicably joined into two large confederations. Distinguished by strips of blue or green cloth tied round their arms, they fought a pitched battle up and down the narrow lanes and twisting alleys.

For some time, neither side was able to gain a telling advantage, until a one-eared, rat-faced boy known as Cheese led a contingent of Blues—a crew known as the Cat Gutters—through a labyrinth of interconnected cellars to fall upon the Greens from the rear. Taken by surprise, the Green leadership was quickly struck down and their followers put to flight. The Blues celebrated their victory by looting the quarter's shops and residences, slaying any who opposed them.

The Severed Head had been fully consumed, but still the fire hungered. It burped, smacked its red lips, and looked about for the next course. Uphill, toward the city center, the houses were largely of stone and brick, many with roofs of tile and slate. Downhill, in the direction of Old Shambles, the roofs were thatch, and the timber frames were old, cracked, and dry—very toothsome! The fire stretched its eager arms.

As the flames streamed down the hill, those citizens still lingering around the Head's charred remains set up a cheer. The Shamblers—for that was how the denizens of the quarter were called—were always causing problems. The respectable burghers were happy to see them burn.

With their attention fully absorbed by the riot, The Shamblers did not at first notice the thick cloud of smoke approaching from the city's higher reaches. They only became aware of the danger when hot embers began dropping from the sky. Fighting and looting immediately ceased as corner boys, footpads, cut-throats, and housebreakers ran to create a firebreak. Thatch was yanked from roofs, wooden shanties were pulled down, bucket brigades formed up at wells and fountains. Green stood next to Blue in defense of their neighborhood.

The Shamblers were never hesitant to murder one another, but old feuds were immediately set aside in the face of a common enemy. And fire was the mortal foe of all.

Under normal circumstances, such disturbances would have forced Sheriff Brandon and his constables to don their armor, mount their horses, and restore order without mercy. On this day, however, the sheriff's attention was elsewhere. For at the same hour that the charcoal burners were attempting to storm the Old Traitor's Head and the corner boys were murdering their neighbors, another great broil had broken out in the Hilltop Quarter.

Hilltop was where the city's nobility and most affluent merchants lived in enormous mansions nestled behind high stone walls. The young sons of such families loved to slaughter one another. They would quarrel over anything—the quality of a flask of wine, the gait of a horse, a hand of cards, or especially the affection of a woman. Young nobles were expected to duel to the death over such meaningless things—how else to establish oneself as a man of honor?

Duels were governed by a strict set of conventions, but they remained deadly dangerous, nonetheless. The light cut-and-thrust swords used by duelists could penetrate an unarmored human torso as if it were made of spongecake. Slain duelists were mourned by their families, but such deaths were looked on as the price of nobility.

The problem was that the scions of wealthy merchant families—rich commoners, in other words—were always trying to ape the behaviors of the social superiors. They, too, took to the streets armed with stylish dueling swords, looking to acquire honor.

This was fundamentally ridiculous because commoners could not possess honor. Honor was strictly for nobles, who were exceedingly jealous of this time-honored right. So when young Maurice de Poot—a lad of fifteen years and the fourth son of a minor lord—saw the equally youthful Thomas Swink decked out in an expensive sword and dagger suite, he felt an overwhelming obligation to put the upstart in his place.

Much to de Poot's surprise, Swink refused his demand to hand over his weapons. Instead, he cursed the lordling roundly and challenged him to fight. This was a serious transgression—law and custom strictly forbade the challenging of nobles by commoners. Even worse, de Poot accepted the challenge, forgetting that a gentleman never condescends to brawl with his inferiors. There could be no honor in it.

The two boys commenced to jab awkwardly at each other—neither was skilled in the use of weapons. With both combatants unwilling to really press an attack, the confrontation might have ended bloodlessly, but then Lady Fortune decided to take a hand.

In delivering a clumsy roundhouse blow, de Poot managed to impale his own forearm on the point of Swink's sword. He fell back, gasping in shock and dismay as his rich noble blood dribbled down his wrist. In a duel between equals, the drawing of first blood was sufficient to satisfy the demands of honor and most often brought the combat to a conclusion. But this was not a duel between equals.

De Poot's comrades, other young ruffians of noble birth, had expected their friend to trounce the presumptuous peasant. Such was their astonishment at his defeat that they could only draw their swords and avenge his injury.

Swink's companions, seeing their comrade beset by a half dozen haughty lordlings, immediately pulled their own weapons and came to his aid.

Thus, a general melee ensued, with more and more people piling onto one side or the other. When cobblestones began to crash through the expensive glass windows of nearby homes, irate householders led their servants into the fray.

When the growing tumult reached Market Square, merchants, craftsmen, and fishwives joined in. There were, by this point, no more defined sides— everybody fought everybody. Farmers pelted soothsayers with beets and cabbages, while poulterers battered cordwainers with the carcasses of geese.

It was at this exciting moment that the constabulary arrived on the scene. Under ordinary circumstances, Sheriff Brandon would have quelled the disturbance by simply riding down everyone in his path. But this rioting crowd was sprinkled with young lordlings, whose lives and property he was sworn to defend. And even the sons of wealthy merchants had to be handled with deference, for their fathers put enormous sums into Earl Ralf's coffers.

Instead of charging straight through the roiling mob, swords slashing and hooves pounding, Brandon and his men were forced to pause on the edge of Market Square. This was their undoing. No one liked the Sheriff or his constables. The rioters surged around them, grabbing at the bridles of their mounts, trying to pull them from their saddles, striking with whatever came to hand.

The constables drew their swords and did their best to defend themselves, but their situation was hopeless. Cobblestones and brickbats were hurled from all sides. One constable was struck in the face by a blacksmith's heavy hammer. Another was dragged from his mount and stomped to death.

Brandon could do nothing. There were too many rioters, and they were in the grip of madness. He signaled for his trumpeter to sound retreat and led his bleeding men back to the safety of City Keep.

The citizens of Hilltop would have to sort things out for themselves.

As bad as things were in the city, conditions were even worse for the Gray

Friars. The monastery was, at the best of times, a steaming pot of jealousy, intrigue, and perfidy. Father Festus, the monastery's abbot, kept his ever-scheming underlings at bay with a time-honored tactic—he kept them at one another's throats.

The feud between Brother Julian, the choir master, and Brother Jerome, the cellarer, had been raging for more than a decade. Both were highly ambitious men with a ceaseless craving to become abbot upon the demise of the distressingly long-lived Festus.

Their ancient grudge had taken a new and dramatic turn when a twelve-year-old novice had spilled a vat of hog's blood over Jerome's feet, ruining his fine leather boots. The lad at once threw himself on his knees and begged the cellarer's forgiveness, but Jerome recognized the novice as being one of the choir master's favorites, so the blood, he assumed, was no mere accident. It seemed that his rival had delivered a declaration of war.

Later that day, a chamber pot was emptied on Julian's tonsured pate as he strode beneath the windows of the dormitory. Though the actual perpetrator escaped unrecognized, the befouled choir master knew without question that Jerome had sent it. He would not endure such indignity—it was time for decisive action.

That evening, a boy of nine years—one of the cellarer's favorites—was dragged behind the stables by four much older novices. There he was ruthlessly beaten and left unconscious on a manure pile, his head stuck in a chamber pot. The next morning, Julian's novice—he who had spilled the hog's blood—was found drowned in a privy with only his two feet protruding up through the hole in the wooden seat.

The situation deteriorated quickly. The monastery's novices and friars, young and old alike, ran to equip themselves with armor and weapons, then joined with either Julian or Jerome. Only a few of the most aged stood with Festus as he attempted to restore order.

The abbot's efforts were futile. He and his followers were swept aside as the factions clashed, the cellarer in the forefront, swinging a spiked flail. The rest fell to, chopping with swords, thrusting with spears, smashing with maces. Soon, even the monastery's servants and workers joined in, hewing at each other with unrestrained fury.

During the tumult, several smaller outbuildings were set alight, and then the big tithe barn went up. This was the source of the smoke that Thurmond sighted from the hilltop.

CHAPTER 7

RETURN OF THE SORCERER

"Skeletons? Damn your eyes, the both of you! Why didn't you warn me I was racin' against dead men? You musta been havin' quite a laugh between you."

Torgul was absolutely shame-faced.

"Nay, brother Roscoe, it 'wasn't like that. I swear by my beard, we would've told you if we could've, but that fat little piggy was somehow stoppin' our mouths. I pledge my word as an Adventurer in good standin'."

Thurmond was equally contrite.

"Torgul speaks sooth—we could not have spoken to save our souls. My tongue felt like a block of wood."

Distraught as he was, Roscoe could not remain angry with his comrades. He knew they were telling him the truth. Lately, he had been getting upset over every little thing. What was the matter with him?

Sarah spoke up, eager to support the others.

"You must believe them, Roscoe. Asmodeus has terrible power—I could feel it. He must have known that Torgul could see through the illusion, so he sent a spell that struck them mute."

At last, the old Adventurer relented.

"Agghh, 'twas my own fool fault, so it was. I should've seen it was all a setup. Only that toad-sucker got to me with his taunts—and I got greedy for the gold."

They sat around the table on the village common. The dwarf poured another round of mead into their goblets. The race had left them confused and worried. They were now under obligation to a capricious sorcerer with seemingly godlike abilities. What was going to happen?

They all had need of a drink and a talk—of much drink and much talk, actually.

Thurmond took a long swig of mead and wiped his lips with the back of his hand.

"Asmodeus said he was coming back with instructions …."

Then, as if the saying of his name were a spell of invocation, the sorcerer swooped down from the sky. He sat upon the back of a huge buzzard—or at least something that resembled one.

It was an ugly, ungainly creature with a wingspan at least five times the length of the biggest buzzard that ever existed. The scaly skin of its head and neck were mottled with blue and red splotches. Its beak was long, narrow, and slightly crooked. Black eyes blazed with obscene malice.

Asmodeus slid from the saddle and stroked its misshapen, reptilian head. He said something in a low voice that caused the creature to shudder with pleasure.

Reaching into a saddlebag, he withdrew a small spiny creature—it looked to be a hedgehog—which he proffered to the hell-bird much as one might give a sweet treat to a child. The little animal gave one small squeak before disappearing down the horror's throat.

Asmodeus had changed his garb, but he still, Thurmond thought, resembled a grape. He now wore a maroon doublet and matching riding britches. His tall boots and leather jerkin were of light, complimentary lavender.

The most striking feature of this ensemble, however, was the codpiece. Projecting from a point much too low—approximately at the level of the wearer's portly thighs—it was at least as long as an average human forearm and decorated with pearls and fine golden chains. As the sorcerer waddled toward the Adventurers, his codpiece swayed to and fro. He wasted no time with mundane pleasantries.

"I trust you are ready to start at once—as instructed."

Asmodeus did not wait for a confirmation.

"You will proceed to the ruin known as the Chapel of Eurea the Ill-Favored. I trust you know where that is."

Again, no pause for confirmation.

"The structure is mostly demolished, but the floor's large paving stones are intact. With your back against the remains of the altar, take eleven paces down the center aisle toward what was once the main entrance."

He turned and pointed directly at Thurmond.

"Use this minion for the pacing—he is the most medium-sized and will be the most accurate. After eleven paces, turn sharply left, and take three more paces. Beneath the pavers you will find an entrance to the Catacombs. The spot may be covered with rubble. If so, you must clear it away. Let no one see you during your search. This must be accomplished with the utmost discretion."

There was no giggling this time—the little man was all business. He went on with his instructions.

"The Catacombs are extensive, as I'm sure you already know. Finding my item would be impossible without magic, so I have brought you this."

He held out a charm suspended on a silver chain—a small human hand also cast in silver, the index finger pointing forward, the other fingers and thumb folded against the palm. He handed it to Roscoe.

"This has been attuned to the psychic vibrations of the item you must seek. Simply hold it by the chain, and it will always point in the correct direction. And do not allow yourselves to become lost. It would be all too easy for you to lose direction and die down there."

Up to this point, the sorcerer had given no one else the chance to speak, and no one was inclined to interrupt him. But when he finally paused to take a breath, Roscoe seized the moment.

"Master Asmodeus, Sir—we will undertake to find your item as agreed. I'm certain we can provide satisfactory service …."

The sorcerer interrupted, his tone was ominous.

"I should hope for your sake that you do, *Master Applehead*."

"Aye, sir, as I was sayin'—we will most assuredly find your … uh … item. But how will we contact you when we have it?"

"You won't have to. I'll be watching, I'll know."

"Aye, sir, as you will, of course—but may I inquire, sir, as to what is happenin' to the folks round these parts? Here and in the city both, they're all at each other's throats, so they are." Asmodeus' face twitched in a grimace of annoyance, but he answered the question.

"In the simplest of terms, something is releasing the hate that's in us all. Men may try to conceal or deny it, but they are no more than ravening beasts, their bellies bloated by fear and greed. Their hunger for power and women and gold is insatiable. Some force is provoking those basic urges."

Roscoe summoned his courage.

"Are you doin' this to us, Master Asmodeus?"

The sorcerer gave him a peeved look, as if the query was utterly absurd.

"Nay, I am not."

"Then are you tryin' to stop it, sir? To set things right?"

Asmodeus obviously found this question even more ridiculous than the last.

"Why would I do that? Times of chaos are times of opportunity."

Without another word, the sorcerer left them, mounted his hideous steed, and flew off in the direction of the city. The four friends stood, mouths open, staring skyward. Torgul finally broke the silence.

"That thing he was ridin' on—that was a demon."

After a pause, Roscoe responded.

"That would be my guess, a demon."

Thurmond nodded.

"Definitely a demon."

Sarah shook her head.

"I'm not certain, but I'd have to guess that it's not actually a demon. I'd wager it's a rather low-level fiendish entity from one of the outer levels— perhaps Limbo. Not intelligent, but capable of being trained to serve under limited circumstances."

Roscoe looked utterly flummoxed.

"I'm sure you're right."

Thurmond was less concerned with the nature of the sorcerer's steed than with the task before him.

"So, what do we do now?" Roscoe was puzzled by this question.

"Get on with the adventure—what else?"

Torgul headed to the armory. Being a dwarf, he was always happiest when his hands were busy, and there were always a thousand chores before commencing an adventure. Weapons and armor take a fair amount of upkeep—there was rust to scrub away, worn straps to replace, loose rivets to tighten. Though he was careful to keep his personal weapons keenly honed, Roscoe and Sarah, he knew, were not so attentive, so there would be need of some sharpening.

Sarah retired to her workshop to gather their occult paraphernalia. She had, during their last adventure, acquired a great pile of charms, philters, and assorted enchanted bric-a-brac, most of which remained unidentified. She did, however, possess one particular item that would prove most useful.

A scroll of fireballs—five of them. Scroll spells were particularly treacherous. These were spells inscribed on parchment that the magic user could unleash by merely reading aloud. The danger was that they were almost always unidentified, so there was no way of knowing what was coming until the spell was read. Anything might happen. The spell-caster might summon a monster or find himself knee-deep in dung.

This scroll, however, was unusual in that it was labeled—*fyf fyrballez*. If the inscription could be believed, this was a most potent weapon. Sarah could only hope that she possessed the psychic vigor needed to guide the fireballs to their intended targets.

She placed the scroll in a wicker pannier with her other essential items—her spell book, her wand, a grimoire she had retrieved from the hut of a dead shaman. There was room to spare, so she gathered an assortment of the unidentified charms and philters.

Roscoe asked Thurmond to join him in a quick journey into the city. They needed to enlist some stalwart fighters, preferably another half-dozen experienced Adventurers, to bolster the strength of their party. The four of them were obviously insufficient for the expedition they were about to undertake. It might not be easy to find willing recruits—the Catacombs were notoriously perilous.

Surviving from ancient Etrusian times, they extended for leagues uncounted beneath the city. They had been dug by ancient builders mining the stone for the city walls, the cathedral, the riverside quays, City Keep, and a hundred other edifices. Over the centuries, the shafts had expanded into a vast and uncharted maze. There had been many luckless wanderers, it was said, who never found their way out.

Moreover, the Catacombs were favored by smugglers who brought the illegal *uisge* from across the river. It was widely acclaimed that many sections were guarded by deadly booby-traps to discourage the pilfering of their highly intoxicating and extremely popular inventory.

The Catacombs were also a haven for unscrupulous miscreants engaged in every kind of corrupt and illegal enterprise—murder, heresy, sedition, and perversion. Child-eating cannibals and depraved priests sought refuge there when the gravity of their crimes denied them sanctuary anywhere above ground. Demented hermits with milk-white skin and huge, round, bulging eyes would lunge from the dark to seize anyone foolish enough to intrude into their domain.

One long section was piled high with human remains—the bones of plague victims from two or three centuries prior. This was a most dangerous passage, for the shades of the dead were angry and confused by their abrupt departure from life. They viciously set upon any living soul venturing into their realm.

But that was not the end of it. Certain old stories claimed that as the ancient miners tunneled deeper and deeper, they had broken into a labyrinth of natural caverns. Nothing specific was known of those dark and gruesome depths, but rumor maintained that few who entered ever returned. Those survivors who managed to crawl back into the light were reduced to mindless, drooling hulks incapable of speech. Better that the lower depths should remain unexplored.

The Catacombs had any number of hidden entrances scattered throughout the city, but venturing inside was strictly forbidden by law. No law-abiding citizen could have a legitimate reason for doing so. No one of sound mind would ever want to.

For several hours, the pall of smoke over the Gray Friars' had been growing larger, darker, and more ominous. Now, as Thurmond and Roscoe rode toward the city, it had spread east to cover the Royal Highway, and south to the outskirts of Grimsgard. More troubling yet, a second and larger smoke cloud was rising from Gorgonholm. The two ill-omened clouds would soon join forces and blanket the entire area.

With the world in such discord, the two Adventurers were well prepared to defend themselves, clad in mail and with swords girded on. Their black hats had been replaced by iron helmets. Shields hung from their saddles. Roscoe brought a crossbow, while Thurmond carried a light spear. Sarah's long dress had given way to a boy's leather breeks. Bodo brought up the rear. He would return the horses to Grimsgard, and the Adventurers would make their way home on foot.

Arriving at the city's South gate, they were surprised to find the massive doors barred and the drawbridge raised. No one would be allowed in or out until the civil unrest was brought under control. A crowd had gathered at the edge of the moat, watching a huge pillar of smoke and ash and embers rising above the city wall. Thurmond was relieved that none of the watchers showed signs of wanting to fight.

There they met three professional men-at-arms, archers who had come to town in search of employment. Newly arrived in Gorgonholm, they had never heard of the Catacombs nor its sinister reputation and were thus happy to be accepted into Roscoe's service.

The archers were Gascars from the kingdom of Gasconia, far to the south. Though significantly shorter than the tall northerners, the archers' upper bodies were massively muscled from years of drawing powerful warbows capable of penetrating mail hauberks. Each wore a stout coat-of-plates and carried a shortsword or small axe as a backup weapon. Lightweight iron caps guarded their heads. They seemed in every way like capable soldiers.

Their names were Wat, Tuck, and Cob. They had come north because the southern realms were experiencing an exasperating period of peace and prosperity. The almost interminable internecine strife between rival barons, lords, and counts had suddenly been allowed to lapse—no one could say exactly why. This unfortunate situation made things difficult for those who made their living by the sword or bow.

Thurmond noticed that each had on the right shoulder a small cloth badge displaying the sun symbol of the Charonite church. This was a little unusual, for the typical soldier was far more devoted to earthly pleasures than spiritual concerns. He decided to ask about it.

"I see the badges you're wearing—were you in the service of some church?"

Wat, who seemed to be the smartest of the three and their spokesman, answered.

"Aye—we was workin' for a priory what was in a feud with a village nearby. They was all the time squabblin' over sumthin'—who got to hunt where and such like. So the Father Prior hired us to help set things straight."

"You are no longer in his service?"

"Not no more. After we shot the lord of that village fulla arrows, the rest of his people got a lot more reasonable. The abbot didn't need us no more, so we hadda move on."

"Yet, you still wear the badge ..."

Cob, the oldest, interrupted.

"Aye—and proud of it, too. We be the obedient servants of Holy Church, just as all men should be. I don't see no badge of devotion upon your own self—ain't you worried for you soul?"

Thurmond knew he was on tricky ground here. His spiritual beliefs were highly ambivalent. He knew that the world was filled with incomprehensible mysteries—he had seen some of them with his own eyes. Yet his distrust of the Church ran much too deep for him to accept the official view of things.

To admit as much was heresy. He could be severely punished, perhaps even hung, for openly doubting church doctrine. Thus, he equivocated.

"I carry my faith in my heart. I respect your right to wear yours on your sleeve, but I am a quiet man who prefers to keep his devotion to himself."

The archer guffawed.

"You northers was always a cold and tight-lipped bunch. We Gascars ain't afraid to proclaim our faith. But if we're workin' for you, then I reckon we gotta put up with your way of doin' things."

Thurmond took an instant dislike to Cob. He was a bit too loud, too eager for a chance to be obnoxious. Yet,1 he did not want to start a row with these three well-experienced archers. They needed their services.

Roscoe named an amount—quite a generous amount in Thurmond's opinion. There would also be a large bonus for good and loyal service. The trio accepted eagerly.

CHAPTER 8

INTO THE CATACOMBS

The Chapel of Saint Eurea the Ill-Favored was located in what, a couple of hundred years ago, had been the prosperous suburb of Shrub located just beyond the city's North Gate. Shrub had flourished until a wave of Keltin invaders had crossed the Mad River and reduced it to rubble. The area had never been resurrected and had reverted to a weed-covered waste.

Most of the fire-gutted buildings had been pulled down long ago, the stones carted away for use in subsequent structures. The walls of the chapel, however, remained intact, though it was little more than a roofless, flame-blackened shell. No one dared take those haunted stones.

Saint Eurea's had been the final refuge for scores of women and children who sought refuge there when the Keltins swarmed up from the river. It was a poor choice. The invaders had set the edifice ablaze, and the unfortunates inside had been roasted alive. Their ghosts, it was said, still wandered about the location, seeking some resolution to their horrible fate. Anyone dumb enough to disturb them would die within a year.

They approached the chapel shortly before moonrise, moving stealthily through the dark. Though the area was supposedly uninhabited, one could never tell who might be lurking about in the shadows, so they had dismounted in the woods, well away from their destination.

Walking quietly was impossible, laden as they were with armor and equipment.

While the Adventurers were locating the hidden entrance, the archers stood to one side, arms folded, faces set in disapproving scowls, occasionally exchanging subdued whispers. Finally, Cob shouted out.

"We'll not stand by and watch you rob Holy Church."

Sarah stood atop a section of fallen column, keeping watch against unexpected visitors. She did not like the tone in the Cob's voice.

"What did you just say?"

"I said we ain't gonna have you stealing God's gold—that's what I said, *girl*."

The emphasis he put on the word *girl* was more aggravating than anything else he said. She was a fully-fledged Adventurer in her own right, the first female to receive such recognition. She had won her black hat and wyvern tattoo by facing off with goblins, kobolds, evil witches, and revenants from the tomb. Aye—and more than a few grubby mercenaries.

Sarah climbed down from the column. She was not about to swallow such disrespect, especially from some churlish southerner.

"Listen, when you were hired, you swore to give loyal service. That means you follow ord …."

Cob interrupted.

"That don't include church robbin'. No oath binds a man to steal from Allfather Charon. We ain't lettin' you do it neither."

Roscoe placed a firm hand on Sarah's shoulder, but his words were directed to the archer. As Adventure Captain, it was his job to keep the peace between party members.

"Friend Cob, what is makin' you think that we'd do such a sinful deed? Would you be so kind to explain?"

The soft tone seemed to anger Cob more than sooth him.

"Don't think you can put me off with a bunch of fancy talkin'. Ever'body knows churches keep their gold hidden under loose stones. We seen what you're up to, *Mister Adventurer, Sir*."

Despite the deliberate affront, Roscoe's tone remained as gentle as before.

"I appreciate your position, so I do. You don't know us, havin' just made our acquaintance this very day, so I can see why you might mistake us for a pack of church-robbin' hobgoblins."

"So, to set your mind to rest, here's what we'll do. You and Tuck and Wat shall be the first to explore what's under that flagstone. If you find treasure, you keep it, all of it, 'cause I know you'll take the honorable course and return it to the Church. But if you find a passageway, then you'll all be followin' my orders from that point without any more fuss. Are we agreed?"

Cob looked at his comrades, who offered him no words of encouragement. This was a difficult moment—he was not accustomed to doing his own thinking. Finally, he shrugged and nodded.

"All right ... I guess ... agreed."

Roscoe smiled.

"And one more thing—I'd prefer to be called Captain, if you don't mind."

Thurmond was greatly relieved that Roscoe had been able to placate their restive hirelings, yet he continued to dislike Cob. Worse still, he knew that sooner or later he would have to reveal the truth about Saint Aphazia's hand. He should have done so before they left home, but his courage had failed him. It was so embarrassing. And this was certainly not the proper time and place.

Despite its age and ruined state, the flooring of Saint Eurea's chapel was stubborn. Try as he might, Torgul was unable to pry the big flagstone loose from the mortar that had held it fast for so many years. He worked a heavy prise bar deep into a crack and tried again. No luck. It galled him to have to ask for help.

"Hey—Roscoe—help me with this sodding thing. I need some weight."

The old Adventurer's voice rose an octave in mock indignation.

"You wouldn't be suggestin' that I'm fat, now would you, my brother? I'll have you know that my girth has shrunk down considerable—shamefully so. I'm right mortified by how lean I've become, so I am."

In fact, Roscoe had not regained the weight he had lost during their last adventure. His once- magnificent paunch—round as a melon it had been—was now no more than a large roll around his middle. He took a position on the other side of the iron bar and gripped it in both hands. He continued to banter, though his voice became strained as he pushed down with all his might.

"And if you're sayin' that I'm fat, I'll be forced to remind you, friend dwarf, that you are yourself, some might say, a tad wantin' in the way of height .... There! We got it! Thurmond—it's comin'. Slip somethin' under it!"

The flagstone broke loose with a *crack*. They lifted one corner high enough for Thurmond to brace it up with a chunk of rock. Now they could get their fingers around it and lift it free. Beneath it, a set of spiral stairs led down a narrow brick-lined passage. It was low—even the short-statured archers were forced to duck. Only Torgul was able to stand upright, so he led the way. Moisture dripped from the ceiling, and their boots squished in the soggy mud on the floor.

The Gascars all carried heavy warbows. Thurmond and Sarah both carried shortbows, but even these would be of no use in such small spaces. Thus, they were now slung over their shoulders. Even Thurmond's broadsword was too long. Torgul slung his long-handled axe and drew his scramasax.

Sarah followed close behind Torgul with the silver hand to guide the way. Then Thurmond and the archers. Roscoe brought up the rear. His great size was typically a huge benefit in a fight, but in a confined place like this, he was at a major disadvantage.

At least they did not have to grope along in the dark. Sarah had learned a new spell, a light spell. When cast upon the adventuring party, it spread over them like a large luminous bubble and moved along with them as they proceeded down the stairway.

The steps ended at a down-sloping tunnel. After forty or fifty yards, they came to a fork in the road—a narrow passage branching off to the right, a wide one to the left. Thurmond watched over Sarah's shoulder as she held the silver hand by the chain as Asmodeus had directed. It began to spin in a slow circle, as if getting its bearings, then came to rest with the index finger pointing down the left-hand path. Off they went.

They came to other passages on either side, but the finger charm invariably pointed straight ahead. After some minutes, the passage brought them to a small room where larger corridors veered off right and left. The finger swung decisively to the left.

More twisting tunnels and corridors, more forks in the road. The finger was leading them through a complicated maze. Thurmond suddenly realized that he had long since forgotten to note the details of their travel. He would never be able to re-trace his footsteps to the opening. Torgul had an uncanny sense of direction, so maybe he would be able to lead them out. But suppose Torgul got killed?

Then he smelled it—a disgusting, lingering reek that he would never forget, no matter how hard he tried. The hideous stench of troll. He had at one point been compelled to scrape the dung from the floor of troll cages. Their unbelievable foulness had so clung to his body that he had been forced to discard his clothes.

The fetor brought the party to a halt. It was getting stronger as they progressed along the corridor, making them reluctant to continue. The silver hand continued to point insistently in that direction, goading them forward. Just ahead, the passage curved sharply to the right. What could be lurking just round the bend? They gathered silently together and listened. Nothing.

Finally, Torgul spoke.

"I'm goin' up there for a look-see. Thurmond—it'd be good if you'd come along behind me just in case somethin' bad jumps out. Sarah—maybe you'd be standin' by with one of your spells or somethin'."

Thurmond could tell the dwarf was frightened. This was unusual, for his reckless courage was typically nonpareil. That's what the stench of troll would do to even the most stalwart warrior.

Now that the corridor was large enough to permit it, Torgul unslung Bloodtroll—his ensorcelled axe—and tip-toed along the wall toward the bend. Thurmond followed close behind. Sarah readied her scroll of fireballs. One quick peek, and the dwarf was coming back, signaling for Thurmond to return to the group.

"There's a door on the other side. It's made outta heavy timbers, but it's all busted up. Like it's been smashed open from the other side. Didn't see nuthin' else. Smell gets worse."

Thurmond knew he had to say something.

"I know what that smell is—I've smelt is before. It's troll."

Everyone immediately paused and took a breath at the mention of the word *troll*. They all knew that they were horrible, brutal, voracious creatures capable of rending and devouring any human unfortunate enough to come within their grasp. At least that is how they were described in the childhood tales that everyone grew up hearing. In fact, none of the group, save Thurmond, had ever laid eyes on a troll.

Trolls were unlike any other living creature. They were warm-blooded and more or less nurtured their young, yet they were perfectly hairless and covered with tiny scales that lent them a distinctly reptilian appearance.

The slightly pointed ears and almond-shaped eyes suggested that trolls might share a common ancestor with elves, but the very suggestion of such a connection would surely have driven an elf to apoplexy. Trolls were too dim of wit to comprehend or care who they were related to.

Trolls possessed an innate ferocity matched only by their ravenous appetite—they were perpetually driven to kill and eat. Their hooked claws, huge incisors, and prodigious strength provided the means for satisfying both of these appetites.

Such was the creature that now lurked somewhere beyond the broken door. Thurmond knew what he had to do.

"Look it—I'll go up and peek through the door, but if there's a troll on the other side, I'm gonna come running back. Get ready to fight. It'll take all of us to kill a troll."

They took their positions, Roscoe standing in front where his large kite-shaped shield could block the way. Torgul just behind him, the long shaft of his axe permitting him to strike out of either side as opportunity allowed. Sarah stood by with her scroll. The archers hung back, as if unsure of what to do.

Thurmond was only gone a moment. Then he was back and reported to the group.

"I looked through the smashed door. I didn't see the troll, but there's scores of small barrels stacked inside. And there's another smell that's unmistakable—uisge."

This was a highly potent distilled beverage obtainable only from the chaotic Keltin tribesmen on the far side of the Mad River. Its manufacture was a guarded secret, and the Keltins would exchange it for nothing less than the finest steel weapons the kingdom of Poitiers had to offer.

Since it was a capital crime to provide arms to such unpredictable neighbors, the smuggling of uisge was the business of the criminal underworld. Roscoe had, in his time, dabbled in this trade. But these days, the enterprise was controlled by the Brethren. To cross this group was to court death in a horrible fashion.

CHAPTER 9

THE STENCH OF TROLL

Roscoe was beside himself.

"Alackaday! So much fine beverage and me with no way to carry it away. It's heart-breakin', so it is."

The casks of uisge were stacked higher than their heads and the stacks extended down the corridor beyond their sight. They had obviously stumbled onto a major stockpile of the Brethren's illicit inventory. There were also crates and crates of axe heads, spear points, and unhilted sword blades packed in straw—the currency for purchasing still more uisge from the Keltins.

Sarah was troubled by the vast quantity of weapons.

"Roscoe, there must be hundreds of pieces in these boxes. Back when you were a smuggler, how many weapons did you carry over the river?"

His response was a bit wistful.

"Oh, nothin' like this. Half a dozen swords or maybe a score of spear points. Course, we was just small-time operators in them days. Nothin' like today with the Brethren controllin' it all."

"Still—there's so much. Almost like somebody is fitting out an army. What could it signify?"

"Nothin' good, lassie, I'm sure of that."

Thurmond called their attention to another disconcerting detail.

"Hey—look at this."

He held a short length of heavy iron chain. One end was fixed to a ring set in the masonry of the wall. The other ended in a broken link. Though the rest of the chain was rusted, the broken place was new and shiny—the metal had been snapped through only recently.

The young Adventurer cast his eyes about the room.

"This place reeks of troll—trust me, I know. He musta been chained here to keep people from stealing the uisge, but he broke loose and escaped."

This caused everyone to look around in apprehension.

Thurmond tried to calm himself and his friends with a happy thought.

"Don't worry. I know trolls. If it was still around, it'd be attacking us at this very moment. It's long gone from here, out looking for something to eat. It wouldn't stick around once it broke free."

While the others were examining the chain, Torgul explored farther down the corridor. Beyond the stacks of casks and crates, he found an area that served as living quarters, complete with bunks, stools, storage chests, and a wooden table.

These furnishings had been thoroughly ravaged—the table and stools overturned and smashed, the chests emptied and the foodstuffs within scattered and chewed. The floor was strewn with the shredded remains of clothing and mattress ticking.

Three dead men lay amidst the wreckage. Where their stomachs had been, only gaping cavities remained.

Torgul called the others to come have a look.

"Who do you suppose these men were?"

Roscoe supplied the answer.

"Smugglers. These poor bastards was left here to guard the goods. They met a sorrowful fate, so they did."

They moved back down the corridor, away from the ghastly, eviscerated bodies. Sarah was uneasy.

"Where's the troll now?"

Thurmond sought to reassure her.

"It's gone. It killed these guys, ate their guts, and broke out through that smashed door. It run off, I'm pretty sure."

Unfortunately, Thurmond's understanding of troll behavior was not as comprehensive as he believed. Otherwise, he would have known that no troll would willingly abandon deliciously decomposing human remains.

No sooner were his words out of his mouth than he was seized from behind by a pair of scaly arms. The troll had, all this time, been lurking in a niche behind the stacked casks. He now emerged from his hiding place and clamped a mouthful of fangs on the young Adventurer's shoulder.

Thurmond screamed and attempted to fight free, but the creature's jaws were immovable. Torgul immediately flew to the attack, his axe streaking red magic as he chopped at the troll's back. But even Bloodtroll's enchanted edge was unable to bring the monster down.

Roscoe jumped in, thrusting at the troll's eyes with his point of his sword. This tactic earned a response. Still holding Thurmond with its teeth, the creature lashed out quick, its claws ripping across the old Adventurer's mail and sending him sprawling into a stack of casks.

Then, annoyed by the axe blows that were stinging its back, the troll delivered a tremendous buffet to Torgul's head. The dwarf went down in a heap.

Thurmond was all the while struggling to pull his sword, but his sword arm was pinned by the troll's fangs. He could only watch as his friends were knocked flat.

Then Sarah unleashed one of her fireballs and a scorching blast of flame exploded against the wall just to the right of the troll's head. It screeched, confounded as droplets of liquid fire sprayed across its body. Unfamiliar with the sensation of fear, uncertain how to respond, it dropped its quarry and backed away.

A second fireball smashed into its face. The nose, lips, and ears fried and shriveled like pork fat dropped on a red-hot griddle. The eyes melted and ran down its cheeks. The creature gave a mind-numbing scream and began to stumble about the corridor, a flailing maelstrom of blind, maddened claws and fangs.

Torgul found his feet and closed in from behind. His axe rose and fell, rose and fell, spattering floor and walls with bits of troll flesh. Roscoe pulled himself upright but held back a bit, wary of the sightless creature's slashing talons. He took his time, found his opening, and then with a single blow almost cut through its neck. With the supporting muscles severed, the troll's head fell limp against its chest.

Released at last, Thurmond—now in his own blind rage—tore his sword from its scabbard and belabored the troll's head and face with all his might. Then it was over. The troll sank to the ground and moved no more.

As Thurmond began to calm down, his bitten shoulder began to ache. He was very fortunate, for the troll had disliked the sharp electric sensation that comes from biting on metal and had not clamped down with the full force of its terrible jaws. Still, his shoulder would bear a large mail-patterned bruise where the iron rings were driven into his skin.

He stared at the battered and roasted remains of the troll.

"We've got to destroy this thing completely. Trolls heal themselves. If we don't chop it into little pieces, its face and neck will grow back, and it'll come back to life."

This was true. Just as some lizards can drop their tails and grow new ones, trolls could regenerate severed body parts and recover from seemingly lethal injuries.

Roscoe rubbed his jaw as if puzzled.

"I dunno, laddie. I've heard tell of such things with trolls, but this bugger seems deader than hell. But we'd best be safe. What should we do first—cut off its head completely?"

Torgul had an idea.

"Let's soak it in uisge and burn it. Remember that oversized slug?"

On a previous adventure, they had been called upon to dispatch a gigantic gastropod. A good dousing with uisge had rendered it into a puddle of goo.

Roscoe was wistful.

"That would a terrible waste of fine beverage—but I suppose we must."

He prodded the troll with the point of his sword, then continued.

"We can't have this fella standin' up and lookin' for another go at us."

Roscoe knocked the bung from one of the casks while Torgul searched through the slain smugglers' scattered possessions. He came up with a dented brass tankard, which he presented to the others with a flourish.

"Makes no sense lettin' all this wonderful drink go to waste. We can at least have us a good snort."

The old Adventurer beamed in approval and filled the vessel to the brim. He drank deep and handed the cup to Sarah. She did her best to follow his example, but the fiery drink was just too strong. It took her breath and made her gasp for air. She passed the tankard on to Thurmond, who also strove to demonstrate his prowess as a drinker. Alas—he fared no better than Sarah. Roscoe's skill with a cup was unsurpassed.

Torgul drank next, then proffered the cup to Cob. The response was entirely unexpected. Instead of expressing gratitude, the archer erupted in a moral outrage.

"Nay—I'll not drink from your cup of sin! Do not try to tempt me with your demon brew."

The Adventurers all turned in surprise. Cob strode angrily to Roscoe and planted himself squarely before him, hands on hips. His head barely reached the big man's shoulder, yet the depth of his conviction made him fearless.

"It's bad enough that you pollute yourself by associatin' with dwarves. But then you drag us down here to the very gates of Hell and thrust us into the jaws of this unholy doorkeeper."

He pointed an accusing finger at the dead troll.

"As if that warn't enow ..."

His paused, his face growing red, his voice beginning to sputter as he worked himself into a righteous rage.

"... but now this stunted, soul-less thing ..."

He indicated Torgul.

"... tries to lure us into corruption with ardent spirits. I'll not stand for it! I won't! Not for a moment!"

He glared defiantly at the old Adventurer, clearly looking for a fight. Thurmond shot a glance at the other archers. He disliked them intensely, Cob especially, and would not be sorry if they came to blows. Yet that was not to be.

The shortest, thinnest archer, Tuck, stood impassively with arms folded, eyes turned away, as if disinterested in the impending conflict. Wat, the smartest of the trio, caught Thurmond's glance and returned a slight shrug and sheepish grin as if abashed by his companion's antics.

Roscoe replied to the vociferous Cob in a calm soothing voice, though his words made his position very clear.

"Friend Cob, I comprehend your ethical misgivings, so I do. Indeed, sharin' a drop of uisge with Torgul and killin' trolls ain't doin' God's work near so well as shootin' some nobleman full of arrows so your preacher friend can poach his stags."

Cob opened his mouth to protest, but Roscoe silenced him with a gesture and continued.

"And I understand, so I do, that you're accustomed to fightin' out in the clean, wholesome air, killin' human folk, instead of facin' off with—what did you call the troll? An *unholy doorkeeper*, I think it was. Aye—that it was."

"So maybe that explains why you three hung back and didn't pitch in with the rest of us."

This was true. The three archers had slunk back and let the others do the fighting. Cob closed his mouth and said nothing, which was wise because Roscoe was determined to have his say.

"So, here's my proposal, friend Cob. I gave you some coin at the beginnin' of our adventure with the promise of more if you gave good service. Well, I'm findin' your service a bit wantin'."

For the first time, his voice rose.

"So be off with you now! Take your two friends and the gold I gave you—which you ain't properly earned—and find your own way out. I wish you no ill, but I'll not put up with more of your foolishness. On your way."

These words brought Cob's complaints to a quick end. Fear gave his voice a slight quaver.

"You don't really mean ...."

Roscoe cut him off.

"I mean exactly what I say, so I do. I left markins all along the tunnel with a piece of charcoal—they'll lead you back the way we come in."

Then another voice—one hitherto silent—spoke up.

"I'll drink with the dwarf! Give me the cup! I'll drink to his health and yours!"

It was Wat. He extended his hand toward Torgul, who obligingly passed him the requested vessel. Then Tuck, as if awakening from a dream, added his agreement.

"Aye, and I as well. Pass the cup, Wat, so I can toast to Lord Torgul's good health."

This put Cob in an awkward position. He was badly frightened by the prospect of negotiating the underground with his two comrades. Doing so alone was unthinkable. Understanding the man's hopeless situation, Roscoe softened a little.

"What about it, Cob? Will you be drinkin' to Lord Torgul's health like your companions?"

The archer hesitated for only a moment before taking the cup. He mumbled something indistinguishable as he lifted it to the dwarf and raised it to his lips. He took only the smallest sip, but it was sufficient to bring tears to his eyes.

In other circumstances, the event might have been a cause for merriment, but their present situation was too precarious for humor. Roscoe looked Cob dead in the eye.

"You've shared a cup with us, and now we're bound together for a day and a night or until the end of the adventure. It's custom, plain and simple, and mighty bad fortune comes to a man who breaks such a bond."

Roscoe was making this up to intimidate the archer. The sharing of a cup carried no such specific obligation.

"I'm givin' you one more chance to live up to your word and give good service. Any more complaints and you'll be left behind for a fact. Do you take my meanin'?"

Cob said nothing, only nodded.

Roscoe and Thurmond were soaking the troll with uisge while Cob sat silent, alone, and glum. Wat hooked Thurmond's arm and drew him to one side.

"You know, Cob ain't really a bad bloke. I mean, he takes good care of Tuck and me—looks after us like we was his little brothers or somethin'. It's just that he wasn't brought up proper, so he don't know how to act with people."

Thurmond was intrigued.

"What do you mean?"

"He was raised by the White Friars. His folks left him in a basket by the church door, and the friars took him in. He don't know nothin' else but what they taught him. It makes it hard for him to get along with normal folks."

Thurmond began to comprehend. The White Friars were the third most powerful denomination in the Charonite religion. Neither as politically connected as the Blues or as wealthy as the Blacks, they maintained a huge following comprised primarily of the lowest social orders. Since there was always a great many poor people, the Whites were never wanting for loyal followers.

Dissatisfied with their third-place ranking, the Whites were far less concerned with spiritual mysteries or ethical teachings than with expanding their powerbase. They therefore kept their dogma very basic. They required little more than total obedience to the church hierarchy, an intense hatred of foreigners and non-humans, and an abhorrence of fornication and strong drink.

These simple dictates could be easily understood and appreciated by the average thick-brained peasant. Fortunately, most of the true believers were redeemed by a healthy dose of wholesome hypocrisy, especially in regard to illicit couplings and excessive swilling.

Cob was different. The White Friar's teachings had been so beaten into him that he could no longer interact with people in a normal fashion. Thurmond understood this because, growing up poor in a small rural village, he had had plenty of contact with White Friars and their devoted followers. He had witnessed what early exposure to such vitriol could do to a person.

The conversation with Wat was interrupted when Sarah hooked him by the other arm and pulled him off to the other side of the corridor. She gave him a hard look.

"Want to come clean?"

"What?"

"Don't *what* me—time to come clean. How do you know so much about trolls? You've never told me anything about meeting a troll before."

This was true. Thurmond had kept the story of his troll encounter entirely to himself. Not even Sarah, his closest friend—and maybe something far more than that—had been told this secret. But now, he knew, he would have to tell all.

"Look, Sarah … it's really embarrassing … that's why I never told you. But …"

He paused, not wanting to continue. She awarded him with an impatient scowl.

"Well?"

"Well … remember that guy Jasper, the one with the troll hand?"

Jasper had been a solider they encountered in the course of their first adventure. His left hand had been lost in a barroom fracas and a troll hand magically grafted in its place.

Sarah wrinkled her nose.

"Of course I remember him. How could I forget something as disgusting as that?"

"I was the one who brought that hand into the city. Just before I met you, I was sent to find this old guy who raises trolls and fetch a hand for Jasper."

The young Adventuress just shook her head.

"Raises trolls? Don't be ridiculous—nobody would do such a thing."

"Nay, you're mistaken—there's a weird old coot who lives out in the woods. He calls himself Trollkeeper."

Sarah was now confused.

"But why?"

Thurmond dreaded telling this next part of the story.

"For wizards or priests—I don't know—to use in their spells. Troll parts grow back, so I guess they're something special. I didn't know why they wanted it, but as soon as we met Jasper, I knew they had stuck it on him."

Sarah's mouth dropped open in horror.

"Oh … I dunno … Thurmond … that's horrible. How could you involve yourself in something so nasty?"

Sarah's reaction was not unexpected. Trolls, along with ogres, kobolds, goblins, and a few others, were the fell creatures—bestial sub-human species that possessed an instinctive hatred for mankind and sought, whenever opportunity arose, to inflict as much misery as possible on their natural enemy.

The fell creatures routinely slaughtered solitary shepherds or small bands of wayfarers unlucky enough to venture near their lairs. At times they grew bolder and raided small caravans and isolated farmsteads. Larger groups might attack a village or sack a remote castle.

Humans returned this animosity measure for measure. There was something about these creatures that was just inherently wrong, that inspired an immediate impulse either to flee for one's life or to attack without mercy. It was simply impossible for people to abide the presence of fell creatures.

The very idea of grafting a troll's hand to a human body was utterly repellent to all right-minded humans. It was also a capital crime and a mortal sin, so Thurmond's involvement had endangered both his life and his soul. But that was still not the worst.

"There's something else, Sarah, something worse."

"It's hard to imagine anything worse."

"After Jasper got killed, the troll hand kept flopping around on the end of his arm. It scared me, so I cut it off and threw it into the river. I thought it'd be gone forever, but that has to be the hand that crawled ashore two Yuletides past. It has to be. That's the hand Asmodeus sent us to find."

Sarah could scarcely believe what she was hearing.

"So, it was your troll hand that Bishop Boniface claimed was the hand of Saint Aphazia."

"Aye, it has to be. If the church ever finds out that I know the truth about their prize relic ... well ... that'll be the end of me. Prithee, don't tell the others. I'm not ready to face them yet."

"It's a little late for that, Thurmond. Look behind you."

Roscoe, Torgul, Wat, and Tuck stood directly at his back. They had overheard every word. Only Cob still sat apart, sulking. Dismayed, Thurmond turned guiltily to Roscoe.

"Do you think Cob heard?"

The question had been directed to the old Adventurer, but Wat answered.

"He's got keen ears, he does. Aye—I 'spect he heard."

Roscoe clamped a heavy hand on Wat's shoulder.

"Of course, you know what must happen if any of you three should breathe the edge of a word about any of this. Do you follow my train of thought here, boyo?"

Wat cringed under the big man's grip.

"Aye—I do. But you gotta understand Cob. He don't see things same as the rest of us. None of this is gonna set well with him."

Roscoe's reply was menacing.

"None of us exactly like it, laddie. Question is—what to do about it?"

Wat replied in low tones.

"Let me and Tuck talk to Cob. Maybe we can make him see good sense."

"You better make sure you do."

Meanwhile, Torgul brought a flint and steel from his pouch and began to strike sparks over the uisge-drenched troll. This was not easy, but thin blue flames finally took hold. Sarah took out the silver hand and held it by its chain. It wavered at first, as if confused, then pointed down the corridor.

CHAPTER 10

SMUGGLERS

Another heavy wooden door secured the far side of the smugglers' lair. The bolt, fortunately, was on their side. With Torgul in the lead and Sarah holding the silver hand, the party again moved off. The passage beyond was wide and smooth. It was obviously the route by which the casks of uisge were hauled to the storage area.

Thurmond sidled up next to Sarah, still feeling the embarrassing sting of his confession. He attempted to ease into a conversation by stating the obvious.

"Can you imagine what it must have been like for those guys we found, living in there with a chained-up troll?"

The young witch's response was cool.

"From what you told me, I think you would be able to imagine it far more readily than I."

She was not, he could see, going to make things easy for him. He would try flattery next. Everyone likes a nice compliment.

"Say—that was pretty smart, shooting that first fireball so it struck the wall next to the troll's head. You got him to drop me so you could let him have one right in the face. Well done—and thanks."

But Sarah remained aloof, refusing his overture.

"If you must know, I wasn't aiming at the wall. I couldn't control the spell properly and the fireball went astray. I tried to send it right between that terrible creature's eyes."

That did it! Enough was enough! He deserved better treatment than this!

"God's lungs, Sarah—I told you I didn't know what they were going to do with the hand. But maybe I would have brought it to them even if I did. They promised to train me with weapons and give me armor—that was all I could think about in those days. Wouldn't you have done something foolish if someone promised to teach you magic?"

This touched her. Indeed, she had done something foolish for that very reason. She had trusted a lying thief called Gavin, and it had nearly cost both her and Thurmond their lives. Yet Thurmond had stuck by her through it all—and without remonstrance.

"I'm sorry. You're right, of course. I'm just a little distracted at the moment. I mean, we're down in a very dangerous spot, we just fought a troll, and who knows what we'll run into next. I was just a little worked up."

They continued down the passageway, following the silver hand. After a number of twists and turns, something changed in the quality of the air. Roscoe voiced what they all knew.

"Smell that—that's the river. I'd know that smell in my sleep, so I would."

The tunnel abruptly opened into a natural cavern so immense that the far walls were lost in the gloom. Huge stalactites hung above them like the fangs of an ancient, calcified giant. Water poured in steady streams from fissures somewhere overhead, feeding an underground lake that looked as black as tar.

Roscoe spoke again.

"We're beneath the river now, that's it passin' over our heads at this very moment."

That was a sobering thought. Uncountable tons of water and who-knows-how-many slithering river monsters were being held aloft by a ceiling that, from the look of the myriad fissures, was ready to crumble at any moment.

Sensing his friends' dismay, Roscoe sought to lighten the mood.

"No need for worry. If these walls have held the river up this long, they'll do it a mite longer while we're down here. We're not so important as to make everythin' come crashin' down on our heads just for spite."

They kept going, following a narrow shelf that curved along the lake's edge. It came to an abrupt end where a wide spot, stacked with empty casks, served as a natural wharf. A small flat-bottomed barge was tied to an iron ring set into a rock. Again, it was Roscoe who assessed the situation.

"Do you see what's goin' on here? Instead of movin' the goods across the river up above, the smugglers have found themselves an easier way across this placid bit of lake. More private, too. The weapons and empty casks go west, the full casks come east. A right jolly arrangement, so it is."

Torgul was not so positive.

"Right jolly for them smugglers, but not so good for us if they find us down here. They won't want nobody knowin' about this place."

Roscoe nodded.

"Aye—you've the right of it, for a fact. Let's conclude our business and get out. The path ends here, so unless someone's minded to take that barge and go explorin' the other side, there ain't no further to go. There still ain't no sign of our quarry—but look!—the wee silver hand is pointin' straight at that stack of casks. Thurmond, you've got experience dealin' with troll hands. Take a look-see at what's behind em."

The young man dutifully drew his sword and began to prod among the casks. At first there was no sign of movement, but then a weird scuttling creature burst from a dark crevice, ran between Thurmond's legs, and attempted to dodge its way through the rest of the adventure party.

It would likely have made it, too, for their natural inclination was to flinch back from the loathsome little entity. But Torgul was in no mood for sport. He brought his heavy boot down as it attempted to scurry past, pinning it to the stone pathway. Seizing it by what seemed to be a boneless section of forearm, he held it up for Thurmond's inspection.

"Is this what we're looking for?"

Thurmond stepped closer, but not too close, for he feared the thing, which continued to flop and twist in the grip of the dwarf.

"Aye! That's it, though strangely changed. It looks bigger now—bloated. And it was cut off clean at the wrist, without that part you're hanging onto. The skin was different then, too. It was smooth with small, fine scales like a snake's. Now it's all rough and ragged, a lot nastier than it was before. But I'm certain it's the same hand."

Roscoe seemed fascinated by the squirming horror. He leaned close to have a look.

"Must be the same one—surely there can't be two such hideous creatures crawlin' about. Let's get it stowed and be on our way."

The troll hand was secured in a stout leather rucksack that was then given to Thurmond to carry. He could feel it writhing against his back, reminding him of how he had previously carried it over his shoulder in a cloth sack. When its claws had begun to penetrate the fabric, he had been forced to bind the fingers into a fist with twine made from blades of grass.

The adventure party was just starting back along the lakeside when, to their dismay, they saw light flooding from the tunnel mouth from which they had recently emerged. Torches! Voices! Someone was approaching. They hurried forward so as not be trapped on the narrow path along the water, but it was too late. A large group of armed men hove into view.

Roscoe gave voice to what they were all thinking.

"Shite on a stick—smugglers!"

The smugglers saw the Adventurers as well, for they gave a shout and came hurrying forward. There was a least a score, perhaps more. Too many to fight, trapped as they were along the water's edge.

The archers, bringing up the rear, immediately fell back. Thurmond assumed they were running away, most likely attempting to escape in the tethered barge while their erstwhile companions held off the attack. Damn their livers, the cowards!

But he was in error, for they retreated only until the curve of the path afforded them a clear shot at the oncoming smugglers. With cool professionalism, the trio began to unleash arrows. A shrill scream and an outraged yelp from the smugglers testified to their accuracy, yet their efforts counted for little. There were just too many smugglers, and the arrow fire only seemed to goad them forward.

There was no way to escape. In front, the first of the smugglers were now on the curving path. Behind, there was only ink-black water. The barge was too small to accommodate them all, and the smugglers would be upon them long before they could untie it and climb aboard. Swimming was not an option—not one of them had ever learned that art, and in any case, their heavy armor would surely drag them to the bottom.

The attackers had closed half the distance when a most unlikely event occurred. A gigantic lamprey with a maw as wide as a church door suddenly launched itself from the water and engulfed the foremost smuggler in a single bite.

So shocked were the smugglers at the unexpected appearance of such a vile and deadly creature that they stood frozen in shock. The lamprey raised itself well above the heads of the men, waggled the barbels surrounding its jawless mouth, and struck again. Another smuggler went down its gullet.

The others could stand no more. They turned and fled back the way they had come, their weapons falling from nerveless fingers. Their torches, also discarded, rolled into the water, plunging their end of the cavern into darkness.

The Adventurers drew together, all the while praying that the lamprey's appetite had been satisfied. Thurmond reached out for Sarah, and to his utter surprise, found her stretched prone on the ground in a swoon.

He whispered urgently in her ear.

"Sarah! Sarah! Can you hear me? What's wrong with you? What happened?"

She groaned softly and began to regain her senses.

"Illusion—it's only illusion—that monster—I made it."

Thurmond felt a huge surge of relief wash through him, for he truly hated the idea of being eaten by a giant lamprey.

"You did that? That was just a spell?"

"Aye—just a spell, but a big one. It took all my energy. I feel so weak. Sick, too. Help me to up, okay?"

Just as movement required physical energy, magical powers drew on psychic energy. An over-expenditure of energy left a magic user nauseous and exhausted. Sarah, a relative novice, had a very limited reserve of such power.

Thurmond helped her up, then turned to Roscoe and Torgul.

"Did you hear what she said? That monster was just an illusion. It can't hurt us."

They had indeed heard the young witch's words. Roscoe, still shaken, peered doubtfully into the water.

"If that was just a vision, lassie, what became of them poor buggers what got swallowed? Are they dead for real or no?"

Sarah's voice was strained—talking was still difficult.

"Not sure. They could be, if their belief was strong enough."

"Could your monster hurt us?"

"Nay—absolutely not. It faded as soon as I ran out of energy."

Torgul started back toward the tunnel mouth.

"We need to move along while the smugglers are still runnin' scared."

Thurmond peered closely at Sarah. She looked worn out.

"Are you able to stand?"

"Aye—just help me to my feet. I'll be fine. Torgul's right—we best get going."

Thurmond caught her around the waist with one arm and steadied her as she rose. As they followed Torgul around the lake, the path was littered with the smugglers' swords and spears. They passed a dead man lying face up with an arrow in his neck. Two more floated face down in the water, the lamprey's victims.

Thurmond was puzzled.

"Sarah—if that monster was just an illusion, what killed those two?"

"Hard to say. Illusions are only as effective as your belief in them. If those two truly believed they were being eaten by a monster, perhaps they really were—at least until the spell faded. Or maybe they just fell in the water and drowned."

"Or maybe they were scared to death? Is that possible?"

"I guess anything is possible, Thurmond. Nothing is certain about magic."

Thurmond found such ambiguity frustrating. When Sarah spoke of the occult, there were never any firm answers, just a lot of unanswerable questions.

The adventure party retraced their steps until they reached the chamber in which they had encountered the troll. The heavy wooden door that they had left ajar was now shut against them. The smugglers had, in their headlong flight, paused at least long enough to close and bar it. Torgul motioned for the others to stand back and remain silent. He pressed his ear to the portal's planks, listened briefly, then returned to his comrades.

"Couldn't make out the words, but they're in there all right. Sounds like they're havin' an argument."

Roscoe considered a moment and then spoke.

"Sarah's monster took the man at the head of their group. He mighta been the leader, probably was. Right now, those boyos ain't got anyone makin' their decisions for 'em. They're arguin' cause none of 'em knows what to do next."

Thurmond spoke up.

"Well, you're our leader, Roscoe. Tell us, what should we do next. Our way out leads through that door."

The old Adventurer scratched his bearded chin.

"Even if we could cut through the door, there's too many of 'em for us to fight. We'd never make it. Let's try that passage that branched off a wee ways back. It's gotta lead somewheres—doesn't it?"

This did not seem like a particularly brilliant suggestion, for it would mean wandering at random through the Catacombs' measureless and perilous depths. Still—none of the others could think of a better plan.

Their encounters in that dismal world were weird and disturbing. Chambers in which human bones were stacked to the ceiling, the heaped skulls laughing in sardonic glee at the Adventurers' futile effort to find their way out. A room filled with the broken and rusted remains of what were once the hideous instruments of torture. Another in which a great yellow serpent coiled in one corner. Disturbed by the intruders, it raised its wedge-shaped head, and warned them away with a menacing hiss.

The most frightening thing of all was that they were completely lost in this hellish subterranean labyrinth. They might well be doomed to traipse aimlessly until they died of exhaustion, thirst, or hunger—or perhaps from sheer despair. They could only push forward in the fading hope of stumbling blindly upon a way out.

CHAPTER 11

THE RAVING OF
THE PROPHET

Lady Fortune gives and Lady Fortune takes. On this day—if it still was day, there being no way to tell—she was generous. Long before they could see the glow, the Adventurers could smell the smoke of a fire. That meant people, people who would surely know the way to the surface. That, at least, was their most fervent hope.

Those people, when they found them, did not inspire much confidence. A more ragged, dejected, and uninspiring lot would be hard to imagine. Bedraggled women, scrawny children, withered old men, pox-ridden cripples, drooling simpletons—all were dressed in filthy, tattered clothing. They sat with their backs against a small, circular chamber, listening to the words of a small, gray-bearded man standing by a tiny fire.

At the appearance of the adventure party, the crowd drew back to the chamber's far side. Only the old man stood his ground, turning his head to reveal white, sightless eyes. His voice, when he spoke, had a liquid, almost musical quality.

"Who comes?"

Roscoe stepped forward, smiled broadly, and addressed the graybeard in his most congenial tone.

"I am Captain Roscoe Franklin, an Adventurer in good standing from the glorious city of Gorgonholm, so I am. Good sir, if I might trouble you for a bit of information. Could you direct us…?"

The old man interrupted, obviously not listening to Roscoe's words.

"What do ye want from us? We are poor people. What ye see here is all that we possess. I beg ye, harm us not."

The big Adventurer did his best to sound reassuring.

"Nay, sir, we will not harm you in any manner. We are lost and need your assistance to return to the upper world. Will you not help us?"

This seemed to get the oldster's attention.

"Aye, help ye we can, if ye will help us. We will guide ye out, but first ye must give us food. Our bellies scream for sustenance."

Roscoe nodded in agreement, forgetting that the man was blind.

"Aye—food you shall have, all that we carry. Half now, the other half when we see daylight. Agreed?"

This was a fair offer, for the Adventurers carried a goodly supply of rations in their rucksacks. But the graybeard did not answer, jumping instead to a new topic as if unable to sustain a coherent conversation.

"Ye say ye be lost. Well, lost ye shall be if ye return to that the cesspit known as Gorgonholm, for there is a curse upon it. I am Zeb, Zeb the Prophet, and I have the seeing of things to be. I tell ye verily…"

His voice grew strident as he warmed to his topic.

"…the end of days is upon us. The river shall run red with blood and frogs shall fall from the sky as rain. Then must the unbeliever know tribulation beyond telling, suffer the sting of his sin upon his blistered tongue…"

Torgul whispered to Roscoe.

"All that talk about bein' hungry—I think they might be cannibals."

The old Adventurer's eyes widened.

"Could be. Anything may be found in this dank underworld."

Zeb, meanwhile, continued to rave.

"…their buttocks beset by boils, their livers with worms…"

Roscoe could endure such nonsense no longer.

"Master Zeb, good sir, I beg you to listen. Are we agreed—that you will lead us to the surface in exchange for the food we carry?"

The mention of food again got his attention, at least for the moment.

"Aye, Aye—for yer food. So shall it be. But know this—if ye would be saved, ye must remain down here, with us."

These last words made Roscoe a bit wary.

"And why, good sir, would you so desire our companionship?"

"Ye are a big man, and strong—yer voice speaks of it. I hear the clank of armor and the clink of coin in yer purse. Ye can go fetch us food—buy it, fight for it, take it from the unrighteous—then come back here to join our company. Keep us safe from the things that lurk in the dark."

Roscoe desperately needed the cooperation of this crazy old man and did not want to offend him, so he made up a lie.

"Your offer is temptin', so it is, and well worth consideration. But for the nonce, we are on a quest of the greatest import. We have been sent to discover the source of the curse upon our city. The source of all our trouble, as it were."

Zeb shuffled forward, cocked his head as if Roscoe finally had his full attention.

"The source of the curse, says ye? The source is in the foul hearts of the city's folk. In their greed and gluttony and lust. They must suffer for their lying, cheating, fornicating ways."

Unable to keep the graybeard on track, Roscoe threw up his hands in frustration. It was now Sarah's turn—young women enjoy unique advantages when it comes to getting a man's attention.

"Father Zeb—I hope I may call you that, for you remind me of my own father."

This was also a lie. Her father was a decrepit nobleman who lived in an opulent mansion. Obscenely old and riddled with disease, Lord Staynes was nothing like Zeb, who in spite of his years and blindness seemed quite hale.

"Father Zeb, our need to return to the city is as great as your need for provender. Perhaps we can discuss this curse as you guide us out."

Zeb seemed startled by the new voice. He stretched his hand as if trying to touch her face.

"A wench! Have ye forsaken the folly of sin, girl?"

"Certes, good father, I have indeed."

"Ye must look to yer soul, girl, for this be the time of tribulation. The Black Stone is risen. Yer sins will gnaw into yer heart like a worm in an apple.

Then must brother turn against brother, father against son, neighbor against neighbor, servant against master until the city burns to ash and lies forgotten in a wasteland. So must it be."

"Aye, Father Zeb—to be sure. So must it be. But, prithee, help us now to find our way home…"

"Can you hear it, wench? The Black Stone's calling? Making yer guts twist in their own sin? Can ye feel it? Can ye, wench?"

"Nay, nay—you misunderstand…"

"Ye stink of sin, and ye be wanting my flesh—I can hear it in the way ye breathe. Yer own sin is driving ye to take me or kill me. That's the call of the Black Stone."

Sarah, quite defeated, turned to Roscoe.

"I can do nothing with this old loon. He's utterly mad. Maybe Thurmond should try next."

Thurmond, however, had slid off to one side to speak with a haggard woman. A brace of dull-faced children clutched the folds of her frayed dress. He spoke to her in a gentle tone.

"Mother, your babes look hungry. Let me give you this."

He held out a small loaf of bread from his rucksack. Her hand jerked up, as if she intended to snatch it from his grasp, but then paused. She said no word, but accepted the gift slowly, graciously, her dim eyes uncertain as she stared into those of the young man.

With trembling fingers, the woman broke tiny pieces from the loaf and gave them to her children, who swallowed them without chewing. She ate nothing.

Thurmond spoke again.

"Mother, do you know the path that leads to the light of day? If you can take us, we will give you all our food. Help us, and your children will hunger no longer."

Zeb continued to rant, seemingly unaware that neither Sarah nor Roscoe were paying much attention as they watched Thurmond and the woman. They did, however, learn that Zeb was a self-ordained preacher of no particular denomination, his congregation being a small band of tattered followers from the poorest of the city's poor.

Three days ago, Zeb had been struck by a vision of horrendous things to come—murder, fire, famine, pestilence, war. He had immediately gathered his flock and led them to the one place where, he believed, they could survive the pending cataclysm. So abrupt was their departure that they had not paused to gather the food needed to sustain them during their sojourn in the Catacombs. Hence, they were now beginning to starve.

All this trouble stemmed, he said, from the waxing power of some baleful influence he called the Black Stone, though exactly what that was, he did not explain.

The young witch began to listen more carefully to the old man's words.

"...reaches right into yer heart just like the hand of some foul demon. Sees all the jealousy and avarice, the lust and the rage that's down deep inside and wanting to boil out. The Black Stone—it tells them to do all those things they never dared before."

The old Adventurer was minded to dismiss Zeb's harangue as mere delirium, but Sarah was not so sure. The graybeard was certainly crazed, but that did not mean he was entirely wrong. Could the Black Stone not have some basis in fact? Something terrible was, after all, currently afflicting both the city and the surrounding villages. Zeb's assessment of the stone's power would explain the sudden violent outbursts.

Sarah was mulling this over when Thurmond returned, leading a girl by the hand. She was thin, pale, and looked to be of about fifteen years. Her hair was snarled and filthy, her dress torn and smeared with grime. She was plainly terrified of the Adventurers.

Thurmond introduced her.

"This is Maud. You saw me speaking to Ellen—she's the woman with the children. Well, Maud is her niece, and she's agreed to lead us back to the city. She knows the way to a secret opening by the river just outside the city wall—don't you, Maud?"

The girl stared at him blankly, then slowly nodded.

"Good girl, Maud. Now, I've agreed to leave half our rations with Ellen. We'll put the rest in one of our rucksacks and give it to Maud when we see daylight. Isn't that right, Maud?"

Again, the slow nod.

This was joyous news. Their negotiations with Zeb had gotten nowhere. Indeed, he seemed to have forgotten about the Adventurers and began delivering a sermon to the members of his flock. Not surprisingly, its subject matter was the evils of lechery, gluttony, ire, and greed. Old Zeb never seemed to tire of discussing those particular sins.

Maud was dull of wit, but her memory was sound. She led them through a warren of tangled passageways without error or confusion. As it turned out, they were quite near the surface when they encountered Zeb and his people, so their trek did not take long.

They stood before a small iron door, its surface scabbed with a heavy coating of rust, the locking mechanism broken and useless. Torgul gave a great push, and it swung open with a loud, abrasive *skreeek*. There was no burst of sunlight, for it was night. They had been underground for at least twenty-four hours. The fresh air tasted wonderful.

Roscoe intended to invite Maud back to Grimsgard where she would enjoy a much better life than she had known to his point. But before the offer could be made, she grabbed the rucksack of food and disappeared back down the tunnel.

The party stepped out into the night and took their bearings. They were on the riverbank, near the south end of the city's western wall, only a few leagues from Grimsgard. The iron door was concealed in a tumble of boulders.

As they headed for home, Thurmond was disappointed. Adventurers were supposed to earn their living by slaying fell creatures and taking their treasure. They had fought and killed a savage troll, but they had found no cache of jewels or gold. It did not seem right somehow.

Sarah kept pondering Zeb's strange predictions. Could the Black Stone be real? Could it be the cause of all the current turmoil? She could not say, but she knew who she could ask about it.

Roscoe was tired and hungry. He longed for one of Florio's lavish dinners and a big flagon of Torgul's excellent mead. Then his bed for a nice, long sleep, and after that a magnificent breakfast. He would ask Florio to make something special for the occasion.

The dwarf drifted to the rear of the adventure party, well behind the trio of archers. They had somewhat redeemed themselves by feathering the smugglers with such alacrity, but he did not really trust them. Dwarves could be stubborn and narrow-minded, stodgy even, but they were dependable. Humans, especially fervent ones like Cob, could be dangerously unpredictable. Best to keep an eye open.

CHAPTER 12
DOOMFUL TIDINGS

The Adventurers arrived home just as the sun was taking its first shy peek over the horizon. Asmodeus was sitting on a bench by the tower's entrance. An empty tankard and a platter of chicken bones testified that Florio, like any good host, had offered refreshment but had wisely not invited him inside.

The wizard was clad in a short jacket and huge, billowing pantaloons, both of crushed velvet in a rich violet hue. Once again, he resembled a grape. Nearby, his demon steed gnawed on something that might have been the carcass of an unlucky cat.

Without waiting to be asked, Torgul unstrapped his rucksack and withdrew the twitching troll hand. Asmodeus seized the appalling thing, cuddled it to his breast, and began to coo as to a newborn.

"Oooo, you're just lovely. Aye, you are. I've got the nicest little bed for you, with your very own satin pillow. And you'll just love scampering about with my other little pets."

Roscoe was impatient to be finished with the wizard. He wanted his dinner and his bed.

"Master Asmodeus, you seem right pleased with your...uh...item. You will then agree that we've fulfilled our obligation to you."

Asmodeus did not look up. He was busy tickling the hand between its fingers, laughing as it squirmed in pleasure.

"Oh, I suppose so, but there is one other small matter I would have you attend to."

Roscoe's reply was grave.

"Another matter, small or otherwise, was not part of our bargain."

The wizard sighed.

"Perhaps not, perhaps not—but bargains are so pedestrian. Anyway, it is a matter in which you have a great personal stake."

"And what would this matter be, if I might inquire?"

Asmodeus's reply was chilling.

"While our city has been embroiled in violent discord, our Keltin neighbors are, I believe, experiencing a period of unprecedented unity. I believe that they are gathering their forces in order to pay us a call."

This was bad news indeed. The Keltin tribes on the western side of the river posed a perpetual threat to the very existence of Gorgonholm. They were smart, devious, and deadly. Over the centuries, they had periodically surged across the river in a wild flurry of killing, looting, and burning.

Though the Keltins had never surmounted the city's massive walls, they brought death to anyone they caught outside its gates, and a small, isolated village like Grimsgard would be swallowed as easily as Asmodeus' demon steed was consuming its cat.

Thurmond was quite alarmed by the wizard's words. Since his arrival in Gorgonholm four years ago, relations with the Keltins had been relatively cordial. But everyone was aware that a period of peace could suddenly end with a bloodbath.

Now his inner voice told him to be wary of Asmodeus, to look for some hidden purpose in his warning. He decided to probe a little.

"I thought you said that you liked troubled times—that they brought you opportunity."

Asmodeus began to caress the hand, as one might stroke the soft fur of a bunny.

"Troubled times, aye—I can make use of them. But it would not be good for anyone to have the county devastated by savages."

Roscoe got right to the point.

"What would you have us do?"

Asmodeus kept his attention focused on the hand as he spoke.

"You will cross the river, locate the Keltin's main force, and assassinate their high king. He is, I am told, a rather charming fellow by the name of Fergis. You must slay him. He is the one bringing them together. Without him, the lesser chiefs will resume their usual childish squabbling and leave us to enjoy our pastimes. You will accomplish this."

Thurmond recoiled in astonishment. He was willing to risk life and limb in deadly combat, and had done so several times. But he was not about to undertake a quest that was so blatantly doomed to failure, that must certainly result in a pointless death.

The Adventurers stood mute—unsure how to respond to such an outrageous demand. Finally, Sarah broke the silence.

"In the Catacombs, we met a man, a crazy man, who spoke of something he called the *Black Stone*. He claimed that it was rising, affecting feelings, making us do evil things. Have you heard of such a thing?"

Now it was Asmodeus's turn to fall into silent reverie. He steepled his fingers and twiddled his thumbs, wrinkled his brow and stroked his chin. When he spoke, there was no longer a trace of his smug, superior air. He seemed genuinely frightened.

"The Black Stone—aye, I know of it. It's an old, old legend. But it couldn't be true. Well—perhaps it could, I suppose."

Sarah was surprised to see the normally arrogant wizard grow so uncertain.

"What is it supposed to be, this Black Stone?"

"Think of it as a demon of tremendous malevolent power. But instead of inhabiting a body with scales and claws and wings like a proper fiend, it resides in a great slab of black stone. It was cast down centuries ago, its power checked. But now, as you tell it, the entity's power is rising again. Give me a moment—I must consult my minions beyond the veil."

Asmodeus drew apart from the others. He lowered himself awkwardly to the ground with his fat legs crossed beneath him. With eyes closed and pudgy hands clasped across his belly, he withdrew into deep abstraction.

Several minutes went by. The Adventurers remained silent and unmoving. Then the wizard's eyes opened, and he rose and returned to the group.

"This person you met—he may well be mad, but he had the right of things—it is the Black Stone. It is at this moment gathering adherents, filling them with hatred and fear, turning them on each other. Now it's reaching out to the Keltins, spurring them to attack."

These words filled Roscoe with cold dread. As a smuggler, he had had enough experience with Keltin tribesmen to understand the grave danger they presented.

"What does it mean for me and my people?"

"It means that you are saved from a trip across the river. I can send some other … hmmm … entities to confound the Keltins for a while. You must go in another direction."

To the old Adventurer, any direction would be preferable to a venture among the Keltins.

"Where do we go?"

"North—to Malachai."

"What's Malachai? A city?"

"Nay—not a city. A superlative magician. Malachai alone will know how to defeat the Black Stone. You must go and enlist his aid."

"Where exactly is this Malachai fella to be found?"

"In the far north, in the moors that border the Cold Sea. I will provide a map that will lead you to his castle."

Roscoe refused to be drawn into the wizard's schemes so easily.

"This ain't an undertakin' for the likes of us. It's the earl's job to hold off the Keltins, so it is. You should be talkin' to him. And as for this Malachai— well, it seems like you and him is old comrades. I'm bettin' he'd be more willin' to talk to you than to us."

Asmodeus was unmoved by his protestation.

"Nay—you must undertake this quest. I will be required here, for there shall be war. I will send emissaries to inform Earl Ralf of this great peril. He will then dispatch messengers to his many feudal vassals, who will in turn summon their levies. All of this will take time—time we don't have."

"I must try to impede the Stone's insidious influence and give the earl time to gather his forces. Thus, I cannot make the journey north. In any case, Malachai and I are far from being, as you put it, *old comrades*. Nay—it must be you who rides north."

Roscoe cleared his throat with a deep, rumbling growl.

"There's only the four of us—well, four of us and maybe them three archers. That's an icy wasteland up there, full of headhuntin' Vanarians and huge, shaggy lions with teeth like sabers. At least that's what I've always heard told. This ain't no job for us."

Roscoe's concerns about the Vanarians were well founded. Those tall, blond savages were the foe of all who cherished peace and regularity. Centuries ago, following the decline of the Etrusian empire, the Vanarians had swept southward, burned Gorgonholm to the ground, and piled the heads of its citizens before the altars of their terrible gods.

The northmen held sway for almost one hundred years, pillaging anything worth stealing and effectively preventing the re-establishment of trade, education, or organized religion. It took the full might of the Seax, a powerful confederation of southern tribes, to finally drive the Vanarians back to their frigid homeland on the edge of the Cold Sea.

Today, the northern warriors were too few to pose any serious threat to the Kingdom of Poitiers, but travelers entering their territory were well advised to be heavily armed and wary. An inclination for brutality still swelled in the breasts of the Vanarians. Young boys could not be recognized as warriors until they had slain a foe and tasted his blood, thereby taking his soul and his strength for their own.

None of this mattered to Asmodeus.

"You would prefer to sit in your miserable little tower to await the arrival of the Keltins? Would you enjoy watching your tenants murder their neighbors as the Black Stone claims their minds and souls? How long will it be before you and your friends turn on one another?"

Thurmond suddenly took the initiative.

"Master Asmodeus, I will undertake this quest. As an Adventurer in good standing, I can do no less for my friends and my city."

This was a bold and rather naïve statement. In spite of their high ideals, many Adventurers were motivated much more by profit than by honor or loyalty. Further, had he thought about it, in pledging himself to the mission, he was committing his friends as well. They would never let him go alone.

Sarah raised her voice next.

"I will go north with Thurmond."

Roscoe shook his head in resignation.

"All right—I yield. We're all brothers here—oh, sorry, Sarah, I just mean that...oh shite! ...you know what I mean. We're all true Adventurers—if one of us goes, we all go."

Asmodeus grinned a sly grin.

"Your young friend comprehends the inevitability of your situation more readily than you do."

"Perhaps so. Thurmond's always been smart as paint, so he has. But I'm not so stupid as to not see through your beguilin' ways. No matter! We'll find this Malachai and enlist his aid in the defense of our city. But you must lend us aid."

The wizard's reply was flat, emotionless.

"You have the wallet of gold I paid you for the hand. Use it to purchase whatever you need. And as I said, all my powers will be needed here to hold back the Stone's influence. You must fend for yourselves."

Roscoe remained undeterred. By now he was far less afraid of Asmodeus than he had been. This was an indubitably foolish attitude.

"And as I said, we are too few. It won't serve to have us butchered by Vanar warriors before we accomplish our task, now will it?"

The wizard was forced to relent.

"Very well, there is a small company of mercenaries with whom I have had dealings. I will send word to their captain and instruct him to accompany you. They number, I believe, about a dozen. Surely that would be sufficient."

"Aye—a dozen experienced men would be good, so it would. But make sure to inform this captain of mercenaries that I am to be the Adventure Captain and that he must serve loyally under my command. That must be understood by everyone. Do you understand that, Master Wizard?"

"To be sure, Captain Appleman. Just as you must understand that delay will be fatal. Thus, you will ride with all possible haste to Visby, there to meet my mercenaries at an inn called Three Fat Friars. Then proceed north."

"I imagine that Malachai will demand some small service in exchange for his cooperation. Do whatever he demands—it is the only way. You must not fail."

The wizard rose from the bench and walked to his steed. Having finished its meal, the creature was asleep with its head under one wing. He kicked it awake, mounted, and soared away into the night sky.

Sarah pointed to the ground beneath the bench.

"Look—he forgot his hand."

Sure enough, the hand lay curled on its side, seemingly asleep.

CHAPTER 13

SO MUCH FUSS AND BOTHER

Roscoe took a huge bite of bread, chewed it thoughtfully, swallowed, then turned to his friend.

"I must be feelin' my age, Thurmond. Time was, I'd have been up and rarin' for an adventure up north, but last night all I could think of was a meal and my bed."

The young man waved a dismissive hand.

"Think no more of it. We were all exhausted. I said I'd go simply to end the debate—I too wanted to go to bed. I must apologize for my hasty words. I had no intention of speaking for us all."

The four companions sat around the long dining table in the tower's Great Hall, still picking at the remains of Florio's glorious breakfast.

"That's all right, laddie. You were right to do so. The Grape was tellin' it straight—it's somethin' we gotta do, so it is."

Roscoe selected a pickled wren from a nearby platter and popped it into his mouth whole. He then paused to spit out the beak and bones.

"Still—I dislike bein' forced into things like we was last night."

He then shouted in the direction of the kitchen.

"Florio! Would you be so kind as to join us, please?"

The elf had been informed of their impending departure, but Roscoe wanted to clarify a few details. He came in from the kitchen, wiping his hands on his apron.

"Milord?"

Roscoe blew air through his nostrils in exasperation.

"Now, Florio, you know well that I ain't a proper lord, and I ain't deservin' of any such a fancy title. Won't you just call me Roscoe like everyone else?"

The elf bowed his head.

"As you will."

They had had this conversation on numerous occasions. Roscoe knew that Florio's acquiescence was feigned and that he would never truly refrain from using the honorific. It forced him to smile, in spite of the serious matter before them.

"You're incorrigible, Florio. But I ain't got time to discuss your personal failins at the moment, grievous though they are. You are once again to have complete authority to do whatever you must to protect this estate. There's plenty money in the strongbox under my bed. Here's the key to it."

He tossed him the item in question.

"I've left you an armory stocked with proper fightin' gear. Not like last time when you was left with nothin'. I hope you won't be needin' to use it, but it's there if you do. Keep the villagers busy, so they won't have time to think up mischief. But you know all that—you handle 'em better than I do. And keep a sharp watch on the river. Any sign of Keltins, you get everybody inside the tower at once. Understand?"

"I do, *milord.*"

The elf let this last word slip out as if by accident, but Roscoe knew better.

"Agghhh—as I said, you're incorrigible. Hey—what you got in the kitchen? I could do with some cake. Could you find me a wee bite of cake?"

Florio knew that Roscoe's idea of a *wee bite* would cover an entire plate.

A scullery girl came in to announce that someone was at the door asking for Roscoe. Florio went out to see what was wanted. He returned almost at once.

"It is a messenger from Asmodeus…."

Torgul interrupted, alarmed, his mouth stuffed with fermented pigeon eggs.

"A demon? Is it a demon?"

"Nay, Lord Torgul. As far as I can tell, he is strictly a man, though a strange looking one, I must admit. He brought this."

He produced a long leather tube, the kind used to carry parchment scrolls.

"The fellow claims that it is a map to guide you to your destination. In addition, he desires the...uh...*thing* that you retrieved from the Catacombs. It seems that his master, in his distracted state, forgot to take it with him last night."

Torgul rose from the table.

"I'll fetch it."

The hand had spent the night locked in an iron cage that had once held Roscoe's hunting ferret. On its first excursion, that ungrateful little beast had taken its prey and run off into the forest. Since then, the cage had sat unused. It made a perfect home for the hand.

Breakfast over, they rose and started preparing for their journey. Thurmond was on his way to the stable when Sarah caught his hand and pulled him aside.

"Can you spare a moment? I have to tell you something."

They sat down on the stone seat of a window niche. The girl put her hand on his knee.

"I feel really shitty about the way I treated you after—you know—what you told me about the troll hand and all. I was pretty shocked, but I shouldn't have been. After all, we were trying to catch the horrible little thing for Asmodeus—that's no better than you bringing it to that disgusting noble who hired you. I'm sorry, Thurmond."

The young Adventurer was touched by her sincerity. Sarah could be headstrong, blunt, demanding and, at times, selfish, but they had shared an intense bond since first meeting almost two years ago. At times, they bickered and disagreed, but she remained his closest friend and ally.

Her words caused him to smile.

"Apology accepted. No harm done. We were all worked up right then— with that cursed troll and all. But thanks for those words."

He rose, put his arm around her shoulders, and kissed her lips. Then he paused.

"This talk made me happy—thank you."

And with that, he was on his way to the stables.

Meanwhile, Roscoe was sorting things out with the Gascars. Cob, who had been the most garrulous of the three, remained morose and silent. Wat and Tuck, however, seemed eager to hear what the old Adventurer had to say.

"All right, laddies—we got off to a bit of a rough start, so we did. But once I made myself clear, you gave good, loyal service. You've earned your pay, and here it is."

He placed a small pouch of coins in Wat's hand.

"Count it if you want—I won't be offended—but it's all there."

Roscoe turned slightly away from the obstreperous Cob and spoke directly to Wat and Tuck.

"I don't know how much of our gab you was listenin' to last night, with that wizard fella, I mean. But we've gotta make a long trip north through some dangerous country. We could use some men who are good with bows, men who give good, loyal service. If you two want to come along, I'll pay you well. If not, well, I understand."

Then he turned his attention to Cob.

"I know you don't like us much, don't approve of the way we do things. That's your business, and I'll not be holdin' it against you. Let us part on agreeable terms."

When Cob failed to respond, Roscoe looked again at the younger archers. Wat shuffled his feet uncomfortably, as if reluctant to say what was on his mind. The old Adventurer had no time for such shillyshallying.

"Out with it, lad. Say what you're thinkin', whatever it is."

"It's like this, Captain Roscoe. I know you don't like Cob—nobody much does. He ain't no good when it comes to dealin' with people. But Tuck and me, we feel different. Cob always sticks by us and watches out so nothin' bad can happen. Real loyal, he is. We wanna come with you, we really do, but we can't leave Cob."

Roscoe nodded.

"I expected somethin' like this, so I did. It's all right, boyo, I understand."

"Nay, Captain, I don't think you do. I'm askin' you to give Cob another chance. Let him come along. There won't be no trouble, none at all—Tuck and me will see to that."

Roscoe stared hard at Cob, who turned away, unwilling to meet his gaze. This did not bode well.

"Cob ain't said two words since we was back there in the tunnels. Been in a funk ever since I give him a dressin' down. I don't believe he'd be wantin' to come with us."

"He'll come all right. Look, Captain Roscoe—we got no place else to go. We don't know nobody hereabouts, and Cob…he don't exactly win us no friends. But he's a grand archer. You saw how he shot against them smugglers. We don't know nothin' about fightin' trolls, but we're good when it comes to killin' men."

Roscoe wanted the services of three experienced men-at-arms. Cob made him uneasy, but he could not deny that he had done well in battle. Right now, he needed men with such skill, even a man like Cob.

"All right, boyo, I'll take you at your word that you'll keep him in line. But know this—at the first bit of trouble, no matter where we be, out he goes. And if that means losin' Tuck and you, well, so be it. Do you take my meanin' clearly?"

"I do, Captain, I truly do. You won't regret this. We're good men, true and loyal—you'll see."

Roscoe could only hope that he had made the right decision. He would have preferred to make a quick jaunt to the city and perhaps enlist a few of the others—fellow Adventurers or experienced soldiers. But the city gates were probably still shut, and there was no time. He would have to make do with what he had.

He decided to groom his horse. He could, of course, have assigned this task to a servant, but the old Adventurer liked to do it himself. It always soothed him to spend time with horses. Unfortunately, he was not to have the pleasant respite he hoped for. Entering the stable, he found Thurmond and Sarah locked in a passionate embrace.

"Burning eyes of God! Why can't you two go to your chambers, or better yet the privy, if you want to carry on like that. It's plumb embarrassin' to an old man like myself."

The two looked contrite, but not overly so. Thurmond cleared his throat.

"Sorry, Roscoe. Well, actually, I'm not really sorry at all. We were just having a moment. You must remember what it was like to be young."

"Maybe so. But I don't like bein' reminded that I'm past the point of playin' kissy-face with a girl in the middle of the day. Have a little mercy."

Sarah laughed, adjusting her bodice.

"You barged in on us. Maybe you should make some noise next time to give us a little warning. Anyway, I want to talk to you. Pozi approached me a few minutes ago. She wants to go with us."

Pozi was a precocious twelve-year-old that Thurmond and Sarah had met in a tiny village in the wild mountains of Carpat. Agile as a cat and utterly fearless, she had guided them up a sheer cliff face to investigate a haunted castle. In exchange, she had been allowed to accompany them back to Grimsgard and escape the dreary existence that awaited her as a village woman. Pozi was now Bodo's adopted daughter.

Roscoe exploded.

"Has the girl gone mad? Absolutely not! Why would you even suggest such a thing?"

He had so many things on his mind at the moment, he did not want to be bothered by the demands of a pesky child. Sarah did her best to calm him down.

"Peace, Roscoe—I was suggesting nothing. I agree with you. The adventure is much too perilous for Pozi to come along. I already told her so. I was just letting you know because she'll come begging and wheedling pretty soon. I thought you'd like to have a bit of warning. You know how she can be."

Roscoe held his hand over his face.

"So much fuss and bother. I got Keltin invaders gettin' ready to cross the river and a demon rock turnin' people's brains. I got a fat, little wizard tellin' me what to do. I got an archer with a bilious disposition and two baby Adventurers who'd rather grope each other than do their work. Now I'm gonna have a contrary child pesterin' me when all I want to do is groom my horse and enjoy my day. It ain't fair. It ain't right. I won't have it."

In Skut, Lord Ubo Futz was lounging in his Great Hall, considering his options. The stone had by now brought him a considerable force, but it consisted almost entirely of untrained, unarmed peasants and woodsmen. Such bastards were worse than useless—undisciplined, dull witted, and always hungry. He needed soldiers, real soldiers, but very few real men-at-arms had deserted their posts to join his throng. He also had a handful of Gray Friars, but these were badly cut up, having just fought a pitched battle with their monastic brothers.

A commotion in the yard below drew his attention. He rose and peered through a narrow window at some ragged serf bellowing his name. He yelled down to the unknown figure.

"Stop that racket, you filthy peasant. How dare you disturb my contemplation with your stupidity?"

"But milord, I bear news—news most important."

"Bah—what could you possibly know that would interest me?"

"Most important, milord, news about...."

He hesitated, obviously reluctant to complete the thought.

"News of what, you lump of dung?"

"About..."

Again, the pause. His reticence was becoming distinctly annoying.

"If you don't speak up at once, dolt, I'll have my men introduce you to their knives."

This threat was sufficient to untie his tongue.

"About the stone, milord, the Black Stone."

Ubo immediately left the window, dashed down the stairs, and ran to where the peasant stood looking stupid and lost. He glared at the man.

"Say no more. Not another word until asked."

He grabbed the peasant's tunic and began pulling him toward the door of his towerhouse. Assuming he was to be killed, the man began to struggle and cry out. Ubo gave him a hard slap with his free hand.

"Stop squalling, you stinking turd, or I'll have your eyes burned out."

The peasant fell silent, and Ubo dragged him inside. The ground floor of the towerhouse served as the storeroom. Ubo threw the man into one corner.

Drawing his dagger, he placed the point under the fellow's chin and pressed just hard enough to make a dark bead of blood trickle down its blade.

"Who are you?"

The man was nearly dumb with terror. He could only stammer.

"I am…I…I am called…Kak.

"And where do you come from, Kak? You're not one of my tenants."

"Nay, milord, I belong to Lord Roscoe—well, you see, he ain't no proper lord really, but…"

"Then why do you style him as such?"

"Whaa?"

"Why do you call him your *lord* if he isn't one?"

"I dunno—we all just call him that because that's what we call him."

Ubo was tiring of this idiot's jabber.

"Let us get back to the real point, Kak. What do you want to tell me? You mentioned the Black Stone."

"Aye, Aye, that's why I come here—to tell you. I was listenin' last night while Lord Roscoe … I mean…oh … I dunno … while they was talkin'…"

"While who was talking, Kak?"

"Lord Roscoe and some wizard what come ridin' in on a demon."

Kak began to tremble uncontrollably. Ubo thought the man might go into a swoon, so he lied a little.

"I'm not going to hurt you, Kak. Not as long as you tell me everything I need to know. Now what exactly did this Roscoe and the wizard talk about?"

"About the Black Stone. I was hidin' in the bushes and listenin' to 'em talk. They was makin' plans to pull it down. To take its power."

"And why would you care to listen to such talk, Kak? More importantly, why would you come tell me?"

"Because I, too, serve the stone. In a dream, it told me to come."

"Well, in that case, tell me everything."

Kak had a remarkable memory for an ignorant peasant and gave a wonderfully accurate account of the conversation that had taken place the night before. He told how Roscoe and company would be heading north to rendezvous with a pack of mercenaries at Visby, then proceeding on to find

Malachai. How Malachai was to be enlisted to overthrow the Black Stone and restore the order of things.

Ubo listened with interest.

"You deserve a reward, Kak. What is it you desire beyond all things?"

"I want only to serve the stone."

"Well then, Kak, you will achieve your heart's desire, for the greatest service one can give is to die for the cause."

PART 2

OF BARBARIANS
AND MERCENARIES

CHAPTER 14
GUSTAVUS SAYS HELLO

They started at dawn the following morning with Roscoe, the Adventure Captain, taking the lead. Torgul rode close behind him. The archers came next, leading a pair of pack mules. Thurmond and Sarah rode side by side at the end of the cavalcade.

The young man chuckled.

"I heard Roscoe had quite a scene with Pozi. What happened?"

"Well, I already told her what he said to me, that she couldn't come along, but she wouldn't listen. Pretty soon, here she comes with her things tied up in a bundle, wanting to know which horse was hers."

"That's when Roscoe stepped in?"

"Aye, he was trying to be very nice about it, trying to make her understand without hurting her feelings."

"What did she say?"

"She informed him that if he didn't let her come, she'd steal a horse and follow along behind until we were too far along to send her back. Then he'd have to let her stay."

"How'd he like hearing that?"

"He said he'd have her locked in the chicken coop, but she told him she'd just pick the lock and escape."

This was no idle boast. Pozi was quite adept as a picklock.

Sarah continued.

"Then he said he'd have her whipped for her cheekiness, but she just laughed and told him that he's much too softhearted to ever do such a thing."

Thurmond raised his eyebrows at that. He had to admit, the girl was cheeky.

"What then?"

Sarah gave a little giggle.

"He growled like an old bear and told her not to pester him with *any more of her accursed jabberin'.*"

These last words were delivered in a comic imitation of Roscoe's voice.

"So, how did you finally change her mind?"

Sarah now grew thoughtful.

"Look, Thurmond, Pozi's no different than the rest of us. She wants something more than the life that was handed to her. She's not about to marry some lunkheaded village boy and raise a pack of brats. She spent the last year learning how to ride a horse, shoot a bow, follow a track—skills that would make her a good Adventurer."

"I get all that, but she's still just a kid. What is she now, twelve?"

"Aye, twelve. But she doesn't see things that way. She feels she's already proven herself."

Pozi's assumptions were not without foundation. On their last adventure, she had repeatedly demonstrated her courage and resourcefulness.

"So how did you change her mind?"

"This may surprise you, Thurmond—I used reason. That's usually the best approach when trying to convince an intelligent young woman. I reminded her of how brainsickly people were becoming and that Florio would need her help while the rest of us were away. That's true enough, and it gave Pozi a feeling that she mattered."

Thurmond shrugged.

"Who knows? Maybe Florio will need her help."

The road north, known as Waddle Street, was a far cry from the great Royal Highway that led to the huge trading cities in the south. Built as an

Etrusian military road, its once-level and graveled surface was now badly pitted and had, in places, fallen away. The bridges that had allowed imperial legions quick passage to the volatile northern border had mostly tumbled into the rivers and ravines they had once spanned.

Waddle Street followed the river for a while, then jogged eastward through a series of small towns and settlements. The city of Visby was almost a hundred leagues distant, so several days, perhaps a week, would be required to join the mercenaries at Three Fat Friars. Roscoe had been up that way before and knew the territory fairly well. Further north, the villages would be small and scarce. Most of the time, they would be sleeping rough.

The adventure party rode all day at a steady pace but was often slowed by the poor condition of the road. Here and there, they were forced to dismount and lead their steeds across especially awkward places. In all, they traveled perhaps eight leagues before the setting sun forced them to halt for the night.

The three Gascars again proved themselves as veteran soldiers. Minutes after the party stopped, they had the gear unpacked, a fire going, and a neat little camp established. They had clearly attended to such tasks many times before.

After a surprisingly good dinner—Florio had packed lavish rations—they sought out comfortable places to hunker down. The archers chose a spot on the far side of the fire, a bit apart from the others. Thurmond volunteered to take the first watch. Torgul would replace him when the bottom edge of the moon cleared the top of the tallest tree.

Thurmond was absorbed in his own thoughts, contemplating the long journey ahead, when the quiet was disturbed by a loud voice from the other side of the fire. It was Cob!

Thurmond rose to investigate and was surprised to find the archer asleep, but with a steady stream of words pouring from his mouth. Unintelligible words, but words for certain, as if drawn from an arcane language.

Then Cob sat up, his eyes wide and blank with terror. Tuck and Wat were now awake and clasped Cob in their arms, speaking softly in his ear. Roused from sleep, Torgul appeared, axe in hand. Roscoe and Sarah were close behind with drawn swords.

When Cob was at last calm and quiet, Thurmond gestured to Wat to join him on the far side of the encampment.

"What's going on with Cob? From the way you and Tuck acted, I'd say you've seen him do this before."

Wat looked thoughtful.

"It's been goin' on for a time. Gettin' worse lately."

"What's wrong with him? Tell me."

"He talks to spirits when he's sleepin'. Least ways, that's what he says he does."

Thurmond was less than sympathetic. He really disliked Cob.

"If he's hearin' voices, he's crazed."

Wat shook his head vigorously.

"Nay, he ain't crazed. When he was little, the friars what raised him knocked him on the head a lot. I think maybe they shook somethin' loose, that's all. It's just his way of dreamin'. Don't mean nothin'."

Sarah stepped forward. She had been standing behind them, listening to their words.

"Maybe Wat's right, but some evil force has been whispering in a lot of ears of late."

Thurmond stiffened.

"If the Black Stone's talking to Cob, then he got to go right now.

Wat raised his hands imploringly.

"Nay, nay—he ain't done nothin' wrong. Only talked in his sleep. Tuck and me told the Captain we'd look after him, and we will. You can't send him away 'til he does somethin' bad—that's what the Captain said."

Thurmond did his best to dissuade Roscoe from allowing Cob to stay with the party. To him, it was an obvious decision. The man was under the influence of the Black Stone, so he had to go. Roscoe, however, remained adamant. He had pledged his word that Cob could stay until he caused a real problem.

Gustavus shielded his eyes from the glare of the newly risen sun. Below him, a narrow section of road known as the Serpent's Back wound its sinuous way along the side of a rock-strewn ridge. His quarry must come this way—there was no other passage north.

He and his men had ridden hard to be in this exact spot before their quarry arrived. He knew the Serpent's Back intimately, knew that this was a perfect place for an ambush.

As a young man, Gustavus had spent two years with a crew of road bandits that used the rugged area as their lair. From here, they could watch for isolated travelers on the road far below, catch and slay them on the narrow trail, and then retreat to their hideout in the upper reaches. When Lord Ubo had ordered him to annihilate the party of meddlesome interlopers, the confines of the Serpent's Back had immediately come to mind.

The location was perfect. A huge, precariously balanced boulder hung directly over the trail. One good push would send it and a cascade of smaller but nonetheless lethal stones down upon the heads of the unsuspecting travelers below. He and his men would pick off any survivors with arrows.

It was well that his plan was infallible, for the men he commanded did not inspire much confidence. Ubo had sent the best six men he had, but none had the look of real killers. Three had been the armed retainers of a rich merchant, one was a city constable who had deserted his post, two were common criminals. The avalanche would have to do most of the work.

Gustavus did not love Lord Ubo—there was nothing lovable about the man. Yet he was used to him. At age nine or ten—no one had ever paid much attention to the boy's exact age—Ubo had been given to him for instruction in the manly art of combat. Gustavus was, at that time, a sergeant-at-arms in the service of Lord Fugar, Ubo's father.

He had been neither kind to the boy nor even a particularly effective teacher. Instruction was given in the most cursory fashion, and mistakes were rewarded with a backhanded blow to the face. Strangely, Ubo had prospered under Gustavus's tutelage, and eventually became quite skilled with lance, sword, and axe.

Now Ubo was middle-aged and Gustavus was old. His eyes had grown dim and his hand was unsteady. But he was still the only man in whom Ubo placed any trust. It had been Gustavus who had warned Ubo about the plotting of his step-mother after the death of Fugar. And Gustavus who helped him arrange the painful demise of her and her children. So it had been Gustavus who had been sent to eliminate the meddlesome neighbor who threatened Lord Ubo's plans.

The long, swift ride to the Serpent's Back had been hard on his old bones, but he had persevered like he always had when carrying out his master's commands. The sun's glare bothered his eyes, but he kept them locked on the trail below.

Just then, a column of eight riders and two pack-mules came into view.

The spring morning was warm and bright, and Roscoe was enjoying himself. It felt good to be out and about. He was always the happiest when heading out on an adventure. His previous weariness had entirely fallen away. Torgul was reciting one of his interminable dwarven ballads.

The trail was twisty and narrow, wide enough for a small wagon but not particularly perilous. They were still within the borders of Poitiers and still relatively close to Grimsgard, so there was little threat of attack. They wore their armor, but helmets were hung from their saddles. Shields and spears were strapped to the pack-mules, as was Roscoe's heavy crossbow.

Torgul and Thurmond rode behind Roscoe, with Sarah next in line. Today, the archers and mules brought up the rear.

Gustavus chose that moment to spring his trap. Far above, two of his men used the trunk of a small tree to lever the big boulder out of balance and send it bounding down the hillside. As anticipated, it unleashed a torrent of smaller stones that would sweep the riders from the trail.

Gustavus had intended the avalanche to strike the center of the column, but his timing was poor. The big boulder struck the trail five feet in front of the old Adventurer's horse and gave a bounce that carried it into the ravine on the other side. Roscoe was able to draw rein and pull back just in time to avoid the subsequent landslide.

Exasperated by the failure of his trap, he signaled his men to finish the job with arrows before the party below could recover from the shock of the near miss. Dutifully, they rose and released a flight into the confused group.

A slight projection on the hillside screened the first three riders from the bowmen's view, so it was upon the middle and rear of the column that their arrows fell. Sarah was hit in the left bicep, the shaft penetrating flesh and protruding from the other side. Another arrow struck the rump of her horse. The beast reared abruptly, throwing her to the ground.

The Gascars were also struck. A shaft rebounded from the iron lining of Cob's coat-of-plates. Another cut the jugular of a pack-mule, which went down in a storm of flailing hooves. A third lodged in the pommel of Tuck's saddle.

Once again, the three Gascars were entirely professional in their response, leaping from their mounts and seeking cover amongst the rocks on the uphill side of the road. In an instant, they had strung their bows, drawn arrows from their quivers, and were seeking targets in the rocks and trees above.

Torgul yanked his axe from his back and began to work his way up the ridge, keeping low, dashing from boulder to boulder. Thurmond drew his sword and followed. He would have preferred his bow at that moment, but it was strapped to his saddle, and his frightened horse had bolted back down the trail. Roscoe saw Sarah on the ground and started toward her, but he was forced back when an arrow cut the air a hand's breadth from his face.

As the adventure party found cover, Gustavus's men ran out of targets. Only Sarah remained exposed. Unmoving, she looked dead, but several shafts were loosed in her direction. One pierced the skull of her mount and sent it crashing down. Fortunately, its carcass helped to shield her from further arrow fire.

Gustavus yelled for his bowmen to rise, to leave their concealed positions on the crest of the ridge and move to more open ground where would again have a clear shot at the people huddled below. At first, they balked, but when he threatened them with the Black Stone's curse—something he made up on the spot—they reluctantly stood and started forward.

The Gascars immediately went into action. Tuck's first took down one of Old Shamble's most notorious thieves, striking him in the throat and knocking him over backward. Cob's needle-sharp bodkin point struck another between two fingers of his left hand, just as he was raising his bow. The shaft pushed up the forearm lengthwise, almost to the elbow. The man screamed, dropped his bow, and ran.

Gustavus watched in dismay as his terrified men fell back to the original positions. He could smell their fear and knew that only by some great act of courage could he propel them forward again. He rose and waved his bow over his head to get their attention.

"Come on, you sons of whores—follow me! Let's go get 'em!"

Two arrows suddenly sprang from Gustavus's chest, one dead center, the other a bit to one side. A third, less well aimed, appeared in his left thigh. The old man died on his feet. With their leader down, the others fled to the far side of the ridge, found their horses, and beat it back to the city with all possible haste.

When the arrows ceased to fall, the adventure party emerged from cover. Tuck, Wat, and Cob stood by, arrow on string. Roscoe ran to Sarah and was relieved to find her alive and conscious.

Her wound was serious but not life-threatening. The arrow's head had passed cleanly through the flesh and muscle of her bicep without touching the nerves or major blood vessels. A foot of bloody wooden shaft projected from the back of her arm.

Roscoe's voice was soft as a mother speaking to her babe.

"Sarah, darlin'—I gotta pull this thing out of your arm. It's gonna come out easy, but it's like to hurt like blazes. Here, drink some of this."

He held a silver flask to her lips.

"What is it? That dwarven stuff?"

On other occasions, Roscoe had dispensed a mysterious concoction of Torgul's making. It was at first wonderfully exhilarating, even to someone bearing a serious injury. The aftereffects, however, could be awful.

"Nay, nay—ain't nothin' but uisge, just good, wholesome uisge. Take down as much as you can."

While Sarah held as still as possible, Roscoe cut off the arrowhead so only an inch of wood still projected from her flesh. He doused this nub with uisge, and then, without warning, yanked the shaft out through the hole in her arm.

Sarah gasped, her eyes filling with tears. Roscoe remained extremely calm as he bound her arm with a long linen strip soaked with uisge. He then fashioned a sling and hung it around her neck. The old Adventurer was well-skilled in the basics of chirurgery.

"Now, your arm's gonna be hurtin' for a time, so you just keep sippin' on uisge, and you'll heal up fine—you'll see. There ain't nothin' to be frettin' about."

By this time, Thurmond and Torgul had arrived at the crest of the ridge, where they found the bodies of Gustavus and the thief, along with an assortment of discarded equipment.

Thurmond rolled the thief onto his back to examine his face.

"I don't recognize either of them. They must be bandits. You figure they're bandits?"

The dwarf grunted in agreement.

"Most like. These hills used to hold a power of bandits. There ain't been none in years, far as I know, but these is strange days we been havin'."

Wat appeared, peeking around a boulder with his bow at half-draw. Tuck and Cob were close behind. Thurmond greeted him with a wave and a grin.

"You three did good work here. You're real fightin' men!"

Wat waved the compliment away.

"Awww, that weren't nothin' special. Them fumble-fingers there couldn't shoot worth piss. It were easy."

The archers searched bodies for anything of value while Thurmond and Torgul proceeded over the top of the ridge and discovered the dead men's horses where they had been abandoned by their fleeing comrades. These were welcome as replacements for Sarah's mount and the slain pack-mule.

Thurmond helped Sarah into the saddle. He knew riding would hurt her and would have preferred to make camp on the hillside to give her a chance to rest, but Roscoe was already mounted and looking back over his shoulder, clearly impatient, as the rest of the party prepared to move out. As Adventure Captain, it was his job to keep them focused on their mission.

CHAPTER 15

INCIDENT AT THREE FAT FRIARS

The Adventurers were more cautious after the ambush. They rode with helmets on their heads and shields on their arms. Roscoe's crossbow was kept in easy reach on the back of his saddle. Thurmond kept his eyes skinned for any indication of a lurking enemy and often rode ahead of the others to scout out suspicious sections of trail.

One day oozed into the next. They rode without incident though a long stretch of evergreen forest. Game was abundant, and the keen-eyed Gascars kept the party well supplied with fresh meat. From time to time, they stopped at the tiny villages for bread, cheese, and ale.

Sarah rode with her arm in a sling, sipping regularly from the flask of uisge. Roscoe's ministrations and a liberal application of Florio's healing balm kept the wound from festering, but she would not be casting any spells for a while. All her energy was required for the healing process.

They were all pleased that Cob seemed to be calming down. The further north they traveled, the less morose he became. Though he continued to remain aloof from the Adventurers, he now conversed with his two comrades in a normal manner, and his sleep was no longer troubled by abominable dreams and fits of screaming.

After days and days of riding—the journey had taken longer than they anticipated—the party crested a small rise, and Visby finally hove into view. It was unimpressive compared to Gorgonholm, with few buildings reaching above one or two stories. Most were built of heavy, square-cut logs cut from the surrounding forests. The better structures were half-timbered, but only one, an imposing castle set on a high motte, was constructed of stone.

The city was girdled by a formidable ditch and bank surmounted by a stout wooden palisade. This was reinforced by wooden towers at regular intervals along its length. A massive wooden gatehouse guarded the only entrance.

Visby was the northernmost city of the kingdom of Poitiers. The blue eyes and blond hair of its inhabitants proclaimed their predominately Vanarian ancestry. Their speech bore a heavy, throaty accent that the Adventurers found hard to understand.

They did manage to ascertain that Three Fat Friars was not actually inside the city, but located in a hamlet a few miles north. It was not an inviting structure. Built of heavy logs with a projecting upper story, it resembled a blockhouse more than an inn. The thick planks of the door were braced with iron bands, as if an attack were imminent.

The proprietor, at least, looked like a proper innkeeper—bald, round, and red-faced. There were, he explained, no private chambers at Three Fat Friars. Half of the upper floor served as a communal sleeping loft, but heavy cloth partitions offered guests a modicum of privacy. He shared the other half with his daughters, who were his cooks and barmaids.

Asmodeus's mercenaries had not yet arrived. Roscoe was frustrated by the delay and considered pushing on without them. In the end, however, caution prevailed, and the party settled down to wait.

Three Fat Friars turned out to be more hospitable than expected. The ground floor was an immense common room with a gigantic fireplace in which slabs of meat were kept turning. The food was undeniably good—thick venison steaks served with beets and onions, roasted haunch of boar, swan stuffed with turnips, smoked trout in a pungent sauce. Not, perhaps, as exotic as Florio's culinary masterworks, but mighty toothsome, natheless.

The innkeeper's daughters were buxom and flirty, but Thurmond knew better than to pay them too much attention, at least in front of Sarah. Because of the cool northern climate, the bedding was less bug-ridden than in the inns down south. The ale, Roscoe declared, was some of the best he had ever tasted.

On the third morning, their breakfast was disturbed by a great stamping of hooves and the rattle of armor. Thurmond peered from one of the common room's tiny windows. A dozen men clad in mail and leather and carrying every imaginable weapon were dismounting in the inn yard. The mercenaries had finally arrived.

Roscoe was just rising from his stool but stopped when a man came through the door. He was of middle height, but stocky and looked strong. His thick blond hair was caught back in a tail that ran halfway down his back. A long scar ran down his left cheek. He wore the white belt of a knight.

Seeing the Adventurers, he stopped short.

"You!"

Sarah was equally stunned.

"You!"

The man remained silent, his eyes filled with distrust.

It was Sarah who finally spoke.

"Roscoe, I'd like you to meet my half-brother, Bart."

Though they had never met him, the other Adventurers all knew about Bartholomew Staynes. He had led a rival party of treasure hunters during their first adventure—a quest to seize a trove of goblin gold.

Bart's face darkened with anger.

"You stole my map."

Sarah's reply was remarkably placid.

"Nay, brother, I did not."

"Don't lie to me, you little..."

Thurmond pushed back his stool and stood up, hatred burning in his eyes. He knew about the vile threats that Bart had made to Sarah, the promises of the unnatural things he would do to her as soon as their father died. His voice was low, menacing.

"Sarah does not lie. I stole your map."

This was indeed true. Thurmond had been hired to burglarize the Staynes's mansion—he had taken the map along with a number of other items. As Bart's hand began to inch toward the hilt of his sword, Thurmond gave him a slight smile. He had wanted this moment for a long time.

The young Adventurer sized up his opponent. Bart was taller and more heavily muscled, but Thurmond was fast and agile. Bart's sword was on his hip. His own was on the table in its scabbard. Could he beat the bigger man in the draw?

Thurmond wore only his tunic and breeks while Bart was clad in mail. This was a telling advantage. Luckily, the knight was not wearing a helmet. His head was covered only by a soft leather cap.

Hate boiled in all four of their eyes. The room stank of death.

Then Roscoe stepped between the two adversaries, extending his hand to Bart. He employed his most respectful tone.

"Milord, we had no idea it would be you we were meetin' here. I bid you welcome. Now, I understand there's some bitter history between you and Thurmond, but we've got an important job of work to do, so we have. Let's not allow past squabbles to keep us from it."

Bart ignored the proffered hand, his eyes shifting between Thurmond and Sarah as if trying to choose the first to die. When he spoke, his voice came through clenched teeth.

"Hardly a *squabble*, old man. I was almost killed by goblins. My men were butchered. I was left alone in that wilderness with nobody, with bloody nothing. It was a miracle I survived."

Roscoe tried to sound reassuring.

"We was all mighty lucky to live through that one, milord. That adventure was a close-run thing, so it was."

"Perhaps so, but you came away with great wealth, so I've been told, while I starved alone in a desolate forest. My only luck was when I found the river and was rescued by some passing boatmen."

Roscoe nodded in sympathy.

"You were fortunate indeed, milord, fortunate indeed. But that was not your only luck."

He indicated the white belt of knighthood encircling Bart's hips.

"May I congratulate you on your newly attained rank? That is no small achievement."

Bart's angry response was as unexpected as it was unnecessary.

"I earned my belt fairly. You have no right to question it, commoner."

Roscoe stumbled all over himself, struggling to make his apology seem genuine.

"Nay, I beg your pardon. I meant no offense, sir knight. My congratulations were sincere, so they were."

While Roscoe distracted Bart, Torgul grasped the back of Thurmond's belt and gave it a hard tug that pulled him back into his seat. Roscoe now turned to his young companion.

"Thurmond, I'd ask you to go to the sleepin' loft and see to our gear. We'll be leavin' shortly. This gentleman and I have business to discuss."

The young man muttered a low curse, rose, and mounted the stairs to the upper floor. Sarah waited but a moment before joining him.

The old Adventurer once more turned to Bart.

"The lad's a bit hot-tempered, so he is. You are older, wiser—I'd ask you to forgive his little outburst."

Roscoe went on.

"Please, sit down and join me in a pitcher of this most excellent beer. These norther folk are fine brewers indeed. It's a heady brew—proper for a fightin' man like yourself. Prithee, have a seat with me and the dwarf. We have much to talk about."

Thurmond was already wiggling into his mail hauberk when Sarah arrived upstairs.

"What are you doing?"

"What do you think? I'm going to kill your brother."

"Nay—you most certainly are not!"

"I am! I will! I must! For the things he said to you—he must die."

"Please, keep your voice down. He'll hear you."

"Good! I want him to hear me."

Quite unexpectedly, Sarah slapped his face.

"Whaaa…?"

She slapped it again.

"Why are you slapping me?"

"To get your attention. Because you're being an imbecile and won't listen to me."

"But Sarah …"

"Be silent! Don't talk! Just listen! I was the one Bart threatened, so I get to decide what to do about it—see?"

"I just…"

"I said, *don't talk*. When I want your protection, I'll ask you for it. Got it?"

"Aye, I got it, but…"

"Not another word! Roscoe is downstairs right now trying to calm down Bart. That probably won't be too hard because he's stupid."

"And you're up here doing the same with me?"

"That's correct. Only it's harder with you because you're so much smarter. At least when you choose to be. So please, choose to be smart now."

"Why is this so important to you?"

"Have you already forgotten why we came here? Or that Bart was sent to help us? If we fail in our quest, Gorgonholm might well be destroyed."

Alas, Thurmond had, in his pique, overlooked that important detail.

Sarah was right about her brother—Roscoe's good humor eventually cajoled him out of his dark mood. He listened to the old Adventurer's tales of high adventure as he swilled the inn's magnificent beer.

As Bart drank, he grew effusive, eager to impress the old Adventurer with exploits of his own. He and his men had spent the last several months in the service of Yorik, Earl of Sark, assisting his efforts to suppress the rebellion of some minor border lords.

The successful completion of this task had left them at loose ends until Asmodeus's messenger, a semi-transparent specter in the form of a talking pig, had instructed them to unite with the Adventurers at Three Fat Friars. They had set out at once because, as Bart readily conceded, it would be sodding madness to disobey Asmodeus.

He had also vaguely alluded to the wizard having had a hand in his rapid elevation to knighthood, but when Roscoe asked for details, he clammed up and would say no more. It was agreed that the Adventurers and the mercenaries would join forces and head north the next morning. Roscoe would, as Asmodeus specified, be in command, with Bart serving as his lieutenant.

The Psiss Marshes, a wide belt of cold, northern wetland, served as a rather nebulous frontier between the kingdom of Poitiers and the homeland of the Vanarian tribes. The Psiss was a dim and doubtful region reputedly haunted by flesh-eating ghouls, blood-sucking vampyres, and faceless, soul-stealing wraiths. This would be the first leg of their journey. Once they entered the land of the Vanar, things would get really dangerous.

While Roscoe and Bart laid their plans, Torgul took the moment to step outside for a look at the other mercenaries. They were milling about in the innyard, watering the horses and exchanging coarse jests with the barmaids who brought them pots of beer.

As the dwarf stepped over the threshold, he stopped short—surprised by the sight of a short, stocky man with dark receding hair and eyes drawn into a permanent squint. Torgul immediately turned about and re-entered the inn. Roscoe was still deep in conversation with Bart. So instead of interrupting their conversation, he shot up the stairs to the loft.

Thurmond had calmed down, removed his mail, and was now packing their gear for departure. Sarah sat on a nearby pallet, talking to him as he worked. Her arm was still too sore for lifting or carrying.

Torgul was barely able to control his agitation as he spoke.

"Thurmond, I gotta tell you somethin' that you ain't gonna like. Here it is…"

Dwarves were decidedly straight-forward in speech.

"…them men down in the innyard, one of 'em is Drax. He didn't die of his wound."

Drax was a mercenary soldier who had joined their party in the aftermath of their goblin adventure. He had initially befriended Thurmond, but had later tried to murder him for the pouch of gems he believed to be hanging around the young man's neck. He had shot him in the chest with a crossbow and was about to finish him with his dagger when Roscoe and Torgul arrived in time to rescue their companion. Drax had caught a bolt from Roscoe's crossbow and fled into the night on a stolen horse. All had hoped that his wound had festered and killed him.

Now he was back.

Thurmond threw down the bedroll in his hands and snatched up his helmet and shield. Reading his thoughts, Sarah took him by the arm with her good hand.

"Thurmond, don't!"

He shook the restraining hand away.

"No choice this time! You were right about your brother. He made threats, but it was all just talk. He never really did anything to you. Plus, I guess we need him. But we can do without Drax. That poxy bastard tried to kill me."

"What do you plan to do?"

"Challenge him to single combat. Then, no matter how it turns out, the quest can proceed."

Sarah saw Torgul raise a surreptitious eyebrow. She again attempted to calm him with reason.

"Come on, Thurmond, you know Torgul and Roscoe won't stand by and let that dog turd Drax kill you. There will be no end to trouble."

"Can't help it, Sarah. I got no choice this time."

The young witch saw how determined he was and had to admit that he was right. Drax was completely untrustworthy, a ruthless murderer. He had to go.

Thurmond headed downstairs, intent on his purpose. Then came to a full stop. Drax stood in the middle of the inn's common room. He was bareheaded, wore no armor, and carried no weapon—at least none that Thurmond could see.

Roscoe, still seated with Bart, spoke gravely to his young friend.

"Drax has somethin' he wants to say to you, boyo—somethin' serious. I'd deem it a personal favor if you'd at least give him a chance to speak his peace."

Thurmond was in no mood for words. There was nothing Drax could say that would signify, but he respected his mentor too much to refuse his request.

"All right, Drax, say what you have to say."

Drax licked his lips and wiped his palms on his dirty breeks. Then he cleared his throat.

"It was a terrible wrong what I did to you, boy. I was plain evil back then,

I truly was. Cared only for myself. Completely taken by greed and strong drink. It wasn't nothin' personal—I always liked you, I did."

Thurmond was unmoved.

"You done? If you are, we have business, you and I."

Drax's eyes grew round with fear.

"You ain't takin' my meanin'. I'm tryin' to say I'm sorry..."

Thurmond cut him off.

"I don't give a fig for your apologies! Get your armor on!"

"I can't fight you, boy. Look what Roscoe's crossbow done to me."

He pointed to his left arm hanging limp by his side.

"I can't lift it no higher than this."

He raised it to the height of his stomach.

"And it's so weak, I can't carry a shield or draw a bow. I'm useless as a fighter. I wouldn't stand a chance against you. It'd be murder—no better than what I tried doin' to you."

Thurmond was not buying any of this.

"Bollocks! You're a mercenary. You fight for a living."

"Not no more. I'm just a scout. I don't own no armor no more. Sir Bart keeps me on 'cause I know the north lands from the old days."

The young man only scowled.

"Fine—I won't use my shield. We'll fight sword to sword."

Drax looked utterly terrified.

"Nay, nay! We don't need to fight at all. I done wrong to you, I admit it. But I'm a whole different man these days. After I was shot, I was found by a bunch of friars. They was kind to me. First time in my life somebody was kind to me. They healed my arm best they could, but it ain't ever gonna be right. More important, they learned me about right and wrong, about how good things come to them what does good."

Thurmond's patience was at an end.

"Save your excuses, wretch. It's time to pay for the bad you did."

Drax's body seemed to sag, his hands hung limply at his side.

"If you're really gonna kill me, I guess that'll be the way of it. But I'm beggin' you, let me finish my story."

"Then talk and be done!"

"Think about how things turned out. I hurt you bad, and I'm sorry, but you healed. From what folks is sayin', you got rich and live in your own castle. And you got that black hat you was wantin'.

"Me? I'm broke and crippled. That's what my sin brought me. See how evil brings evil? Bart—he don't pay me but half of what the others get 'cause I can't fight no more. I don't even own a sword. So if you're gonna kill me, come do it right now. I won't try and stop you."

Thurmond did not know what to do. His very soul lusted for Drax's blood, yet he could not slay a defenseless man. He glanced at Roscoe, who gave his head a very slight shake—*don't do it*. That settled it. He stepped so close to Drax that their noses almost touched. His voice was a low snarl.

"Stay away from me. Don't talk to me, not ever. Give me any reason, and I will kill you with a smile on my face."

Then he turned and stomped back to the loft.

When he was gone, Roscoe addressed Drax.

"He means what he said, boyo, so I hope you was listenin'. We need you, Drax, 'cause you know the country, but I won't lift a finger to save you."

Then he turned back to Bart and resumed their conversation.

CHAPTER 16

ACROSS THE PSISS MARSHES

The combined parties left Three Fat Friars before noon. They enjoyed several days of relatively easy progress through the high pasturelands of northern Poitiers before the ground dropped lower and lower into the Psiss Marshes.

This extensive wetland proved to be as nasty and dangerous at they had heard. Their path was little more than a slippery game trail threading through a deadly maze of peat bogs, stagnant sloughs, and pools of deadly quicksand.

The trailsides were shrouded with thickets of hazel and massive tangles of creepers and bracken. Stands of birch, alder, and swamp pine obscured the cold northern sun. Many of these ancient trees were twisted into fantastic shapes with long branches resembling the grasping hands of dead men. Strands of gray moss hung nearly to the ground.

Worse still, the air was suffused with a foul stench far worse than the musty reek of decaying vegetation—more like that of a battlefield strewn with rotting bodies. Thurmond tied a rag over his mouth and nose. Several of the others immediately followed his example.

The Psiss insects were unrelenting in their assaults. Tiny blood-sucking midges swarmed over every inch of exposed skin. Huge, black, biting flies plagued horse and man. Dragonflies the size of small birds darted menacingly at their eyes.

By the end of the first day, the Adventurers were exhausted and miserable. The damnable swamp seemed to suck the energy right out of them. Their bodies itched from innumerable bug bites, and the foul odor seemed to have permeated their skins.

They began to search for a spot to make camp, but most of the ground was soggy with fetid swamp water. Finally, just as the long summer day was drawing to a close, they lucked upon a sedge covered hummock, dry and open enough for the party to spread their cloaks and blankets.

They divided into two groups. Roscoe's people spread their blankets on one side of the hummock, Bart move his mercenaries to the other side. Roscoe observed this with a wary eye, for it signaled the distrust and potential hostility that lay between the two groups. That did not bode well for their mission.

Bart was sullen. Clearly uncomfortable around Sarah and Thurmond, he eschewed any unnecessary conversation with the Adventurers. He even kept apart from his own men, who he regarded as mere underlings undeserving of regard.

The Adventurers enjoyed a more accommodating spirit. The Gascars gathered wood, built a fire, and prepared a meal, while Thurmond and Sarah tended to the horses. Torgul scouted the surrounding area for signs of danger.

As they ate, the old Adventurer addressed Wat and Tuck.

"When we finish here, I want you boyos to make friends with that lot over there. We're gonna need each other before this quest is over, so it won't do to have us sittin' and scowlin' at each other. Think you can do that?"

Wat nodded.

"Sure, Roscoe—them are just soldiers like us. They won't much care about the bad blood between the rest of you."

"Well and good. I'll send over a skin of wine I was savin' for my own drinkin'. That should help ease things along."

As bidden, the three archers joined Bart's men around their campfire. As first, all went well. The wineskin was passed hand to hand, and they were soon laughing and exchanging coarse soldier jests. Roscoe's strategy seemed to be working.

Then all went wrong.

The jovial banter was drowned by angry shouts and the smack of a fist striking flesh. A body was flung out of the dark to land squarely in the campfire, scattering sparks and hot coals in every direction. The figure rose, only to receive a savage kick in the sternum that sent him back in the blaze. This time, he rolled away from his assailant and regained his feet. It was Cob!

The archer's adversary now stepped out of the shadows—one of Bart's men, a burly sergeant-at-arms called Gorb. He stepped around the fire, looking to renew his attack, but Wat and Tuck rose and barred his way.

This brought the rest of the mercenaries to their feet. The three Gascars found themselves surrounded by the scowling faces of men with whom they had, only moments before, been drinking and laughing. A bloody battle seemed inevitable.

But before anyone could draw steel, Roscoe burst in among them, Torgul, Thurmond, and Sarah close behind.

"Here now! What's this all about? Stand back, all of you! I'll kill the first man who draws a weapon, no matter who it be! Is that understood?"

The men shuffled a few inches backward, none eager to test the mettle of the huge Adventurer.

Roscoe grabbed Cob's arm and pulled him forward. The archer's nose was bloodied, and a large bruise was forming on his cheek. Protected by his armor, he was not badly burned.

Roscoe glowered at his hireling.

"All right, Cob, how did this begin?"

"I was just tryin' to show this man…"

He pointed to Gorb.

"…that what he was sayin' was plain heresy. He wouldn't listen, so I was…"

The Gascar was interrupted by Gorb's angry ejaculation.

"Heresy, my arse! My family's always been true believers. I tithe to the Blue Friars same as my father and grandfather. But this stinkin' foreigner says only White Friars are proper Charonites—that I'm goin' to Hell for thinkin' different."

This was an old story. The rivalry between the various Charonite sects often manifested as intolerance between their followers. Oceans of blood had been spilled in identical disputes.

Roscoe turned angry eyes on Cob.

"I told you before to stop this kind of shite, but I guess you didn't hear me. Well, you better hear me now. You make one more problem, and I'll leave you in this swamp without a horse or food or your bow or nothin'. Did you hear me this time?"

Cob nodded but said nothing.

"That's right fine, Cob, so it is. Now, I want you to beg pardon from this soldier and swear that you won't ever bother him with your nonsense again. You got that?"

Cob said nothing, just stood with eyes downcast.

The angrier Roscoe got, the calmer he became. His voice was now a cold, quiet whisper.

"Listen to me, laddie—this is your last chance. You'll be out in the dark if you don't speak up now. Better do as I say."

The archer remained defiant.

Finally, Tuck interjected.

"Do it, Cob—do as the man says."

Then Wat.

"He's right, Cob—you better do it. You're my sworn companion, but you brought this on yourself. If you get banished, Tuck and me, we ain't goin' with you. So, do it."

Cob's eyes were suddenly filled with terror. He had obviously never considered the possibility of being left alone. His voice, when he spoke, was contentious.

"All right—I shouldn't have said nothin'. It's just that…"

Roscoe stopped him cold.

"You ain't beggin' the sergeant's pardon. Now do as you was told."

With no other choice, Cob finally gave in

"I beg your pardon, mister. I won't be botherin' you again."

Roscoe sighed in relief and turned to Gorb.

"Okay, he apologized and promised not to make no more problems. This quarrel is over—got that? Don't be startin' it up again, or you'll get what I promised Cob."

The old Adventurer raised his voice and addressed the group.

"What I just said goes for everybody. The only way we're gonna survive this adventure is by workin' together and lookin' out for one another. This kind of bickerin' just won't do."

There was some shuffling of feet, but no one raised his voice to object. They all knew Roscoe was right. Then Bart sneered at Roscoe.

"I would have let them fight it out, man to man. My Gorb could tear the balls off your preacher boy."

The old Adventurer turned away in disgust. There was no point in arguing with this arrogant ass. Sooner or later, he knew, there would be a confrontation, but it would have to wait until they completed the task at hand.

Thurmond drew the third watch, the dark, forlorn stretch of night between the hours of the Twa Witches and the Deadman. Standing alone in the gloom, he thought he must go mad. There was too much noise— unseen creatures rattling the underbrush, twigs snapping, water gurgling and splashing. Sometimes he heard what sounded like distant voices

Weird blue lights winked on and off, first on one side, then on the other. Shadows shifted shape. Just before the end of his watch, Thurmond watched a pale, spectral figure drift across the sky.

The next day was much like the first—all bogs and bugs and stink. Fortunately, they encountered no ghouls, vampyres, or wraiths. Thurmond hated the region and inwardly renamed it the *Piss Marshes*.

Roscoe's archers and Bart's mercenaries put their feud behind them and resumed their soldierly bantering. Fighting was their trade, so they were seldom eager to draw steel unless they were getting paid for it. But all believed that a showdown between Thurmond and Drax was inevitable, and coin was secretly wagered on which would survive.

An unlikely friendship grew between Drax and Cob, the former being the only member of the company willing to tolerate to the proselytizing. On the second evening, the scout huddled with the archer to pray and receive instruction. The next morning, Drax was seen wearing the religious badge that had previously adorned Cob's shoulder.

Whatever failings Drax possessed, he proved to be an excellent guide, bringing them through the marsh without mishap. And he was careful to keep his distance from all the Adventurers, Thurmond in particular. He clearly wanted to avoid a conflict.

Their track finally brought them back to solid ground, a barren expanse of low, weed-covered hillocks. This was the bleak Vanarian homeland. Countless small streams trickled into brackish pools from which man and horse were reluctant to drink. Kites screamed overhead and long-legged waders picked at the edges of the streams and pools, but no other wildlife did they see.

Roscoe searched the terrain for a landmark shown on Asmodeus's map. He found it on a nearby hill—the foundations of a ruined fortress. The tumbled stones marked the northernmost boundary of the Etrusian Empire in its failed attempt to dominate the world. The party was exactly where they were supposed to be. Drax's guidance had been spot on.

CHAPTER 17

WITH THE BLUE HORSE PEOPLE

They came to a large earthen mound topped by a pyramid of human skulls. A tall wooden post, rising from its center, supported a horse skull painted with intricate blue whorls.

Roscoe brought the party to a halt and called to Drax.

"What's all this about?"

The scout took a deep breath and let it out slow.

"It's a warning. This here's the territory of the Blue Horse People, the ones I told you about. Big tribe. Real dangerous bunch. The Blue Horses don't like strangers comin' into their lands. If they catch you, your skull goes on the pile."

Without waiting for a reply, Drax urged his horse a little ahead of the party, searching the landscape.

Bart growled in disdain.

"That don't scare me. Nobody really dangerous would pile skulls like that. It's just bluff."

Thurmond had often heard Sarah describe Bart as a blustering buffoon, and this seemed to prove her point. To him, the warning looked entirely sincere, but he kept his opinion to himself.

Roscoe shrugged.

"Whatever it means, we can't stop now, not for a pile of old bones."

And so, they entered the lands of the Blue Horse People.

The day, though bright, remained cool. The column moved through an endless series to low grassy ridges that had, perhaps a thousand years before, been sand dunes. All was quiet save for the sigh of the wind and the occasional shriek of a kite.

Desolate as it was, the country reeked of danger. They rode with their helmets buckled beneath their chins and their shields strapped to their arms. The Gascar archers kept their bows strung and their arrows close to hand. Sarah had her wand in easy reach.

Yet for all their apprehensions, no foe came boiling over a ridgeline. As the day wore on to late afternoon, Thurmond began to relax a little. Perhaps their fears had been exaggerated. Then he heard Bart's condescending, artificial laugh.

"See? I told you, didn't I? No pack of barbarians are gonna attack armored soldiers like my men. They're hidin' someplace, hoping we'll pass through and leave 'em alive."

Drax turned slowly in the saddle and stared into the knight's face.

"Take a look over there…"

He pointed to a ridgeline on their left flank.

"…and tell me what you see."

Bart remained as oblivious as ever.

"I see a little rimple of dirt. Why? What am supposed to see?"

"Look a mite closer, milord. You'll catch a little gleam of light from time to time. Maybe two or three of 'em."

Sure enough—careful observation revealed pinpricks of reflected sunlight. Drax now turned away from Bart, choosing instead to speak to Roscoe.

"Them are spearpoints. The Blue Horses, they use real long lances. Sometimes they forget to keep 'em hid below a ridgeline.

The old Adventurer grew deadly serious.

"Why didn't you tell us this before?"

"'Cause I wasn't sure until a just a moment ago. I thought I seen somethin' in the corner of my eye, you know how that goes, but I wasn't sure what it was. I didn't want to put you in a panic 'til I knew for certain."

Roscoe was plainly dissatisfied with Drax's answer.

"I think you can see, I ain't in no panic. Now tell me what you think we oughta do."

"Ain't nothin' much we can do but try and get away. Right now, some warrior is ridin' hard to fetch some more of the tribe. You don't wanna get caught by them. The sun is startin' to go down. There ain't much dark up here this time of year, but maybe we can lose 'em in what little bit we got. I doubt it, but we can try."

"Are these boyos good trackers?"

"The best."

Luck was with them—a thick blanket of clouds obscured the moon, making the night darker than most. At Roscoe's command, the party zigzagged several times, backtracked for a couple of miles, then hunkered down in a rocky ravine between two small hills.

It was uncomfortable with so many horses and riders crammed into so small a space, but they stretched out as best they could. Sore and exhausted from the long ride, Thurmond fell at once into a deep and dreamless sleep. It seemed, though, as if he had no more than closed his eyes when he was prodded awake by the toe of Roscoe's boot.

"Rouse yourself, laddie. I've got something to show you."

The sun was up. All around him, men were climbing to their feet, saddling horses, pissing, snatching a quick mouthful of food. Torgul was putting a fresh edge on his axe.

Sarah's hair was tangled, and her eyes were swollen with sleep. Thurmond was tempted to give her a good morning kiss, but he held back. This was neither the time nor place for affection.

Roscoe yanked him by the arm.

"Come on, laddie, and stop moonin' around. I need you to see somethin'. Sarah, you come along, too."

He led them down the ravine until they came to a low spot.

"Climb up there, laddie, and tell me what you see. Keep your head low."

The young Adventurer did as bid, then slid back down beside his friend.

"I saw half dozen riders with long lances sitting on a ridgeline. They seem to be waiting for us."

"Aye, so they are. That's exactly what they're doin'. And I'll tell you somethin' else—there's another group just like 'em waitin' on the other side. Now what do you think we ought to do?"

"We outnumber them. We should charge out of here and slay the first group as quick as we can. Then turn on the second group."

Roscoe rubbed his beard thoughtfully.

"Now that's a thought. Torgul suggested the same thing. But tell me— how exactly is that gonna help us get on with our quest?"

"It'd be better than getting trapped in this stupid ravine. It'd give us a chance to get away."

"Maybe it would, but this land belongs to those boyos, and I don't think there'll be any getting' away from 'em. Drax don't think so either."

Thurmond considered for a moment

"Well, maybe Sarah could make some kind of illusion. Something to distract them while we ride away. Could you do that, Sarah?"

"I doubt it. My arm is still healing, so my energy is still low. Anyway, they're in two different groups and too far away."

"Could you disguise us somehow? Maybe call down a big blanket of mist?"

"Nay, our party is too big for me to cloak with my magic, even if I was up to it."

"You brought along all of those charms and amulets. Could you use one of them?"

"I still don't know what they do. I have some spell scrolls, but you know how dangerous they are. I won't use them until we're about to die."

Roscoe came to a decision.

"Alrighty then—seems like there's nothing for it but to do as Drax says and just keep ridin'. If they're willin' to talk, maybe Sarah can throw her charm spell on the leader. Or maybe I can challenge their champion to single combat. You never can tell with these barbarian fellas—they got real funny ways of doin' things."

The company mounted their steeds, and Roscoe led them out of the ravine and into a broad, flat plain. Drax scanned the countryside, checked the position of the sun, and stuck out his tongue to taste the wind. Then he turned them north toward the Cold Sea and the abode of Malachai.

The two groups of warriors stayed with them, one well to the front, the other keeping its distance in the rear. They made no effort to conceal themselves, but neither did they show any hostile intentions.

The column crossed the plain and entered a shallow valley running between two low grassy ridges. Suddenly, war parties of a hundred or more warriors appeared upon the ridges on either side. Two long lines of riders dressed in fur and leather and mail. Each wore a pointed iron cap and carried a very long lance.

The Blue Horse tribe had arrived in force.

Thurmond knew he was looking at death. There was no way they could prevail against so many. He wheeled his mount, seeking a way out, but too late. A third group of Vanarians had already ridden down to block the valley behind them. Still more filled the valley to their front.

It was Drax who saved their lives, spurring forward and proclaiming loudly in a weird, yowling tongue that brought to mind the cry of an angry owl.

He stopped before a man so huge that it seemed impossible that his small steed could bear his weight. Long blond braids fell past his shoulders, a gigantic mustache hid his mouth. His helmet was topped by a horsetail crest that hung past the center of his back.

The big man, obviously the leader, sat unmoving as Drax continued to yammer. The scout then pulled back the sleeve of his tunic and held up his right arm—his good arm—for the tall man's inspection.

Thurmond turned to Roscoe.

"What's he doing?"

"Bart told me about this back in the inn. Seems that Drax was in this country when he was young—learned their talk and their ways of doin'."

"What's he showing that big fellow?"

"Tribal tattoo. Drax claims he did somethin' wonderful back then—slew somebody they didn't like or some such—and got himself adopted into their tribe. I figured we'd need him to get us through these parts. That's why I didn't want you to kill him."

"Why didn't you tell me this?"

"'Cause you're still a baby Adventurer, and I wanted you to figure things out for yourself. Drax is a bad 'un all right, but he don't deserved to be murdered for what he done. Some of the things he said was right, so they were."

This was not the first time that Roscoe had shown such mercy to an old enemy. The young man found it hard to understand how he could be so forgiving.

Whatever Drax said to the big blond man, it worked. When he turned and rode back to the Adventurers, he was smiling. He reined in by Roscoe and Bart.

Thurmond drew back just a bit. He was desperate to learn what the leader had told Drax, but he did not want him to know it. His loathing for the man was so deep that he did not want to appear interested in anything he had to say.

The scout's grin widened as he related his news.

"Lady Fortune loves us today. These is Blue Horse riders, just like I said. We're in real luck here. That big warchief there—that's Brodar Eaglebeak. He was just a kid when I was here afore, but we got lucky—he recalls me."

Roscoe raised an eyebrow.

"So that means they like us?"

Drax cocked his head to one side and looked sly.

"Not exactly. It means they like me, but they ain't made up their minds 'bout the rest of you.

Bart's lips curled in disgust.

"What do they want? Gold? How much should we offer them?"

"Nay—not gold. If it was just your gold they was wantin', they'd kill you and take it."

Roscoe gave him a long look.

"If it ain't our gold they're after, what's on their minds?"

"Brodar ain't decided yet. They don't catch a big bunch like us very often, so this is a special occasion. Somebody'll probably make up a song about it.

He's gotta take us back to his town and talk it over with the tribe's elders. They'll get drunk and argue back and forth just like they always does."

The old Adventurer raised his other eyebrow.

"If we decline their hospitality, will they take it as an insult?"

Drax gave a dry chuckle.

"I doubt it—they ain't so sensitive. But if you don't do what they say, they'll kill all of you right where you're standin'. If you wanna live, you gotta take off all your armor and weapons and put 'em in a pile."

With no other option, both mercenary and Adventurer complied. Surrender was humiliating to be sure, but it was preferable to being slaughtered by the scores of horsemen who lined the ridges. Shields, swords, axes, bows, spears, mailshirts, helmets, even short daggers and knives were dropped into a heap. Most reluctantly, Sarah added her wicker pannier of magical items.

CHAPTER 18

VANARIAN HOSPITALITY

The Blue Horse riders surrounded their unarmed captives and herded them like livestock. As they rode, with Brodar in the lead, Roscoe continued to question Drax. He wanted to learn as much as he could about their captors.

"How'd you manage to get so friendly with these boyos, if I might ask?"

Drax laughed out loud, delighted to get to tell his tale.

"I come up here with a pack of merchants who wanted to trade with these blonde devils. They had mules loaded with knife blades and axe heads and iron kettles—stuff they figured the Vanar would be eager for. I was just a kid, younger even than Thurmond, but I was took on as one of their guards.

"Problem was, the Vanar don't hold much with tradin'. They like takin' better than buyin'. So they killed them merchants and took their goods. All the other guards was killed right off. But me? I fought so hard I killed two Blue Horses afore one of 'em snuck up and cracked me on the head with a club.

"When I come to, I was all tied up—they was gettin' ready to make me a sacrifice. They do a lot of that with prisoners."

Roscoe did not like what he was hearing.

"How did you escape?"

"I'm comin' to that. Their warchief back then was an old graybeard name of Njark. Anyways, he liked my style and decided not to sacrifice me but to give me a chance to do a worthy deed.

"See, he wanted this woman, some princess or somethin', but she was already married to the warchief of the Snow Panther People, and they been the mortal enemies of the Blue Horses since afore the beginnin' of the world. The only way to get her was to steal her, and that would be a worthy deed for certain 'cause the Snow Panthers is ever' bit as mean and tough as the Blue Horses."

"And you got her? How'd you do it?"

"Nothin' much to tell, really. I just climbed over the village wall one night in a snowstorm, and crawled on my belly to the warchief's hut. Then I slipped in nice and easy and cut his throat while he was sleeping. I knocked the woman out cold and carried her back to Njark. He was so happy he made me a brother of the tribe."

The old Adventurer continued to probe for useful information.

"Tell me more about these people. What exactly is a Blue Horse?"

"It's the name of their tribe, but it's also a spirit. Kinda like a god that watches over 'em all. It's supposed to look like a regular horse 'cept it's blue and all glimmery with sparks and shit. Somethin' like that. I never paid much attention—I didn't get mixed up in their religion."

"So, it's a big tribe?"

"Aye, great big tribe. But it's made up of a bunch of separate clans spread out all over their territory. They come together when the warchief calls 'em up—like now. When he heard about us, Brodar sent riders around callin' for his warriors to join him."

"Where are they takin' us?"

"To Oohl, it's the Blue Horse's only town. Most of the tribe lives in little thorps scattered 'round the country."

Drax's description proved accurate. The captives were led through any number of tiny villages. Grubby, fair-haired children emerged from the low wooden huts to watch them ride by. Smaller, meaner hovels built of mud, reeds, and sticks clustered in modest fields of barley and oats.

Drax pointed these out to Roscoe.

"Them little shacks are where the thralls live. Thralls, that's what they call slaves in these parts. They do all the work.

"The warriors spend their whole lives in the saddle. Real proud, they are—they'd rather starve than touch a plow or a rake. They won't even tend their own pigs and cows and sheep. That's all thrall work."

"And the thralls—they ain't nothin' to a Blue Horse. They can kill 'em, take the women, do whatever they wanna do. Nobody cares what happens to thralls."

Roscoe was almost afraid to ask the question that came to mind.

"Where do the warriors get their thralls, Drax?"

Drax remained entirely unconcerned as he answered the question, as if the implications of his words were lost upon him.

"Some is born to it—the children of thralls always stay thralls, but a lot of others is took in raids."

Roscoe nudged his horse forward. He had had enough of Drax for a while.

Oohl sat upon the summit of a cone-shaped hill that leapt out of the surrounding grassland like a wart on the end of a goblin's nose. Brodar led them up a winding trail and through wooden gates set in a stone wall twice the height of a man.

It was not an impressive town—perhaps five score stone houses covered with thatch. A gigantic longhouse with a high, pitched roof towered above the rest. Goats, pigs, and chickens fled for their lives as the column of riders trotted through the narrow pathways that served as streets. They burst into the town center, the riders hallowing in exultation. One of them began blowing a bronze trumpet.

Women and children streamed from the houses in answer to the call. Several warriors emerged from the longhouse. All were big, hairy, frightening fellows, but one stood out as the most horrible of all. A huge brute, naked to the waist, as tall as Brodar but much broader of shoulder, his girth swollen to monstrous size by enormous rolls of fat.

He was ugly, too, with greasy, matted hair, narrow porcine eyes, and jowly cheeks. His face, arms, and huge round paunch were covered by blue tattoos. He was chewing the last strands of meat from a large beef bone.

The sight of the prisoners seemed to enrage the ugly man. He howled, sending bits of meat flying from his mouth, and launched the bone directly into the face of one of Bart's mercenaries. Struck in the forehead, he tumbled from his saddle.

Blue Horse warriors immediately ran to the unfortunate fellow's side, spears poised, and Thurmond feared that they would skewer him before he could rise to his feet. Brodar, however, motioned them away, allowing the bleeding mercenary to rise and remount his horse.

Blue Horse humor was apparently of the coarsest nature, for the warriors laughed and laughed at the man's distress. The women and children joined in. The big, ugly man bellowed loudest of all.

The war party drew up before a trio of standing stones so tall and thin as to resemble needles. Within this triangle, another painted horse skull stared down from a tall wooden pole. A similar skull was fixed over the door of the adjacent longhouse.

Here, they dismounted, captor and captive alike. Blonde servant girls immediately brought the warriors large horns of ale. Brodar strode to a group of warriors standing by the entrance of the longhouse. Their gray beards suggested that they were the elders he would have to consult. Drax also joined this group.

The prisoners were prodded at spearpoint into a large circular enclosure. Its high stone wall and heavy wooden gate proclaimed that this was no pen for livestock—it was made to confine men. A guard climbed onto a tall wooden platform from which he could keep watch.

Thurmond's stomach seemed to have tied itself in a knot. Terror, rage, confusion, and frustration washed over him in a series of unrelenting waves. He had heard Drax speak of the Blue Horse practice of sacrificing their prisoners. Was that in store for himself and his companions? Or were they destined to live out their lives as miserable thralls, mucking in the dirt for some merciless master? Which was worse?

Their only hope was Drax. He had gone off with the one called Brodar, so maybe he was trying to negotiate their release. But would Drax really do that? The young Adventurer suddenly realized that his fate was in the hands of a man he had sworn to kill.

And Drax had every reason to want him dead.

Hours passed. The captives were given neither food nor drink. They could hear the Blue Horse warriors laughing and carousing all around the enclosure, no doubt celebrating their easy victor over the foreign intruders.

Bart withdrew to the far side of the enclosure and sat by himself. Several of his men stretched out on the bare ground and went to sleep. One curled up in a ball and wept. Cob prayed and insisted that Wat and Tuck join him. The Adventurers sat in a circle, looking at each other but not speaking—nothing to say.

More hours passed, but the summer sky stayed light. Still no food or drink. The prisoners sat, slept, wept, or simply stared, depending on their individual inclinations.

At last, the gate creaked open and Drax appeared. He approached Bart, but when the entire group crowded around him, he squatted on his heels and addressed them all.

"Them old roosters ain't decided nothin' yet. Same old thing—they'll sit in the longhouse and argue forever about every little detail, just 'cause they like hearin' theirselves crow. The only thing for sure is that you ain't gonna be thralls. They know you're fightin' men—you could never be made into good thralls."

That was encouraging news, and Thurmond began to feel a glimmer of optimism. It lasted only until Roscoe asked a fateful question.

"Now that's good to hear, Drax, so it is. I've never felt a callin' for bein' of a slave. But tell me straight—if they ain't gonna make thralls of us, what are they squabblin' about all this time?"

The scout gave him a smug, knowing look.

"They got a big Blooding comin' up soon. A mighty important one, 'cause this is the ninth year."

Thurmond did not like the implications of the word *Blooding*. Neither, apparently, did Roscoe, for his expression darkened.

"What exactly might that be, boyo—this Blooding?"

Thurmond watched Drax's expression carefully. He seemed to be struggling to suppress a smile.

"It's this religious gatherin' when the Vanar come together to honor their gods. It's gonna be midsummer pretty soon, and that's a special day for prayin' to their war god, askin' for victory in the comin' year."

"The celebration goes on for days. Lots of drinkin' and feastin' and screwin' and fightin'—all the things the Vanar like best."

"And how would we be fittin' into this holy rite?"

"Maybe not at all. That's what they're tryin' to figure out right now."

Roscoe grew weary of Drax's evasiveness.

"Explain yourself. What precisely are you dodgin' around? What are them blue devils tryin' to figure out?"

Thurmond thought he saw the corners of the scout's mouth move slightly. Was he trying to hide an evil grin?

"A big part of a Blooding is the sacrifices. They offer up pigs, sheeps, horses—even dogs and geese and chickens. They stab 'em first, then hang 'em from the limbs of some special trees."

Drax paused in his narration as if savoring the moment. The old Adventurer gave him a dire look that spurred him on.

"They sacrifice men, too. Not just thralls, neither. They offer up warriors who are worthy of joinin' the god's warband."

Roscoe's face became a flat, blank mask.

"So these savages are lookin' to sacrifice us?"

"Well, maybe. Some of 'em are sayin' they should, you bein' fightin' men and all. But others are holdin' out, sayin' you wouldn't be fittin' on account of you not bein' Vanar. Sendin' foreigners to the god might offend him."

"How are such questions finally resolved?"

"Usually the elders keep drinkin' and jawin' until one side passes out and hits the floor. Then the other side gets their way."

Drax rose to his feet, obviously preparing to depart until Roscoe laid his heavy hand upon his bad arm.

"I appreciate you bringin' us this news, Drax, bad as it is. And we'd all be grateful if you'd convince our hosts to send in some meat and bread and beer. It ain't proper for them to be starvin' their guests. Would you do that for us?"

The scout shrugged.

"I can try, but I don't know that they're in a mood to listen."

With that, he hollered something in the Vanarian tongue, and the enclosure gate swung open a crack. He slipped out and it slammed shut behind him.

Neither food nor drink ever appeared.

Night arrived very late, shuffling across the sky like an old man with the gout. Its appearance did not interrupt the revelry in the streets of Oohl. The shouting, hooting, and whooping went on and on until Night got fed up and slunk back over the horizon for a much-needed nap.

Thurmond remained awake, listening to shrieks of passion mingling with the bull bellow of the hideous tattooed giant who had thrown the bone. He was certain that he could hear Drax's distinctive chortle amid the raucous hilarity coming from the other side of the wall.

CHAPTER 19

THE RITES OF BLOODING

When Daybreak pulled itself from bed and took its first peek over the city wall of Oohl, a gruesome sight met its eyes. The streets were strewn with fallen bodies as if some great plague had struck down man, woman, and child with one terrible blow.

They lay in great communal heaps and small family groups. Some lay on their backs with hands folded sedately on their breasts. Others in contorted postures suggestive of great agony. Some lay in pools of blood or vomit. Many were naked.

Daybreak was relieved when it saw some of the figures begin to shift and stir. The citizens of Oohl were far from dead, it realized. The scene of carnage was nothing more than the aftermath of another Blue Horse revel.

Blue Horse warriors were not, by nature, an energetic bunch. Unless an opportunity for battle came their way, they were typically given to sloth. Had members of a rival tribe appeared, they would have been in the saddle in an eye-blink, lance in hand. But without such stimulus, they found it much more rewarding to simply lie wherever they had dropped the night before.

So, it was well into the afternoon before the town got to its feet. Once up, however, the warriors shook off the effects of the previous night's excesses. They were, to a man, seasoned revelers who recovered quickly from drunkenness. Vanarians were muddle-headed most of the time anyway.

After so many hours without food or water, the prisoners were in worse shape than their hungover captors. Thurmond lay in a stupor—weakened, nauseous, apathetic. In no mood for what was about to happen.

The enclosure gate banged open, and a dozen spearmen surged inside. Shouting in their unintelligible tongue, they jabbed at the stuporous captives, forcing them to rise and stumble out through the gate. Thurmond found his feet and snagged Sarah's elbow and helped her up. They then followed the others out the gate.

Both sides of the narrow street were lined with townspeople—young mothers with babes at their breasts, toothless grandams, snot-encrusted children, dim-eyed old gaffers. Behind them, on horseback, Blue Horse lancers discouraged any thought of escape.

The crowd jeered, taunted, and spat at the captives as they shuffled down the street. Rosy-cheeked girls pelted them with rotten cabbages. Their younger brothers threw horse turds, and their grandfathers brandished knives.

Thurmond stayed close to Sarah, attempting to shield her from the bombardment, but that was impossible. There were too many townspeople hurling too many unpleasant things—sticks and stones, putrefied entrails, a dead hedgehog.

A bald, scar-faced man suddenly reached out and gave the young Adventurer a hard shove. Unbalanced by the unexpected blow, he stumbled sideways against Sarah, sending her sprawling against a rotund, gray-haired matron. Infuriated by this affront, the woman snarled and pushed her violently back into the street.

There was no sign of Drax or Brodar, the warchief. Today, the ugly tattooed brute was clearly in charge. His arrogant swagger and haughty manner proclaimed him a personage of some importance. More animal than man, he rode among the warriors, roaring commands in his inhumanly loud voice, gobs of spittle flying from his lips.

He was as eager as the townspeople to terrorize the captives. Seizing a heavy spear from one of the warriors, he swung it as lightly as a willow wand, and used the butt end to deliver hard thrusts to the faces and bellies of the passing prisoners. Crowded together, unarmed and surrounded by a hostile crowd, there was little they could do to escape the painful jabs.

Tiring of this game, the bellowing beast smashed the spear's thick shaft on the shoulder of one of Bart's men. As his victim crashed to the ground, he brayed like a mule, laughing so hard that he choked on his own spit and was seized by a violent fit of coughing. When the spasm ceased, he hawked up a tremendous wad of phlegm and spat it into the group of captives, striking Wat.

The lines of shouting townspeople extended all the way to the city gates. The spearmen forced the prisoners forward until they were outside the town wall. Here they were thrust into a circle of stones as big as a good-sized farmyard. Behind them, the townspeople streamed out of the gates and crowded around the circle's outer edge, eager for the pending spectacle.

The guards motioned for the captives to sit. Sarah took hold of Thurmond's sleeve and drew him into the center of the group where they were somewhat shielded from view. With one quick motion, she pushed something up the sleeve of his doublet.

He reached for it, exploring the shape through the cloth. It was a short-bladed knife.

"Where'd you get it?"

"From that big woman with the long gray hair, the one who pushed me. I pretended to fall against her, then slipped it from her belt while she was distracted."

"Well done!"

Brodar and the elders now appeared. Many were reeling drunk, having imbibed heavily during the long debate. Then Drax pushed his way through the throng of gawkers.

"It ain't lookin' good. I told 'em how you didn't mean 'em no harm comin' here—how you was just lookin' for some wizard name of Malachai. And 'cause I did such a good job of explain' things, and tellin' 'em how brave you all was, Brodar was about convinced that you was all worthy warriors. I thought maybe they'd let you go.

"But Vanar warchiefs ain't like kings back home. They can't do just whatever pleases 'em. They gotta listen to the elders and obey custom and not offend the gods. They got lots and lots of old-fashioned ideas.

"Well, the elders decided you gotta be sacrificed at the Blooding—it's about a month away."

These words kindled a small flicker of hope in Thurmond's heart. Many things could happen in a month. Perhaps they could change the elder's minds or arrange an escape. These hopes were dashed when Drax continued.

"Problem is, see, they don't want all of you. They sacrifice nine of everything at Blooding—nine goats, nine pigs, nine horses, nine men. So now you gotta fight one another 'til there's only nine of you left. Look over yonder—they got all your armor and weapons piled up over there. They'll take you over one at a time and let you choose whatever weapon you want except bows. And you can't have no armor or shields—them'll just slow down the killin'."

Roscoe's face assumed the same flat, blank expression as is had the day before.

"What comes next, Drax? What do they want us to do?"

"That's pretty obvious, isn't it? Fight it out. They'll pair you up two at a time until there's only nine of you left. They'll be the worthiest warriors and most pleasin' to the war god. So whoever's still breathin' will be kept until Blooding."

Roscoe glared at Drax.

"What about you, boyo? What happens to you?"

"Like I told you—I'm part of the tribe. So they wouldn't sacrifice me unless I asked 'em to. It's funny—some of these crazy buggers actually ask for it. I never could figure that out."

Bart had been strangely quiet since their capture. Now his rage exploded.

"You treacherous bastard! You led us right into this trouble. I'll kill you!"

Drax shook his head.

"Nay, that ain't gonna happen, not with all my Blue Horse brothers standin' by. You gotta believe me, I didn't want none of this to happen. I warned you these parts are dangerous, but you wanted to come up here anyway. And I done my best to get you set free, but the elders wouldn't listen. Nothin' else I can do. So no hard feelins, okay?"

Thurmond harbored plenty of hard feelings. He had always distrusted the perfidious scout, and he did not believe that he had truly advocated their release. It seemed more likely that Drax had urged their destruction in order to evade a later reckoning with himself.

Then, out of nowhere, the faint shadow of an idea crept shyly across the surface of his brain. He hated to have to speak to Drax, but he had no other option. Reluctantly, he pointed his thumb toward the tattooed brute, who was swilling from a drinking horn.

"Drax, tell me—that big barrel of guts over there, who might he be?"

Drax glanced at the subject in question.

"They calls him Grinder, and he's a bad 'un. Strongest man in the whole tribe. A fearsome bloke, he is. They say he can tear a man apart with his bare hands. Nobody messes with Grinder."

"His own people are afraid of him?"

"For good reason, I say. He turns hisself into a bear when he fights—at least he thinks he does."

The conversation aroused Roscoe's interest.

"How do you know so much about him, boyo?"

"They was discussin' him in the longhouse. They're thinkin he's sure to challenge Brodar to be chief of the tribe. A duel to the death kinda thing—it happens from time to time. That's exactly how Brodar got to be warchief, by challengin' the old one."

This information raised both of the old Adventurer's eyebrows.

"So Brodar and this Grinder fella ain't exactly friends."

"God's bollocks, nay. Brodar would kill him if he could, but he's gotta be careful 'cause Grinder's part of a big, powerful clan. Killin' him would start a blood feud inside the tribe, and that's the worse crime a Blue Horse can commit."

Roscoe saw the possibilities of this situation.

"This Grinder—if he's lookin' to become the chief, maybe he'd be lookin' for allies. Could you talk to him for us? Maybe see how he'd feel about the idea."

Drax's face turned crafty.

"I know what you're thinkin'. You're tryin' to figure a way to start a feud so maybe you could escape somehow. Forget it! Nobody wants the tribe to start killin' its own warriors—not Brodar, not Grinder, not nobody."

"The Blue Horse got rules for how their chiefs get chosen. It ain't like down south where you can kill your neighbor any old way. Everybody's gotta follow the old customs in these parts—you included."

"So that's why you're gonna have to fight each other. There ain't nothin' you can do about it."

CHAPTER 20

IN GRINDER'S EMBRACE

Actually, there was something that could be done, and Thurmond knew exactly what it was. He walked to where Grinder was sitting on a little bench with spindly legs that looked far too frail to support his enormous bulk. The young Adventurer stood before him, hands on hips, feet spread, in an unmistakable posture of challenge.

Drax's life had been spared because he had done a worthy deed. Specifically, he had completed a difficult task that the warchief needed done but that none of his warriors could manage. Brodar saw Grinder as a rival, but he dared not kill him. He ought, therefore, to be grateful if Thurmond took care of it for him. That ought to qualify as a worthy deed.

The brute said something obviously intended as a warning, his voice sounding like the roar of a boar-hog being gutted with a rusty scythe. When Thurmond failed to retreat, the giant began to rise. The young Adventurer kicked him squarely in the balls. Taken by surprise, he grunted and fell backward, landing on the bench with such force that the legs snapped and he was thrown to the ground. Before he could rise, Thurmond kicked him in the face, hoping to stun him or at least knock him flat so he could stomp him into lifelessness.

But Grinder refused to go down. Instead of being flattened by Thurmond's kick, he hurled himself forward with remarkable speed for a man so large, caught his attacker in a chest-to-chest bear hug, and proceeded to squeeze all the air from his lungs. Thurmond opened his mouth to scream, but nothing came out. His chest burned as if filled with hot coals.

Fighting back a rising wave of panic, he pulled the concealed knife from his sleeve and drove it under his opponent's chin so that its tip was visible inside his gaping mouth. That should have at least slowed Grinder down, but it produced no significant effect. The brute only bellowed, splashing them both with blood.

Grinder tightened his grip, and Thurmond felt his ribs begin to give way. Unable to draw breath, his strength began to ebb. If he did not escape the brute's terrible grasp, he would surely die.

The young Adventurer gave the dagger a hard shove, pushing it through the hard palate. He expected his foe to release him at once, but Grinder only squeezed harder as the blade penetrated his sinuses. With consciousness slipping away, Thurmond pulled the dagger free and thrust it at man's face, burying the point just below his left eye. But again, incredibly, the monstrous warrior would not release his hold.

Grinder did, however, shift his grip in an effort to avoid the blade, expertly spinning Thurmond around so that the young man's back was now pressed to his chest. This allowed the Adventurer one quick, hot breath before the crushing pressure was renewed.

Thurmond stuck wildly behind him, crisscrossing the brute's scalp with deep gouges, opening his cheek from ear to mouth. But still the inexorable pressure continued. The point, at last, found the right eye, and with the last of his strength, Thurmond drove the blade to the hilt into Grinder's skull.

For a moment, nothing happened. It seemed as if the huge man did not require a brain to live. But then his grip began to slacken, and he oozed to his knees as if his bones had melted. Thurmond slipped free and fell to the ground, unable to move. He was in terrible pain. His ribs felt like they had been ground between millstones. Breathing was sharp, shooting agony.

Sarah immediately ran to his aid. The Blue Horse warriors stood in awed silence. None of them, Brodar included, would have dared to challenge Grinder hand to hand.

Roscoe was not slow in exploiting Thurmond's victory. He had understood at once what Thurmond had been hoping to achieve. He stood beside his gasping, suffering friend and proclaimed loudly.

"Was that not a worthy deed? This stripling lad has defeated your greatest champion, so he has. Who among you could have done so well? Such a lad deserves his life and freedom."

He shot a hard look at Drax, who caught the meaning and began translating the old Adventurer's words into the Vanarian tongue. The elders began to murmur amongst themselves until, finally, Brodar spoke aloud. Drax nodded in comprehension.

"He says this ain't the kind of worthy deed they really wanted to see, but he has to admit that the kid's got real courage. No matter what he's sayin' to his tribe, Brodar's real happy to have Grinder dead. That's why his men ain't killin' you right now. He signaled them not to."

Brodar summoned Drax to his side. After a few moments of head nodding, he returned to Roscoe. He was smiling.

"I got great news. Seems like Thurmond solved a lot of problems for everybody by killin' Grinder. Nobody much liked him, and none of them elders wanna see his clan takin' over the tribe. So Thurmond done a worthy deed.

"I'm pretty surprised at how easy goin' they're bein' about things. Brodar says Thurmond can go free. And he can buy the rest of your lives by givin' him a gift that's proper for a warchief. Somethin' worthy. Then we can all ride on."

Bart was immediately suspicious. Generosity was unnatural to his nature.

"What do they want?"

"Nothin' much—only Sarah. Brodar likes her. He says she's kinda old for him, but he'll take her anyway. Then the rest of us can go."

The Adventures were shocked at this announcement. Before Thurmond could object, Roscoe spoke up.

"Has your brain withered in its skull? What makes you think that we would even consider such a thing? That ain't gonna happen, boyo."

"You ain't got no choice, Roscoe. You can refuse, but then they'll just kill you and take her anyways."

Hearing this, Sarah's mind began racing at full speed, seeking an alternative. Then she had an idea.

"How about a fine weapon? A man like Brodar can surely have any girl he desires. And I'm seventeen. Like he said, that's far too old for a man of his standing. A weapon is a much more fitting gift for such a great warrior. Tell him that, Drax."

Drax translated, sending the elders off into another screaming, jabbering argument. They poked fingers into each other's chests. Clenched fists were waved beneath noses. The warchief was right in the middle of them, waving his arms and yelling as loud as he could. It was a typical Blue Horse discussion.

Then, inexplicably, the clamoring came to an abrupt halt. Brodar spoke to Drax, who rendered his words into the common tongue.

"Brodar says he accepts your offer, but he will choose for himself the weapon he wants from among our pile of gear."

This presented a whole new problem. The weapons of the Adventurers and mercenaries were nothing more than plain, soldierly tools. The only exceptional piece was Torgul's axe.

It was a truly magnificent weapon, a masterpiece of dwarven workmanship. The highly polished head was inlaid with silver and gold in a complex pattern of interlaced figures. If the Vanarian chief tried to claim it, there would most certainly be trouble, for Torgul would fight to the death before surrendering his prized possession.

Brodar began searching through the pile of weapons and armor. He examined a couple of the better pieces but quickly rejected them. Then he picked up the axe.

Torgul gave a tight-lipped little grin, the dangerous expression he reserved for the moment just before committing an act of extreme violence. Roscoe saw the look, understood its meaning, and would have restrained his friend, but he was too far out of reach. If the dwarf launched himself at the warchief, they would all be slain.

Then something else caught Brodar's eye, prompting him to drop the axe as if it were no more than a simple wood-chopper. He grasped instead the hilt of a sword projecting from the heap of nicked and rusty blades. It was the finest sword the warchief had ever beheld.

The dome-shaped pommel was resplendent with gems and lavishly embellished with knotwork cast in gold. The ends of the crossguard took the form of savage horse heads. The long, double-edged blade was heavy enough to sheer through the stoutest mail, yet remarkably light and agile in his hand.

Brodar's heart leapt up! Here was a sword worthy of a Blue Horse warchief! He signaled for Drax and spoke to him in his barbaric tongue. The latter again translated.

"Brodar made his choice—he's takin' that sword."

Roscoe wiped his brow in relief.

"We're free to go then?"

"We are. But we still got a problem. When Grinder's brothers find out what we done to him, they'll come ridin' hard and fast."

Roscoe looked grave.

"How many?"

"Five brothers, but they'll bring their whole clan. I dunno...dozens... scores maybe."

"How long 'til they get here?"

"Somebody's already gone to tell 'em what happened. They'll be here by sometime tonight."

Bart scowled.

"What happens then?"

"You gotta understand—you're in a blood feud. We all are. Grinder's brothers won't care which one of us actually killed their kinsman. They'll see us all part of the same clan. We gotta get outta here, and we gotta do it right quick."

Bart remained unmoving as if he failed to comprehend these words. Drax, his voice rising, continued to prompt him.

"We're gonna die if they can catch us, count on it. And Brodar will stand by and let 'em kill us—that's the custom in a feud. And our deaths ain't gonna be easy ones like Thurmond give Grinder."

The rest of the company understood and sprang to the pile of gear. Mercenaries and Adventurers began strapping on armor and belting on swords. Brodar's warriors brought forth their horses, saddled and ready.

Sarah did her best, but she could not manage to drag the nearly insensible Thurmond to his feet. He seemed to have no strength, and his breath was coming in terrible rattling gasps. Wat and Tuck came to her aid. Taking him gently beneath the arms, they lifted him into the saddle.

They rode through the night. Fortunately, the moon offered enough light to prevent a madcap plunge into an unseen gorge or unexpected river. Following the map, Roscoe aimed them at the constellation called the Coupling Goats, specifically at the tip of the left horn of the uppermost goat.

Grinder's squeezing had left Thurmond in a terrible state. Every breath he drew was a moment of torment, every jolting hoofbeat brought a surge of pure misery. Roscoe gave him frequent swigs of Torgul's energizing potion, but it did little for the pain. They dared not stop, for the pain, as bad as it was, was preferable to what he could expect from Grinder's kin.

At daybreak they could go no farther. The horses were as exhausted as their riders. A low, rocky hillock offered the only high ground in the otherwise flat landscape. Its defensive value would be minimal, but better than nothing at all. They could not light a fire lest their pursuers spot the smoke.

While Torgul and Drax kept watch for approaching horsemen, most of the others fell into a deep sleep. Bart sat glum and brooding, as if angry about something. Finally he rose and approached Roscoe, who was sitting with Sarah. Thurmond lay beside them, either asleep or unconscious.

Bart assumed his typical haughty manner.

"When I answered Asmodeus's summons, I never expected anything like this. I was told to keep you safe while you talked to some wizard. Nothing was said about tangling with barbarians."

Roscoe rubbed the back of his neck as if giving Bart's words careful consideration.

"I see what you mean, milord, so I do. I'm none too pleased myself, and that's a fact. These Vanarians are a rough lot, I'll grant you that."

These words were especially displeasing to Bart. The old Adventurer was agreeing with him when he had hoped to provoke a confrontation. Frustrated and afraid, he needed an outlet for his inner turmoil.

"Maybe it didn't occur to you, old man, that even if we get away for now, we've still got to come back through these parts going home. Those bastards will be waiting for us, you know they will be."

Roscoe remained cordial despite Bart's insulting tone.

"Aye, you've the right of that as well. Like yourself, I've been givin' that problem a lot of thought. Don't be worryin' overmuch, sir knight. Many things can change between now and then. Maybe the magician will kill us all, so we won't be goin' home. Or maybe he'll like us so well that he gives us some magic charm to bring us through safe."

Bart was irritated by Roscoe's attempt to sooth him. He wanted an excuse to pick a fight.

"You're not the only one who thinks, old man! I've been thinking too— thinking like, where did that fancy sword come from? I never saw it before, but there it was in our pile of gear. So tell me, where did it come from?"

Sarah gave him a satisfied smile.

"I can answer that. It was my sword, a light one with a narrow blade and a simple hilt. Didn't look special at all until I put a glamour spell on it. I knew there'd be trouble if Brodar tried to take Torgul's axe."

Bart had never liked his half-sister, even before he learned that they were blood kin. Smart women annoyed him in ways a man never could. At this moment, he liked her less than ever before.

"I thought you were too injured to cast spells. That's what I was told."

"My arm is getting better, so my psychic energy is returning, and it was just a little spell. It's probably worn off by now, so Brodar no doubt hates us, too."

Bart's response oozed sarcasm.

"And that doesn't worry you even one tiny bit?"

"Of course, it worries me, Bart, but we needed to get away from those people, and that was the only way. And like Roscoe says, we have lots of time to try to work things out."

Getting nowhere, Bart threw up his hands and returned to his brooding. Roscoe and Sarah turned their attention to Thurmond. Ever so gently, they lifted his tunic to examine his damaged ribs. A wide band of black bruise extended around his chest and sides where Grinder's arms had so mashed his flesh so that the veins had burst beneath the skin.

Even the lightest touch made him squirm and groan, though his eyes remained closed and he said nothing.

Roscoe spoke in a low voice.

"His ribs is likely busted or at least cracked some. Ain't much I can do for that. You can't splint 'em like you does for an arm or leg. They just need time to heal. At least there ain't no bones poking through the skin—that's somethin' anyway."

Sarah was not reassured.

"Those bruises look really bad. And he's in a lot of pain. Don't you have something to give him?"

"Only uisge or some more of Torgul's special elixir. But I'm thinkin' neither one of them is gonna do the laddie any good right now. He needs sleep more than anythin'. Don't be frettin' about them bruises. They'll heal up all by themselves. Why don't you take a wee nap yourself? I'll keep an eye on him while you do."

They decamped a little before midday. By now, Thurmond's injuries had stiffened, so mounting his horse became even more painful than before. He gulped down a generous slug of uisge from Roscoe's flask and gave his friend a silent nod of appreciation. It hurt too much to talk.

By Drax's best reckoning, it would take another day of steady travel to reach the seacoast. They would then have to find some landmark to determine their exact location before heading either east or west toward Malachai's castle. It was assumed that the Vanarians, aware of their destination and familiar with the area, would try to cut them off before they reached their goal.

They stumbled along, hungry, bleary-eyed, and drooping with fatigue. Their mounts on the point of collapse. There was a brief stop in the dead of night for the sake of the horses, but it was not nearly enough to restore their strength and spirits. They had to keep moving or fall prey to the pursuing horsemen.

The shore was still somewhere up ahead, but they knew they were getting close. Gulls soared overhead and, after a time, the air grew tangy with salt. The breeze carried the brisk chill of the sea. All of this was new to Thurmond and Sarah and most of the others, who had never before seen an ocean. Roscoe recognized the signs. So did Drax.

And then, spreading before them like a gray mass of fog, was the Cold Sea. Wind-whipped waves battered the jagged rocks of a desolate and inhospitable coastline. The tide was out, exposing a stretch of pebbly beach. Several riders dismounted and made their way down the cliffside to the water's edge, drawn, as men have always been, to the sea's cold embrace.

Under normal circumstances, Thurmond would have joined them, but he was in no shape for such endeavors. Sarah was highly intrigued by the sea's awesome power, but elected to remain with Thurmond. Roscoe, Torgul, and Bart studied the map, trying to determine some specific feature that would give them their bearings.

When no likely point was found, they decided to head east along the shoreline, hoping to come to the long, narrow foreland on which Malachai made his home. If that failed, they would have to reverse direction and head west.

CHAPTER 21

LORD UBO VISITS THE GRAY FRIARS

Lord Ubo sat on his horse, smiling as the gates swung open. A lantern appeared, bobbing up and down three times—the signal. All was working perfectly.

Two days ago, six Gray Friars had left his fief and returned to their monastery. They had groveled before the new abbot, begged his forgiveness, and presented him with the purse of gold sovereigns Ubo had provided for this purpose. After a severe reprimand for their apostasy and a promise of dire consequences should they ever again deviate from their vows, the six were allowed to resume their previous positions.

Actually, Abbot Jerome, the former cellarer, was secretly quite happy to receive them—he needed people. The order had been reduced by more than a third during the internecine butchery of two weeks past. The dead included his chief rival, Brother Julian, struck down by Jerome's own flail, and Festus, the previous abbot, smothered with a pillow while asleep in his bed. No one knew by whom.

Jerome was completely unaware that the prodigal friars had no genuine interest in rejoining their order, that they were feigning repentance only to gain admittance to the monastery's grounds. Their real purpose was to slay the monastery's guards and throw open the gates to Lord Ubo's forces lurking just outside.

All went just as Ubo had envisioned. The brace of sentinels was disposed of quickly and silently by a quick slash of a blade across the men's unsuspecting throats. Then the gates were unbarred, and Ubo's men came rushing silently from the darkness.

These men were not soldiers, only peasants and woodsmen armed with improvised weapons. Ubo had sent his only real fighters off in pursuit of some meddlesome Adventurer, and they had not returned. But even this piss-poor rabble would be adequate for the task at hand.

Within moments, they were through the gates. Ubo urged his horse forward, followed by his personal retinue—a dozen of the most likely of his followers. Even before he entered the monastery grounds, the screaming began. Guided by the renegade friars, his men were now bursting into the various cells and chambers in which the friars reposed. Half asleep and in their nightclothes, they were cut down without mercy.

Only Abbot Jerome, Balthazar the treasurer, and a half-dozen others were spared. These were stripped naked and brought into the courtyard where Ubo sat on his tall horse. Thrown to their knees before him, they began to beg for their pitiful lives. Torches were lit, revealing faces white with fear.

Ubo looked down on them with disgust.

"I would have thought holy men such as yourselves might possess a bit more dignity—but no matter. I have come for the treasure that you have extorted from the people of this county for years beyond count. Give me what I want, and I will leave you with your vapid lives. Defy me, and you will suffer."

He signaled to one of his men—a fellow armed with a heavy hunting spear.

"You, fellow, show him I mean what I say."

Without hesitation, the man pushed his spear through the back of one of the kneeling friars. The man writhed and screamed until silenced with a second thrust through the heart.

Ubo continued.

"I require the key to your strong-room. But I am not so naïve to believe that the bulk of your wealth resides therein. You have a secret hoard somewhere. You will show it to me."

Abbot Jerome began to protest this outrage. It was one thing to murder his friars, but quite another to steal his money.

"Profaner! Recreant! Scoff-law! The gold here belongs to Allfather Charon…"

Ubo signaled again, and Jerome was struck in the mouth with a heavy club, breaking his front teeth.

Ubo looked slightly amused.

"Your yawping has just cost the life of another of your people."

He gestured, and another friar was thrust through with the spear.

Now Ubo frowned, all trace of amusement gone from his face.

"I tire of this game. You will tell me what I want to know or I will have my men disembowel the next man. He will see his own entrails slither to the ground before he dies. We will then move on to the next, but he will die even more slowly, more painfully than the last. Each will receive, in turn, a more terrible death than the man before. You, Abbot, shall be saved for the end."

That was enough for Balthazar the treasurer—it was the Abbot's money, anyway.

"I'll tell! I'll tell! The key to the strong-room is hidden in the Abbot's bedchamber. Only he and I know where it is kept. The treasure cache is under the floor of his private privy. I'll show you."

Ubo dismounted.

"Take me there."

He gestured for the men of his retinue to follow along, and then turned to the man with the bloody spear.

"Slay the Abbot and these others—they are of no further use."

Ubo had spoken the truth when he told Jerome that he had come to take his treasure, but not the whole truth. In fact, he was specifically there to seize the monastery. The treasure was but a secondary consideration. It was all part of his great scheme. He had always before been contented to sate his simple appetites within his own demesnes. But lately, Skut had come to seem a dreadful little place, entirely unfit for a man of his abilities.

Ubo took stock of his position. Under normal circumstances, the seizure of a monastery and the slaughter of its inhabitants would have an immediate reprisal by Brandon, the county sheriff. But Brandon was fully occupied in containing the civil brawls that continued to erupt in Gorgonholm with distressing regularity. He would not interfere with Ubo's plan.

The only person who might intervene was Earl Ralf. But he, too, had other, more pressing problems. Several of his normally compliant vassals had risen in rebellion, and the county's towns and villages were torn by insurrection. The earl would have no time for a pack of friars.

The monastery was only the first step. It was to be the base Ubo needed to move on to the second and third phases of his plan. There, he would gather his forces before undertaking the conquest of this city of Gorgonholm. Then the county of Avincraik. Then...who could say. He would expand his holdings one increment at a time. He could not fail.

When every Charonite symbol had been pulled down and smashed, when every holy item was destroyed, then would the Black Stone be brought to the courtyard, there to be raised and venerated by an ever-growing host of devotees.

Lord Ubo would then come into his rightful destiny.

On the far side of the river, Fergis listened to the pounding of the drums with a joyous heart. They beat out a song of victory, of vengeance, of vindication. Countless generations of his people had been waiting for the old days to come again. For the land to be cleansed of the *laigi*, the weak city people on the far side of the river. For his tribe to range, as they used to, through the rich lands of the east.

This was, at last, the destiny foretold in the stories of the old times. Never before had the tribes mustered with such shared purpose. Marching from their remote woodland glens and stony duns, Warriors of the Bear-Breeks clan, the Hardshod, the Black-Spear, the Quickthrottle, the Long-Tooth—bitter enemies all—had put aside old grievances to unite against their common foe.

Wily Hamish Wolf-Eye had brought his clan, as had old Cannok Mor and young Cannok Beg. Coinneach mac Coinneach had led more than a thousand spears from his great roundhouse on Ben Wyvis. Most surprising of all was the arrival of the notorious outlaw leader, the Tyree, and his host of renegades.

The Painted Men had come from the stygian forests of the far west—tattooed warriors with dark skins and smoldering blue eyes, who fought with stone axes and stabbed with flint-tipped spears. They moved as silently as a breath of wind.

The painted ones would go in first. They would scale the high stone walls on rawhide ropes, cut the throats of the sleepy sentries, and open the city's great gates. Then they would move through the houses, killing the hated laigi in their houses in the dark, in their beds.

The iron armor of the laigi would avail them not. Their steel swords and long lances, their prancing horses and far-shooting crossbows would be useless against the creeping death of the forest men. With warriors such as these, what need had he of iron armor?

At the same moment, he would lead the gathered tribes over the river. They would burn the city, pull down its tall towers and foul churches. They would exterminate the laigi, and in so doing, bring again the old days and the old ways—the only proper path for men to follow. Fergis's name would be praised for a thousand years.

The attack would commence as soon as the bulk of his force had assembled—hopefully by the next full moon. Until then, his shamans would beat their drums, summoning the spirits of the four elements to their aid.

Though Fergis knew it not, there was something else arousing his martial ardor—a dim voice calling him from the far side of the river. The voice of the Black Stone promising conquest, riches, and renown.

Sir Brandon Phugg, sheriff of Avincraik, stood on the crenellated roof of City Keep and stared down at the streets below. They were littered with fractured bricks, bits of torn clothing, broken crockery, and the smashed remains of furniture hurled down from the high windows of the houses. He saw none of the hawkers, laborers, or housewives who, in normal times, filled the lanes with bustle and chatter. The houses, like the streets, were soundless, with doors and shutters closed and barred.

Brandon did not know what might be going on inside those houses. He did not want to know. But he did know that the present quiet was deceptive, that at any moment those doors might fly open, the inhabitants spilling into the street to fall upon each other with whatever weapons came to hand.

In the distance, lazy columns of smoke drifted skyward from the smoldering remains of shops and houses. Half of Old Shambles was reduced to ash. Good riddance.

Brandon was a practical man and decidedly not given to heroism. Nonetheless, he and his two-score constables had made a genuine effort to quell the rioting that kept erupting throughout the city. It was his sworn duty, after all, to protect the rich against the deprivations of the poor.

But his men were, in truth, little more than fat, lazy gate-warders with scant skill with arms and no real appetite for blood, particularly their own. They had fled in a panic when attacked by a population gone mad.

Since that first day, two weeks before, many had deserted, either slipping away to the countryside or going over to the rioters. Those remaining steadfastly refused to leave the safety of City Keep.

In desperation, Brandon had sought the aid of the city's privileged classes—the nobility and wealthy merchants. Such men regularly kept armed retainers for their personal security. The sheriff assumed that they would be willing to use them for the defense of the city. He was wrong. The Quality kept their men-at-arms at home.

His repeated appeals to Earl Ralf were also denied. A curt message informed him that the earl was beset with his own problems—peasant uprisings, rebellious vassals—and that restoring civic order was his, Brandon's, responsibility. He was expected to attend to this duty with all alacrity.

The sheriff was not an especially astute man, but he was keenly aware of the bind he was in. Without sufficient forces at his back, any attempt to take control of the city would be doomed from the start, nothing more than an empty gesture that would most likely result in his death. But were he to do nothing, Earl Ralf might decide to remove his head.

Florio stood on Grimsgard's common, staring westward, listening to the pounding of faraway drums, their rhythm monotonous, relentless— BOOM-boom-boom-boom, BOOM-boom-boom-boom, BOOM-boom-boom-boom. Day and night for the past three days. Getting steadily louder as more drummers joined in.

The Keltins were undeniably gathering. Laying plans, getting things in order, singing their battle-chants, and sharpening their spears. Distaining the soft city folk to such degree that they made no effort to conceal their intentions.

How long did he have until the last savage tribesman arrived to add his bronze-headed battleaxe to the swelling Keltin host? Until the last spear was honed to a needle point? Until the clans were driven to frenzy by their murderous songs of war?

And what was he to do? He had, not long ago, held off a band of mercenaries who attempted to seize Roscoe's towerhouse. But there had been no more than a score or so of them. How many thousand would come sweeping up from the river? No amount of planning or preparation could stem that red tide.

PART 3

MALACHAI

CHAPTER 22

IN THE MANSE OF THE MAGICIAN PART ONE

Perhaps it was the jolting, uneven gait of his horse in the sandy soil. Perhaps the damp sea air carried an effluvium that vexed his damaged lungs. Whatever the cause, in the early afternoon, Thurmond began to cough. It started as a dry, annoying hack but steadily progressed to a wet, painful wheeze. By late afternoon, he was bringing up blood.

He grew weaker and weaker until he could no longer sit unsupported in the saddle. Sarah began leading his horse by its bridle, while Roscoe rode with one arm stretched around the young man's shoulders. As the day wore on, he worsened, his breath now coming in slow, painful gasps.

Roscoe called a halt. He saw his friend was dying and wanted, at very least, to make him comfortable. As the old Adventurer lifted him from the saddle, Sarah spread a cloak on the ground. She then rolled another for his pillow. Neither spoke.

Torgul gestured for the three Gascars to scout ahead. The mercenaries flopped to the ground, glad for the chance to rest. All but Bart, who stalked toward Roscoe. Torgul read his angry, impatient expression—he would berate the old Adventurer over this delay, demand that Thurmond either ride or be left behind.

The dwarf unslung Bloodtroll and stepped between the knight and his comrade. Feet apart, weapon horizontal across his waist, eyes boring into the Bart's. Nary a word was spoken, but his meaning was indubitably clear—Thurmond's final moments were not to be interrupted by inane blather.

Seeing Torgul's determination, Bart flushed red with rage but turned away, saying nothing. His mercenaries, sprawled on the ground, watched the scene unfold and wisely remained mute. Drax permitted himself a secret smile.

All this silence was suddenly shattered by the return of the archers, galloping, waving their arms, shouting something that no one could make out. The reclining mercenaries jumped to the feet and drew their weapons. Leaving Sarah to tend Thurmond, Torgul and Roscoe ran to see what had befallen.

It was neither Grinder's brothers nor the warriors of Brodar Eaglebeak that had prompted the shouting and waving. As he drew rein in front of Roscoe, Wat was actually smiling.

"There's a sodding big castle just a bit further along—sittin' out on a long point of land. That's what you told us to be lookin' for. Well—we found it."

As gently as possible, the wheezing, blood-spattered Thurmond was restored to the saddle, and the party set on with the archers in the lead. Sure enough, as Wat had promised, they soon came to a large stone edifice set high above the sea at the end of a narrow headland, thrust like a bony finger into the sea.

It was a mansion, not a castle, as it boasted neither towers nor parapets. No moat, drawbridge, barbican, or coign of vantage. The windows were large and wide rather than glowering slits. The only feature suggesting defense was a high stone wall across the base of the headland, isolating the house from the mainland. The wooden gate stood open, and as they drew nigh, a man stepped through it.

He was middle-aged, balding, and dressed in the smock and breeches of a typical servant—obviously a gatekeeper. Roscoe began the formal speech he always used when introducing himself in an official capacity.

"I am Captain Roscoe Franklin, Adventurer in good standin' from the City of Gorgonholm. My companions and I…."

The man began speaking as if unaware of Roscoe's words. His voice was flat and inflectionless, his face void of expression.

"You are expected. You may enter. The master awaits."

As he rode through the gate, the old Adventurer took a careful look at this fellow. His eyes were as lifeless as his voice.

The promontory jutted straight into the churning water of the Cold Sea, so that the waves came crashing in from both sides. Their ceaseless pounding made the ground shake as if the entire point was about to crumble into the sea.

They met no other servants or workers. There were no outbuildings, no livestock, no orchards or crops, only a single path leading from the gate to an immense edifice constructed of sandstone blocks. It looked as gray and cold as the water below, and it filled them with dread.

Sarah could feel an intense psychic vibration permeating the air around them. She shuddered, wondering how so large a structure could have come to be built in such a remote spot. Had it, she wondered, been raised by infernal hands?

The main doors stood open—more expectation than invitation. Roscoe looked at Sarah, his eyes filled with grim determination.

"We got no time to be wastin' here, lassie. We gotta get our boy some help or we're gonna lose him for a fact. If that magician fella is as powerful as Asmodeus seems to think, then he oughta be able to do somethin'. Let's get him inside."

Thurmond was by now so drawn and pale as to resemble the corpse he would soon become. They lifted him from his horse, and Roscoe carried him like a child in his arms through the waiting doorway. Sarah was at his side. Torgul started to unsling his axe, thought the better of it, slipped it back into its baldric, and followed his friends.

Bart hesitated on the doorstep, obviously reluctant to enter. Then he gave a low curse, spat, and stepped in behind the others. He had never intended to pass through the magician's portal, but when Sarah had done so, he knew he had no choice. Where a girl dared to go, a knight could not hold back.

They found themselves in a long entry hall, its walls hung with rich tapestries but otherwise empty. At the far end, a wide set of stairs led to the mansion's upper reaches. A small man stood in the hall's center. He wore a black robe with long, drooping sleeves. His face was sallow, his nose narrow. When he spoke, his voice was dry and reedy.

"I am Malachai. I have been aware of your approach for some time, but your purpose is not known to me. Why have you entered my domain?"

Before they could answer, he pointed at Thurmond with a thin, delicate hand.

"That one reeks of death. Can't you smell it? He will pass within the hour."

All Roscoe could smell was the damp, mildewy air of the hall.

"Master Malachai—you've got to help this poor laddie. He's our boon companion and a fine young man…."

The magician waved his hand dismissively.

"People die, that is their fate. What matter if it comes sooner or later? This is his time."

Fear, rage, and frustration swelled in Roscoe's breast, but he did his utmost to appear calm.

"Maybe it is and maybe it ain't…not yet anyways…not if you can help him. We'll be needin' his skills to fulfill our quest, so we will. We can't possibly carry on without him."

A look of mild annoyance crossed Malachai's face, the look of a man with an annoying pebble in his shoe.

"Oh, very well."

The magician neither spoke nor gestured, but almost immediately a tapestry was drawn back and a servant appeared. He carried a stoppered flask of opaque glass on a small silver tray. His eyes were as lifeless as those of the gatekeeper.

Malachai indicated the flask.

"A potion of restoration. If he drinks of it, he will live, though two days will be necessary for him to recover full health and strength. Be aware—I do nothing for nothing. If you accept this potion, you will owe me a service."

Roscoe did not bother to answer. With Thurmond still cradled in his arms, Sarah began to trickle the liquid into his mouth. Barely conscious, the young man gasped, choked as if he must retch, but then began swallowing the concoction. Within moments, his breathing became easier and his eyes closed.

The magician resumed their conversation.

"He will sleep, perhaps for more than a day, while the potion does its work. Now you will answer me—why are you come here?"

Roscoe once again assumed his formal role.

"Master Malachai, I am Captain Roscoe Franklin, Adventurer in good standin' from the city of Gorgonholm...."

Once again he was cut off before going any farther.

"Your name and rank are of no consequence. You will answer my question. What would you have of me?"

The old Adventurer towered over the small, dark magician, yet the smaller man seemed the far more menacing of the two.

"Well sir, to get right to the point, our quest is of great import, so it is. Our beautiful city is imperiled by some demonic force, and your old comrade Asmodeus suggested that you was the only one that could save us."

Malachai's brow creased in what might have been a tiny frown.

"You believe Asmodeus to be my comrade? He told you that?"

Realizing he had made a mistake, Roscoe tried to back up.

"Perhaps he didn't say comrade. It may have been *old acquaintance*, he said. Aye—that was it."

"Hardly a mere acquaintance. We are much more closely connected than that."

Unable to read the depth of the magician's displeasure, the old Adventurer sought to equivocate.

"Kinsman? I seem to recall him saying such like. A distant kinsman, maybe? A second cousin once removed?"

"Rather closer."

"A brother then, mayhap?"

"We have no common parentage. Perhaps the relationship is best left undefined."

There was no discernable family resemblance. Asmodeus was fair of complexion, rotund of build, and sanguine of humor. He was also given to flamboyant dress and outlandish displays of whimsy. Malachai was dark, thin and phlegmatic. His attire was subdued and his manner grave.

Roscoe was flummoxed by the magician's cryptic remarks.

"Well now…ain't that somethin'…him bein' some relation or other."

"We are estranged. It was, in fact, his doing that led me to seek refuge in this desolate land while he resides in comfort and luxury. So he has no reason to presume upon my good will."

Roscoe's heart sank, as did Torgul's and Sarah's. They had suffered much injury and deprivation, in their long journey north. Was it to be for naught? And what would become of Gorgonholm if the Black Stone's grip was not loosened by Malachai's magic?

Roscoe cleared his throat.

"Master Malachai, we don't want to stir up no bad feelin's between you and your kinsman—by God's knobby knees, we truly don't. We only come up here because he told us that you was the only one that could save our city. Right now, the folks there are killin' each other for no reason at all. Burnin' down their houses, causin' no end of misery and mischief."

"And when we left, the tribes across the river was gettin' ready to come across. If they do, and our people are all busy fightin' one another…well… it'll probably mean the end of everything. And all because of somethin' called the Black Stone."

The magician's eyes widened slightly. This was, for Malachai, a lavish display of emotion and led Roscoe to suppose he was now intensely interested. His next words confirmed this assumption.

"Tell me about this Black Stone."

Roscoe proceeded to tell him in detail about the terrible discord that had erupted so suddenly and for no appreciable reason. About the frightful predications of Zeb the Prophet. About the legend of the Black Stone as told to them by Asmodeus.

Malachai listened intently, though his expression remained impassive. Then he spoke.

"Asmodeus is correct—the Black Stone is a powerful entity, a malevolent demon in lithic form. It has arisen many times throughout the centuries, always with the direst consequences for those on whom it feeds, for it has an insatiable appetite for human pain, fear, and despair."

Roscoe's mouth was dry as he asked the most important question.

"You will help us to destroy it, then?"

The magician stared into the old Adventurer's eyes, causing a thin chill to course down the length of his spine.

"The Black Stone cannot be destroyed, that is beyond my power, beyond the ability of any man."

Roscoe felt as if he had been struck by a club.

"Master Malachai, we must at least try. I can't just sit by while a demon eats my town."

"Understand this, I care nothing for Gorgonholm or its people. The life of a city is of no more importance than those of the men who live within it. All must, in their time, droop unto death.

And yet I am moved to involve myself in this matter. Though the stone cannot be destroyed, it may be possible to cast it down and return it to the earth until it's time once more comes 'round."

Roscoe sensed he was being baited, that the magician was about to name some fantastic price for his services.

"And what exactly, sir, would you be demandin' in return?"

The reply was surprising.

"From you, nothing at all. The reasons for my involvement will remain entirely my own."

The old Adventurer was much relieved to hear this, yet the magician's words somehow filled him with foreboding. He smiled his most winning smile.

"Well now, that's mighty gratifyin' to hear, so it is. How soon can you get ready?"

The answer was disconcerting.

"A day or two, perhaps longer. I must study the stars and consult my allies beyond the veil. There is much to be done.

"You will remain my guests while I do so. My servants are even now preparing chambers for your use. A feast will be served you as soon as you are settled."

None of the Adventurers liked this idea. Every hour spent dallying here could bring new wrack and ruin to Gorgonholm. Moreover, they did not want to be quartered in the magician's ominous mansion. Roscoe began to object, but was silenced before he could truly begin.

"Your friend needs to gain strength. That will, as I said, take some days. And forget not, you must perform the service you agreed to by accepting the potion of restoration. Your soldiers will remain outside. They will be provided everything required for their comfort and convenience.

"The stairs at the end of this hall lead to your chambers on the next floor. Come and go through this entry hall as you please. The front door will remain open. But under no circumstances must you attempt to venture into my private chambers in the upper stories. Be warned, there is danger there."

Then he turned and disappeared behind a tapestry.

CHAPTER 23

IN THE MANSE OF THE MAGICIAN PART TWO

The staircase brought them to a dining hall on the second level. In its center, another dead-eyed servant was placing cups and plates on a long trestle table. He finished his task and withdrew without a glance or a word. At the far end, a large fireplace was flickering with a newly-kindled blaze.

Doors were set at intervals around the walls, opening into individual sleeping chambers. One was designated as a sick room for Thurmond. Sarah took the room next to it, Roscoe and Torgul chose one next to the stairs.

Bart despised Sarah more and more, resented her uncanny knack to thwart him. Without a single word, merely by being herself, she had compelled him to enter this hellish abode. He was uncertain which was worse—being at the mercy of a vile magician or being forced about by some bastard girl.

He claimed a large chamber at the far end of the room and shut the door behind him. Here, at least, he could be free from their low-born company. Asmodeus's commands compelled him to treat with this rabble, but when this obligation was fulfilled, all that would change. Then he would settle the score with his self-proclaimed sister and repay the sneaking little thief who had stolen his treasure map.

The dining hall and sleeping rooms were large and well appointed, yet all were fraught with the same sour smell as the reception hall. The servants had made only the most cursory efforts in preparing the rooms for the guests. The center areas had been swept, but the corners abounded in cobwebs and dust. The glass windows were heavy with grime, the linen damp and yellow with age.

The feast, when it arrived, was dismal. The wine had long since turned to vinegar, the bread was sodden and lumpy. The meat, which they assumed to be pork, was spongy, gray, and so foul of flavor that the diners immediately spat their first bite onto the floor.

The Adventurers, like all people of their time, were quite accustomed to the taste of partially decayed meat. Hunters routinely hung their grouse and heron until the neck rotted and the body fell from the head, lending the flesh a gamey flavor that many found delectable. Roscoe was quite fond of a well-hung bird.

But Malachai's pork tasted like something exhumed from a grave. A troll might find it toothsome, but no human could ever stomach such putrefaction.

Outside, the soldiers were having a similar experience. Malachai had, true to his word, provided them with everything necessary for their comfort and convenience. The servants brought iron spits and kettles for cooking, thick felt tents, fodder for the horses, casks of ale, and an abundance of meat and bread. But the ironware was encrusted with ancient rust and the tents were heavily spotted with mildew. The ale was flat, the fodder moldy, and the meat was the same gray horror served to the Adventurers.

The soldiers at least had access to the rations carried by the pack animals. The Adventurers made do with the unpalatable bread and whatever scraps they could find in their rucksacks.

The rest of the night was equally unpleasant. Restful sleep was impossible, for the clammy air carried the vague murmurings of spirits unseen. Sarah found her chamber insufferable—the dank bedclothes seemed a very shroud. When she could stand it no longer, she got up and padded around the room in bare feet.

She knew what she had to do. It would be a desperate risk, and the others would try to dissuade her if they knew, so it would be better if they remained unaware. She harbored grave suspicions regarding Malachai and his intentions. If these proved to be true, they must flee at once from his evil abode.

No stairway connected the guests' dining hall with the upper floors—the only way to go was down. Sarah descended the stairs to the entry hall, intending to try the passages concealed behind the tapestries. She found only blank stone walls. Her search for hidden doors revealed nothing—no telltale outlines, no concealed keyholes, no secret latches, nothing.

She returned to the dining hall and examined the windows until she found one she liked. The wooden sash was ancient and swollen, unwilling to open. Sarah secured a knife from the eating-ware scattered about the dining table and began to scrape away at the putty holding the glass in its frame. The stuff was old and crumbly—easily removed—and in short order, she had the glass out, filling the room with cold night air.

The young witch wiggled out the opening, scrambling a bit until her feet found a ledge running along the mansion's second level. Luckily, it was wide enough that she could stand upon it without too much fear of falling.

Looking up, she spied a light pouring through a window two stories above her and half the building's length away. It might, she decided, be possible to climb to that window, for the damp sea air had crumbled the mortar between the mansion's stones, forming many gaps in which her fingers and toes might find purchase.

She wished that Pozi was there. That girl could climb like a spider on a waterspout! She would be up that wall in an eyeblink, delighted for a chance to prove herself. But Pozi was not there, so there was nothing else for her to do.

Sarah began to slide along the ledge until she stood directly beneath the lighted window, then she began to climb, wedging her fingers and toes into the narrow cracks. Her progress was slow and painful, but she gradually approached her objective.

A sudden thought caused her to freeze in fear—would the descent not be more difficult than the ascent? Could she make it without falling to her death? She must, she knew, put such fatal thoughts from her mind. Steeling her resolve, she resumed her upward course.

The young witch gasped with relief as she at last pulled herself onto the ledge running the length of the fourth level. Moving as stealthily as she could, she peeked into the lighted room. Malachai sat in a posture of meditation in the center of a magic circle. His lips moved as if he were chanting, yet no sound came to her ears. A narrow-bladed sword lay across his outstretched palms.

She scanned the rest of the room, seeking any detail that might suggest the magician's true intentions. The walls were lined with high shelves crammed with magical bric-a-brac. Many held what looked to be large glass jars, others bore long rectangular tanks, also of glass. Parchment scrolls were stacked on a nearby table. She could see nothing more.

Malachai ceased his soundless chanting and opened his eyes. He looked up as if aware that he was being observed. Sarah ducked back from the window and fled back down the wall as fast as she was able. Under such conditions, the descent was much easier than she had anticipated. Back in the dining hall, she replaced the glass in the sash and secured it in place with lumps of soggy bread.

When she turned to go back to her room, Roscoe was standing directly behind her, hands on hips.

"Learn anything?"

Sarah did not know how to reply—she felt like a child caught by her mother at some mischief.

"Nay, I just...."

"Then try again tomorrow night. Just make sure Torgul doesn't see you slipping out—he'd want to go with you. And as long as you're awake, how about taking a turn sitting with Thurmond?"

Roscoe went off to bed, leaving Sarah alone and rather amazed in the dining hall.

Morning finally arrived. At some point in the night, unseen servants removed the uneaten remains of the bad dinner and set out a breakfast of the same sorry fare. Always a vigorous and enthusiastic eater, Roscoe was beside himself with disappointment.

"It seems our good host is not much given to the pleasures of fine victuals.

If this nasty slop is the best he can offer, I'm like to wither and starve, so I am—and I don't want to wander these halls as a hungry ghost."

These words had scarcely left his mouth when he noticed the magician standing at the top of the stairs. He had heard every word.

"Is something the matter with the food?"

Roscoe immediately shifted to a more respectful tone.

"Oh, nay, nothing the matter, as it were. First class viands, to be sure. It's just…"

When his voice trailed off, the magician pressed the point.

"Just what?"

"Well, sir, the fare is perhaps a bit too rich for our simple tastes. Take the wine, for instance. It's been aged a considerable time. Now I'm aware there's gentlefolk what like their wine old—the older the better, in fact—and pay a high price for it. But we're just simple people what ain't used to such fanciness."

Malachai's face displayed no trace of emotion.

"Anything else?"

"Nay, nay, nothin' else, nothin' at all. The bread is quite good—just like I like it—a bit damp and doughy inside. But some of the others…well…they prefers their bread a bit more baked. And the meat was a tad too high for their tastes. Myself, I prefers a well-hung bird or hare. But it's the girl, sir—she's needin' somethin' less strong, so she is."

Malachai said nothing, in no way acknowledged Roscoe's words. Then Sarah spoke up.

"Master Malachai! I would speak to you as well."

The magician replied with a slightly impatient look. Again, he said nothing.

"Master Malachai, I have with me a number of magical items that remain unidentified—talismans, charms, potions. Would you be willing to establish their purpose? They might be very useful in our quest."

The magician replied.

"As I have said, I do nothing for nothing. I will identify the nature and purpose of your trinkets, but for a price. If I do this thing, you must allow me to choose any three of them for my own—my choice, no matter how valuable they might be. Do you agree?"

"Aye, sir, I do. You may take any three of the items for yourself. Please proceed."

She dug into her pannier and spread them on the table—medallions, amulets, fetishes, scrolls, a ring, and a small padded box. Malachai's interest must have been great, for his brow wrinkled slightly as he examined them.

"None of these possess great power. Use them once, perhaps twice, and their psychic energy will be exhausted. Most are for humble purposes. This charm, for example, will draw redworms to the surface—good for a fisherman in search of bait. This other is for the harvesting of nuts—it causes them to fall from the tree on command.

"Some are cures. This potion will drive away boils or chilblains. Wear this medallion to ward off the bloody flux. This small black charm will cure sheep of the shaking sickness."

He opened the padded box to reveal six small glass bottles packed within.

"These are potions of restoration, the same as I gave your friend. You might find them very useful. All except this one...."

He removed one of the bottles and ran his thumb along its side. A skull and crossbones appeared, then disappeared.

"That one is a deadly poison, so beware."

The magician replaced it in the box and picked up a plain silver ring.

"Now this is unusual. It allows you to understand the cries of the Great Oog."

This piqued Sarah's curiosity.

"If I may ask, what is an Oog?"

"A gigantic terror bird. Its beak will rend a man as readily as you tear a piece of bread."

"I've never before heard of such a creature."

"That is because it does not exist in this world. But should you ever come across one, you will be able to comprehend its cries as it eats you."

Was this intended as a joke? Did Malachai have a sense of humor after all? Sarah was uncertain, but she guessed that he probably did not.

The magician next held up a small yellow feather and a tiny whistle made from the bone of a bird's leg.

"More bird magic—surely the work of a shaman. Wave this little feather to invoke a gentle breeze to cool a hot summer day, but be careful—the more you wave it, the harder the breeze will blow. The whistle will allow you to summon and, to a degree, control a flock of birds."

He next examined an assortment of small glass vials sealed with wax.

"The liquid inside this clear vial will dispel any illusion, even the most potent. Simply smash it to release the essence inside. This brown one will emit an unendurable stench—break it at your peril. Drinking this red potion will enable a man to jump across a gulf of twenty feet. The blue one will let sing you like a castrato in a cathedral choir."

A small golden amulet drew his attention.

"Now here's a talisman of greater power—it will compel a cacodemon to reveal its true name."

Malachai next pointed at a small brown item that resembled a dried human tongue. His eyes seemed to gleam with repressed delight—well, almost.

"Place this under a man's bed to induce the most dreadful dreams."

He turned to the final item.

"This necklace of teeth is interesting—it will cause the wearer to perform an act of reckless courage."

Sarah indicated the scrolls.

"I have two of these, each carries three unknown spells. Can you identify them?"

"Nay, to read a scroll spell is to cast it."

Sarah nodded, she had expected such a response.

"I thank you, Master Malachai. Some of these charms will be of great service, I am certain."

"I will now make my selections."

Strangely, Malachai's first choice was the charm to summon fishing worms. Was he an avid angler? Sarah could not imagine him with a pole and creel. He then selected the talisman for compelling a cacodemon—no surprise there. And lastly the ring of the Great Oog. The magician apparently desired to hold discourse with a nonexistent creature.

Malachai's attention returned to Roscoe.

"I would remind you that you owe me a service for saving your friend. I expect you to undertake it this very day."

Roscoe held out his hands, beseechingly.

"Now, sir, you said it yourself, so you did, poor old Thurmond ain't goin' to be up and about for another day or two. And it wouldn't do to go off without him. Young as he is, he's our best fightin' man."

This was a lie. Thurmond's fighting skills were progressing rapidly, but his skill level still lagged behind those of Roscoe and Torgul. In reality, the Old Adventurer was unwilling to leave his helpless friend alone with Malachai.

"Very well, but the task must be completed by tomorrow evening. I will spend tonight and tomorrow in a deep state of trance as I complete the... instrument...that will cause the defeat of the Black Stone. It must be carried south in two days."

Roscoe had another important question to ask.

"Would you care to reveal, sir, the exact nature of this *task* we are to perform for you?"

"A gang of rampaging giants have been plundering the fishing villages nearby. You must destroy them."

Giants!

Did such a creature even exist? They had all grown up on tales of giants, though no one had ever seen one. Or knew of anyone who had. Or had even heard of someone who had. Surely such abominations dwelt only in old stories and legends.

Giants were said to be as tall as trees, stupid as a pile of rocks, and mean as a dozen drunken werewolves. They possessed ravenous appetites and devoured any human luckless enough to fall into their hands. Giants were also said to be great hoarders of gold.

Roscoe cleared his throat.

"You said a *gang* of giants, Master Malachai? Not just one giant?"

"Nay, there are several."

Roscoe swallowed hard, clearing his throat.

"Then wouldn't it be wiser to send some demon to kill 'em off, or maybe smite 'em with some deadly curse?"

"Not so. I do nothing for nothing, and the miserable fishermen could never meet the price of such intervention."

"And yet you're helpin' 'em by settin' us to this task."

"The villagers provide me with certain useful things, so I will not have them eaten by monstrosities. There are other reasons, but they will remain my own."

"How will we find these brutes?"

"Ride east along the sea cliff until you pass the third village. The giants are living in hillside caves half a league onward. And remember, the task must be fulfilled by tomorrow night. Fail in this, and you will know my profound displeasure."

CHAPTER 24

SARAH'S FRIGHTFUL DISCOVERY

At a little past midday, Thurmond opened his eyes. He felt weak, but the pain was entirely gone. He also felt thirsty—and hungry—and he really needed to pee. Sarah sat in a chair nearby. Weary from the previous night's escapades, she was fast asleep.

He tried to call to her, wanting a drink from the pitcher that stood on a nearby table, but his throat was so dry that his voice resembled the rough squawk of a crow. Sarah awakened with a start, saw his open eyes, and emitted a little squeak.

Thurmond pulled himself upright, snagged the pitcher, and drank until it was empty. Sarah gave him a smile.

"So slugabed, you're finally awake."

"Aye, and hungry. What's to eat?"

"Not much, I'm afraid. The magician's board is unspeakably vile, but we've brought in some of our rations from the pack mule."

Though his throat was still parched, he gave her his best Roscoe imitation.

"Would you be so kind as to bring me a great pile of victuals, lassie. I'm a man with a mighty appetite, so I am."

This made Sarah laugh.

"I see you're not only awake, you're feeling playful. I think you might live after all."

She brought him a plate of salt meat, hard cheese, and a small loaf of Malachai's soggy bread. Thurmond thanked her and began shoving it into his mouth with both hands. Finished, he climbed from bed and headed for the garderobe to empty his bladder. On his way back, he encountered Roscoe and Torgul coming up the stairs.

They were delighted to find Thurmond awake and out of bed. The lad was clearly on the mend. But they also brought some troubling news—one of Bart's mercenaries, the fellow known as Gorb, had inexplicably disappeared. He had been present in camp at mid-morning, eating, jesting with his comrades, tending the horses. But then, for reasons unknown, he was simply no longer there.

A search of the small encampment disclosed nothing. Bart had posted sentries at both the curtain wall gate and at the door of the magician's manse, but these men swore that the missing soldier had not passed their way. The only plausible explanation was that he had stepped too close to the cliff's edge, perhaps for a piss, and tumbled to his doom.

That evening's meal was better than that of the previous day. A man in tattered, salt-stained clothes had arrived at the manse with a basket of fresh fish for the soldiers. In the dining hall, the pork, though tough and stringy, was at least fresh. The wine was thin and sour, but drinkable. Only the mushy bread remained the same.

As night fell, the soldiers applied themselves to the magician's flat ale. Some began to sing. Others sharpened their weapons, for word had spread that tomorrow would be a day of battle. Cob and Drax, by now close comrades, went off to pray.

None of the men had yet been told the nature of the enemy they must face. Bart was livid when told about the giants and flatly refused to participate in such a suicidal venture. Roscoe plied him with Malachai's sour wine and wooed him with promises of great glory. No good. He described the fabulous treasure found in every giant's lair, but still to no avail. It was only the threat of the magician's *profound displeasure* that finally convinced the petulant knight to throw in.

Sarah waited until the hour of the Maiden's Ghost before squirming through the window and climbing to the ledge on the mansion's fourth story. All was dark. The magician was either asleep or in a magical trance. She inched along, window to window, searching for a way inside—a loose pane of glass, an unlatched latch.

Finally, at the corner, she found what she needed—a wooden sash rotted by long exposure to the rays of the sun. The pulpy wood gave way easily to the blade of her knife, and in a moment, the glass was removed. She laid it carefully on the ledge beside her. Upon leaving, she would fasten it in place with soggy bread.

With only a pale fragment of moonlight to guide her, she slithered into the magician's lair. The room was dark, but she could make out high shelves laden with books and scrolls, apparently a library. In the center, a large parchment lay unrolled on a long table, three of its corners held down by books, the fourth by a large bronze key. She pocketed the key and replaced it with a carved wooden box. Keys were always useful.

Sarah glanced quickly at the parchment. There was just enough light to make out a diagram of nasty-looking symbols she did not recognize. She left it and proceeded to a door in the far wall. It was locked, of course, but opened easily with the bronze key.

Sarah found herself in a windowless corridor. Here the darkness was absolute, forcing her to grope her way along with her hands. She left the door behind her unlocked—an unimpeded flight might become necessary—and moved down the corridor to the door of the chamber she sought, the one in which she had observed Malachai in meditation. Here, she reasoned, would be her best chance of discovering the real intentions of their mysterious host.

The door was locked, but gave way readily to the bronze key. She slipped inside but remained for only seconds. What she saw in the dim moonlight was enough to send her fleeing wildly back down the corridor, all thought of stealth forgotten, her hand clamped over her mouth to keep from screaming aloud.

Back through the library she flew, the door left open behind her. Climbing out the window, her foot struck the displaced pane of glass and sent it spinning to the ground. Her descent to her own room was so rapid, so heedless, that she was lucky not to have fallen to her death.

"Heads! Heads in big glass jars! Human heads floating in some kind of liquid. They were staring as if they could see me. Some had no eyes, but they surely knew I was there."

Sarah sat by the fire with a blanket wrapped around her shoulders and a cup of wine in her hand. She had finally stopped sobbing, but the uncontrollable trembling continued. The three Adventurers and Bart stood clustered around her.

Roscoe tried to sooth the young woman.

"Now lassie, I'm sure it was a terrible sight, so it was. But try to put it out of your mind. Them ain't but the heads of dead men, probably servants who died of sickness or old age or such. Maybe that's what they do here when somebody dies—they keep the head—instead of buryin' 'em proper like we do back home."

Sarah shook her head emphatically.

"Nay! They weren't really dead, that's what scares me. They were alive somehow."

Thurmond laid a comforting hand on her shoulder.

"It was just a fancy, Sarah. You had a bad shock, seeing something so horrible, and your mind played a trick on you, that's all."

Again, she refused the simple explanation.

"Nay! They were alive! They talked to me…but without words. Like they were right inside my brain."

This caught Thurmond's interest.

"What did they say?"

"They wanted me to help them."

"Help them how?"

"By killing them. They want to die. They were like lost souls with no way to escape. Malachai did that to them, and that isn't all, isn't the worst of it."

The girl's body was wracked by an intense shudder. Roscoe patted her shoulder. He felt terribly guilty for having suggested her second nocturnal exploration. Thurmond knelt down and took her hands in both of his. Torgul stood silently, his brow creased with concern.

Bart gave her an impatient look, then strode to the table and poured himself a large tankard of wine.

When her shaking abated, Roscoe spoke again.

"Go on, lassie, tell us the rest of it."

Sarah wiped her eyes with her fingers and blew her nose on the tail of her tunic.

"Like I said, there were these big jars with heads inside. Living heads. But also big, square, glass boxes with all manner of body parts. Some had arms or hands or fingers. Some had feet and toes. There were jars of eyeballs and tongues, plus all the things we have on the inside—livers and lights and hearts. But that still isn't the worst of it."

"Stretched out on a table, there was a body that he, Malachai, has been stitching together from different parts, like he was making a doll from old rags."

She paused, seized by another fit of trembling, then blurted out.

"That's still not the worst of it!"

Roscoe gave her shoulder a gentle squeeze.

"Go on, Sarah—just say it."

"You know Malachai's servants, the ones with the empty eyes? They're walking dead men. He sewed them together out of parts and brought them back to life."

Bart drained his tankard, refilled it, and drained it again. His voice was seething with rage and thick with drink.

"And maybe that still isn't the worst. You know that gray meat we tried eating, the stuff we thought was rotten pork? Have you seen any pigs here? Or any other livestock? I'm betting Malachai cooked up one of his dead servants. That's why it tasted so foul—it came from some jar in his workshop. And then today we got fresh meat. Tasted pretty good, uh? Maybe it won't taste so good if I tell you where it came from. I figure we ate Gorb, my man who disappeared this morning."

All conversation stopped. Sarah put her hand over her mouth as if trying to keep from retching. Thurmond's stomach clenched like a fist. Torgul turned an odd shade of green.

Finally, Roscoe spoke.

"This is grim speculation, so it is. Sir Bartholomew, you might have the right of it, about the nature of our meal here tonight, but we can't know that for sure. And it'll be best if we never know, of that I am certain. So let us agree to never mention it again. Not another word. Not to one another, not to no one. Let us bury that terrible thought for all time."

Thurmond's guts were trying to rip themselves loose from their moorings. He held his stomach in both hands, trying to restrain its convulsions. He addressed his old mentor through clenched lips.

"What do we do, Roscoe? Malachai's worse than a necromancer. We've got to get out of here before he cuts off our heads and sticks 'em in jars."

"Aye, laddie, that we do. But we'll do it in a nice, orderly manner—nothin' panicky. Malachai's a minion of evil, that's a fact, but I don't think he's out to pickle our heads just yet. If he truly wanted 'em, they'd be floatin' in jars already.

"We're more important to him alive. He wants us to kill some giants. I think that's maybe a test to see if we're worthy of some bigger task. Did you see his eyes light up when I mentioned the Black Stone? There's somethin' he's wantin', and he sees us as the best way to get it."

Sarah spoke, her voice shaky.

"I hope you're right, but you didn't really answer Thurmond's question. What are we going to do?"

"We're gonna pack up our gear, right here and now. Bart and me, we'll go down and get the men doin' the same. And as soon as it's light out, we'll all go and see about killin' some giants. Are you agreeable with that, sir knight?"

Sir Bartholomew was far from agreeable. He would no longer knuckle under to these stinking peasants. When he spoke, his voice quivered with repressed fury.

"I've had all I can stand of you and your adventure, old man. First you get a tribe of barbarians screaming for my blood. Now you put me at the mercy of a black magician who keeps heads in jars. One of my men has gone missing, and I probably ate him. Now you want me to go fight giants."

"Are you utterly mad? My men and I head south tomorrow. You may go fight the giants, or don't, just as you please, but I'm through with this whole shitting mess."

Roscoe recognized the look in Bart's eye, knew that the young knight was looking for an excuse to draw his sword. He would need Bart on the morrow, so he could not afford to kill him—not yet, at least. So he kept his voice soft and gentle.

"Sir knight, I understand your feelin's. There's a lot of truth in what you're sayin', so there is. Right now, things is lookin' dire, but maybe not so bad as all that when you really think about it."

"Take the giants—all I really want to do is go have a look-see. Maybe we won't have to fight 'em at all. If they're as slow-witted as they're said to be, then we'll outsmart 'em somehow."

"And the barbarians? Those Blue Horse fellas? Well, we ain't had no problems stayin' out of their way so far. I'm bettin' we can keep outta sight in a country as big as this one."

Bart remained unmoved.

"Bollocks! I'm through listening to your equivocation. Your schemes have brought me nothing but trouble."

Roscoe gave the knight a pitying look.

"You have to do what you deem best for own self, so you do. And you don't have to explain anything to me. But you might have a tad bit of trouble gettin' Asmodeus to understand—bringin' you on this adventure was his doin', not mine. And Malachai made his expectations very clear."

The old Adventurer's reasoning was impeccable. Seeing he was trapped, Bart threw his tankard at the wall and stormed off down the stairs. He was angry and needed to take it out on someone—anyone—maybe that one-armed cripple, Drax.

CHAPTER 25

A GANG OF RAMPAGING GIANTS

They rode out before dawn in a column of twos, passed through the gate in the curtain wall, and headed east along the seacoast. A narrow track took them through the dunes to the first of the fishing villages—a cluster of decrepit hovels interspaced with long racks of drying fish. Ropes, nets, and wicker baskets were piled next to tiny boats that looked far too fragile to withstand the buffeting of the sea.

The fisher folk took one look at the Adventurers and fled for their lives, the women and children seeking refuge in the hills and ravines just behind their cottages, the men taking to their boats.

They found the giants just beyond the third village, just where Malachai had said they would be. Four of them squatting in a circle next to the mouth of a large cave. They were eating, wholly unaware of the two Adventurers watching them from a grass-covered hummock.

The giants were hideous creatures—huge, misshapen things clad in odd bits of clothing much too small for them. Thurmond raised his head higher for a better look, but Roscoe pulled him back down. Only then did the younger man notice the broad grin on his comrade's face. What could be so pleasing?

They slipped back to where the rest of the party lay concealed in a small ravine, the old Adventurer chuckling all the way. When the company was gathered around him, he explained the reason for his good cheer.

"Them little fellas ain't giants at all— ain't nothin' more than ogres. There's only four of 'em, and they're so busy with their breakfast that they ain't keepin' watch. We can take 'em easy."

Thurmond had, of course, heard of ogres but had never before encountered one.

"What are ogres, Roscoe?"

"You seen 'em, laddie—kinda like men, but a mite bigger. Not near so big as giants. Real stupid, they are, too. So here's what we'll do…."

The Gascar archers rose from their concealed position and let fly with their powerful warbows. Three broadhead arrows buried themselves in the back of the nearest ogre. At the same moment, Roscoe fired his heavy crossbow, driving a bolt clean through the neck of a second.

This should have slain the creatures outright, or at least caused them grievous injury. But the ogres seemed to suffer no ill effects despite the blood that oozed from their wounds. All four stood and scanned the landscape for the source of the irritation.

The archers fired a second volley, striking their target in the chest this time. But again the arrows had scant effect. While the Gascars were laying a third arrow to string, the ogres spotted their attackers, roared, and charged.

Roscoe tossed aside his crossbow—it was a very powerful weapon but too slow in the loading. He strapped his shield on his left arm and drew his sword with his right. At his signal, Bart's mercenaries rose from behind the archers, moved forward, and formed a battle-line.

Three pairs of sword-and-shield men comprised the first row, with each pair directed by a spearman standing directly behind them. Protected by their shields, the swordsmen would occupy the ogres with a ferocious attack, while the spearmen, striking over their shoulders, would thrust at their faces, chests, and bellies.

Bart, armed with a glaive, stood behind the line with two more sword-and-shield men. They were the reserve and would advance to defend a weak point or exploit an advantage. Roscoe stood slightly to one side, ready to join any group in need of his strong right arm. The archers drifted right and maintained a steady barrage of arrow fire.

Roscoe had expected the dimwitted ogres to attack at a slow shuffle, but they came on quickly, unhurt by the arrows, undaunted by the size of the opposing force. As they grew closer, they began to pick up speed, gaining momentum with every step. They would strike with the force of a battering ram.

When half the distance had been crossed, Thurmond, Torgul, and Sarah emerged from concealment on the ogre's right flank, and Sarah read the three remaining spells on her scroll of fireballs. She had intended to read them one at a time, aiming each magical incendiary at a specific target. But her skills were insufficient to firmly control spells of this magnitude, and all three went off at once.

She got lucky with the first—it struck an ogre directly in the face and burned its head to a cinder. He dropped and moved no more. The second spiraled violently, then shot straight up into the air. The third exploded in the air midway to its target, throwing back a wall of heat that burned Sarah's face and singed her hair.

Just as the ogres were closing in on Roscoe's battle-line, two more of the creatures emerged from the cave and made for the young witch and her companions, standing isolated on the flank. The archers saw them coming and directed their fire at this new threat, but once again, their shafts failed to bring them down. Though not badly burned, Sarah was too disoriented by the blast to throw another spell. She scrambled behind Thurmond and Torgul, who now stood shoulder to shoulder to receive the onrushing foe.

The first was a rangy, long-legged brute clad only in a ragged tunic that failed to cover below its hips. The open jaws revealed a mouthful of ragged, yellow teeth. Thurmond delivered a hard, clean shot to its temple that would have cut halfway through a human skull, but the blow only seemed to anger the ogre. With one mighty heave, he sent Thurmond crashing to the ground, then stooped and lashed out with long, hooked claws.

Flat on his back, Thurmond could only scoot frantically away as the deadly talons scythed a hand's breadth from his face. Luckily, the ogre was slow, its attacks awkward, affording the young Adventurer to draw his knees beneath him and rise to a partial sitting position. From there, he could fight back.

He struck again and again at the monster's arms, hands, and fingers, but the foul creature seemed not to notice the long gashes made by the sword's sharp edge. Finally, recalling his fight with Grinder, Thurmond plunged the weapon's tip into the ogre's eye, but the thing still did not die. He did, however, leave off his attack and began a howling, clomping dance of agony with his hands clamped over the ruined socket.

The young Adventurer regained his feet and moved to his opponent's blind side, all the while snapping blows at his face, trying to take out the other eye. The ogre, snarling and grunting, lurched about in a circle as it attempted to come to grips with his unseen enemy.

Meanwhile, Torgul's ogre, possessing obscenely fat legs and freakishly large feet, was attempting to stomp its much smaller foe into the ground. The agile dwarf evaded this clumsy attack and while doing so began slicing meat from the thing's bones, his magical axe, Bloodtroll, proving quite useful in this regard.

Then, dodging left, he raked the edge laterally across the ogre's stomach, spilling its guts to the ground. It yowled and lunged at the dwarf while the loathsome feet stomped the blue mass of its own entrails into the mud. Another blow of the axe removed its head, yet even then, the creature took three more faltering steps before tumbling lifeless to the ground.

Sarah sought to help Thurmond, who was still engaged in a grotesque jig with his slavering foe. She tried a sleep spell, hoping to at least slow the creature, but saw no discernable effect. Then an illusion spell—the image of an enraged troll—but the ogre failed to respond. Perhaps it was too stupid for illusions.

It was Torgul who brought the combat to a happy conclusion. Approaching from the rear, he sheared off the back of the creature's skull with a single blow from Bloodtroll. The ogre fell facedown but continued to lash out with its arms until Thurmond moved in and scattered its brains like so much pink gruel.

Bart's mercenaries fared less well. Though pierced by arrows, slashed with swords, and stabbed with spears, the three surviving ogres tore through their battleline like a charge of heavy cavalry. Gobbets of flesh were ripped from bones. Blood sprayed as hairy feet stomped human faces. Their thirst for gore as yet unslaked, the ogres rose from the carnage, regrouped, and charged Bart's reserve group.

The first ogre was massively fat, yet surprisingly agile in spite of his bulk. Head down, flabby arms spread wide, it smashed into the sword-spear trio. They fell as one, and the monster trampled their recumbent forms.

Then one of the swordsmen—bloodied but not dead—lashed out from the ground as the ogre was crushing the skull of the spearman. His blade severed the creature's heel tendon and sent it crashing to the ground. Dazed and bleeding though they were, the surviving mercenaries rose and plied their weapons until the fallen monster moved no more.

The ugliest of the three, a hideous brute covered with white-headed boils, slammed into Bart and sent him flying backwards. The knight did, however, manage to plunge his glaive into the center of his assailant's chest before the shaft was torn from his hands.

Seemingly unaware of its injury, the ogre continued to charge forward, burying the glaive's butt in the soft dirt. The long blade pushed through its body until the curved projections on its socket brought him up short. Only then did the creature notice that it had been impaled. It stopped, gave a howl and sought to pull the weapon from its torso.

The monster was so occupied with this task that it failed to notice as Cob glided in from the side and sank his battleaxe into its forehead. The ogre turned savagely, wrenching the weapon from the archer's hand. But Cob was too agile, too battle-wise to be caught so easily. He dodged back, easily avoiding the claws that sought to snare him.

Then Tuck and Wat, creeping up from the rear, struck the creature's neck, left and right. They chopped again and again until the spine was severed and the monster fell to his knees, his head dangling from a tangle of muscles, veins, and tendons. Cob seized the head by its long, matted hair while Wat sawed it from the shoulders with the edge of his blade.

The third ogre bore down on Roscoe with the force of a falling boulder. It was the largest of the three, clad only in a filthy goatskin tied around his neck. The old Adventurer tried to sidestep his charge, but the creature's shoulder caught the corner of his shield and bowled him off his feet. But just as it was reaching for Roscoe's face, Sarah's errant fireball, the one that had flown straight into the sky, reached the apex of its upward journey and plummeted back to earth to land at the ogre's feet.

The old Adventurer was trying to rise when the fireball struck, knocking him flat. His beard was badly singed, and his eyebrows were burned off. The ogre staggered but kept its feet. However, its greasy goatskin was set alight, engulfing the monster in magical flame. It began to squeal, his voice as high-pitched as a goblin, as hair and beard frizzled in the heat of the fire. Its flesh blackened, cracked, and split. The eyes and nose burned away. Blood ran and fried, fat oozed and flared. Arms, chest, and belly were consumed by the inexorable blaze.

The ogre shrieked and began to run in blind circles, beating frantically at the flames. Finally it fell, and the shrieking ceased. Roscoe and the others watched as the hideous creature was reduced to a pile of charred bones.

Torgul scratched his head.

"Somethin' ain't right here. These ain't proper ogres at all. Least ways, they ain't like any I seen before. This one's got the tusks of a boar-hog."

Thurmond prodded a monstrous carcass with the toe of his boot.

"You've fought ogres before, Torgul?"

"Time or two—but they wasn't like these fellas. Much more like regular men, they was—wore clothes and could talk. These things just ain't natural. None of their body parts match up right. Either their arms is too long, or their heads is too small, or their legs is too big."

Thurmond nodded.

"They don't seem to feel much pain either, and they don't die until you chop 'em apart."

The dwarf growled in agreement as they strolled to another sprawled body.

"Unnaturally ugly they are, too. Regular ogres ain't what I'd call handsome, but these things are right brutal to the eye."

Roscoe and Sarah were tending the surviving mercenaries. Four had been killed outright. Three had received serious injuries. All were scratched, bruised, and sore. Bart sat a bit apart, still dazed by his hard fall.

Sarah's brow was creased with worry.

"I don't know what to do for these injured men, Roscoe. This one's unconscious from a blow on the head. That one's got a broken leg, and the end of the bone is poking out through the meat. He's in terrible pain. And that last one got stomped on the stomach—he's got blood coming up in his mouth. You know a lot of chirurgery—what do we do?"

"Ain't much we can do for these poor fellas, lassie. We can splint the leg, but that's about all. I don't think there's much chance for any of 'em. They can't ride with us, and we sure can't take 'em back for that damned wizard to put in his jars. Maybe we can get 'em to one of them fisher villages and at least make 'em more comfortable."

Sarah looked grim.

"If it's really that hopeless, then maybe I've got a solution. I've got six healing potions in my pannier—at least that's what Malachai said they are—but one of them is actually a deadly poison. Malachai revealed a skull and crossbones on the bottle, but it disappeared, and I can't find it again."

The old Adventurer squinted his eyes in consternation.

"But you recall which bottle it was—don't you?"

"Nay—I can't—it's like the memory has been blotted from my mind. The poisoned bottle is like a magical trap. Malachai could see it, but I can't."

"What do you have in mind, lassie?"

"Give them potions. The odds are only one in six that they'll get the poison. If they're going to die anyway, they've got nothing to lose."

"That's what we'll do. The potion will cause 'em to sleep, so we'll leave 'em here with Drax while we search for whatever treasure these monsters may have hidden away."

CHAPTER 26
IN THE OGRES' LAIR

Sir Bartholomew Staynes was livid with rage. His head throbbed unmercifully, and his cheek bore a nasty gash from the ogre's claw. He would be fortunate if the wound did not fester and kill him. Half his men were dead or badly injured.

Worst of all, that old man—that jumped-up peasant—had outsmarted him again. Had prodded him with dark warnings about incurring the *displeasure* of Asmodeus and Malachai. Had lured him on with beguiling promises of great treasure.

But the ogres' cave contained no gems or gold or precious items, only the remains of their disgusting breakfast. Gnawed fragments of human arms, legs, and ribs. A skull from which the brains had been scooped. It was not even a real cave—no more than a deep dent in the hillside with just enough overhanging ledge to keep out the rain.

Roscoe stepped beside him. Half of his beard had been burned off by the fireball. Bart wished it had taken his entire face. The old Adventurer's soothing tone infuriated him all the more.

"I know what you're thinkin', sir knight. You're wonderin' where all the treasure might be—the gold and gems I said them ogres was sure to have. Am I correct? That's what you're thinkin'?"

Bart gave him a sour look and said nothing. He could not trust himself to speak at the moment. He was too likely to blurt out something that would reveal his true thoughts. There would be time for all that at some later day.

Getting no response, Roscoe continued.

"Well, don't despair quite yet, sir knight. This ain't their proper lair, ain't nothin' more than where they stopped to have a bite of breakfast, which looks to be some poor fisherman unlucky enough to get hisself caught."

Roscoe pointed toward the nearby hills.

"Their real lair is somewhere in them inland hills—not too far away, I should think. All we gotta do it follow their tracks and find it. Then we take whatever's worth the takin', so we do."

He nodded toward a line of footprints pressed deeply into the mud.

"Them was weighty buggers, so their tracks will be easy to follow. Want to go find some gold, sir knight?"

Bart had a variety of bad traits. He could be vindictive, selfish, overbearing, obnoxious. But he was not entirely stupid. He learned from his mistakes, and experience had taught him to be cautious when dealing with the wily Adventurer. Especially when he was attempting to be charming and convincing.

He had also learned to be wary of invading a monster's lair. He had narrowly escaped death after brashly charging into a goblin cave. A deadfall of boulders had slain many of his men, and a subsequent assault by the outraged goblins had accounted for most of the others. He was not about to repeat that mistake.

"Listen to me, Roscoe—half of my men are down. I'm not leading the rest into some ogre cave. We came on this quest to guard you, not fight monsters! If you Adventurers want to get yourselves killed by ogres, well, go do it. My men and I will wait for you here."

Roscoe nodded and smiled.

"Now that's mighty fine, so it is, so it is. Mighty generous of you to decline the spoils that we'll be gatherin' in. That's a right noble gesture, and I thank you for it. But I have to wonder just how you'll be explainin' to your men why they ain't gettin' their share. How exactly do you plan to do that, sir knight?"

Bart's dislike for Roscoe turned to loathing. The old man had outmaneuvered once again. He could not order his men to stand aside while the Adventurers claimed all the treasure. Not after they fought and died for it.

"All right, we'll go. But your people will go first if there's a cave. You're supposed to be experts at fighting underground."

Roscoe nodded.

"Agreed."

"And one more thing—I will require three-quarters of anything we find. My company took most of the hurt in our battle with the ogres."

The old Adventurer could only smile at this.

"Sure, it's true, your men took most of the pain. But my people did most of the killin'. Here's what we'll do—we can split the treasure right down the middle, or you and yours can go find it yourselves and keep it all. Or you, sir knight, can stay here, and I'll lead your men without you. What's your choice?"

Bart's face burned with frustrated anger. He could never out-think this despicable old man. Roscoe gave him a mischievous grin.

"Don't let this situation fret you. I'm pretty sure the ogres, or whatever they was, are all dead, so I don't expect trouble when we explore their den. Won't take long at all. We go in, grab whatever we find, and shank it back to Malachai with the good news that the ogres won't be botherin' his fishermen no more. Then we go home."

"We'll leave your wounded here with Drax to tend 'em. Sarah dosed 'em with her healing potions, so they're all three asleep. None of 'em has died, so it looks like she didn't give 'em the poison. You still got five hale soldiers. Let's go find some treasure."

Torgul led the way, followed by the other Adventurers and the Gascar archers. Bart and his men brought up the rear.

The ogres' footprints were big, deep, and easy to follow. They proceeded in both directions, indicating the creatures had made frequent passage between the breakfast cave and their regular lair. The way was further marked by large piles of their noxious dung.

The trail first led inland and then west, cutting across the small cape on which the fishing villages were perched. Their morning ride had taken them the long way along the meandering coastline. Thurmond turned to Roscoe.

"If we keep heading in this direction, we're gonna see Malachai's tower sooner or later. It's gotta be somewhere beyond those hills in front of us."

"Funny you should say so, laddie. I was just now thinkin' the same thought, so I was. Aye, seems like this is a shortcut back to where we come from."

But before the magician's tower hove into view, the trail came to an abrupt end at the mouth of the cave, which was cut into a sandstone hillside. A wide scattering of bones from both beast and man told plainly that this was indeed the ogres' primary abode.

As they prepared to enter, Roscoe gave the party their final instructions.

"Sarah's gonna cast a light spell over us, so seein' won't be a problem. Stay close together or you'll be out of its range and find yourselves lost in the dark. Ogres ain't smart enough to set traps and ambushes like goblins do, but who knows what other creatures might be waitin' inside. So keep quiet and keep your eyes skinned for trouble. Signal me if you sees anythin' suspicious-like."

The cavern was far larger than expected. The floor was littered with more bones and more piles of dung. There was certainly nothing like treasure.

Thurmond had never seen a cavern so immense. It stretched before him like the mouth of some colossal subterranean monster ready to swallow them up. The stalactites covering the ceiling were its fangs. The slippery, uneven floor, its tongue. The lingering ogre stench, its breath.

But he had chosen the path of the Adventurer. The wyvern tattoo on his arm testified to his willingness to face the terrors of the underground, so he kept close to Torgul's back, sword and shield at the ready. He could not hear Sarah's light footfall behind him, but he knew she was there, set to unleash a blast of magic at any attacker. And Roscoe would be there too, watching out for them all.

The four of them had faced down many dangerous foes. Monsters far more powerful than themselves, men better armed and more numerous than themselves, witches and warriors more adept in the skills of battle. Yet they had always prevailed despite the long odds against them.

Their successes, Thurmond knew, were due to the unique spirit of teamwork that made them greater than their individual attainments. That was what being an Adventurer was.

Torgul's harsh whisper put a sudden end to his reverie.

"Stay put. I see somethin' up ahead."

The dwarf's keen eyes could see almost as well in the dark as they could in the daylight. He moved forward, beyond the glowing aura of the light spell, and was soon lost to view. Thurmond stepped back to stand beside Sarah and Roscoe, as did the three archers. Bart drew his men up as a separate group in the rear. Mercenary and Adventurer strained eyes and ears for any possible threat.

Then Torgul was back.

"This is a big mother of a cavern, but it tapers down on the other side and narrows into a tunnel. Looks natural, like it was made by water or ice or somethin'. Ain't been carved out by hands, I'm pretty certain."

Roscoe signaled to Bart to join the group of Adventurers. Then he spoke to Torgul.

"Is that tunnel big enough for the ogres to use?"

"Certes—without havin' to duck their heads or scrape their shoulders."

"Then here's what I'm thinkin'—that this still ain't their proper den. Maybe more like their banquet hall from the looks of all them bones. But this ain't where they been sleepin', and this ain't where they kept their treasure. That's somewheres down that tunnel."

Bart now cut into the discussion.

"Send the dwarf to have a look!"

His tone was deliberately abrasive, challenging. Roscoe was just turning to confront the arrogant knight when Torgul touched his arm.

"He's right. I can slip down real quiet and take a look-see. Makes more sense than all of us chargin' down there."

Thurmond knew it was time to show himself worthy of his tattoo. He did not want to accompany Torgul, but he knew it was the right thing to do.

"I'm coming with you."

Torgul shook his head.

"Thanks, boy—that's a nice thought. It'd be a comfort to have you. But it's real dark down there, and you can't see like I can."

Sarah spoke up.

"I could use my light spell to put a little glow on his sword. Just enough so he can see."

"Aye, that might work. But keep the sword sheathed unless we run into trouble. I wanna sneak up on anything that's in there. So just hang onto the back of my belt 'til I say different."

The casting of the spell took only a moment. Moving as quietly as possible, the two Adventurers crossed the cavern and entered the passageway. Once inside, Thurmond could see nothing and held tightly to his companion's heavy sword belt.

The tunnel proved to be quite long. Thurmond tried to judge the distance by counting his steps, but he lost track somewhere around two hundred. He moved as quietly as he could, but that was difficult while groping blindly in the dark. His boots kept scraping on the uneven floor. After a long time, Torgul spoke in his ear.

"We're outta the tunnel now. Take out your sword and have a look. But be mighty careful when you look down."

Thurmond drew the weapon, and a mild glow extended a spear's length before them. They had entered another huge cavern, the walls and ceiling of which were lost in gloom. Then the young man looked down, and what he saw made him shrink back in alarm.

They were standing on the very edge of a yawning chasm. One step forward would have plunged them into its unknown depths. The dwarf grabbed Thurmond by the arm.

"I told you to be careful lookin' down! Get hold of yourself, boy. I don't want you gettin' nervous and flingin' yourself over the edge."

Embarrassed, the young Adventurer made a supreme effort to regain his composure.

"How deep do you think it is?"

"Don't know—deep enough I can't see bottom. Let's find out."

Torgul tossed a fist-sized rock into the darkness and began counting on his fingers. He reached five before they heard the sound of impact. Thurmond took a careful look over the edge.

"Pretty damned deep, I'd say. And the wall is straight down. I don't think even Pozi could climb down there. Looks like we're going no further."

Torgul chuckled softly. This was disturbing, for he was stern by nature and rarely smiled or laughed. His laughter could, most typically, be prompted only by the direst of circumstances. Standing on the edge of an inky precipice, the chuckle did not bode well.

"What's funny?"

"It's like this—the light from your sword don't carry very far, but I can see pretty good out across this cavern. This hole we're standin' on is fair deep, but it ain't wide. Just a big trench cut in the cave floor. Can't be more'n twenty foot over to the other side."

"Twenty feet? It might as well be twenty leagues unless you plan to sprout wings and fly across."

"That's what I'm laughin' about, boy. It ain't me gonna fly across there. It's you."

CHAPTER 27

A LEAP IN THE DARK

The entire company of mercenaries and Adventurers milled about the second cavern. Some dropped stones into the chasm and counted the seconds until impact. Others waited silently for instructions from their leaders. In the glow of Sarah's light spell, they could make out a large square structure on the far side of the gulf.

Bart remained aloof and sullen—he hated the underground. Sarah sorted through the magical paraphernalia in her pannier. Thurmond, Torgul, and Roscoe stood in a group on the edge of the precipice.

The dwarf snorted.

"Then I says to him, I says, it ain't gonna be me jumpin' across that hole, boy. It's gonna be you."

Torgul guffawed as he told the story, causing Roscoe to smile broadly. He was by nature as gleeful as the dwarf was dour. Assuming this was all a jest, Thurmond grinned along with them.

"All right, all right—I'll fly over there just as soon as you can tell me how I can sprout a pair of wings."

At these words, Roscoe grew more serious.

"I don't think you really fathom what we're gettin' at, boyo. You gotta jump over there for real, so you do."

The young man was nonplussed.

"Just how do you expect me to do that? Torgul calls it a score of feet to the other side."

"Remember when Malachai named all the charms in Sarah's basket? One of the potions will let a man jump that far. That's what he said, ain't it Torgul?"

The dwarf nodded.

"Aye, leap over a twenty-foot gulf. That's what he said."

Thurmond came to the terrifying realization that their jesting was not jesting at all. They really expected him to do this suicidal deed.

"If I did such a thing, I'd likely be killed. Why do you find that so funny?"

Roscoe saw the dismay in his face and placed a hand on his shoulder.

"Forgive us, lad, we meant no harm. Sometimes things is so serious that there ain't nothin' else for it but to laugh."

Torgul's voice was rough, but his words were contrite and sincere.

"God's balls, Thurmond—sorry. It was just a stupid joke. Didn't mean no harm. I'd jump over there myself, 'cept, you know, my legs are too short."

Roscoe spoke again.

"And I'm too old and fat. Sarah could maybe make the jump, but we don't know who's over there. It's gotta be somebody that can swing a sword."

Thurmond jerked his thumb toward the mercenaries.

"How about sending one of them? Why does it have to be me?"

Roscoe shook his head.

"Which one of them numbnuts do you trust not to muck it up? Crazy Cob maybe? Vainglorious Bart?"

Thurmond knew Roscoe was right. The strengths and weakness of Bart's mercenaries were still largely unknown to them. Bart himself was little more than a bumbling fool. The Gascar archers had proven themselves to be capable soldiers, but their skill with edged weapons was far less than their expertise with the bow.

"If I do this—and I'm not saying I'm going to—but if I did do it, what in hell am I supposed to do after I get over there?"

Torgul pointed off into the dark.

"See that dark shape that looks kinda like a big wooden tower?"

Thurmond was incredulous.

"A tower? You want me to attack a tower?"

"Let me finish, boy. That ain't no tower. You're lookin' at the timbers that support a drawbridge. All you gotta do is drop it across the gap. Then the rest of us will come over and help you."

Their conversation was interrupted by Sarah, who drew an item from her pannier and held it up with a flourish.

"Found it! It had sunk all the way to the bottom, but I got it. I knew as soon as I saw that chasm that we'd be needing it."

She held the small blue vial that Malachai had identified as the leaping potion.

"Drink this, Thurmond, and you should be able to make it to the other side."

"Should be able? What if I don't make it?"

She could only shrug.

Thurmond had additional concerns.

"You don't even really know what you have there. I know what Malachai said it is—but why should we believe him?

Sarah unbuckled the chinstrap of her light, open-faced helmet.

"You're right. He's a creature of evil. We have no reason to trust him."

Thurmond continued.

"How can we be sure the potion would really carry me twenty feet? What if Torgul's wrong about how far it is to the other side?"

The young witch removed her helmet and unbuckled the heavy belt cinched about her waist.

"Right again—the plan is extremely dangerous."

"What if there's more ogres over there, hiding in the dark. I'd be by myself. What could I do except die?"

Sarah bent forward and wiggled out of her mailshirt. This finally caught the young man's attention.

"What are you doing? Why are you taking off your armor?"

"Because I'm going to make the jump. It might be a stupid plan, but it's the only way to see what's on the other side. If there's any treasure over there, I want my share. I've come too far to back out now."

Thurmond threw up his hands in resignation. He would make the jump. He knew Sarah was not bluffing, that she would make the jump if he refused.

Roscoe put in a reassuring word.

"Don't be frettin', boyo. I'm fair certain there ain't nobody over there. We're standin' here in a big bubble of light, more than a dozen of us, talkin', laughin', throwin' rocks, yet there's been nary a peep from the other side. No horns or drums soundin' the alarm. No arrows flyin' across the gap. Nothin'. That's 'cause there ain't nobody there."

Thurmond was unconvinced.

"Maybe they're just keeping quiet."

"Could be, but I don't think so. Ogres ain't smart enough to lay low. And Torgul would have spotted any of them buggers that was movin' around over there. He sees real good in the dark, so he does."

Sarah dug into her pannier and retrieved a strand of large, pointed teeth suspended on a leather thong, presumably the fangs of some ravening monster.

"Malachai called this a necklace of reckless courage. I was going to wear it if I jumped. Do you want it?"

That settled it! There was no way to back out now. He had known from the beginning that this jump was inevitable, but had not wanted to admit it to himself.

He shook his head.

"Nay! I am not wanting for courage—save it for yourself. Help me off with my armor, I'll carry nothing more than my sword."

And so it was that Thurmond made the leap across the Cimmerian abyss. A running start and away he flew, bounding like a roebuck in pursuit of a doe. Clad only in breeks and his quilted arming doublet—sans shield, sans helmet, sans mailshirt. Sword strapped tightly to his back.

He was halfway across when, most inconveniently, Sarah's light spell flickered once and went out. She frantically attempted to re-cast it, but in her haste fumbled and produced but a single bright, blinding flash. Thus it was that Thurmond hit the ground in complete darkness.

The potion enabled Thurmond to cross the gap but did nothing to cushion his landing. He hit hard, pitching forward, his shoulder slamming into the cavern's hard, rocky floor. His hands and arms were badly skinned as he rolled over and over.

The young Adventurer was bruised and abraded but thankfully unbroken. He lay unmoving, flat on his belly, ears straining in the dark for any indication that he was not alone.

When nothing came, he rose carefully to one knee and struggled to unstrap his sword. The light spell on its blade would allow him to see. He pulled the weapon from its scabbard, discovering, to his immense relief, that the spell was still active. Its dim glow seemed as bright as the sun in that lightless grotto.

Roscoe had been correct—no ogres stormed out of the dark to attack him. On the far side of the gap, Sarah finally managed to rekindle her light spell. Thurmond felt a surge of confidence. His former fears now seemed childish. What had been so frightening, after all, about a leap in the dark?

The drawbridge was small and flimsy, quite unlike those spanning the moats of castles and walled cities. Too narrow for a wagon or even a cart. Too lightly constructed for a horse and rider. It was held upright by an iron chain affixed to a wooden windlass. One pull of a lever would release the windless, dropping the bridge into place. Easy!

Thurmond was just reaching for the lever, when he discovered to his dismay that his optimism had been premature. Not all monstrosities take the form of misshapen ogres—the thing that that crawled from beneath the windlass was far more hideous.

Its round, humped body was the size a large washtub. The head was small, the long snout sported a multitude of jagged teeth. Both head and body were covered in a series of articulated plates resembling those of a common woodlouse. A long, heavy tail whipped to and fro like that of a hunting cat.

It scuttled forward on short, powerful legs, allowing the startled Adventurer no opportunity to retreat. Rearing up, it struck with its taloned forepaws, left and right. Thurmond dodged the first blow and blocked the next with his sword. He immediately slashed at the thing's head, but the boney plates kept the edge from cutting deep.

The thing snarled and reared as if to attack once again with its paws, but then it lashed out with its tail, striking Thurmond's shoulder like a blow from a barbed whip, the sharp scales tearing though his doublet and abrading the skin beneath.

The young Adventurer delivered blow after blow, but the creature's tough armor kept it from suffering injury. The thing was relentless in its attack, continually pushing forward, rearing up, slashing with its talons.

It struck once more with the tail, this time at Thurmond's face. Luckily, he saw it coming, sidestepped, and severed its tip with a sweep of his sword. The maimed appendage began to thrash wildly, casting gouts of blood in every direction.

The enraged creature yowled, raised itself fully upright, and waddled forward on its hind legs, obviously intending to catch its prey in a bear-hug and rend him with claws and teeth. This was a mistake, for it exposed its vulnerable underside.

Thurmond's broadsword was not balanced as a thrusting weapon, and was not particularly effective as such. It was specifically designed to deliver cutting blows powerful enough to cleave through mail. But it did possess a tip sufficiently pointy to pierce a soft abdomen, and this is exactly what occurred as the creature came into range. Thurmond rammed it squarely into its belly, then ripped upward.

The thing screamed and toppled onto its armored back, the legs flailing wildly as it sought to right itself. Thurmond never gave it a chance. He stabbed again and again into the pulpy remains of the stomach until the screams stopped and the legs ceased to flail.

He pulled the lever releasing the bridge, and in a few moments his companions stood at his side. Roscoe inspected his wounded shoulder, which felt like it had been set aflame.

"You've taken a hard shot, boyo. You lost a bit of hide, so you have, and you'll be getting' a dandy bruise. But ain't much. Nothin' a wee drop of honest uisge won't set to right. Here—we brought your armor."

Thurmond's breath came in hard gasps. He was still winded from the extreme exertion of the fight.

"What was that thing, Roscoe? I've never seen anything like it before."

The old Adventurer bent over the mangled remains.

"Whatever it was, it weren't no natural creature, kinda like them ogres.

There's somethin' about it that just ain't right. It's like somebody sewed up the worst parts from a whole parcel of unlikely beasts. Powerful ugly it was."

Thurmond began pulling on his armor.

"It was mean, too. It came at me right off and didn't stop until I killed it."

"Probably hungry, laddie. I don't see no signs of it bein' well fed—no gnawed bones, no piles of shite, nothin'. You probably looked like a proper snack."

Bart approached and poked at the dead monster with the toe of his boot. Something inside it burst, releasing a most vile stench. He turned to Roscoe.

"This is as far as we go, old man. And don't be thinking to turn my men against me. We're all agreed—not one step further."

Roscoe smiled and boomed out loud enough to be heard by all.

"It's amazin', so it is, how two intelligent gentlemen so often arrive at the same thought at the same moment. I was just now tellin' Thurmond here that we dare not proceed without leavin' somebody here to guard this bridge, and now here you are volunteerin' for that very duty. I salute you, sir knight. Rest assured that you and your men will receive half of any treasure we may find."

Bart was, as always, angered by Roscoe's words. The old Adventurer had a way of making him feel cheated even when he gave in to Bart's demands. Before he could respond, Roscoe grinned and walked on, leaving him standing by the bridge.

Searching along the cavern's wall, Torgul discovered another tunnel, and again the Adventurers set off into the darkness. This time, however, the Gascar archers followed close behind the dwarf. Thurmond and Roscoe brought up the rear.

The tunnel was another long one, running—like its counterpart on the far side of the chasm—straight through the heart of the hill with neither side passages nor diversions. The air grew chill and damp. The floor and walls began to tremble at regular intervals as if seized by an ague.

The passage ended abruptly at an iron door set into the rock. Roscoe rapped his knuckles on its rusty surface, producing a dull *thunk*. The door was solid and heavy. It boasted neither keyhole nor latch.

Sarah turned to the old Adventurer.

"You know, of course, where we are?"

"Aye, that I do. We're inside that needle of rock leadin' out to Malachai's mansion. The waves are beatin' it from both sides, givin' it the shakes, so they are."

"And you know where this door leads?"

"I'd have to say to the magician's cellars."

"What do you think is really going on here?"

"Well now, that's somethin' of a mystery. Here we are, deep underground, and what do we find but a drawbridge and an iron door. Somebody, it seems, is determined to keep somebody else out, and it's my guess that the party bein' excluded is them ogres we slew."

"And what of that thing Thurmond slew?"

"Hard to say. Maybe a watchdog. Maybe somethin' else."

"Where do you suppose the ogres and the watchdog first came from?"

"That's a mite easier to answer, Sarah darlin'. Such twisted horrors can only be the progeny of Malachai, our gracious host. First, he created 'em, then for reasons of his own drove 'em forth to blight the world."

Sarah gave the door a hard look.

"I may be able to open this with my knock spell, but I imagine it's heavily barred on the inside. Opening it will take all my psychic energy, might even put me in a swoon. I'll be useless until I can rest and renew my strength."

"That won't be necessary, we'll not be passin' through that portal."

Hearing this, Thurmond ceased buckling his chinstrap and confronted his old mentor.

"We're not going on? You've always told me that a true Adventurer never stops 'til he finds treasure. We can't stop now!"

Roscoe shook his head.

"Nay, lad, this situation is too delicate. We've still got to take Malachai back to Gorgonholm, so we can't afford to anger him. Anyway, he scares the shite out of me."

"What do we do, then?"

"We report back to him, maybe bring him the ogres' heads to prove we took care of things. He oughta like that—he can put 'em in jars. Then he and us all ride to Gorgonholm to knock down a black rock."

"We aren't going to loot his cellar?"

"Doesn't seem like a good idea."

"Why did we come down here then?"

"I had to be sure. Sarah and me both figured them ogres were Malachai's creations, and it wasn't hard to figure that the tunnel we found would lead us back to his mansion. We've gotta long ride with him, and there's a lot at stake—our own lives, the life of our city. I needed to know what kind of a man I was dealin' with."

"Did you find out?"

"Indeed, I did, boyo. Indeed I did."

CHAPTER 28
CHANGE OF PLAN

The Adventurers returned to the drawbridge. Two of Bart's men had lit a torch and crossed back over the chasm. Exploring the far corners of the chamber, they discovered a foul nest of branches and rags that the ogres had used as a bed. The pair adamantly denied finding anything worth taking, which was probably the truth. With their task completed, the party headed back the way they had come, eager for daylight and fresh air.

They retraced their steps back to the ogre cave where Drax was tending the wounded. Roscoe was happy to find them still alive and continuing to sleep under the influence of the healing potion. He was also pleased that Drax had constructed three crude sledges by lashing together scraps of brushwood. The wounded, unable to sit a horse, could be dragged back to the fisher villages on these contrivances.

The old Adventurer was not dissatisfied with the day's work. They had, it was true, lost four men, but they were mercenaries, and violent death was the very nature of their trade. His own people—Torgul, Thurmond, Sarah, and the archers—were safe and sound. Moreover, they had accomplished their mission. Malachai's rampaging giants were lying dead on the ground all around him.

Roscoe was feeling his age, his bones ached and his muscles were sore. He sat down in the late afternoon sun with his back propped against a boulder. One by one, the other Adventurers joined him there. Thurmond was deeply frustrated by their failure to win any treasure. Finally, he could keep silent no longer.

"Roscoe, back in that tunnel, you said you're afraid of Malachai. I am too—he's scary. But we've never just run away like this before. Not from goblins or trolls or nothing. We've always been willing to take risks to win treasure. It doesn't seem right just to walk away without even trying."

The old Adventurer shook his head.

"I was tellin' you true, boyo. Malachai is a bad one, so he is. Not just a foul necromancer—and that's bad enough—but somethin' else. Somethin' there ain't even a name for. That creature you fought by the bridge—no natural man could ever dream up somethin' that horrible.

"I ain't never been much for religion, but I do believe there's things that's right and there's things that's wrong. That thing was plain wrong. It was the blackest sin to create such a creature."

Thurmond shrugged, not caring to engage in a philosophical debate.

"Well, I slew it, so it can't bother anyone ever again. Whatever else is down there, we can kill it too."

"I ain't so much worried about our own skins, laddie. I'm thinkin' of our beloved city. I can't see no good comin' from breakin' into Malachai's cellar. Maybe we find treasure and maybe we don't, but he's sure to find out, and we can't afford to lose his assistance."

"How do you know he'll find out? He can't know everything."

"Can't take the chance, boyo. Gorgonholm was destroying itself when we left. Malachai is the only solution."

The sun was just going down as they rode back through the gate in Malachai's curtain wall. He met them at the mansion's entrance.

"Have you completed the errand I assigned you?"

Roscoe produced a weary smile.

"That we did, good sir. We killed a full half-dozen rampagin' giants, just as you asked us to, and we brought you their heads as token of our achievement—left 'em in a pile outside your gate. Fearsome brutes they was. Seven of our men were slain in the doin' of it."

This was untrue—only four had died. The three badly wounded men, still under the soporific effect of the healing potions, were sleeping at a fisher village. If fit to ride on the morrow, they would rejoin the party. Those unable to sit a horse would have to be left behind.

As expected, Malachai was unmoved by loss of the mercenaries.

"Fine, fine—the giants are dead, and you have lost some men. Spare me the details. Now listen carefully, I spent the afternoon gazing into my scrying pool. Events in Gorgonholm are growing darker. You will need to depart at once."

Roscoe cleared his throat.

"We can leave at first light, Master Malachai. Will you be riding your own horse, or will you be needin' one of ours?"

"What inanity is this? My place is here."

Roscoe heard these words with both relief and confusion.

"Master Malachai—I had assumed that you would be coming with us and would throw down that bloody stone yourself. Was I in error?"

"What? Don't be absurd! I made no such statement. I have created a most potent instrument to divert the stone's power back to the stars from whence it came. Your young witch will have to carry out the actual operation. I will instruct her."

A servant stepped from the house with a wooden chest the length of a man's forearm. It was bound with bronze and secured with a heavy lock. He handed it to Roscoe, who was surprised by its weight. The servant then produced a key, which he also handed over.

Malachai abruptly reached out and touched Sarah lightly on the forehead. She was jolted as if slapped or perhaps stung by a wasp. Gradually she began to regain her composure.

"I...understand. I will do as you have bidden."

The magician returned his attention to Roscoe.

"It would be ill-advised to open the chest or disturb its contents in any manner. You would find the result unpleasant. I have just given the girl complete instructions, so guard her as closely as you do the chest. Our business is complete. Now be off."

With nothing else to do, the company turned their horses and rode back to the fisher village.

The fisher folk loved the men who had delivered them from the ogres. Long had those creatures feasted on their friends and relatives. Now their appreciation was expressed in every conceivable fashion.

A lavish banquet comprised of their most appetizing delicacies was set before them. The menu included dried fish, dried turnips, dried parsnips, dried radishes, and coarse bread made from dried lentils. The beer, brewed from dried lentils and flavored with dried fish-eyes, made up in potency what it lacked in flavor.

The village women—blushing young maidens, zestful wives, and well-experienced granddams—were eager to reward the martial prowess of their guests. Bart's men, sufficiently befuddled by many cups of lentil beer, rose to the occasion in spite of the rotten teeth, facial hair, and physical abnormalities borne by many of their hostesses.

Cob, of course, firmly disapproved of such lascivious goings on, and strictly forbade Tuck and Wat to indulge in the proffered delights. The Adventurers, too, resisted the charms of the local ladies. When a buxom village lass with a remarkable hare lip plopped herself on Thurmond's lap, he shot Sarah a quick look. She returned an intense stare that led him to gently set the girl aside.

Bart sat and scowled at the whole proceeding. At about midnight, he rose, kicked a drunken soldier soundly in the ribs, and announced that the evening's festivities were at an end. The company must, he declared, leave at dawn, so they could not spend the night in wanton debauchery. For once, Roscoe agreed with Bart's course of action.

Thurmond and Sarah endured a miserable night huddled on the cold dirt floor of a tiny, bug-infested hut that, according to Drax, was considered luxurious by local standards. They shared the space with the fisher family whose house it was—a father, mother, and an uncountable number of filthy children. They had all swilled great quantities of lentil beer and spent the night flopping, bickering, pissing, and farting.

Unable to sleep, Sarah rolled onto her side and found herself staring into Thurmond's open eyes. He was intensely awake.

"Damn it, Sarah, I was ready to give up on our last adventure, but you and Roscoe wouldn't let me. You and me alone—we faced the Old One in Castle Sathas. Malachai can't be any worse than her. But this time you're ready to walk away empty-handed because you're scared of some scrawny runt of a magician."

"That was different. We can't afford to anger Malachai. We need his help to defeat the Black Stone."

"Do we really? We've got his magic doodah, and you know how to use it. What do we need him for? Anyway, I bet we can still slip into his cellar, find something worth taking, and sneak out again without him ever knowing we've been inside. I want to try, and I wish you'd go with me. If you don't, I'll go alone."

Sarah bit her lip in frustration, not so much because she feared Thurmond's proposal but because it was the same argument she routinely used on him. She could not refuse him any more than he could refuse her.

"All right, Thurmond, but let's try to persuade Roscoe to come with us. I'd feel a lot better with the whole company along."

In the morning, Sarah checked on the injured mercenaries. The man with the crushed stomach had died, but whether his hurts had been too severe for the healing potion or whether she had administered a slow poison, there was no way to ascertain. Head-Wound and Broken-Leg were still deeply asleep.

Thurmond, meanwhile, approached Roscoe and Torgul with his scheme to re-visit Malachai's cellar. He had expected to encounter staunch resistance, but Torgul was enthusiastic from the start and welcomed his suggestion with glee.

Roscoe was in a more agreeable mood after a good feeding and a sound night's sleep, but he continued to hem and haw, reiterating the same objections that he had given the day before.

Thurmond had watched carefully as his mentor had time and again manipulated Bart by challenging his courage and pride. He smiled inwardly as he now turned the same trick on his friend.

"Do you recall, Roscoe, when we were in the mountains of Carpat and Torgul was nearly killed by that shaggy snow beast?"

"Aye, course I do."

"Maybe you remember that I was pretty frightened because you were gonna carry him back down the mountain, which would leave Sarah and I alone up there. Remember that?"

"Aye, I do."

"And do you also remember what you said to me when I wanted to go down with you?"

The old Adventurer knew what was coming. He glared at his young friend.

"Can't say that I do."

"Well, I can recall your exact words. When you said 'em, I had no choice but to continue on, even when it seemed like Sarah and I were going to certain death. Shall I tell you what you said to me?"

Roscoe growled like a troll with an ingrown claw. He knew exactly what Thurmond was about to say.

"All right, if you must."

"You told me that I had to keep going because…"

Here he affected Roscoe's lilting accent.

"…*that's the way real Adventurers do things—they don't give up 'til they're dead.*"

Roscoe knew he must yield to his young friend's suggestions, had known it all along really, but he refused to submit without a fight. Actually, it amused him greatly that Thurmond was able to turn his own favorite tactic against him, though he was not about to admit it.

He stepped close until their faces were only inches apart. His voice was a menacing whisper.

"Your mother must have mated with a river eel for you to be such a slippery bugger."

Thurmond stood stock still, attempting to gauge the sincerity of Roscoe's anger. Then his face split in a wide grin.

"You think it's a grand idea then?"

Unable to maintain his wrathful façade, Roscoe also began to smile.

"Nay, laddie, I think it's a dreadful idea and likely to get our heads pickled in jars. But takin' terrible risks is how us Adventurers earn a livin'. So if Sarah and Torgul are in accord, we'll do it."

The dwarf was always ready for some desperate undertaking and nodded his head vigorously. Sarah assented but remained dubious, having been, like Roscoe, ensnared by Thurmond's cleverness.

They began to work out details.

"Sarah darlin', when we leave the cellar, will you be able to lock the door behind us? Make it look like we were never there?"

"Nay, a more powerful magician could reverse a knock spell and lock a door, but it's beyond me. Anyway, I doubt I'll have any energy left after getting it open."

"That's all right, girl. You'll do your share just gettin' us through the door. We'll shut it behind us. Maybe nobody'll notice it's unbarred."

"Thurmond, when we're finished, you'll be raisin' the drawbridge back like we found it and jumpin' back across. You're willin' to do that?"

"Uhhh...I don't think so, Roscoe. I drank the entire jumping potion yesterday, and it stopped working after a few minutes."

The old Adventurer hesitated.

"Okay, then—can't be helped. The drawbridge stays down."

They then apprised Bart of their plan. Roscoe gave him a knowing look.

"Care to join us, sir knight?"

"Nay, neither myself nor my men will again venture into that hell-hole. Only a madman would do so."

Roscoe smiled pleasantly.

"Just as you say, sir knight."

Bart's refusal was welcome, for the mission ahead called for stealth rather than a company of clanking, cursing, hungover mercenaries. Even the three Gascar archers would be left behind.

CHAPTER 29

BEYOND THE IRON DOOR

"We're all set, lassie. Cast your spell."

Sarah was still uncertain about the wisdom of their undertaking, but did as instructed. She could feel the spell trying to work, but the stout door was resisting her effort. She focused her will, directing more and more of her psychic energy to the task. Her ears were filled with a loud buzzing and her temples began to throb as if her brain might burst.

Torgul kept his ear pressed to the door as she worked and was gratified, at last, to hear the distinct *clink* of bolts being withdrawn and the *clunk* of a heavy bar dropping to the floor. He gave a push and the portal swung open.

Another passage—this one short, brick-lined, and clearly the work of skilled hands. At the far end, a chamber emanated a pale blue light.

As predicted, the spell required the entire reserve of Sarah's power. Drained and woozy, she placed her back against the wall and sank slowly to the floor, where she sat with her forehead resting on her knees.

She felt nauseous, as she always did after exhausting herself to such a degree. Her legs were too shaky to support her weight. She needed to sit and rest for a while, and could barely manage to raise her head as her companions disappeared down the passage. Roscoe and Thurmond went side by side with swords and shields raised, Torgul close behind, gripping his axe in both hands.

Then, to her amazement, Roscoe came slamming back through the door, sword and shield gone, the heels of his hands pressed against his eyes as if trying to shut out something dreadful. Tripping on the uneven floor, he fell forward and sprawled on his belly.

Thurmond was right behind him, also weaponless, right arm thrown across his face. He tripped over the prone body of his friend and lay groaning on the floor.

Torgul came last, eyes wide but unseeing, likewise seized by stupefying fright. He too stumbled and fell, then curled up in a tight ball with elbows and knees drawn tight to his chest.

Sarah was dumbstruck. She had seen her comrades face the deadliest of perils, but nothing had ever reduced them to blind panic.

It took all her strength to pull herself to her feet. Her legs trembled weakly as she made her way to Thurmond who lay groaning as if in unendurable pain. She placed her hand on his shoulder. His muscles were clinched tight, and his right arm was firmly clamped across his eyes.

"Thurmond, what is it? Where are you hurt? What happened to you?"

He remained at first unresponsive, then seemed to become aware of her words. He spoke like a child having a bad dream.

"Terrible pictures…in my mind…won't stop…horrible things…ooooh."

His voice trailed off into a soft moan.

Sarah attempted to roll him onto his back, but she was still too weak. Her legs gave out, and she slumped down next to her friend.

"You're seeing things? Bad pictures in your head? Thurmond, tell me what you're seeing."

He moved his head from side to side without removing his arm from his eyes. He groaned quietly.

"Oh horrible, horrible."

She shook him gently.

"Thurmond, whatever you think you're seeing, it's not real. It's just an illusion in your mind. You've got to disbelieve and make it stop."

Once again, he was slow to respond, but gradually seemed to comprehend her words.

"Listen to me, Thurmond, it's only an illusion. Just disbelieve and it will stop."

He began to mumble.

"Disbelieve…disbelieve…disbelieve."

Sarah saw his muscles suddenly relax, then he withdrew his arm from over his eyes.

"Oh, Sarah, it was so bad. I could see…."

"Never mind what you saw—it was only an illusion. Nothing more than a bad dream. I've got to help Roscoe and Torgul. They're still under the spell."

The old Adventurer lay where he fell, his palms still pressed to his eyes, his breath coming in short, painful gasps. Torgul's eyes bulged in terror as if pinned by some indescribably horrific sight.

Thurmond moved to the dwarf's side.

"Torgul! Torgul!"

Getting no response, he gave his beard a vicious yank. This, at last, got his friend's attention. Though he spoke no word, his eyes regained their focus.

"Torgul! Damn it! Hear me! It's only an illusion. Disbelieve it and break the spell."

It took several more moments of encouragement and a couple more tugs of the beard before he could do as instructed. He sat up and looked around as if in a state of utter confusion.

"What happened to us?"

"An illusion spell set to drive away intruders. It filled our minds with the vile thoughts. I saw hideous things, things I had never imagined before."

"Aye! Me, too. But funny thing—they're all slipping away now. Like when you're havin' a dream but forget it soon as you wake up. Kinda like that."

"Exactly—I can't recall what I was seeing, but I know it was disgusting, dreadful."

By now, Sarah had administered to Roscoe and had him sitting up. His normally booming voice was subdued.

"God's blue tongue—that was a right ghastly experience, so it was. Can't remember ever havin' such atrocious thoughts in all my life. Not somethin' I'd care to do again, I'll tell you that."

Thurmond got to his feet.

"My sword! I dropped my sword and shield in there."

Roscoe looked about.

"By God's great rump, I'm right ashamed to say I musta done the same thing. Dropped 'em and run off like a laddie in his first battle."

Torgul nearly expired from shame when he discovered that he had abandoned his magical axe, Bloodtroll. His voice was heavy with dismay.

"Woe to the dwarf who throws down his axe and runs away. I am disgraced. I'm naught but a weak-kneed craven, a cringing poltroon. I've brought dishonor on my whole clan. There must be...an atonement."

He drew his scramasax. For one awful moment, Thurmond thought he meant to gut himself, but instead he cut a good foot from the length of his beard.

Sarah laid her hand on Torgul's arm.

"There's no shame in what happened. You've done no disgraceful deed. Your mind was full of magic. You are not to blame."

The dwarf shook his head and turned away.

"I know you're bein' nice, girl, but you don't ken our dwarven ways."

"Then maybe there's a way to win your honor back. Would you be willing to go back in there to break the illusion and retrieve your axe? Such a deed would require supreme courage. It must surely restore your good name."

Torgul's eyes widened in fear. When he said nothing, Sarah continued.

"Since the chamber is guarded by magic, we must use magic to defeat it. I have a potion that will break the spell. Malachai said smashing the vial will dispel even the most powerful illusion."

The dwarf's eyes went blank, his face drained of color. The mere suggestion of re-entering that appalling chamber had driven him to the quivering edge of panic.

Sarah turned her eyes toward Thurmond and Roscoe.

"If we're going forward, someone has to do it."

But both her friends looked off, unwilling to meet her gaze. No one was willing to face that abhorrent chamber.

Then a low, growling voice startled her.

"I'll do it."

It was Torgul.

"Give me the potion, missy. I'll carry it in."

Sarah at once began to dig through her pannier.

"Here it is. And here is the necklace of wolf teeth. It'll help you overcome the fear. It's no weakness to wear it, it's just using magic against magic."

Contrary to Sarah's expectation, the dwarf seemed glad for the necklace. That such a strong, proud, and courageous soul as Torgul could be so reduced by fear testified to the awesome force of the illusion. She could only hope that the necklace's reckless courage would be sufficient.

Torgul wasted no time. With the vial in one hand and his scramasax in the other, he charged down the tunnel into the blue-lit chamber. After only a moment, he shouted back to the others.

"It's all right—things is clear now. Sarah, you've gotta see this."

Thurmond was next down the tunnel. Roscoe helped Sarah to her feet and supported her with an arm around her waist.

"Come on, lassie, let's go have a look-see."

The first chamber proved to be empty save for the Adventurers' weapons, which they quickly recovered. Several adjoining rooms, however, were cluttered with the implements of the darkest magic. Bones of all descriptions, human and otherwise. Black, evil-smelling candles. Stewed entrails and rotting flesh. Snakes, toads, and furry insects pickled in vinegar. Noxious herbs and pots of noisome balms. Even Sarah, who was largely inured to the foulness of occult paraphernalia, was forced to suppress an impulse to gag.

Then they found the heads, dozens of them, each in a large covered jar. Severed heads are bad under any condition, for their sorrowful eyes and mournful expressions invariably convey a deep sense of regret and desperate longing.

These heads were far worse because they spoke. Not with words—a head in a jar can have no actual voice. They spoke with thought, sending brief pictures flashing into the Adventurers' minds, images that begged for the release of true death.

One jar in particular caught Thurmond's eye.

"Roscoe, look at this one. Isn't that…?"

Indeed, it was the head of Gorb, Bart's missing mercenary, the one they had most likely eaten for dinner two days ago. The old Adventurer sighed.

"Well now, this is truly a grim turn, so it is. But it confirms our suspicions about Malachai. He's a far sight worse than a mere necromancer or black magician. We were fools to trust him. And yet..."

Thurmond finished his thought.

"And yet we're bound to him. He's our only hope for preserving our city. At least that's what Asmodeus claims."

Thurmond gave Gorb's head another look. It did not speak, yet the dead eyes pled desperately for succor.

"Can we at least do something for Gorb? He was one of us, and he doesn't look happy in that jar."

"Nay, boyo, best leave it. We don't want to leave no trace that we was ever here. I'm afraid old Gorb's gone to whatever fate he deserved."

Torgul interrupted their discussion.

"Come and see what's in the next room."

The chamber in question contained a number of large stone slabs, roughly the size and shape of a bed. Each held a recumbent human body, nude, motionless, either drugged or dead. The pale forms drew no breaths.

Torgul pointed to a youngish man with dirty blonde hair.

"Recognize him? He's the servant what brought our wine the first night. These are Malachai's people, 'cept they ain't really people. At least not no more."

Sarah suddenly called out.

"Here's something else!"

Another body, much too large for a slab, was stretched on the floor. It's immense size and grotesque proportions left no doubt—the malformed ogres were another of Malachai's malignant creations.

Roscoe's brow furrowed in disgust.

"Just as I thought—he built them things in this room, then drove 'em out over the drawbridge. No right-minded man would do such a deed, but that's what he's done. When they got outta hand and started eatin' the fisher-folk, he sent us to kill 'em off. A foul business, so it is."

Torgul gave his old friend a hard look.

"Whadda we standin' around gabbin' for? There ain't no treasure here. Let's keep movin' and see if we can't find some gold."

Roscoe nodded in agreement.

"No truer words was ever spoke."

CHAPTER 30

THE GUARDIAN

They searched and searched, prying into iron-bound chests, rummaging through cabinets and drawers. Torgul turned his dwarfish eye to the walls and floor, hunting for secret hidey-holes. Nothing. No horde of ancient coins, no heap of gold bars, no jewel-encrusted goblets, no enchanted weapons. Only room after room of abominations most vile.

Sensing the frustration of his comrades, Roscoe did his best to keep their spirits up.

"At least there ain't no more ogres. I thought maybe Malachai would have some in here as guards."

As if summoned by these words, Malachai's guardian emerged from his hidden niche. A foul, lumpish, blasphemous creature possessing the most forbidding features of man and beast. Its body and limbs were of human form, yet grossly misproportioned. The nude torso, sagging with fat, was swollen to the girth of a barrel. The thick, flabby legs were far too short, while the heavily muscled arms were much too long. A thick coat of long gray hair hung from its thighs and shoulders.

The creature's head was the most ghastly of all—human in size and shape, but with the stubby snout of a pig. Long tusks jutted from the lower jaw. The ears hung floppy like those of a goat. Its eyes were convex and expressionless, the eyes of a fish.

It moved slowly at first, as if awakening from a long nap, but its sluggishness did not last long. The Adventurers scarcely had time to turn and brace themselves for the attack.

Thurmond was the first to engage. His opening blow, a straight shot aimed at the beast's snout, was stopped short when his sword caught the edge of a bookcase. The cellar's confined space made swinging a long weapon next to impossible. He next sought to drive the point into the softness of its belly, but the creature shifted and caught his sword arm with its remarkably human hand.

The monstrosity lifted Thurmond as if he were a child and hurled him backwards into Roscoe, who was moving up on his left. The impact knocked the old Adventurer from his feet so that he landed on his back with the younger man atop him.

Then the creature was on them, its long arms reaching, its powerful hands seeking a grip. Thurmond managed to drive the edge of his shield straight into its snout. The results were surprising. The hideous thing drew back, opened its mouth, and gave what looked to be a long, silent howl. Was it mute? Whatever it was, its nose was sensitive.

The two Adventurers barely had time to scramble to their feet before it was upon them again. They both struck at the nose, but it was impossible to deliver a proper stroke, standing as they were among high shelves, tall cabinets, and counters laden with glassware.

Thurmond's first blow shattered a jar of pickled eyeballs. Roscoe missed the nose, but did manage to lop off one of the goatish ears. Thurmond's next shot opened a deep gash in the sloping brow.

The creature seemed not to notice either injury. It seized Thurmond's shield in both hands and pushed him backwards into Roscoe. This time, however, they all went down, with the creature uppermost.

Torgul came barreling in from an adjoining room, axe at the ready. But he, too, was hampered by the confines of the magician's workroom—it was no place for his two-handed weapon. Nor did he want to strike recklessly at the pile of bodies sprawled on the floor, where it would be too easy to injure friend rather than foe.

He paused for a moment to draw his scramasax. This hesitation was costly, for the creature rose with unlooked-for speed and dealt him a backhanded blow that lifted him from his feet and sent him smashing into a counter laden with jars of heads.

Sarah, still drained of energy, read from her scroll of unidentified spells. This was risky, for the results were entirely unpredictable, but she read it anyway. Her friends were about to die and there was nothing else she could do.

The creature had seized Thurmond by the foot and was trying to twist it loose from the ankle when the cellar was suddenly filled with locusts, thousands upon thousands of them, a rasping, whirring, biting swarm that flew into their faces, entered their mouths, and scratched at their eyes.

Ravenously hungry, the insects immediately assailed every inch of uncovered skin with their saw-like mandibles. The Adventurers were well protected by their armor and thick clothing, and had only to guard their exposed faces. The creature, however, was stark naked save for patches of straggly hair. Thus, it became the target of hundreds of the flying pests that attacked from all sides.

The creature dropped Thurmond and began to bat frantically at its tormenters. Its mouth stretching in a silent scream, it flung itself to and fro in a vain attempt to dislodge the multitude of tiny jaws. This movement seemed to attract rather than discourage the insects, for more and more took hold on its head, body and limbs.

The magical swarm was short-lived. As quickly as it had appeared, the ravenous insects suddenly vanished. The misbegotten creature, driven to madness by their innumerable bites, jumped to renew his attack.

When the locusts first appeared, Thurmond dove beneath a table, curled into a ball, and covered his face with his arms. Next to him, two large jars exuded a familiar smell, that of a highly volatile liquid Sarah kept in her workroom. It was exactly what he needed.

As the beast approached, he rose and flung the contents of one jar directly in its face. The thing began once more to crash about the room in silent agony as the noxious substance burned its eyes. Seizing the second jar, Thurmond poured it over the thick hair on its back and shoulders. Sarah snatched a burning oil lamp from beneath an alembic. One quick touch of the tiny flame was all it took—the liquid ignited with a resounding *whoosh*, engulfing the creature's body in fire.

If that poor, blighted beast ever needed to scream, it was now, but it remained silent as it blundered about the cellar, smashing glass, overturning tables, upsetting shelves and bookcases. The more it ran, the more it burned, and soon the flames were spreading to the flammable substances spilled from the broken vessels. In desperation, the creature fled to the far reaches of the workshop, bringing fire with its every step.

Though sorely battered, none of the Adventurers were significantly hurt. They rose to their feet as the flames were taking hold of the smashed furniture and torn books. The chamber began to fill with smoke.

Roscoe grabbed Thurmond's shoulder and pushed him toward the door.

"Time to go, laddie. Be quick now."

The young man was still dissatisfied. He had fought ogres, jumped over a chasm, slain the misbegotten monster by the bridge, endured the most hellish of illusions, and now fought Malachai's horrendously powerful guardian. He was not about to leave this place without some sort of compensation, something of value to reward him for his pains.

Unfortunately, he saw nothing of interest. He most certainly did not want a head in a jar. But then he spotted a small, leather-bound book lying on an adjacent counter. He slipped it into the pouch on his belt. Sarah would like it—she was always interested in weird old books.

Roscoe gave him another push.

"Get crackin', boyo, unless you're lookin' to die in here. The smoke's getting' right bad, so it is."

Thurmond hesitated one more moment. Gorb's tortured face was staring at him from its jar. He swept it to the stone floor, where the glass was smashed to tiny shards. As he ran from the room, he thought he heard a grateful sigh of relief.

By now, the workshop was well ablaze. Perhaps the fire would conceal their incursion into Malachai's abode. Perhaps he would blame the roasted guardian for the destruction.

Bart and his mercenaries remained in the fisher village while the

Adventurers were effecting their subterranean trespass. As he waited their return, the knight fumed over the inequity of his lot. Five of his men were dead. How would he replace them? Trained soldiers would be impossible to come by in these desolate regions.

The two wounded men galled him as well. They would remain, he was certain, hopelessly crippled. Broken-Leg's shattered bones would leave him lame, and Head-Wound would be a drooling imbecile. It would have been much better had they died. Such broken remnants were of no use to him.

Worse yet, he would receive no payment for this ill-fated adventure, nothing to compensate for his suffering and costs. He had accepted the mission to discharge his debt to Asmodeus, but he had expected to come by some sort of spoils along the way. Was he not entitled to something for his pains? Roscoe had promised him exorbitant wealth, but he had received not a farthing.

Roscoe—that damned old man. Bart had hated him deeply for some time, but he suddenly realized why. His father. The Adventurer reminded him of his father. The two bore no physical resemblance, quite the opposite. Roscoe was large, loud, and hale. Lord Percy Staynes was frail, emaciated, and ravished by disease. He looked to be a thousand years old. His life, Bart suspected, was preserved only through some forbidden diabolic rite.

Yet they both had the same knack for thwarting him. Lord Percy might look like a walking wraith, but he possessed a will of iron, and it had always been his pleasure to keep his son squarely beneath his thumb. Since childhood, Bart's greatest ambition was to be trained at arms and become a knight, but Lord Percy had stubbornly denied him the thing he most desired.

Driven by a desperate need for glory, for recognition, for something of his own, Bart had organized the abortive goblin adventure. It had brought him nothing but failure and disgrace. A sizable portion of the family fortune had been squandered. He had almost died.

He could not return to the family home after that. Did not dare to face his father's vitriol. Far better to die a broken man, a homeless, penniless wanderer. Better to be hanged as a common thief.

Lord Percy, that vindictive old man, would never forgive the disobedience, the tearing free from his hideous grip, the spending of his money. He would most certainly deprive Bart of his inheritance—the titles, estates, and family fortune that should be his by right of birth. Just to spite him, his bastard half-sister would most likely get it all.

Then a chance encounter allowed Bart to achieve his long-denied dream. He met Asmodeus, and through a skillful manipulation of circumstances, found himself with a white belt and a golden chain. But they had come with a price. He owed the wizard a service.

Bart's wandering thoughts returned to Roscoe. The old Adventurer did not look like his father. Perchance that was why it took so long for him to recognize their similarity. But like Lord Percy, he had a smug, commanding air, an overweening confidence that he was always right. Like Lord Percy, Roscoe always managed to twist things so that Bart had no choice but to play the follower. Above all else, Bart hated being made to feel small.

Bart would never stoop to patricide, but he had no qualms about settling with the Adventurer, who was, after all, nothing more than an upstart peasant. And he would need to remove his sister. She would have a hard time inheriting if she were in her grave. Also the stable boy. He still nursed a grudge over the stolen mirror and map.

The Adventurers exited the cave complex, mounted their tethered horses, and set off for the fisher village. Only then did Thurmond recall the book he had tucked in his pouch.

"Hey, Sarah, I have something for you."

"What is it?"

He drew it out and handed it to her.

"I took this from Malachai's workroom. I wasn't going to go through all that trouble for nothing. I saw it lying on a table and thought you'd like to have it. It was going to burn up anyway, so he won't even know it's gone."

It was a small book bound with exceptionally smooth, supple leather. Sarah studied it closely, turning the pages in rapid succession. When she finally turned to Thurmond, her eyes were filled with apprehension.

"God's holy molars, this is Malachai's spellbook. It's where he writes down all his formulas for the animation of dead flesh. We better hope the whole cellar burned up. If it did, maybe he'll assume the book went up with it. If not, he'll definitely come looking for it."

She continued to scan the pages.

"Oh! There's something else in here. Oh! Lungs of God! These are his notes on that magical instrument he gave us. Thurmond, there's a demon in that box."

"Is that a problem? You carried around a beer jug with a demon trapped inside. He did us no harm."

"Not the same, not at all. That was just an imp, a very minor demon. He was stupid and weak. And even so, if you recall, his dark influence almost turned us against one another. This one is something else. I'm not sure what it is, but it's much more powerful, more intelligent, more evil. And Thurmond, I know you stole this book for me. Thank you. But now I want you to take it back."

"Take it back? Why?"

"It puts out a—I don't know what to call it—a vibration of evil. You're not attuned to psychic energy, so I doubt you'll even feel it. But it's intensely disturbing to me."

"What should I do with it?"

"I don't know. Throw it away. Burn it."

"Do you think it's valuable?"

"To the right person, I'd imagine it is."

"All right, give it back to me. I'll hang onto it. Maybe Jarvis would be interested."

Jarvis was Gorgonholm's premier dealer in unique and unusual goods. For many years, Roscoe had sold him the plunder from his underworld adventures. More recently, the canny merchant had brokered the deal that brought about the old Adventurer's acquisition of Grimsgard.

"Maybe Jarvis. But in the meantime, you have to tell Roscoe about the book and the demon."

Thurmond urged his horse forward so that he and Roscoe were side by side and quickly told him about the book and the demon in the box. The old

Adventurer's reaction was less severe that Thurmond expected—he cursed for no more than two minutes before lapsing into a morose silence.

Thurmond was encouraged. If Roscoe was this constrained, perhaps their situation was not as dire as he thought. But Roscoe's next words quickly dispelled this illusion.

"So now we've got to pack around another demon, and a far worse one this time. That's bad enough, so it is. But did it ever occur to you, laddie, that the well-bein' of an entire city depends on us getting back home alive? Sarah says Malachai will probably want his book back, and he ain't likely to ask for it nice-like. Maybe you should've thought of that before you went stealin' trinkets for your lady-love."

"Sarah's not exactly my...."

"Shut up and just listen—that's somethin' you haven't quite managed to learn yet. You bein' light-fingered maybe puts us in a bad place."

"Roscoe, we're Adventurers. We're supposed to take great risks and win treasure. Well, we didn't find any gold, so I had to take something, didn't I? And if we'd taken Malachai's gold, wouldn't that have angered him just as much?"

Roscoe dismissed that argument with a wave of his hand.

"Nay, stolen gold wouldn't rile him near so much. The book is somethin' special, and you takin' it were a stupid boy's trick to win a girl's favor, so it was."

"Okay, maybe so. You're right. I admit it. But I think I have a way to make up for it."

"Bein' what?"

"You and the others head for home as fast as you can. I'll take the book back to Malachai. I'll tell him it was me that broke into his cellar and stole the book. I'll make up some story and blame the guardian for the fire. Then I'll apologize. Maybe he'll let me go. If he does, I'll ride like hell and catch up with you."

"And if he don't, you'll end up with your head in a jar."

"Could be—but I'm a pretty good talker when I have to be. Maybe I could reason with him, use some logic."

The old Adventurer was moved by Thurmond's suggestion.

"Now that's a right generous offer, right courageous and noble. But I'm not about to let your head get stuck in no jar. We'll stick together, just like always. What comes to one, comes to us all. That's the logic what has seen us through many a desperate scrape, so it has."

"So what do you want me to do?"

"Just keep mum. I'll explain things to Torgul, but don't say a word to nobody else. Especially to Bart. Especially about the demon in the box."

They arrived back at the fisher village, where another round of intense celebration was underway. Both Head-Wound and Broken-Leg were awake and declaring, in no uncertain terms, that they were fit to ride and would accompany the party when it departed at dawn.

PART 4

NARROW ESCAPES

CHAPTER 31

DANGERS, DELAYS, AND A SLICE OF FRUIT

The Black Stone dozed in the bright afternoon sun. A blackbird perched on its top and shat down its back. Only yesterday, the impudent creature would have been smitten with death long before it could perpetrate such outrage, but today the Stone barely noticed, and the bird remained unscathed.

The stars were wrong. The Failed Maiden was giving way to the Fecund Mule, a sign associated with increase and commerce rather than despair and discord, so it was not the best time for a demon-possessed rock to take over the world.

It had, when first raised, needed a good feeding of the fear and hatred that humans exuded so readily. Thus, it had sown a bit of chaos, turning neighbor against neighbor, father against son, servant against master, and gobbled up the consequent suffering.

Now, however, was a perfect time for a nap after an excellent repast of human misery. When the stars came 'round again, there would be plenty of time to fulfill its greater desires.

Lord Ubo burned with frustration. His plans had begun so well, but now they were lurching along at the pace of a blind beggar. Recruitment, at first so brisk, had fallen off. Woodsmen, road travelers, and townsfolk still trickled in, but in nowhere near the numbers as when the Stone had first been raised in the monastery's courtyard. He could not understand how things could have changed so abruptly.

His army included too few trained soldiers. His best men were deserters from the city constabulary, and they were more over-fed extortionists than real fighters. One or two of these men had once served as mercenaries, and he set them to train the rest of his force in the use of arms.

The results were disheartening. Farmers, charcoal burners, and runaway apprentices were not by nature amenable to military discipline. And there was not enough armor and weapons to properly equip his retinue. The Gray Friars' armory had been woefully under-supplied with the necessities of war— swords, spears, shields, helmets, mail. It had been too many years since the Grays had been forced to defend themselves.

His food supplies were also running short. The monastery's larders had, it was true, been filled to bursting with every kind of meat, cheese, bread, grain, and vegetables. With wine, beer, mead, and illicit uisge. But his band of hungry peasants was eating its way through this stock with alarming rapidity. He must, he knew, find additional food sources or this army would dwindle as its bellies grew empty.

Ubo had hoped to lie up in the monastery and gather strength, to remain undercover until he could launch a sudden and devastating attack on the city. But that was not to be. He lacked the strength for this decisive move, and his army was ill-equipped. But perhaps a change of plans could solve both problems.

He would raid the neighbors. The small fief to the south, a small dreary place called Grimsgard, would be a good place to begin. The small tower looked strong, but there were, he knew, no soldiers to defend it. His spies reported that the estate was managed by an elf—an elf, by God's fiery breath! —and inhabited by no more than two- or three-score peasants.

The raid would give his ill-trained men some valuable experience, and the village's storehouses would provide needed foodstuffs. There were cows in the pasture and sheep in the fold. The tower might yield up some armor and weapons, perhaps even some gold. Any peasants fortunate enough to survive would no doubt be eager to join his victorious force.

That would be a good start, but Ubo's eye was on a more lucrative target. Lying a few leagues further to the south, the monastery of the Brown Friars was famous for its spectacular mead. There would be much food there, and a great hoard of gold gleaned from decades of selling this renowned beverage. Perhaps a fine store of weapons and armor.

He would fall upon them without warning, in the dark of the night, giving them no chance to arm and prepare themselves. The monastery had no curtain wall, only a thick thorny hedge. His peasants would breach it with pruning bills, then swarm inside. Anyone left alive would either join him or die.

Two such victories would lend his men skill and confidence in preparation for the bigger battle yet to come—the storming of Gorgonholm.

Sheriff Brandon sat on his big white horse, a heavy war-sword strapped to its saddle. He wore a long-sleeved mailshirt reinforced with iron plates at shoulder and elbow. A visorless basnet guarded his head.

Brandon's wary eyes swept the bustling array of farmers and merchants as they set up their booths and stalls in Market Square. Everyone was on edge—this was the first market day since *the Troubles* began. The city gates had been opened for the first time this morning to allow food and other necessities to be hauled in.

The Troubles—that was what they were calling the chaos and madness that had begun a score of days before. Things were better now. The streets were calming down. The fires had finally been extinguished. Armed mobs no longer engaged in pitched battles. Those small altercations that did erupt were quickly contained by Brandon's constabulary.

This was quite different than the first few days when he and his men could only cower in City Keep while the citizenry slew their neighbors and burned their houses. After the initial savage eruption, there had come a lull in which the citizens, like exhausted pugilists, had drawn back to rest their battered bodies. And at that moment, Brandon had done his best to take his city back.

Urgent pleas for aid were dispatched to the powerful and influential—the nobility, the various orders of clergy—and to wealthy merchants and guildsmen. Even the Brethren received an appeal for support.

Few responded, at least at first. But then Bishop Boniface provided a contingent of Blue Friars from the cathedral. These well-trained fighters came heavily armed and were a welcome addition to Brandon's shoddy force of city constables. Quite unexpectedly, Lord Drakar sent three-score mounted men from his personal retinue, seasoned warriors all.

With this force, Brandon had slowly wrested control of the streets from the rampaging citizens. Rioters rich or poor were ridden down without mercy. A dusk-to-dawn curfew kept the streets clear at night. Anyone caught out after dark was summarily hanged and left as a warning to other nocturnal skulkers. The city gates were kept firmly barred, only official messengers being permitted in and out of a small postern.

These harsh tactics had worked. Things were now sufficiently calm to allow the re-opening of the market. This was a necessity, for even a city in chaos needs to eat, and Gorgonholm's cupboards were bare. Word had it that some citizens were reduced to eating rats, while the denizens of Old Shambles, it was said, were cooking their own dead.

Market day was a risk. Hungry people were arriving in droves, eager for the fish, flesh, and vegetables brought in by farmers and rivermen. The wafting smells from the cook-stands—the baking bread and roasting meat—drew even more famished folk from their nearby houses. Having this many people together was dangerous. The slightest provocation could send the crowd into another orgy of blood-letting.

There were no foreign merchants today, no exotic spices or fine brocades from the east, nor delicate lace or smooth, crisp parchment from the cities of the south. The last caravan had arrived at the height of the Troubles. Its merchants, guards, and teamsters had been slaughtered, their goods pillaged. After that, merchants prudently kept their distance.

Sheriff Brandon sniffed the air as if discord had a discernable smell.

Market day might be necessary, but the sooner it was over and the streets cleared, the sooner he could begin to relax.

He was ready should things go badly. A phalanx of blue friars was drawn up before the cathedral, while mounted soldiers—Drakar's men—stood ready at each of the streets branching off from Market Square. At his command, a trumpeter would blow a special call. The horsemen would seal the exits, and the friars would advance, pikes leveled.

No prisoners would be taken.

Ubo had his problems, Brandon his concerns, but Fergis, the *Ard Righ*, the High King of the Keltin tribes, was plagued by the most vexing situation of all. His great strategy had been stalled by a series of maddening delays.

In order to slay the laigi and burn their city, he must first carry his army across the river that had, for centuries, protected the soft city folk from his valiant ancestors. To surmount this obstacle, Fergis had a plan—he had set his men to building hundreds of small, skin-covered boats known as *currachs*, and scores of large, wooden rafts.

The currachs would carry the Painted Men on their silent mission to scale the city wall, open the city gates, and slay the laigi in their beds.

The little boats would also bring the men with the strongest backs and the mightiest shoulders. These stalwart fellows would use long, hempen ropes to draw the rafts over the river and ferry the bulk of his army into battle. When enough warriors had been landed to protect the crossing, the rafts would be lashed together to form a floating bridge. Nothing like that had ever been attempted before, but Fergis was certain the idea was sound.

But he could not put his plan into action because neither the rafts nor the currachs were ready. There had been unforeseen problems and inexplicable setbacks. The wooden planking of the rafts split, cracked, and broke. The leather sides of the currachs rotted and fell to pieces, as did the long ropes for drawing the rafts. A sudden fire consumed much of the available building materials. Tools mysteriously disappeared.

Fergis thought, at first, that angry forest spirits must be behind these aggravating mishaps, or perhaps he had offended the gods in some way. He immediately undertook a painful ritual of cleansing and appeasement, but the mischief continued unabated. He had sacrificed goats, pigs, dogs, a prized bullock, a trained falcon, and finally his favorite horse. No results.

He was contemplating the soft, white necks of his own children, considering his next step, when a thought struck him—Oengus! His older brother Oengus had always been jealous of his successes. He had always resented that he, the eldest, had not succeeded their father as Ard Righ. Always felt that he had been deprived of the prestige and privileges he rightfully deserved.

If the invasion failed or was sufficiently delayed, Fergis would lose the confidence of the lesser kings. When that happened, he would be, according to custom, ritually slain and replaced by the council of clan chiefs and lesser kings. They might well turn to Oengus, the other son of the legendary Brude mac Boru.

Fergis stared across the camp to where Oengus stood talking to the men of his personal war-band. They burst into laughter as if some uproarious joke had been told. What, Fergis wondered, could these grim warriors find so amusing?

He was forced to ask a terrible question—could Oengus be the source of his ill fortune? Could he be so treacherous that he would imperil their great conquest to advance his own prospects? Absolutely! His older brother had, since childhood, been selfish, small-minded, vindictive. He would dash Fergis's aspirations for the sheer pleasure of doing so.

Something would have to be done. Even if Oengus was not plotting against him, he would remain a threat for as long as he lived. Fergis recalled the advice of one grizzled under-king on the day of his election as Ard Righ. He had whispered that royal siblings must always be a threat to a king's position. Oengus, he suggested, should be strangled without delay.

Fergis was the Ard Righ. Duly chosen by the council of kings, he had passed the Test of Seven to determine his fitness—the Threefold Ordeal of fire, water, and stone, then the Long Tribulation of dark and cold and hunger. Finally, there had been the terrible Night of Blood. He had survived, and in so doing had confirmed his right to be anointed by the high priest beneath the sacred oak.

He now, for the first time, began to seriously consider the old under-king's advice. As Ard Righ, did he not have a duty to his people, an obligation that rose above the family bond? Could he allow Oengus to threaten the well-being of all Keltin people? Something would have to be done.

That was but one of Fergis's problems. There were other, more immediate concerns.

He had, it was true, a greater fighting force than he had ever imagined possible, and it was growing still larger every day. Far-flung clans continued to arrive from the far west. Their chiefs were typically stubborn, stiff-necked men, notoriously resistant to showing deference, yet now they came, ready to submit to his authority.

Even the Small Folk were coming in—diminutive warriors, scarcely the size of children, said to dwell in underground houses hidden in the deepest woods. Their tiny flint-tipped arrows, it was rumored, were smeared with a deadly poison. In sooth, few men had ever set eyes on the Small Folk, and never in such numbers.

The sheer size of this host was Fergis's most pressing problem—he had no idea how to keep so many warriors fed. He had, in preparation for his attack, laid in a vast store of food, but it was sadly inadequate for so many hungry mouths. His hunters and fishermen were out every day, bringing in what they could. But game was getting increasingly scarce, and his men's appetites were not abating.

The Ard Righ knew if he did not cross the river soon, his hungry army would slip away.

From the uppermost window of the tallest tower of his opulent hall, Asmodeus contemplated his garden. He took great satisfaction in the vast collection of exotic trees, vines, and flowers. Many were of his own creation, the product of his magical sleights. Others had been brought hither from lands unknown to the most learned human geographers. Some were from still further away.

Through a window of the clearest glass, the wizard gazed down on tiny trees bearing the most delectable nuts and fruits. One of his servants was just then plucking a blood-fig for the master's morning snack. There was no need for illusion in the privacy of the garden—the hand that held the fruit was that of an animated skeleton. The magician had named him Knuckles.

The garden held many delights. Succubus vines clung to the garden wall with desperate sincerity. Giant succulents presented themselves in a variety of erotic postures and strangely inviting shapes. Thorny shrubberies thrust out spines the length of small daggers.

Asmodeus loved the flowers best of all. They covered the grounds below like the mottled garb of a mad harlequin—blooms of all sizes, shapes, and hues. Some so tiny as to be nearly unseeable to the naked eye. Others were large enough to swallow a man. The blossoms of one shifted continuously from color to color. Another would emit a deep warning growl if disturbed.

Their fragrances were just as appealing. A brief whiff of the bloom he called *purplecup* gave a stimulating intoxication, while *brownshadow* induced slumber on restless nights. The cool essence of *bluebreeze* provided a pleasant pick-me-up, and *redsnake* kept his garden free of pests. His favorite, though, was the pungent scent of an orchid he had named *lightlove*.

The wizard's estate was protected by defenses both mundane and magical. A cordon of invisible imps was enough to discourage all but the most intrepid intruders. But should a determined housebreaker chance to defeat the imps, they would be forced to scale a twenty-foot wall topped with the sharpest volcanic glass—poisoned, of course.

Should the wall prove insufficient, there was the garden. His loyal vegetable friends would sting, strangle, enfold, and digest any thief luckless enough to enter their realm.

A skeletal servant brought the blood-fig on an alabaster plate. It looked something like a small human heart. When sliced, the juice, velvety and red, oozed out like thickening blood. Asmodeus took a bite—exquisite!—intensely sweet, yet just tart enough to be interesting. The servant—this one known as Teeth—departed, his bony toes clicking on the tiled floor.

As he finished his snack, Asmodeus's mind turned to other things, and he gave a perverse giggle. He often did when his machinations discomfited those who stood in his way. His minions, his creatures of the air, had unleashed a torrent of decay on the boats and rafts of the Keltin fleet. They would not be crossing the river any time soon.

More importantly, his artificial sprites had induced into the mind of the Keltin king unwholesome ideas that could only distract him from his larger purpose.

CHAPTER 32

A LONG, HARD RIDE

They stayed well inland, avoiding the coast and Malachai's ill-omened mansion on its barren promontory. From the direction of that edifice, a huge plume of black smoke twisted into the sky, testifying that the conflagration still raged in the magician's cellars. Or had it escaped to the mansion itself, rising level by level, to engulf the entire structure?

Perhaps, if they were very lucky, the fire had caught Malachai in a deep state of trance and consumed him along with his property. If not, his wrath would be incalculable. He might be, at this very moment, taking measures to avenge his loss.

It was time to put a great distance between themselves and Malachai's domain.

The summer days were long that far north. Full dark lasted perhaps two hours, so they rode late into the night, allowing themselves only the shortest snatches of sleep before pressing on once again. The vernal sun failed to produce much warmth, and a cold wind blew lonely snowflakes into their faces.

The landscape was gray, bleak, monotonous, just a flat, windswept grasslands broken here and there by low, rocky hillocks. Cold and treeless, almost devoid of wildlife, and silent save for the mournful shriek of an occasional seabird.

They were a sorry, ragged lot. Their wounds had stiffened and throbbed more painfully than on the previous day. Those who had partaken too liberally in last night's merriment now leaned in their saddles to vomit fisheye beer. All were exhausted and out of sorts.

They headed west rather than straight south, hoping to avoid the tribal lands of the Blue Horse People. Grinder's brothers, maybe even Brodar and the entire tribe, might still be on their trail. All day they rode without encountering another human soul. This was good. The Adventurers had no desire for company as they made their way toward home.

Though utterly worn out, they paused only to keep the horses from dying beneath them. At noon, Roscoe approached Drax.

"We been headin' west now for a day and a half. Is this still Blue Horse land, or have we crossed over into somethin' else?"

Drax scratched the back of his neck as if carefully considering the question.

"Years ago, the Slow Worm River was always the boundary line 'tween the Blue Horse and the Snow Panthers. You'll know it when we come to it—it's the most beautiful color blue you ever saw. All milky lookin'. It don't even look like it's made of water."

"And when can we expect to come upon this amazin' spectacle, if I might ask?"

"Any time now, best as I can recall."

"Once we cross it, we'll be safe on the other side?"

Drax made a wry face.

"Hell, no. Nobody's safe in these parts. First off, tribal boundaries always shift, dependin' on who won the last war. So that river might not mean nothin' to nobody these days."

"Second, the Panthers don't take to uninvited guests any more than the Blue Horses does. Some might' say they're worse. And you better pray none of 'em recognize me as the one who killed their old warchief."

Roscoe did his best to conceal his apprehension. Behind them, an infuriated magician was perhaps summoning demons to rend their souls.

Hordes of savage horse-barbarians lurked on all sides, lusting for their blood. At home, a fiend-possessed rock was inciting riot and invasion in their city. And if that was not yet trouble enough, they carried a powerful demon locked in a casket in Sarah's saddlebags.

"Friend Drax, what do you suppose we should do next?"

"Keep low, keep quiet. Cross the river and turn south. Hope nobody sees us."

"Do you suppose Grinder's brothers are still out huntin' us?"

"Not a doubt in my mind. Blue Horses got long memories. They'll be holdin' a grudge against us for a hundred years, maybe more. Their poets will make up songs about how Thurmond snuck up and stabbed Grinder in the eye while the poor guy was sleepin'."

The old Adventurer grew indignant.

"Didn't happen like that, not at all."

"That don't matter, they'll remember it like they want to. By now, the whole tribe remembers it like that."

They reached the Slow Worm at early evening. It was, as Drax had described, a most striking shade of milky blue. Wide and shallow, it oozed through the flat, barren steppe in a multitude of sleepy bends. The party splashed across without incident.

On the other side, Roscoe again sought Drax's counsel.

"All right, Drax, we're across. What now?"

"Keep goin' west 'til we're out of sight of the river, then turn south and ride like hell for home."

"If Grinder's people find our tracks, will they cross the river?"

"Certes! They're always raidin' other tribes' territories. And there's a fair good chance they will pick up our trail at some point. Blue Horses are expert trackers. So we gotta keep movin'."

Another night of short sleep, another long day in the saddle. At mid-afternoon, they paused atop a low ridge that afforded a good view of the flat, grassy expanse over which they had traveled. With a cry of alarm, Sarah pointed into the distance. Her voice was shrill with urgency.

"Look straight out, just to the left of that rocky outcrop."

Sure enough, a clump of dark dots was moving steadily in their direction—riders. They watched with dismay as the dots followed their trail with unerring accuracy.

Torgul's voice was a low, disgusted growl.

"Buggers are on our track all right. There's a lot of 'em, must be close to a hundred."

Roscoe's reply was sharp and decisive.

"Mount up! We've got to keep ahead of 'em. Maybe we can lose 'em in the dark, it's our only chance."

Thurmond took a last look before stepping into his stirrup.

"Who are those guys?"

Roscoe was already spurring his horse. He shouted back over his shoulder.

"Don't make no difference, boyo. Blue Horses or Snow Cats—none of 'em are gonna be friendly, so hold your gab and just ride."

They rode and rode, then rode some more. At every rise and hillock they cast anxious, searching eyes over the landscape behind them. The dots were always there, gradually growing larger and more distinct as the pursuers drew inexorably closer.

Finally, in the gloaming of the evening, Roscoe called a halt. Horses and riders alike were on the quivering edge of collapse.

"It's getting' dark, so our friends back there will have a harder time followin' our tracks. We've been goin' straight south, but now it's time to veer off. Maybe we can at least confuse 'em for a bit and delay 'em. Dismount—we'll lead the horses for a while. Single file, now—follow me."

Roscoe led them in a zigzag course, bearing generally west by southwest, but veering at times toward every point of the compass. They came at last to a dry watercourse whose rocky streambed would show little evidence of their passing. Here they mounted and began picking their way through the loose, clattering stones.

Thurmond was astounded when he realized that the old Adventurer had turned them north rather than south.

"Roscoe, what are you thinking? You're taking us away from home, back toward the barbarians."

"Only for a wee bit, laddie. If they follow us as far as this streambed, they'll have a hard time findin' any tracks. So they'll probably assume we're still goin' south, the way we've been headin' all day."

"We'll fool 'em by going the opposite way?"

"That's the idea, boyo, so it is."

They rode for some time. A cold wind rose, tearing at their faces like the claws of a small, angry animal. They drew their cloaks around their shivering bodies and continued on.

The streambed abruptly petered out, leaving them once more on the soft, sandy soil of the steppe where their tracks would be easy to follow. It would soon be daylight.

After days of hard riding and so little rest, neither man nor beast could go any farther. Roscoe scanned the surroundings for some place of concealment in the barren wasteland. In the distance, he spotted a small, round hill topped by something that resembled a structure.

They made their weary way to the top of the mount, where the emerging dawn revealed the crumbling remains of an ancient ringfort with a wall something higher than a tall man's head. A ragged opening was all that survived of what had once been a gate. Inside, stone foundations told of the houses that had once circled the inner wall. All other traces of human habitation had long since disappeared.

As a defensive position, the fort left much to be desired. The ancient walls were of unmortared stone and broken down in many places. They might delay an attacker slightly, but they were too low to be much of a hindrance. There was no way to barricade the broken gate.

But at least the walls offered welcome protection from the biting northern wind that had made the day's ride so miserable. And they would conceal them from probing barbarian eyes.

"I'm against it!"

Torgul's voice was harsh, his tone adamant.

"You never want to hole up in a buildin' when somebody's after you. First place they're bound to look. Better to lay down flat in the grass."

Sarah was of a different mind.

"The horses can't go any further, not even to find a patch of tall grass to lie down in, and I can't either. I'm so tired, and the wind is so cold—it seems like it's biting right into my bones. At least this wall will protect us from it."

Torgul remained unmoved.

"Better cold than dead, girl."

Thurmond rose in her support.

"Sarah's right. I'm done in. I'm so tired that my body can't seem to warm itself. Let's stop here."

Roscoe pondered a moment before coming to a decision.

"All right, the fort it is. We've got to stop—all of us is plumb wore out. We won't linger here long in any case."

Torgul harrumphed.

They pulled the saddles from their horses and turned them loose to nibble the grass that grew inside the enclosure. Thurmond tied a rope back and forth across the gate to keep them from wandering out.

They would sleep for four hours. Pairs of sentries were assigned one-hour shifts, pairs because they could help keep each other awake. They would mount the parapet on the top of the wall and keep watch. With any luck, their pursuers would lose the trail in the dark. By the time they found it and resumed the chase, the Adventurers would have rested and moved on.

Thurmond and Torgul took the first watch, using a small hourglass to mark the time. Roscoe and Sarah were to take the second, but when the old Adventurer was roused to start his shift, he refused to have his watch-partner awakened.

"Let the girl sleep—she needs it. I'll be fine on my own, so I will."

Good to his word, Roscoe stood his watch alone and duly awakened the next pair of sentinels, a pair of Bart's mercenaries known as Toss-Pot and Goose. Then he rolled up in his cloak for some desperate rest.

Perhaps it was the secret flask of uisge that Toss-Pot kept hidden in the bottom of his saddlebag. Or it might have been that the weariness of the preceding days was just too great. Whatever the reason, both sentries were soon snoring at their posts.

Malachai's eyes were unexpressive, his countenance vague, as he surveyed the smoldering remains of his workshop. The destruction was total. His potions and compounds had burned very hot, so anything flammable was reduced to ash. Non-combustibles—metal, glass, crockery—were either melted into puddles or fused into unrecognizable lumps.

Even the psychic signatures of the intruders had burned away. Not that it mattered. He knew exactly who had invaded his cellars and destroyed his property.

He should, he knew, be furious, but he was involved at that moment in a matter of such greater import that the burning of his workshop seemed trivial. The old man—Roscoe, he was called—must bring the girl and the instrument safely to the Stone. Then she must employ it correctly. If all went according to plan, he would no longer require a workshop for the quickening of dead tissue.

Indeed, the fire was a useful thing, for it had swept away the accumulated baggage of the past. There were many side tunnels lined with iron-barred cells in which some of his early experiments had wailed, flopped, and beat the walls with their skulls. He should, he supposed, have disposed of them decades ago, but he had never quite gotten to it. Well, they were gone now.

There was, of course, the matter of the book. His personal notebook, bound in an enchanted hide that only an infernal flame could ignite. It would have unquestionably withstood the blaze, and yet it was gone. Taken by the intruders.

He would have it back. Let them first return home and employ the instrument. But afterwards—aye, afterwards—he would have it back, and they would learn the error of their thieving ways.

CHAPTER 33

SARAH WHISTLES A LIVELY TUNE

Shortly after sunrise, Torgul awoke with his bladder bursting. The early morning air was freezing, and he hated to leave the warmth of his cloak, but there was nothing else for it. He climbed to the top of the broken wall, intending to relieve himself over the edge, but he would have to endure a long wait before he could accomplish that task.

"Up! All of you up! Fire and damnation! You sons of dogs, get up! We're under attack!"

Torgul ran through the camp, screaming, exhorting, kicking the prone shapes huddled beneath cloaks and blankets.

In moments, the company was roused with bows strung, swords drawn, shields raised. They had slept in their armor, so it was only necessary to clap helmet on head.

A line of warriors was approaching on foot through the morning mist, two score or more armored swordsmen with large round-shields followed by spearmen with long lances. Behind them came a contingent of archers. A large group of horsemen sat to one side, ready to cut off any attempt to flee.

The Adventurers and mercenaries quickly took positions along the parapet, but their resistance must be futile. There were far too many attackers, and the fort's tumble-down walls would be but a momentary barrier. They would be pinned inside and slaughtered.

The attackers were, it appeared, unaware that they had been spotted by the men in the fort. They were still in open formation, their shields held low and to the side. They came on slowly, quietly, steadily.

Cob, Wat, and Tuck nocked arrows and stood ready. The fort's walls were still well beyond the range of the attackers' shortbows, but the advancing line was within reach of the Gascars' powerful weapons. Roscoe wound his heavy crossbow.

The first volley of arrows took their assailants by surprise. Two men died, shot in the chest and throat. A third dropped, an arrow's wooden shaft protruding from his thigh. Roscoe's bolt dumped one of the horsemen from his saddle. The remainder spurred their mounts to a different hummock that was out of crossbow range.

The oncoming warriors knew their business. Their shields immediately snapped into position, covering their bodies between the lower leg and the top of the head. As all wore iron helmets, they were all but invulnerable to arrow fire. Then they closed ranks and overlapped their shields, forming a solid wall behind which the spearmen and archers huddled. Then they dropped to one knee and waited.

Thurmond looked at Roscoe, who was rewinding his weapon.

"Why'd they stop? They should hurry forward—shouldn't they?"

"Aye, that's what I'd be doin' if I were them fellas'. I guess they was tryin' to sneak up on us, and we gave 'em a bit of a shock. But I don't guess they'll be waitin' there for long."

One of the horsemen, obviously a leader, now rode forward. With an elaborate flourish, he stuck the point of his long lance in the ground. Then he removed his helmet and hung it on his saddle. He retained his sword, but it remained in its scabbard.

He nudged his horse slowly forward, right hand raised, obviously wanting to parley. He passed the shield wall, drawing rein when within shouting distance.

Bart pulled Drax onto the dilapidated parapet.

"Who are they?"

"I don't know—I'll ask 'em."

Drax yelled something in the Vanarian tongue, and the rider shouted back.

Drax turned to Bart.

"Shit! This is bad—they're Snow Panthers."

"What do they want?"

"Dunno, I'll have to ask 'em."

There was another exchange in Vanarian.

"They don't want to kill us, they want to take us prisoner."

"Why?"

"Gimme a minute."

Another brief conversation ensued.

"He says they want to sell us to Grinder's brothers."

Sarah spoke up.

"I thought they were bitter enemies with the Blue Horse People. Why should they help them catch us?"

Drax shrugged.

"You don't understand these people. They hate each other, but they can forget about that when there's gold involved. It's the way things work here."

The young witch was confused.

"That's right, I don't understand. Why would they tell us what they have in mind for us? Now that we know, we'll never surrender."

"Girlie, the Snow Panthers ain't never been what you'd call smart."

Thurmond also had a question.

"Why didn't they come in here last night in the dark, when we were asleep? They could have taken us so easy."

"Dunno, I'll ask 'em."

Drax once again hollered over the wall and received an answer.

"He says they been trackin' us since yesterday. They knew we was here, but they didn't wanna come in the dark. This old fort is haunted, and they was afraid of the evil spirits. They waited for sunup when the spirits can't hurt 'em."

Sarah had an idea.

"They're afraid of spirits, that's good! Then maybe they'll believe this—tell them you have a witch with you who will summon spirits to carry their souls to Hell."

The scout looked at Bart, who gave a slight nod. He yelled over the wall, and the horseman yelled back.

"They don't believe me. They say they know who we are, the Blue Horses told 'em everything."

Sarah cast her eyes into the sky. Luckily, it was a clear morning, so she could see a long way. Finding what she was looking for, she began to delve in her pannier. Her voice was sharp as she spoke again to Drax.

"Tell them they must depart at once and leave us in peace, or I will call a troop of demons to eat their eyes and livers."

The scout again glanced at Bart, who again gave him a nod. There was more conversation across the wall.

"They ain't buyin' it, girlie. They say that any liver-eatin' that gets done, Grinder's kin will likely be the ones doin' it. They say if we don't come out now, they'll be comin' in."

Sarah took another quick look at the sky.

"Tell them they must leave at once—this is their last warning."

Drax again looked to Bart, but this time there was no nod. Sarah grew impatient.

"Tell them, Drax."

Bart gave his sister a hard look.

"I don't know what your game is, Sarah, but let me remind you that Drax is my man. You don't give him orders."

Sarah rolled her eyes in disbelief.

"I'm trying to save our lives, you great oaf, so kindly order *your man* to do as I told him."

Roscoe did not wait for Bart's reply.

"Do it, Drax."

The scout, still uncertain, continued to look at Bart. The knight's countenance flushed with hatred as he finally spoke the words.

"Do it."

Drax shouted at the rider, who yelled something in reply.

"They're callin' your bluff. They want us to leave our horses and all our armor and weapons inside. Then come out real slow with empty hands."

Sarah stamped her foot in frustration.

"Tell them they were warned, so what happens now is on their own heads."

Drax had no chance to relay these words, for the horseman abruptly rode off. Roscoe considered shooting him in the back, but held his hand—the man was still under the protection of a truce.

Then a horn blew, and the wall of shields resumed its advance.

The Gascars began a slow, deliberate fire, taking careful aim before each shot, doing their best to hit an exposed face or foot. One attacker was struck in the knee, but they suffered no other injury.

The shield wall grew closer and closer. Reaching the effective range of their bows—perhaps a hundred paces—their archers released a swarm of arrows at the fort. The steady rain of shafts forced the defenders to shelter behind the safety of the parapet while the shieldwall closed the remaining distance at a fast trot. The inevitable end was very near.

All the while, Sarah had continued to dig through her pannier. Finally, she found the object of her frantic search, the little whistle carved from the bone of a bird's leg.

She took another quick look at the sky, raised the whistle to her lips, and blew. The gulls that had been circling aimlessly overhead at once began to descend toward the ringfort. She blew again and again and yet again. More gulls appeared, joined now by terns, grebes, petrels, and gannets.

She blew again, drawing down egrets and pelicans, and swans. Herons, storks, and bitterns rose from the marsh in answer to her call. Partridge and grouse left their nests in the tall grass.

She blew and blew. Now came the kestrel, the merlin, the osprey, the kite. And finally, from the very top of the sky, huge black-beaked eagles.

Focusing her will to the utmost, Sarah swept her wand in a circle, pointing at both shieldwall and riders. Then she blew with all her might.

The birds fell upon the riders like the demons she had promised them. Curved beaks tore at their eyes, sharp talons ripped their faces. The horses, maddened by the savaging of their nostrils and ears, bucked and stampeded.

The riders, distracted by the flapping horror in their faces, lost their balance and fell to the ground. The birds continued to peck and scratch and gouge.

Sarah blew the whistle until it splintered into a hundred shards. That broke the enchantment, and the attack was abruptly ended. As quickly as they had come, the flock rose and began to disperse.

But the birds had served their purpose. The Snow Panther warriors, believing themselves to be the victims of infernal assault, broke ranks and bolted. Terrified, bloody, and in some cases blinded, they discarded their weapons and shields. The Adventurers could hear their frightened cries long after they had disappeared from view.

Roscoe was ecstatic.

"Now that was a fine a piece of work as ever I've seen, so it was. You've grown into a fine, cool-headed Adventurer in every way worthy of your black hat, just like I always said you was."

This was not exactly true. Roscoe had long resisted initiating a female into his organization.

Thurmond, equally pleased, put his arm around her shoulder.

"Roscoe's right, that was very well done. But how did you control that flock? How did you know what to do?"

"Well, I didn't really. Malachai said the whistle would summon birds and allow me to control them *somewhat*, but I had no idea what kind of birds would come or how many I'd get. I figured controlling them was a matter of focusing my will—that's how all magic really works. So I did my best. I'm shocked by how well it came off."

Drax was especially happy. The tribesmen in these parts had long memories. Had some old Snow Panther warrior recognized him as the youngster who had murdered their chief, his death would have been slow and hard.

Only Bart held back, peeved that Sarah had challenged his authority so successfully. She had called him an *oaf* and gotten away with it—at least for now.

CHAPTER 34

VARIOUS CONVERSATIONS

They camped in a small dell, well concealed by a thick growth of bracken. The wind died, and the night was not so cold. They were all still exhausted and looking forward to a good sleep. Unfortunately, they were not destined to enjoy the restful night they longed for.

Sometime before moonrise, the entire camp was aroused by hideous screaming. Everyone assumed Cob was again in the grip of night terrors, but this time it was Bart. He screeched and shrieked, wholly consumed by a dreadful dream and unresponsive to their attempts to wake him, at least until Drax emptied a water bag over his head. Even when restored to consciousness, Bart continued to be wracked by intense shuddering. When the others returned to their beds, he sat wrapped in a cloak, silent, befuddled.

When his fear at last abated and all seemed to be back to normal, the knight returned to his blankets, desperate for the rest he so badly needed. But no sooner had he fallen into slumber than his soul was again torn by harrowing visions. His gasping sobs woke the entire camp, and Drax was once more forced to employ a water bag.

Bart sat up for the rest of the night, while the others returned to their blankets to garner whatever sleep they could find.

In the morning, Sarah approached Thurmond as he was tightening the cinch strap of his saddle. She gave him a quizzical look.

"It seems the Tongue of Dreadful Dreams was taken from my pannier last night. Do you have any notion as to who might have done it?"

The young man's eyes widened in surprise.

"Really? I have no idea. Why would anyone want to steal something so revolting?"

"Maybe to hide beneath Sir Bartholomew's blankets."

Thurmond gave a slight shrug and a not-so-innocent smile.

"Not a bad idea, now that you mention it. Your brother is such a bloody bunghole—he deserves some torment. Don't you think?"

"No doubt, but just make sure that the Essence of Unendurable Stench remains where it is. Understood?"

"Not really. Why are you telling me this?"

Another day's ride brought them to the Psiss Marches. Though they remained unmolested by ghouls, vampyres, or wraiths, the passage was difficult. The air was bad, and several men developed a wheezing cough. A pack-horse bearing much of their provender floundered in a bog and was lost.

The nights were again the worst. It was difficult to find dry ground, and there always seemed to be a malevolent presence lingering just beyond their range of vision. The last stale loaves of fisherman bread grew green with mold, and their supply of salt fish was almost exhausted.

During these dismal days, Drax renewed his friendship with Cob. The two could often be seen riding together, engaged in quiet conversation. Most everyone assumed that Cob was again providing spiritual guidance to the formerly wayward scout.

Thurmond, however, observed these conversations with the darkest suspicions. Cob's religious fanaticism was well seasoned with madness. He was capable of anything if he believed it was the will of God. Wat and Tuck had promised to keep him out of trouble, but could they prevent his falling under the influence of that perfidious mercenary?

Drax might claim to be a changed man, to have renounced the treachery of his earlier life, but Thurmond did not believe it. It was just another ploy to regain their ill-deserved trust so he could betray them for his own gain. He should have been slain back at the beginning of their journey.

Thurmond wondered what Cob and Drax could be discussing at such great lengths. Not religion, surely. They occasionally broke out in peals of laughter. Certainly, the devout Cob would find nothing humorous in the workings of God. What was really going on between them? What were they plotting? Whatever it was, they needed watching.

By the time the party reached firm ground, everyone was filthy, hungry, and worn thin. But now the ride became more pleasant. The grey marshland and stinking bogs gave way to grassy hillsides and evergreens. Wildflowers sprinkled the meadows, and birds made melody all through the night.

They made better time through the open, gentle countryside. Though they kept a wary eye, no horse-riding savages came pounding over the horizon, no flesh-rending demons came screaming out of the night. Indeed, their only significant problem was an unfortunate encounter with a flock of carnivorous sheep.

Accordingly, the Adventurers' mood began to lighten. Sarah stopped wearing her helmet and let her long brown hair cascade across her shoulders. The mercenaries sang their nasty songs as they rode at the rear of the party. Even the horses seemed happier, putting a bit more prance in their step.

Only Torgul remained glum. He had been out of sorts since he lost his axe and cropped his beard with his scramasax. His comrades at first attempted to make light of his plight, but his anguish was too genuine, too profound.

Finally, Thurmond could stand it no longer. He reined his horse next to Torgul's, and blurted out what was on his mind.

"Hey, Torgul—you've been in an ill-humor for days now. I've watched you pulling on your beard like you're trying to stretch it longer. Come on! We all ran away in that hellish tunnel, even Roscoe. We had no chance against that magic. You're not disgraced, and your beard will grow back. Let it go!"

Torgul grumbled something that sounded like *mmdrrfkrr*. Encouraged by even this sullen response, Thurmond endeavored to keep the conversation going.

"What did you say? That was the dwarfish tongue, wasn't it? What did it mean?"

"It means I just want to be let be. I don't feel like havin' a chat right now."

But the young man was determined to draw his friend from his funk.

"Nay, that's not what it meant. What does it really mean?"

Torgul threw him a weary look.

"If you gotta know, it was a dwarven curse word."

This excited Thurmond. Exotic curse words were always intriguing.

"Meaning what? I've hardly ever heard you speak dwarven. You have to tell me what you said."

"It doesn't translate well."

"Tell me anyway."

Torgul shrugged in resignation—there would be no escape from his friend's nonsensical questions.

"It means *three hundred hairy bears*."

Thurmond started to laugh.

"Three hundred hairy bears? That's what dwarves say when they stub their toes?"

"Sometimes."

That line of conversation exhausted, Thurmond tried a different tack.

"You never say much about your home or family, Torgul. Why is that?"

"Some things is better left unsaid."

"Do you ever miss them?"

"Not much, but sometimes I do miss good, solid dwarven food. Stuff that really gives your jaws a workout. Human food is too easy, and it's got too much flavor."

"Your mother is a good cook?"

Torgul stiffened and his eyes grew grim.

"We'll not be discussin' her or any member of my family, understand? There's too much hard feelin' between me and them."

Knowing he had blundered, Thurmond made a quick verbal retreat.

"My apologies, Torgul, I meant no offense."

After a few moments of silence, he attempted to renew their conversation.

"I know you come from Spear Mountain, but you've never said where that is exactly."

Still annoyed by the reference to his family, Torgul was in no mood for further chatter. His reply was gruff.

"Nor will I ever. You're my sworn comrade, you've saved my skin just as I've saved yours, but no human—not you nor Roscoe nor nobody—can ever learn the whereabouts of my homeland."

Thurmond was shocked by the vehemence of his friend's words.

"Why is that?"

"Us dwarves learned centuries ago that our survival depends on keepin' apart from humans."

The young man was confused.

"But you're not like that. You live with us."

"That's my problem. I'm different."

With that, Torgul urged his mount forward, ending the discourse. Thurmond heard him mutter one final word.

"*Mmdrrfkrr.*"

Frustrated and a little hurt, Thurmond reined back next to Sarah, who had been observing their exchange. She, too, was concerned about Torgul's state of mind.

"How's he doing?"

Thurmond cast his eyes skyward as if seeking divine intervention.

"Grumpy."

She nodded.

"I guess a human can never comprehend the relationship of a dwarf to his beard."

They rode along, enjoying the warm afternoon sun. After so many days of danger and discomfort, it was good to relax a bit and engage in conversation. Thurmond grew thoughtful.

"I woke up for a while last night. While I was lying there trying to go back to sleep, I had the strangest idea."

Sarah's response was playful.

"An idea? Really? You? First time for everything, I guess."

She expected some witty repost, but the young man grew serious.

"It seems like things are changing around us."

"Changing how? And even if they are, what's so strange about it?"

"I guess...I mean… things aren't like they used to be."

"What does that mean? Do you think the sky is turning green?"

"When I was growing up, I was always told that the world is like it is because that's how it has to be, so nothing can ever really change."

"You're confusing me, Thurmond. What are you saying?"

"Well, here we are—a runaway apprentice, a girl, a dwarf, and an old fruit vendor—we're riding halfway across the world, fighting monsters, and trying to save our city from a demon. Doesn't that seem wrong?"

"Wrong how?"

"You know the old stories. It's a job some great hero should be doing. Or some powerful noble. Or at least some valiant knight. It shouldn't be up to us to do these things. Something is different when important quests are left to people like us."

He paused, trying to formulate his thoughts.

"Things aren't like they were. I think the world is changing. Maybe the way people see things is changing."

"I dunno, Thurmond. I think maybe the real change has been in you. You grew up believing all those old legends, but they were never true."

Thurmond let his thoughts wander for a while, and then recalled another question he had been meaning to address.

"Hey, Sarah, it must have been a shock to you to find out Bart was alive. I mean, we thought he'd been killed by the goblins. How do you feel about that?"

"How do you think I feel? He's a selfish, mean-tempered, ill-mannered bully. But he's still my half-brother, and we grew up in the same household, so my feelings are complicated. I despise him, but I still don't wish him dead."

"That's not what I meant. He's alive, and that changes everything for you. You were in line to inherit your father's estate, maybe even his titles. But now that he's back, everything goes to him."

This was true. Sarah's father, Lord Percy Staynes, was a nobleman of considerable wealth. Although Sarah was the illegitimate issue of his dalliance with his chamber maid, Lord Percy formally recognized her as his daughter. With Bart dead, it was conceivable that she could fall heir to his name and property. With Bart alive, she would get nothing.

Sarah cocked her head to one side.

"It's funny, you know—when I met you two years ago, I really loved the thought of being Lady Sarah. I grew up not knowing who I was. I wasn't a servant, but I was certainly not one of the family. I needed something definite."

"From what you've told me, you were treated far better than Lord Percy treated Bart."

"That's true. I guess I was kind of pampered. But still, I never felt like I belonged anywhere. Having a title would have given me a definite place in the world."

This was a sensitive topic. Sarah's craving for social position had at one point come close to destroying their friendship with Roscoe. Thurmond knew he had to tread lightly.

"But you seemed to have changed."

"I guess I have. I always assumed that once I knew my place in things, I'd know what I should be doing, that I wouldn't always be struggling to figure things out. Well, being accepted as an Adventurer gave me that place, but I'm still often confused."

"I dunno, Sarah, it seems to me like you can figure things pretty good."

"Well, how about your own life? You really wanted a black hat. Now that you've got it, do you have all the answers?"

"I never looked at it quite that way. I see what you mean, though. I always thought I'd feel a lot more confident, that I'd know how to handle problems. But I still have to rely on Roscoe to make most of the decisions."

"That's exactly what I'm talking about. Being an Adventurer or a noble doesn't make you any smarter or wiser or braver. You're still just yourself underneath."

"You don't care about being Lady Sarah anymore?"

"Not so much. Do you still like being an Adventurer?"

"I do, but it's a lot different than I expected."

Sarah reached over and punched him in the arm. The links of his mailshirt hurt her knuckles.

"We better stick close together, Thurmond. It's going to take us a long time to get smarter and wiser and braver."

CHAPTER 35

INCIDENT AT THE BLIND PIG

The track climbed to a large plateau dotted with prosperous farmsteads with broad fields and verdant pastures. Men were busy everywhere with plow and harrow. Their wives and children walked behind them, casting seeds.

Eager for news of the outside world, the farm-folk welcomed the Adventurers. Friendly farmwives sold them soft cheeses, fresh meat, newly-baked bread, and wonderful ales made from their homegrown barley. Clean stone barns provided comfortable nighttime accommodations.

They came at last to a town—a real town, not just a cluster of huts. A town with merchants, craftsmen, and, best of all, an inn.

The Blind Pig was by no means a regal inn. It boasted no individual chambers, only a large communal sleeping loft, but the food was plentiful and tasty, and the bedding acceptably clean.

The Pig did have one unique feature, a bath house. This was a simple shed in which a large brick tub was fed by an adjacent hot spring. The bath was available to all the inn's guests free of charge.

Bathing was a common practice in the North, especially during the bitter winter months. In the more temperate climate around Gorgonholm, it had never caught on. Thurmond had grown up hating baths. His mother had called it a filthy and immoral practice that was guaranteed to bring disease.

But Sarah had taught him otherwise. She had a large copper tub in her chamber at home, a most rare and exotic item left behind by the former occupant. It had taken quite a bit of convincing, but she had eventually coaxed him into giving it a try.

All his childhood baths had been in a pond or stream, where he scrubbed himself with leaves pulled from a nearby bush. They had served a single purpose—to remove some offensive smell or foul substance from his body. Often he had not even bothered to remove all of his clothes.

Sarah's tub offered an entirely different experience. Surrounded by candles, with steaming hot water up to his chin, he would enter a dreamy euphoric state closely resembling the effect produced by Florio's addleberry wine.

After the long, painful ride, he was quite eager to enjoy the tub at The Blind Pig. He tried his best to get Sarah to come with him, but she begged off. She could be so unreasonable at times. But no matter. He would go by himself.

After the evening meal, a tankard of ale in hand, he set off for the bathhouse. The water was almost too hot, but he finally managed to enter the tub and stretch out. He closed his eyes and relaxed. The cool night air streaming in through the open door felt good on his exposed face and shoulders.

He heard the scrape of the footstep coming from the direction of the door. Sarah! She had decided to join him after all.

Without opening his eyes, he reached behind him for his tankard and was surprised when a heavy boot came down on his hand, trapping it against the bricks. He looked up, astounded, to find himself staring into the malevolent face of Drax. The scout held a crossbow aimed squarely at his chest.

Drax leered wickedly.

"Seems just like before, don't it?"

Thurmond was too startled to reply, so Drax continued, eager to gloat.

"Bart wanted you for himself, but I been such a good scout, I convinced him I was entitled to a little bit of fun. So he gave you to me."

Thurmond finally found his tongue.

"Your arm—I thought you couldn't lift your arm."

Drax grinned.

"That's right—that's exactly right—I couldn't. But then back in that fisherman village I stole those healin' potions outta the witch's basket. Been drinkin' just a little every night so it wouldn't put me to sleep like it did you and the others. And whadda you know? Little by little, my arm come back. I can move it real good now."

"What do you want, Drax?"

"I'm gonna kill you, you little piece of shit. You was all set to murder me when I was a helpless cripple. Tell me, boy, how's it feel to be helpless and lookin' at death?"

Thurmond fought to subdue the panic that was surging through his body. His voice with tight.

"What did you expect? You tried to murder me before."

"Maybe so, but that time don't count 'cause it was just business. This here is strictly personal."

Just as his fingers began to tighten on the crossbow's trigger, the weapon was suddenly dashed from his hand. Cob stood beside Drax, holding a shortsword. Wat and Tuck glided in behind him.

Now it was Drax's turn to be surprised.

"Cob—whadda you doin'? You're supposed to be keepin' watch, not messin' up the plan. What's the matter with you?"

Drax reached for the fallen bow, but the archer kicked it away.

"You ain't gonna kill him, Drax. You reach for that bow, and it'll be the last thing you do."

The scout's voice was tight with rage and frustration.

"You dolt—the kid's a heathen. He hobnobs with witches and dwarves. You said you'd help me kill him."

"I was lyin'. That's a terrible bad sin, but not when you're talkin' to a dirty snake like you."

While they argued, Thurmond scrambled from the tub, pulled on his clothes and boots, then buckled his swordbelt around his hips. Ever since his near-fatal encounter with the charcoal burner, he always kept his sword nearby.

Dressed and armed, he felt much surer of himself. He drew his weapon.

"Stand back, Cob. Drax and I will settle this by ourselves—fair fight."

Drax snarled.

"I ain't got no sword. I got nothin' but my little belt knife. What kinda fair fight is that?"

Before the young man could respond, Wat dropped his shortsword at Drax's feet.

"Here, Drax, you're welcome to borrow mine."

Thurmond's voice was hard.

"Pick it up, Drax. It's time to settle up."

Then he shot a look at Wat.

"Whatever happens, don't interfere. This is between him and me."

Drax weighed the odds carefully. Thurmond was younger and stronger, but he was more experienced and far more cagey. Moreover, he was entirely unencumbered by the concept of fighting fair, a foolish ideal that might hamper his naïve young adversary. The shortsword would be light, fast, and much more suitable to the limited space of the bathhouse. Neither of them wore armor, so Thurmond's heavy broadsword would offer no advantage.

With the speed of a striking snake, Drax scooped up Wat's blade with his right hand and a small, three-legged stool with the left. Now he had a shield of sorts. With the odds on his side, he sneered.

"Come on, you egg, let's dance."

"I'm ready, you shaggy-eared scum."

For all his bluster, Thurmond knew he would have to be very careful. Drax' advantages were not lost upon him. If his blade were to lodge in the soft wood of the stool, the weapon could be wrenched from his grasp. If that happened, he could only pray that the three archers would intervene.

Drax was on him in an eye-blink, getting in close with the shorter weapon, slashing at his throat, his belly, his face. Thurmond was able to parry the first two blows with the flat of his sword. He jumped back from the third, but the tip of the shortsword opened a shallow wound along the line of his jaw.

Thurmond punched the scout's chest with his pommel, knocking him back a step, then cut down hard at the base of his neck. Drax side-stepped, then moved in again before his opponent could throw another blow.

They slammed together, chest to chest, Drax endeavoring to work his point into stabbing position. Thurmond again shifted back, striving for the space to bring his longer weapon into play. His legs struck the brick lip of the bathtub. He could retreat no further.

Drax pushed in again, still trying for the stab. In desperation, Thurmond dropped his blade and grasped his adversary's sword arm while Drax attempted to brain him with the stool. They grappled awkwardly against the edge of the tub, shoving, fumbling, losing their balance, until with a final stumbling lurch, Drax propelled Thurmond backward into the water.

He landed on his back with Drax on top of him. Both were entirely submerged in the near-scalding bath. With his right hand, the scout sought to draw his belt knife while he drove his left forearm into the young man's throat, pinning him against the tub's brick-lined bottom.

Thurmond's dagger, worn stylishly across the small of his back, was out of reach. He struggled desperately to dislodge the arm from his throat, but Drax's grip was too strong. Finally, gathering his legs beneath him, he stood, lifting both of them from beneath the water, then threw himself forward so they fell once again, but this time with Thurmond on top.

Drax's back smashed against the hard, sharp bricks of the bathtub's rim. Something inside him broke with a sickening *crack*. He groaned and slipped once more beneath the surface. Bubbles gushed from his open mouth.

Thurmond retrieved Wat's shortsword from the tub's floor, then reaching down, pulled Drax's head from the water by his hair. The scout's eyes were wild with terror. He coughed and coughed, while water ran from his mouth and nose. When he at last regained his breath, Thurmond placed the point of the sword against his throat.

"Can you think of any reason why I shouldn't finish you off right now?"

Drax was not listening. He began waving his arms in a frantic motion as if attempting to fly. When he finally spoke, he seemed to be talking to himself.

"Can't move my legs—can't even feel 'em. I can move my arms, but not my legs. Ohhhh—I'm bad hurt. What's gonna happen to me now? What'll I do?"

Thurmond had, in the past, given the mercy blow to a badly wounded opponent, but something now kept him from killing this broken, miserable, luckless man. Drax would no doubt die from his injury—ruptured spines were notoriously fatal—so he left him there to live or die as Lady Fortune would have it.

The young Adventurer addressed the three archers, who stood by the door with drawn weapons. He had no doubt they would gladly slay Drax for him.

"I want to thank you—you men saved my life...."

He faltered, unsure what to say, especially to Cob for whom he had always felt a deep dislike. Wat grinned at Thurmond's uneasiness.

"Aw hell, we saw Drax was a bad one right from the start. So Cob decides to make friends with him to see what he was up to. Tonight he tells us about Bart's plan and how Drax gets to be the one to deal with you."

"What's Bart's plan?"

At that moment, a chorus of shouts and screams, accompanied by the clang of steel on steel, erupted from the inn.

CHAPTER 36

BETRAYED IN DEEPEST CONSEQUENCE

The Blind Pig's common room resembled the streets of Gorgonholm after a full-scale riot. The floor was strewn with overturned furniture, shattered crockery, and lots and lots of blood. The kindly innkeeper and his family crouched in an alcove beneath the stairs to the loft. Two dead bodies lay face down on the floor. Five of Bart's mercenaries, three of them nursing bloody wounds, sat on the floor against the back wall.

Sir Bartholomew Staynes stood unarmed and bare-headed in the center of the room. Next to him stood Torgul, his left arm dripping blood, his right hand holding a gore-bespattered scramasax. Roscoe, sword in hand, stood on Bart's opposite side, where he could also keep an eye on the men against the wall.

The old Adventurer glanced over as Thurmond and the Gascars charged into the room.

"Well now, there you are. About time you arrived. We could've used you a moment ago, and that's a fact."

"What went on here, Roscoe?"

He nodded toward Bart.

"Seems our friend here blames us for himself bein' an incompetent oaf. Seems he wants to kill me and Sarah and you for him not bein' able to lead his own men in a proper fashion. Maybe there's other reasons, but it's all a lot of childish blather, whatever it may be."

"He attacked you?"

"That he did. We was sittin' here, enjoyin' a mug of ale after that roast beef dinner, havin' ourselves a fine time, when these here miscreants crept up and looked to stick us in the back with knives. They was thinkin' we'd be in our cups and unable to defend ourselves, but we showed 'em different."

Hearing this, Thurmond could barely keep himself from striking Bart dead.

"Drax attacked me in the bath! That's where I've been—fighting him off. The Gascars say they've been planning this all along."

"So they have, laddie, so they have. But Wat over there tipped us off, so they didn't take us unaware. Sir Bartholomew here ain't as smart as he thinks."

Thurmond grimaced.

"I wish somebody'd told me. Drax took me by surprise. Why didn't you warn me, Wat?"

"No time—it all happened pretty fast."

Roscoe concurred.

"He's right, boyo. Wat slipped me word just before they made their move on us, then him and Wat and Cob went off to warn you. So old Drax turned out to be ever' bit as bad as you said he was. Did you finish him?"

"He drank Sarah's healing potions, so he wasn't a cripple anymore—but he is now. I left him with a broken back. He can't move his legs. Hey!— where's Sarah?"

Roscoe pointed to one of the dead mercenaries with the tip of his sword.

"One of them fellas threw somethin', a tankard, I think it was. She got hit in the head, but she'll be all right. She's up in the loft, puttin' a bandage 'round her brow."

Thurmond rose, intending to ascend to the loft, but at that moment, Sarah climbed down the ladder and joined her companions. A linen bandage tied around her head was stained with a spot of blood. Thurmond took her hand.

"Roscoe tells me you're all right."

"I'll live—just a bump on the head."

"You're sure?"

"I'm fine. Now go keep an eye on my brother so I can tend to Torgul. He's the one that got hurt."

The dwarf had sustained a bad cut on his left arm, which continued to drip blood. While Sarah bound Torgul's wound, Thurmond drew his sword and laid the razor-sharp edge against Bart's neck.

"Drax said you *gave* me to him, sir knight. What do you have to say about that?"

When Bart failed to reply, Thurmond almost chuckled.

"That's what I thought. There's not a lot you can say, is there, sir knight?"

Roscoe addressed Bart, his voice utterly cold.

"Sir Bartholomew, I accuse you of bein' a foul oath-breaker and a betrayer, a false knight and a blackguard. In fact, I suspect you was never a true knight at all, just a mountebank paradin' around in a white belt and gold chain posin' as one."

"I can forgive your men. They're just hired killers who took your money and followed your orders, but you are bound by a code that you have most grievously violated. So I will ask you one question—how would you like to die? By the blade or by the rope? That's the only choice you have."

Bart's mouth fell open. He stared into Roscoe's eyes without comprehension, as if those fatal words had been spoken in a foreign tongue. When he said nothing, the old Adventurer asked again.

"I'll ask you only one more time, sir knight—how would you like to die? Speak up now or your head comes off right here."

It was Sarah who finally resolved the issue.

"Nay, Roscoe, nay. Slay him not. Loathsome as he is, Bart is still my brother—well, my half-brother anyway—so we are bound in blood. Ask whatever you want of me in exchange, but spare his life, please."

Thurmond's retort was angry.

"You want us to spare this treacherous slug, even after he tried to kill Roscoe and Torgul? After he sent Drax to kill me?"

Sarah was suffused with conflicting emotions.

"Nay—well, aye—but nay, not really. Oh, Thurmond, I'm all mixed up.

I just know that he's my brother even if he's vile in every respect. I beg you, do not slay him."

Roscoe gave Sarah a long, sorrowful look.

"Remember, lassie, your brother here was out to kill you, too, so he was. He wasn't about to show you no mercy. And if we let him go, you can bet your last silver penny that he'll be back lookin' for revenge when you least expect it. He ain't gonna be grateful to you, not one bit. He'll blame you for the shame he's feelin' right at this very moment."

Roscoe had the right of it. Bart would have liked nothing better than to throttle Sarah on the spot. Never had he hated anyone so much, not the upstart stable boy or the old Adventurer, not even his father.

Sarah remained unmoved.

"I understand what you're saying, Roscoe, and I don't doubt you're right. But such reasons really do not matter. Please spare my brother's life."

The dwarf finally settled the question.

"God's bloody bladder, Roscoe, let 'im go. The world's full of double-dealin' knights. What difference can one more make? He ain't no worse than any of his kind."

So Bart was allowed to live, at least for the time being.

A group of armed citizens arrived under the command of a constable. The perfidious mercenaries, Bart included, were taken to a stone barn, where they would be held until judgment could be passed by the local baron. Their guilt being evident, they faced whipping, mutilation, perhaps hanging.

Men were sent to bring Drax from the bathhouse, but the maimed scout was not to be found. Drag marks in the dirt suggested that he had pulled himself from the tub and into a nearby farm field. There they lost him, but the search would continue after daylight the next day.

The old Adventurer and the constable held a brief, private discussion. It was agreed that Bart and his men would forfeit all possessions of value—all money, armor, weapons, horses, saddles and bridles, tools, cooking gear, bedrolls and cloaks. All extra hats, boots, and clothing. The prisoners were left, in the end, with nothing but the thin clothes on their backs.

This booty was divided equally between Roscoe and the constable, though the former immediately awarded his share, along with an additional sum of gold, to the traumatized innkeeper. It was important to keep him in good spirits, as he would serve as the primary witness in the upcoming legal proceedings.

The constable had at first insisted that the Adventurers be detained to stand before the baron, but another handful of gold soon convinced him that their presence was unnecessary. They could leave in the morning.

Later, as Thurmond and Sarah lay wrapped in each other's arms beneath a counterpane, she related her version of the night's events.

"I got knocked flat right at the start, so I didn't see much. Roscoe signaled me to get ready, that there was going to be trouble. I was going to throw a sleep spell, but then something struck my head. I was so stunned, I missed most of it."

"They thought they were going to take us by surprise, but Roscoe knew what was coming. So it was us who surprised them. Torgul fought like a demon. He killed two of Bart's men right off, and that took the spirit out of the rest of them. When Roscoe waded into them with his big sword, they started throwing down their weapons and begging for mercy."

Thurmond could feel her trembling, still upset by the bloody onslaught. He spoke quietly.

"What about Bart? What was his part in all this?"

"He just stood to one side—didn't even draw his sword. When he saw how things were going, he unbuckled his swordbelt and let it drop to the ground."

Thurmond growled softly.

"Coward."

Sarah shrugged.

"He's not much of a fighter, so it would have been suicide to cross blades with Roscoe. Surrendering was his best option."

Thurmond found her rationale distressing.

"But he's a knight! Has he no sense of honor?"

"None at all. Not one bit. I grew up with him, so I've known what he was like since he was a little boy. He's selfish, spiteful, envious, petty, greedy—anything but honorable."

"And I'll tell you something else—all that talk about the nobility being bound by a code of honor? It's all just crap. When I was a girl, I saw lots of nobles. I witnessed how they treat people. Most of them are just as bad as Bart, some of them are worse."

Thurmond stroked her hair.

"You used to want to be one of 'em."

"Let's just say I've seen the error of my ways. Anyway, Bart's childish and vain, but he isn't the person who really offends me."

"Who is it then?"

"It's those two men, the ones I saved from certain death, the one with the broken leg and the other with the head wound. They were right in there with the rest of them, looking to kill us. How could they do such a thing?"

"They're mercenaries, loyal only to whoever gives 'em gold. You can't expect anything else from men like them."

"Well, at least Adventurers aren't like that. They stick by one another."

"Some of them do, Sarah. I'm not sure they're all as loyal as Roscoe and Torgul."

Sarah snuggled against him.

"At least we have each other. The only reason we're still alive is that we can trust one another."

"You're right! Roscoe's always asking me what I learned from this or that. What you just said—that we have to be true to each other—that's the most important lesson of 'em all. But you have to learn that lesson in your own way. Nobody can just tell it to you."

Thurmond had a random thought.

"Hey, I just remembered, did you ever look in your basket? Was Drax telling the truth about stealing the healing potions?"

"Aye, he did indeed. He took them all but left the box they were packed in, so I didn't notice they were gone. He even put rocks inside so it would weigh the same."

"But didn't you say that one of the potions was really a deadly poison? Why didn't it kill him?"

"That's what Malachai told me, but maybe he was lying. I have no idea."

She poked him playfully in the ribs, hoping to lighten the mood. The mention of Drax reminded her of something.

"There's something I just have to ask you about. Wat told me that just before you and Drax fought it out, you called him a shaggy-eared scum. What's that supposed to mean?"

"I dunno, it's just what came out. He called me something first, and it was the only thing I could think of to say."

"What did he call you?"

"An egg, he called me an egg."

"An egg? Why an egg? Is that an insult?"

"I guess. I was so angry right then, anything would have pissed me off. So egg was quite sufficient. Didn't you ever notice Drax's ears?"

"God forefend, nay. I always found him filthy and repulsive. Why would I look at his ears? What was wrong with them?"

"They had black hairs growing out of them. Lots of old people get hairy ears, but his were especially so."

"Ugh, I don't ever want to see hair growing out of your ears—got that?"

"I'll do my best."

CHAPTER 37
FLORIO'S GRAVE MISTAKE

T he Black Stone awoke and licked its lithic chops in greedy anticipation. The celestial influences had come right once again, shifting from the sign of the Fecund Mule to that of the Rampant Weasel. The terrible planet Bale was in conjunction with Thanos, the realm of the cursed dead.

Now, its vigor and influence restored, it could afford to act with greater deliberation, and it craved a banquet instead of a nibble. There would be no more inane street brawls or casual highway murders. Let rapport replace discord. Let the humans join into vast armies, united in their hatred of each other. As they destroyed themselves, the Stone would glut its insatiable appetite for agony and death, supping on misery just as a hungry schoolboy might gobble his plum pudding.

The sun was rising over the city when Asmodeus entered his divinatorium, a small, hexagonal chamber devoted to the seeing of far off things or future events. Its furnishings were sparse—a padded stool, a carved wooden cabinet, and a bronze table cast in the likeness of a raptor's taloned foot and leg. A brace of lamps burned atop the cabinet, their light reflecting in a great sphere of flawless crystal resting on the table's small, square top.

He unlocked the cabinet with the key he wore as a ring and drew forth a three-legged brazier, which he place on the cabinet's top. A single snap of his fingers ignited the charcoal in the brazier's bowl, and it began to burn a dull red. From his pocket, he withdrew a cube of some waxy substance and set it on the smoldering coals. The room at once filled with a thick, sweet smoke.

The wizard took several deep breaths, holding the smoke in his lungs until he felt its magic surging in his veins. He then sat on the stool, folded his hands in his lap, and gazed intently into the crystal sphere. As the smoke took control of his mind and body, the walls around him faded into darkness, leaving only the bright, round light of the sphere. Pictures began to form within it—a thin, crooked road running along a mountainside, then a second, wider road passing through grass-covered hills and tracts of forest. He saw plodding pilgrims and shuffling wayfarers, creaking farm carts, and slinking reprobates.

He did not see the party he was looking for.

Things had not been going his way. During the past two weeks, the stars had worked for him, permitting his ethereal helpers to impede the schemes of the Keltin high king. But as the constellations moved across the sky, the might of the Black Stone was again growing. Its dread authority had struck the wizard's minions with terror, causing them to abandon their tasks and flee back to the empty plane from which they had been summoned.

Thus, there would be no more burning of boats nor broken ropes, no more poisoned words poured into the ear of the Ard Righ, warning of his brother's machinations. The Keltin horde could now advance without hindrance. If the Adventurers did not fetch Malachai's instrument soon, they would be well advised not to return at all.

His mind was deeply fogged from frequent exposure to the magical smoke. He disliked the feeling, but his growing anxiety compelled him to gaze often into the crystal sphere. Always, he searched the road north, and this time, to his immense relief, he spied a party of eight riders heading south along the winding track known as the Serpent's Back.

The wizard strained his will to focus his vision, and for a moment, he saw them clearly—a big man on a black stallion, a dwarf, the girl, the others. They should be back in a day and a half. He could only hope they would be in time.

Lord Ubo Futz smiled in satisfaction as he watched the line of men advance through the trees. It was still early morning, so they were concealed by a lingering ground fog. These were all experienced woodsmen, so their progress was silent and swift. Almost three hundred of them—far more than required for the immediate job, but today would be good training for the harder objectives soon to come.

Reaching the edge of the woods, the line paused as instructed. Ubo urged his mount forward—he and his bodyguard were the only ones on horseback—until he, too, reached the tree line.

It was just as his scouts had reported—a small towerhouse and a tiny village. Peasants going about their ordinary tasks. No sign of soldiers. Perfect. He had, as expected, taken them entirely by surprise. One quick swoop and it would all be over.

Lord Ubo smiled again—that made two smiles in one day. Such unrestrained jocularity was unusual for him, but it felt good to indulge a bit, for this was a most singular day. He had seized the Gray Friars' monastery by stealth and guile. Today, like a true warrior, he would triumph by force of arms. It was to be but the first step in a long, long chain of victories soon to come.

Ubo had not tasted battle for many years, since he was a young man called up for duty by his feudal overlord. As the insignificant son of a very minor noble, he had never been given the chance to demonstrate his true prowess or achieve great glory. That would change now.

He pushed his horse through the line of woodsmen and proceeded across the large beanfield separating the village from the wood. His company of bodyguards followed. They, like Lord Ubo, were dressed in leather and mail, their heads protected by iron helmets. All were well armed with swords, spears, and crossbows.

These were a recent and most welcome addition to his forces—a dozen

Royal Road Guards who had abandoned their duties and ridden though his gates to offer their services. Tough, ruthless soldiers, hardened by life in the saddle and well-schooled in no-quarter combat with desperate brigands.

He had immediately appointed them as his personal guard and named their leader, an ugly, one-eye scoundrel named Pons, to be his new sergeant-at-arms. Had he possessed a hundred such men, he would have led his army against Gorgonholm that very day.

The woodsmen came behind the guard. They wore no armor and carried improvised weapons—splitting axes, crude spears, and small hunting bows. Some bore only knives or wooden clubs. No matter, there would be no real fighting.

Though he knew nothing of the power of the stars, Ubo could feel the return of the Stone's awesome strength, making him supremely confident in his own ability. His mind was clear, and his body pulsed with energy. His soul burned for the attainments fated to be his.

Others seemed to be feeling it too, for in the last few days, the previous trickle of new devotees had once more swelled to a steady stream. Not so many, mayhap, as at the very beginning of his enterprise, but enough to restore his faith in his destiny.

The villagers spotted the intruders as soon as they moved into the open. A horn began to blow. Men and women dropped their tools, snatched up their children, and fled to the towerhouse. A few, too far afield to reach that edifice in time, ran as fast as they could to the shelter of adjacent woods.

Ubo allowed himself to laugh. There was no place for them to run to. Any of these peasant bastards lucky enough to survive would soon be cowering with heads hung low, begging to be accepted into his host of loyal followers.

As he approached the tower, a high-pitched voice came from a window somewhere near its top.

"Go no further or I shall fire. State your business."

He ignored the voice and rode forward, his guards closing in tight on both sides. It had to be the elf he had been told about. He need only make a convincing demonstration of his strength and the spindly creature would be eager to capitulate.

Without warning, a heavy dart the length of a man's arm struck a guardsman in the chest, lifted him from his saddle, and sent him flying backward.

At that same moment, bowmen rose from the parapet on the tower's roof and launched a volley of arrows. The first struck Ubo but failed to penetrate his heavy, reinforced mail. A guardsman was hit in the shoulder, a horse in the flank.

This was not supposed to happen! What was the matter with these people? Did they not realize the hopelessness of their situation? Did they not recognize his natural superiority? His military acumen?

Another salvo of arrows. Another horse was hit and whinnied in agony. A woodsman went down, shot in the stomach. The guardsmen wheeled about in confusion as they sought to control their frightened steeds.

Lord Ubo was not about to endure such insolence, such wanton disrespect for his position. If the degraded villains in the tower refused to recognize his authority, he would simply leave them to their wretchedness. He turned his horse abruptly and dug his spurs into its flanks, forcing it back through the line of woodsmen. He spurred again, sending his mount galloping into the cover of the trees.

His guardsmen were happy to follow his example. They had no desire to storm a fortified tower. The woodsmen, abandoned by their leader, grabbed their wounded comrade and melted back into the woods as fast as they were able.

Inside the tower, there was much cheering and slapping of backs. The villagers were delirious with joy. Fat Annie broached a cask of ale and began filling cups to toast the elf's military genius. Others began to belt out a special song in his honor.

On the roof, Bodo was similarly praised for building the wonderful ballista that had knocked the raider so smartly from his horse. The three-man crew lifted the one-legged carpenter onto their shoulders and paraded around the war engine in a transport of delight. It was called *Mother* in honor of Bodo's wife, Bess.

This was the second time Florio had saved the villagers from marauders. The first battle had taken place six months prior when a maniac with an especial grudge against the Adventurers had attempted to seize the tower in their absence. That fight had been a much bloodier affair, with the villagers suffering numerous dead and wounded. Nonetheless, he had held off the attackers until the returning Adventurers joined him in driving them away.

Florio hated war, he found it stupid, destructive, pointless. He was terribly afraid of being killed or wounded and grieved sorely when he saw his villagers slain. Yet he had to admit, he felt a profound degree of satisfaction in defending Grimsgard in Roscoe's name.

The elf had long ago left his father's household, and the old Adventurer had been the only human willing to offer him a position. He felt respected here, appreciated, perhaps even liked. Such things were worth defending.

Still, as he looked down on the motionless body on the ground below, he was filled with apprehension. He feared that the villagers' celebration was premature, that their elation was based on a serious misunderstanding of circumstances.

As he watched the attackers approaching, he had assumed they were Keltins. This conjecture was not unreasonable. He had, for weeks, been listening to the pounding of Keltin drums and knew that he could expect visitors from across the river.

During that time, Florio had done his utmost to prepare for an attack. Each man or woman was set to a specific task. Weapons and armor were readied. During the previous battle, such items had been almost nonexistent, but Roscoe had, as a precaution, brought in an adequate supply of basic wargear. Food and drink had been gathered and stored against a siege.

But despite the preparations, he expected to die, for the ferocity of the Keltin warrior was legendary. They would come in thousands to swarm over the tiny village of Grimsgard and its little tower. It was odd, therefore, that the attackers had been so few in number. It was even more peculiar that such vaunted warriors could be driven away so easily.

When it seemed safe to do so, he ordered the tower's door unbarred. When no danger presented itself, he stepped cautiously into the open and examined the body of the fallen rider.

Bodo's ballista had done its job admirably. The stout bolt had punched cleanly through the man's armored body so that its head and most of the shaft protruded from his back. The dead man's face, he thought, bore an expression of hurt surprise, as if a friend had done him a dirty turn.

Something about the man did not look right. Florio was not especially informed about the battledress of Keltin warriors, but he assumed they wore little or no iron armor. The mail-clad corpse lying at his feet looked more like the mercenaries he had seen in the streets of Gorgonholm.

The elf bent and looked closer. To his horror, he saw that the fellow was most certainly not Keltin. Then he noticed a medallion bearing the royal seal hanging on a leather lace around the man's neck—the badge of the Royal Road Guard. This had been no forest savage, but a royal soldier, a king's man!

Florio had made a ghastly mistake. The attackers had not been attackers at all, but had been sent by someone of royal authority, most likely Earl Ralf, to protect Grimsgard from the Keltins. Yet he had, after a single shouted warning, ordered Bodo to commence firing.

The elf knew his voice was less powerful than that of most human males. Perhaps it had not carried far enough, perhaps they had not heard the order to halt. Or maybe the leader had never dreamed someone would actually fire on him.

The elf began to tremble. What would happen now? The soldiers would obviously return, but this time they would be angry and vengeful. They might burn the village and slaughter its inhabitants.

There was, he realized, only one thing to do. Upon their arrival, he would throw open the door of the tower, present himself to the leader, and beg that the villagers be spared any punishment. He would take the full blame.

PART 5

THE BATTLE OF
GORGONHOLM

CHAPTER 38

THE GATHERING STORM

Asmodeus did not consult his crystal sphere that night. His previous exertions and the ill-effects of the smoke had left him too foggy-brained to muster the necessary concentration. He needed to rest and restore his powers for the climactic battle about to begin.

If the Adventurers returned as expected, they might still employ Malachai's instrument to cast down the Black Stone and thereby disrupt the unity that had welded the normally querulous Keltin tribes into a cohesive fighting force. With any luck, their immense horde would begin to melt away. Old rivalries might turn the tribes against one another.

But even then, the Keltins would remain a deadly threat. Stone or no Stone, their numbers were so great that they might still storm the walls of Gorgonholm and butcher its population.

That was not the only danger. Unless Malachai's instrument worked perfectly, the Stone would release such an intense blast of infernal energy that a person such as himself, a person with one foot in the otherworld, might be consumed in an instant.

Unfortunately, Asmodeus was, at this moment, too weak to protect himself from either demonic or human foes. He summoned a servant, the one called Knuckles, to fetch a sleeping draught. Downing the mixture, he retired to his featherbed for a night of undisturbed slumber. Only sleep would bring the regeneration he so badly needed.

Had he gazed into his crystal sphere that night, he would have been pleased to see the Adventurers pushing toward home even in the dark. They rode through broadleaf woodlands and rolling hills, across rocky streambeds and grassy valleys, the road steadily improving, their pace quickening, as they grew closer and closer to home.

Had the wizard then turned his eyes to the west, he would have spied shadowy masses moving stealthily through the trees, always in the direction of the river. Near the bank, screened from view by a dense growth of bushes and reeds, men and oxen hauled heavy rafts to the water's edge. Others carried light currachs suspended on wooden poles.

The most venerable of the Keltin kings waited with their warriors. They would, by ancient right, lead the main assault—Ferkin of Kilconaquer, Black Dingus of Dalraden, Dermot mac Quaddy of Dunayre, and ill-tempered Colin Red of Brae.

All around them, the massed clans waited, panting for the day of reckoning that the ancient legends promised. Warriors of the Hornfinger clan, the Dancing Snake, the Fire Leapers, the Chewbone. Thousands and thousands of tattooed faces alight with battle lust. Spearpoints glinting in the moonlight. Bronze-bladed swords clutched in gnarly fists.

With them stood the shamans, naked save for feathers, twigs, and dried serpent skins twined in their dung-encrusted hair. They shook rattles and waved bones, chanted and pranced. They would call down the fury of nature on the accursed city. Savage winds would tumble the towers, temblors cast down the massive gates. Rats would rise from the sewers in a ravenous brown flood and consume all in their path.

Further upstream, the Painted Men squatted silently by their currachs, their naked bodies smeared blue with woad. They would be the first to cross, the first to spill the blood of the detested laigi. Moving silently through the night, they would be over the city wall before the sleepy sentries awoke to their presence. Then they would slay and slay and slay.

The Small Folk had been set to a task uniquely suited to their capabilities. These little men spent much of their lives in extensive *souterrains*, venturing forth only to hunt or gather. Thus, they would be sent into the Catacombs. They would follow the underground passage by which uisge was delivered to laigi smugglers, and then cross the subterranean lake in tiny coracles. When the city's defenders were fully engaged with the assault upon their walls, the Small Folk would spill from concealed openings scattered throughout the city and fall upon them from behind.

Fergis was busy that night. An unending procession of messengers came and went, came and went. Kings awaited his counsel, chieftains his commands. Wild-eyed shamans brought their prophecies. Famous warriors waited patiently for a chance to bend their knee and swear an oath of fidelity. Beautiful young women offered their services in more personal ways.

Quite unexpectedly, his brother Oengus had appeared before him and begged to pledge his loyalty upon Fergis's stone scepter, the ancient symbol of kingship. This was the most sacred of vows. Should Oengus betray Fergis now, his own children would be cursed for seven generations. Far worse, he would be remembered as an oath-breaker in story and song.

So Fergis could trust his brother for the moment. He would still have to kill him, but not for a while at least.

The Ard Righ was pleased. The ill-fortune that had delayed his plans had finally passed. The boats and rafts were almost ready. His men were taking their appointed positions. All were in good spirits and eager.

The attack would commence the next night at the rising of the moon.

On the river's far side, many leagues beyond Gorgonholm, a vastly different force was approaching from the east and south. Avincraik's most experienced and celebrated warriors, Baron Phineas Hardbottle, Lord Pikadilly Fudg, and Sir Marmaduke Twaddle, answered the summons of their feudal overlord, Earl Ralf Mortimer. Above their heads, proud heraldic banners proclaimed their illustrious lineage.

With them came their personal retinues of knights, squires, and men-at-arms—battle-hardened veterans in leather, mail, and plate. Then the long lines of foot soldiers—tough spearmen and keen-eyed archers clad in padded jacks and iron caps. And, finally, the peasant levies, untrained but eager for blood, armed with the savage weapons of the farmyard—grain flails hastily fitted with crude spiked collars, heavy wooden mauls, razor honed sickles, pruning bills.

This mighty force grew with each passing league as other lords, greater and lesser, joined its ranks. Sir Bors of Ballycock, Sir Stefan Greenwald, Sir Henry Bone, and Lord Balin Runt were eager to fulfill their feudal duty. This great host would join Earl Ralf beneath the walls of Gorgonholm.

Nor were the nobles of the city wanting in courage and devotion. As if awakening from a dream, they suddenly became aware of their plight, stopped their internecine bickering, and turned to face their common foe. Lords Wiffie, Hooey, de Wanque, and de Poot added their armed retainers to the earl's ranks.

The city's militia, the Trained Bands, assembled at the municipal armory, each craft guild fielding its own company. Potters, glass-blowers, barbers, clothiers, masons, wheelwrights—Gorgonholm's stalwart backbone—were issued pikes and crossbows, breastplates and kettle-hats. They followed Sheriff Brandon through the South Gate, determined to defend their shops and homes. Men too old or infirm to march out would guard the gates and man the city walls.

Clerics of all denominations—Blue, Black, White, Brown and even a few surviving Grays—would fight alongside the Trained Bands. The Whites, an especially numerous sect, fielded a large contingent of pikemen. The Blacks, smaller but much wealthier, formed up as a squadron of heavily armored cavalry. The Blues and Browns provided a mixed contingent armed with swords, spears, and crossbows. Charonism was not a pacifistic faith.

Bishop Boniface, the city's spiritual leader, rode at the head of the holy men. Armed cap-a-pie in plate, he brandished an oversized ceremonial mace. Behind him, young acolytes carried the cathedral's sacred relics and swung censors of burning herbs to inspire martial ardor.

The women of Gorgonholm, led by a scurrilous fishwife named Barberry, mounted the battlements to stand shoulder to shoulder with their menfolk. They were of all ages and occupations—brawny washerwomen and submissive housewives, bright-eyed ale-pourers and wrinkled crones, unrepentant harlots and habited nuns. They brought hot water, paving stones, and pots of human waste to drop on enemies beneath the walls. Their children were sent to gather cobblestones, broken bricks, and fallen roof tiles—anything that might inflict injury.

The city's magician's guild, The Most Sacred Fellowship of Spell-Casters, Alchemists, Diviners, Sorcerers, Philter-Mixers, and Thaumaturgists, gathered in their meeting hall. Armed with amulets, potions, and rods of power, they searched moldy books and crumbling parchments for useful spells of destruction and desolation. Hellish entities were summoned and dispatched on errands of ruin. Wards were laid to counteract the enemy's psychic attacks.

Bartos Freez, Gorgonholm's chief engineer, opened the corroded lock and forced apart the creaking doors of dusty warehouse where the city's war engines were stored—disassembled springalds, ballistae, and mangonels. After years of neglect, the iron fittings were rusted and some of the wood was split and decayed. Most, however, were thankfully sound. Beams, braces, and throwing arms were loaded onto carts and carried to the walls for assembly.

The citizens of Old Shambles—smugglers, pimps, cut-throats, and corner boys—stood by to do their bit. A destroyed city and massacred populous would be, after all, distinctly bad for business. They would not join the Trained Bands nor man the walls. The Shamblers preferred to handle things in their own way.

The famous Hawkwood rode in with his company of hard-bitten mercenaries, famous for their fierce tenacity in battle. Numbering nearly five hundred, they were a most welcome addition to the city's forces.

And then came Lord Drakar de la Pole, the most fearsome warrior in all of Avincraik—and beyond. The cunning survivor of fifteen mortal battles and dozens of skirmishes and raids. Thrice had he slain his foe in trials-by-combat. Lauded for his hatred for all things Keltin. Infamous for his merciless cruelty.

With these resources, Earl Ralf laid plans to preserve his country from the Keltin onslaught. He would do as the Mortimers had always done—defeat the savage invaders or die in the attempt.

Lord Ubo was unaware of any of these developments. He was concerned only with the humiliation he had suffered during that morning's abortive raid on the towerhouse. He brooded far into the night, and his thoughts were red thoughts. He would slay all those wretched peasants and drink the blood from their veins, pull down their miserable tower so that not a single stone stood atop another. He would....

Another thought struck him. The peasants had been insolent beyond words, they would all most certainly die, but they had not been the true cause of his defeat. It had been his own men, the woodsmen, who failed. They had refused to press the attack, had routed to the cover of the woods at the first sight of blood.

Their cowardice had given him no choice but to retreat. He and a handful of guardsmen could not have stormed a stoutly defended towerhouse by themselves.

His rabble had cost him a much-needed victory. Worse, they had sullied his honor by forcing him to withdraw most ingloriously in the face of the foe. Something must be done to avenge this affront. Blood was always the best remedy.

He summoned his one-eyed sergeant.

"Pons, assemble your men. Then round up those whey-faced woodsmen who deserted us today. They fled while you and I were facing a deadly storm of arrows. Facing a ballista!"

"Remove the head from every tenth man and arrange them by the main gate. Turn the faces forward—I want their friends to recognize them. Let the message be clear—I will not tolerate poltroonery."

The sergeant shifted his feet uneasily. He was more than happy to let the woodsmen take the blame, but he had no wish to tangle with the tribe of untamed forest dwellers.

"I dunno, milord. There's lots of them woodsmen, and ain't but eight of my men fit to fight. Two of 'em is hurt bad."

Ubo was in no mood to hear his excuses.

"Make it happen—I care not how. Get the charcoal burners to help you— they bear little love for the woodsmen. You must make haste. Tomorrow night I will reduce that vile little tower to rubble."

CHAPTER 39
THE MASTER RETURNS

Roscoe and company arrived at Grimsgard late that night. Drawing close to his towerhouse, he was surprised to see helmeted heads moving atop the battlements.

"Holla! Holla in the tower! It's me, Roscoe! I'm back! Open the bloody door, by God's holy backside!"

Bodo peered down between two merlons, torch in hand.

"Roscoe! Is that really you? And Thurmond and Torgul and Sarah? Oh, this is wondrous indeed! If ever we needed…."

Roscoe grew impatient.

"God's twelve toes, Bodo, leave off with all the jabber and get that door open. I'm tired to the very bone, so I am, and sufferin' from a mighty appetite. Get crackin', boyo!"

Bodo disappeared from the parapet, and soon the heavy door of the towerhouse swung wide. But so great was the rush of happy villagers from inside that Roscoe and the others could only stand and wait for the way to clear before they could enter.

Roscoe had hoped to enjoy a long and leisurely dinner in the comfortable surroundings of his own great hall. Florio, he was certain, would be delighted to prepare a lavish banquet for his newly returned master. After so many days of salt meat, dried peas, and hard bread, he really needed a good meal.

These hopes were dashed the moment he stepped in the door. The towerhouse was crammed to the rafters with supplies stockpiled for the expected siege, the ground floor storeroom with barrels of beer, baskets of dried fish, and bags of oats.

Ascending the stairs, he was dismayed to discover his great hall had become a stockyard filled with goats, sheep, pigs, and cows. Geese, ducks, and chickens roosted in the chandeliers and overhead beams. The floor was spotted with their droppings.

Every available space, it seemed, was crowded with something—bedding, clothing, tools, sheaves of arrows, firewood. The tower was intended to house a force of perhaps a dozen, but more than three score now huddled within its walls. The place reeked of human and animal waste.

Amidst all the turmoil—excited voices, crying children, squawking poultry, and lowing, bleating, grunting livestock—Florio tried to explain.

There would be no fine feast. The toothsome delights of peace had given way to simple fare of war. Florio sent a serving girl for what remained of the evening meal—salt meat, dried peas, and hard bread. He could offer them beer, of course, but someone had surreptitiously consumed the entire store of Torgul's mead.

Even their private chambers had been taken over by the village's displaced tenants. Torgul's room now housed an extended family of Gock the cowherd. This included his grandparents, parents, siblings, children, aunts, uncles, cousins, and nephews.

Roscoe booted a pair of amorous newlyweds from his quarters and invited the dwarf to share it with him. Thurmond was horrified to discover his room filled to capacity with assorted villagers. Fat Annie stood in the doorway with crossed arms, as if daring him to try to evict her.

Sarah's quarters remained thankfully untouched. Nothing could induce the villagers to approach the witch's workroom or sleeping chamber. They were firmly convinced, perhaps inspired by Florio's occasional remarks, that a ferocious demon resided therein and would rend anyone foolish enough to enter.

Sarah hooked Thurmond by the arm.

"Come on, you can bunk in my room."

He was not reluctant to agree to this suggestion.

Roscoe needed sleep almost as much as he needed a grand feeding, but he must first listen to Florio's account of that morning's unfortunate incident, how he had mistaken royal soldiers for Keltin raiders. The elf began to weep as he apologized for his stupidity, and he did his desperate best to assure Roscoe that he would personally suffer whatever dire consequences came their way.

Roscoe was moved by his reeve's sincerity, but he was too worn out to offer much in the way of reassurance. All he could do, in the end, was pat the elf's arm and give him a wink.

"Don't be frettin' about it, Florio. I ain't gonna let nothin' bad happen to you."

Early the next morning, a small contingent of armed riders bearing a black banner came galloping across Grimsgard's village common and drew rein before the towerhouse. A gust of wind spread the banner wide, revealing the heraldic arms of Lord Drakar de la Pole—in silver, a viper swallowing an infant.

Peering down through an arrow-slit window, Florio suppressed an urge to vomit. There could be no mistake, he was looking at his own death. The men he had slain must have belonged to Drakar, a notoriously vindictive and vengeful lord. He could only pray that his demise would not be slow and agonizing.

It had been his ill judgment that brought this catastrophe upon them. Therefore, he must surrender himself, confess his culpability, and endure whatever fate Lord Drakar decreed. He had just started down the spiral steps to the ground floor when a harsh voice came from outside.

"Roscoe Appleman! Freeholder of Grimsgard! Show yourself in the name of Ralf, Earl of Avincraik!"

The elf froze in mid-step, one pointy-toed shoe suspended in the air. *In the earl's name*—what could that portend? Would it be better or worse for him?

He resumed his trek down the stairs, but before he reached the bottom,

Roscoe, who was already in the tower's ground-floor storeroom, opened the door and stepped out to face his visitors.

"I am Roscoe, the franklin of this holding. What would our most gracious earl be havin' of me?"

The reply was curt and gruff.

"You are commanded to join the armed forces of Gorgonholm, appearing at the South Gate no later than sundown this very day. You will bring yourself and five others, all well-armed and mounted. In addition, you must supply six lightly armed spearmen or archers, on horse or afoot. Be not late!"

A thudding of hooves told that the riders had ridden away.

Florio placed his hand on the wall, dizzy with relief. It had been a summons to arms. There had been no mention of the man he had slain.

When he finally reached the door, Roscoe was standing with hands on hips, watching the riders canter away. He looked at the elf and grinned.

"You hear that? I figured them fellas was here for your hide, so I did. But they didn't say one word about yesterday's little misunderstandin'."

Florio hung his head.

"I was going to give myself up to try to save everyone else."

The old Adventurer exploded.

"Don't talk rot! You'll do no such thing! I need you to run this place. I'm no good at it. Nay, laddie, you're goin' nowhere. Especially now, what with me goin' off to war."

"What do you need me to do?"

"Well now, this ain't gonna be easy. We're plumb wore out after our long ride, plus we got a demon to destroy. But a summons is a summons, so I ain't got no choice. You'll be takin' charge here. I hate to leave you in such desperate times, but you've got the tower as ready as it's ever gonna be. And you got Bodo. He's a good man, so he is."

"Who goes with you?"

"Torgul and Thurmond and Sarah, of course. And those three Gascar archers. That makes seven, so I'll have to take five villagers to round out the dozen. You know 'em better than I do—who do I want? Are any of 'em good with a bow?"

"Aye, they've had plenty of practice poaching your game."

"Good! Pick out five of the best and fix 'em up with some armor best you can. Also, we'll be needin' food and drink for a couple of days."

The elf nodded.

"I'll see to it at once. All will be ready by midday."

"Oh, and one more thing, Florio, what's for breakfast?"

"I have salt meat and lentils."

"What? God's liver and lights! Is that the best you can offer a starvin' man?"

"I do but jest, milord. I've prepared a simple but tasty repast of creamed raven's eggs spiced with bittersweet herbs. Next a savory stew of red and black squirrels. Lastly, a small compote of spicy yarbleberries in red wine. I pray it will be adequate."

Before breakfast could be served, Asmodeus swooped down from the heavens on his demon steed. He hopped from its back and strode to the tower's door, where the elf and the old Adventurer stood.

The wizard was as dapper as ever, bedecked in magenta riding breeches and matching doublet. A black leather skullcap was buckled beneath his chin. Black knee-high boots completed the ensemble.

He wasted no time on pleasantries. There would be no evil giggles today.

"You were very long in returning, Appleman. By my calculations you should have been back a week ago. I allowed ample time for you to complete your task and get back. You must have been dawdling along the way."

Roscoe was too tired and hungry to fear the wizard's displeasure. He just wanted his breakfast.

"By your calculations, mayhap. But did you figure on us bein' captured by Vanir warriors or Thurmond havin' his chest crushed? Then there was that necromancer Malachai, right pleasant fella he was with his heads in jars. Oh, I nearly forgot, there was also this gang of rampagin' giants that needed killin'. Then still more Vanarians. And just when we was finally in the clear, we was attacked by the very mercenaries you sent to guard us. So I guess we got a tad behind schedule."

Asmodeus dismissed these words with a wave of his hand.

"Pishposh, we all have our difficulties to overcome. I never said your quest would be easy."

Roscoe huffed.

"Well, Master Asmodeus, you have the right of that, so you have. Easy it wasn't. But we're back now, and we've brought the thing you sent us for. Just a moment, I'll fetch it for you."

Real fear filled Asmodeus's eyes.

"Nay! Bring it not! I must not touch it nor even see it. I can't be near it. I can feel its hellish power even as we speak."

Roscoe cocked his head, uncertain.

"You can feel its hellish power? I've felt nothin', and I've been ridin' with that thing for days and days."

"Of course not, for you are bound entirely to this plane. I, on the other hand, am…"

He paused.

"…otherwise."

The old Adventurer was by now growing more and more fed up with the wizard's haughty demeanor.

"God's webby fingers! If you won't take it, what am I to do with the damned thing? Answer me that."

Asmodeus pressed his palms together as if praying.

"You are more correct than you know. Malachai's instrument is precisely a *damned thing*. An infernal entity resides within it. You will release it from its bonds and set it against the Black Stone."

"Nay! I will not be releasin' no demons from bondage. I will not! You do it, you're the magic man. It's your rightful job, so it is!"

Two stories up, in a chamber overlooking the tower's door, Thurmond and Sarah were awakened by the uproar below. Sarah opened a window so they could hear more readily the details of the dispute.

Asmodeus's voice was now as loud and angry as Roscoe's.

"You must, you fool! Either you or that little witch of yours. It's the only way. I can't, the instrument's power would consume me in an instant. You'll be safe enough. Your humanity will protect you."

"And just what are you meanin' by that?"

The wizard raised his eyes in exasperation.

"Both the Stone and the instrument exude infernal power. They touch everyone to a greater or lesser degree, depending on their natural disposition. You being the bumbling dolt you are, with your idiotic ideas about honesty and loyalty, you should be safe. At least for long enough to employ the instrument."

Roscoe was intractable.

"I will not! I *am* an honorable man, just as you say, and I will not soil my soul by releasin' no hell-spawn into the world. Neither will my people."

"Then we must all perish as the Black Stone continues to feed."

"Find someone else. Maybe one of your skeleton men. I already did my bit by bringin' it here."

"There is no time, you big buffoon. It must be done tonight at the hour of the Howling Basilisk. The Keltins will cross the river at any moment. The Stone is drawing them on, unifying them like they've never been before. Only by breaking its hold do we have any hope of defeating them."

Sarah could stand the racket no longer. She hollered down from the window.

"Roscoe, I beg you, lower your voices. Such squabbling accomplishes nothing. So leave off."

Roscoe, still irate, shouted in her direction.

"You don't know what he's askin' of me, girl. He's wantin' me to…"

She cut him short.

"I'm aware. I heard all. It's all right. I'll release the thing in the box. Give me a minute and I'll be right down."

Sarah pulled a dress over her linen chemise, stuck her feet in slippers, and dashed down the stairs. Thurmond was close behind her, doing his best to make her change her mind.

"This is madness, Sarah! You saw what happened to Renata when her demon got loose. It tore her to pieces, and you said it was just a little one."

But the young witch was not inclined to listen.

"Enough, Thurmond, please. Asmodeus knows what must be done. It'll all work out, you'll see."

"I see nothing except that you'll very likely be killed, maybe worse."

She looked back over her shoulder as they spiraled down the stairs.

"I seem to recall facing death once or twice before. You didn't make such a fuss those times."

"Demons are different. They're too powerful, you can't fight 'em."

"Certainly you can. You just have to have the right weapons."

They crossed the threshold into the open air. The wizard was calmer now, his voice normal.

"So, you will do this deed?"

Sarah nodded.

"I will."

"Then I must instruct you in its proper employment."

"Malachai told me much. I believe I'm ready to proceed."

"Sit down and listen. There may still be a few things you need to know."

CHAPTER 40

THE RISING OF THE MOON

Roscoe and company presented themselves as ordered at Gorgonholm's South Gate where an officious marshal assigned them to Lord Drakar's contingent and told them to await the arrival of their commander. Though they sat for some time with nothing to do, their wait was far from tedious. All around them, a great army was taking form.

Thurmond had, since childhood, loved tales of legendary heroes and monumental battles. Stories in which vast armies collided in a maelstrom of thundering hooves and flashing blades. Battles in which thousands of men were swept away by the scythed wheels of chariots.

He had discarded his given name, Wido, in favor of Thurmond, a celebrated hero of song and fable. In one epic conflict, the legendary Thurmond had crushed the huge army of King Doophz, seized his crown, and married his daughter. Our Thurmond was especially fond of that tale.

Now, it seemed, he was to be part of such a glorious undertaking, for all around him men were gathering for war. Knights and horses beyond count. Wanes piled high with all the implements of battle. Endless lines of plodding infantry. Banners waving, trumpets blaring, men shouting. The young man tried to absorb it all but found he could not, there was simply too much going on.

He was particularly taken by the fine plate armor of the nobility. No Adventurer wore such cumbersome harness. The huge warhorses were equally impressive. The charge of such massive beasts must crush anything in their path.

And Thurmond was not the only one thrilled by the scope of the mustering forces. Roscoe, Thurmond, and Sarah were equally awestruck. None of them had ever seen such an army before.

With a great flourish of trumpets and drums, Drakar arrived to assume command of his troops. He immediately began to assess the various units assigned to him. Coming to Roscoe's group, he did not like what he saw.

He stared hard at the old Adventurer.

"You are Appleman, I remember you."

They had indeed met once before when Drakar had, at Earl Ralf's behest, handed over the charter that granted Roscoe the freehold of Grimsgard.

Drakar's gaze hardened.

"Indeed, I recall you, Appleman—a fat, crippled drunk reeking of cheap ale. A jumped-up peasant now posing as a gentleman.

"Quite a following you've brought me, a dwarf, a wench, and other assorted peasant scum. You will guard the baggage camp while the rest of us do the fighting. You are fit for nothing better."

These words hurt, yet there was some truth in what Drakar said. On the morning they met, Roscoe had been severely hungover from too much good cheer the night before. And he had been crippled then. An old wound had left him with a painful limp. Luckily, that malady had since been cured. Alas, he had to admit that from Drakar's viewpoint, he was nothing more than a jumped-up peasant. To the nobility, birth was everything.

Roscoe was, however, seriously stung by Drakar's assessment of their fighting skills. Keltin warriors were deadly in battle, true enough, but they could hardly compare to a gang of rampaging giants. Still, he said nothing. It was never prudent to disagree with Lord Drakar.

Thurmond was mortally offended by Drakar's arrogance, and railed loudly as soon as the fearsome lord was out of earshot. Sarah's efforts to quiet him were ineffective.

"Damn his bloody bowels, Sarah, didn't you hear what he said about Roscoe, about all of us? We're only fit to guard the baggage."

"Be still, Thurmond. Drakar's a noble, and nobles get to say whatever they want."

"It doesn't matter who he is! Nobody has the right to say such things."

"You're wrong, he has every right. That's just the way things are."

Thurmond's voice rose with his frustration.

"But that pig doesn't even know us!"

Sarah put her hand over his mouth.

"Mind your tongue! Keep wagging it like that, and he's likely to have it removed. He can do it, too. Anyway, you're forgetting something."

The young man was exasperated by her lack of outrage.

"What would that be?"

"You're forgetting that we've got a more important job than guarding baggage or fighting Keltins. We've got a demon to release, and to do that, we need the freedom to move about. Being camp guards will make that much easier."

Despite his indignation, Thurmond found himself liking the baggage camp. He had imagined it as a collection of carts and wagons, but he found instead a small city in which a legion of camp followers were raising tents, setting up kitchens, butchering livestock, digging latrines. Children scampered underfoot, dogs barked, women sang as they worked.

Huge heraldic banners flew above the encampments of the leading nobles. The earl's servants had raised a pavilion the size of a large house. The open flaps revealed rich tapestries and thick carpets, long trestle tables and high-backed chairs.

Buxom servant girls darted about, unpacking silver tableware from wooden crates and arranging it on an elaborately carved sideboard. When Earl Ralf traveled, he preferred to do so in style.

Here he would, as custom demanded, entertain his favorite minions with elaborate banquets. His stewards would pour the best of wines, while his cooks prepared the most delicious and exotic comestibles. His guests would be regaled by musicians, jugglers, and contortionists.

The camp was under the command of Lord Beaufort de Oinque. He, by the strangest chance, was the minor lord who owned the small village in which Thurmond had been born. Lord Beaufort was a small-boned, shaky fellow, not at all a robust or forceful leader of men. That is why he had been assigned to the camp.

Thurmond knew him at once, but there was next to no chance that the little old man would recognize Thurmond. The strapping young Adventurer bore scant resemblance to the obstreperous boy who had run away from his village four years ago.

Thurmond's mother had always maintained that Beaufort was his father, but the young man doubted this. Most nameless peasants claimed to have noble blood in their veins. He thought the village's drunken carpenter was a much more likely candidate.

Beaufort was a lackadaisical camp captain. He assigned the Adventurers no duties other than to stay out of the way of the workers. This was fortunate because it gave them the chance to devise a plan of action. Sarah told the others what Asmodeus had told her about the Black Stone.

"Some crazed noble found it in a village deep in the woods, some place called Skut, and he's started a murderous cult that took over the Grey Friars' monastery. That's where the Stone is now. That's lucky because it's a lot closer to here, but also unfortunate because the monastery is surrounded by a wall and heavily defended. We'll have to figure a way to get inside."

Roscoe raised an eyebrow.

"And how are you figurin' to do that?"

"I'll cause a lot of fuss with an illusion spell. Something horrible, maybe one of Malachai's ill-formed giants. That should scare the hell out of whoever's watching the gates. I'll slip inside while the guards are running for their lives."

Roscoe remained unconvinced.

"What happens if the spell fails or if the guards disbelieve the illusion?"

"Then I'll need a backup plan, but maybe there won't be any guards. Maybe the gates won't even be shut. There's no time to spy things out first, I'll have to play it as I find it."

Thurmond could stand no more of this.

"God's eyeballs, Sarah! You keep talking like you're in this by yourself—*you'll* do this, and *you'll* do that. But you damn well know when you volunteered to release that demon, you volunteered me too. Don't argue with me, you know it's true."

Torgul spoke up.

"He's right, missy. We're all stickin' with you, even Roscoe, and he's horrible scared of your demon."

The old Adventurer shrugged, embarrassed by the dwarf's disclosure, but he did not deny that the words were true. The very thought of demonic release filled him with cold dread.

Sarah sighed in relief.

"I thank you. I'm grateful because I'm plenty scared."

Thurmond was still not satisfied.

"Tell me exactly what you're going to do. I want to know how this instrument thing is gonna work."

Sarah pursed her lips.

"I'll do my best to explain. The Black Stone's some form of a demon. It doesn't just live in the stone, somehow it *is* the stone. I don't know how that can be, but it is. We're going to release a different kind of demon to take its power."

"And how will it do that?"

"They use opposite kinds of energy. Put them together, and they'll suck the power out of each other. That's the best I can tell you. The instrument can't destroy the Black Stone, but it will take its energy, so it won't be able to rise again until the stars are just right years and years from now."

She cast a worried glance at the sky.

"And speaking of the stars, we don't have much time. The sun is going down now. As soon as it's dark, we've got to sneak away from this camp and get over to the monastery. The ritual must be carried out during the hour of the Howling Basilisk. That's just a couple hours after moonrise."

Inside the Gray Friar's monastery, Lord Ubo was deep in his cups. The friars had possessed an excellent wine-cellar, and Ubo was making liberal use of it. But despite the comforting effects of the vintage, he was nervous. He hated to admit it, even to himself, but he had come to doubt the reliability of his followers. The poor performance of the woodsmen had made him notice just how slovenly and inefficient they were in all respects.

The wine could not quell the rage and frustration that gnawed in him like the sharp teeth of a rat. He was Ubo! It was his destiny to prevail. To dominate. To destroy. No craven lackey or defiant peasant would stand in his way.

That wretched little tower would be razed this very night, just as soon as it got good and dark. He would take his entire force—charcoal burners, villagers, renegade cityfolk, wayfarers. All except the craven woodsmen. Those unworthy cowards had cost him his first battle, they would not be allowed to do so a second time.

He paused in his reverie to look out the window. The pale edge of the moon was making its first shy appearance in the wine-dark sky. The hour had come for screams and blood and fire.

Lord Ubo was not the only one drinking that night. Pons and the guardsmen, aware that their lord was again befuddled with wine, had broached the cask of uisge they had found stashed in the monastery's kitchen. They were beginning to entertain serious doubts about their new master, and a wee drop of uisge made them feel better.

Despite their inebriation, the guardsmen responded with consummate professionalism when commanded to prepare for war. Horses were saddled, armor buckled, swords girded on. In short order, they were mounted and ready to go.

The deportment of the rank and file was altogether different. Always happy to follow the example of their leaders, they too had been partaking in the ardent beverages that are always present when people gather in groups. Barrels of wine, beer, and ale were broached. Stone bottles of mead and uisge were passed from hand to hand.

When Ubo led his small army out through the monastery's gates, many of his men were rollicking drunk. They staggered as they marched, singing, laughing, slurring their speech.

Left behind, the disgraced woodsmen, overjoyed by the departure of their angry master, slaked their thirst with gusto unrestrained. The unsupervised gate guards soon abandoned their lonely posts to join in the revelry.

CHAPTER 41

THE HOUR OF THE HOWLING BASILISK

Precisely at moonrise, the invasion began. The first currachs were pushed into the water by the Painted Men. They paddled furiously, for the river was wide and the current strong. More and more pushed off behind them until the surface was covered with tiny boats.

Once on the other side, the warriors splashed ashore and headed inland while the boatmen turned about to fetch another load. More boats arrived with the long ropes that would bring over the heavy rafts. All was going according to plan.

Hundreds of painted warriors made their way toward Gorgonholm's city walls. Skilled climbers all, they would storm over this barrier by means of grapnels fixed to rawhide ropes. They would be the first to enter, so the richest pickings would be theirs. Designated groups would seize and open the south and west gates, while others spread death and terror amongst the inhabitants.

Unfortunately for Fergis and his warriors, Lady Fortune hates a well-executed plan. Too much order breeds complacency. A bit of chaos promotes awareness and innovation. She smirked and gave her famous wheel a spin.

The Painted Men were denizens of the deep woods, so none had ever seen a city before. They could not envision the sheer size of Gorgonholm, the enormity of the gates, the loftiness of the towers. Thus, when the walls of the Grayfriar's monastery loomed before them, they naturally assumed it was their intended target.

The Painted Men were amazed by the carelessness of the laigi—they lacked the sense even to mount a guard on their city. The uproarious laughter and roaring songs from within testified to woeful lack of discipline and fortitude. Such people obviously deserved to die.

The Painted Men scarcely needed their ropes and grapnels to scale the monastery's modest walls. The first dozen warriors were over in an eyeblink. They opened the gates and started killing. The savage fighters slashed into the unarmed crowd of drunken revelers, the vast majority of which—taken completely by surprise—could do little except stand and be slain.

A few held out for a while, barricading themselves in the stable and holding off the attacks with shovels and pitchforks. The invaders, however, had no time for such nonsense, not when there was such rich booty to be had, so they set a torch to the stable's thatched roof and let fire do their work for them.

Then the pillaging began. The invaders looted the dead woodsmen of their woolen caps and leather belts. They snatched up clay cups and iron cooking pots, pulled curtains from the windows, fought over spoons and eating knives.

Storming into Ubo's sleeping chamber, the Painted Men were awestruck by its lavish appointments—the carved escritoire, the canopied bed, the embroidered hangings—all of which had, until recently, belonged to Abbot Festus. The warriors assumed that only a great king could enjoy such opulence. This must be, they reasoned, the private apartment of the Ard Righ of the laigi.

They discovered their mistake soon after when scouts brought word that the city—the real city—was still half a league to the north, that they had captured nothing more than an outlying fortress. They quickly abandoned their fun, coiled their rawhide ropes, and set off to complete their real mission.

The Adventurers arrived at the monastery while the butchery was at its height. The air was rife with the screams of the dying and the victory shouts of the painted invaders. Flames from the burning stable cast weird shadows and lent the scene the red glow of Hell.

They were too late—the invasion had already begun! Their objective was already swarming with enemy warriors. A score stood armed and ready at the gate. Others moved to and fro along the battlements.

Thurmond whispered in Sarah's ear.

"Illusion spell?"

"Nay, there's too many of them. And they're too spread out. It wouldn't work."

"Invisibility?"

She had once used such a spell to invade a goblin lair.

"Nay, I've not the power."

There was nothing to do but hunker down in the weeds and wait. Any attempt to enter the monastery now would mean immediate death.

Sarah scanned the night sky with growing anxiety. The Drowned Cockerel was high in its nightly orbit across the celestial sphere. When it reached its zenith, The Howling Basilisk would appear on the eastern horizon. She had very little time.

As they waited, the screams grew louder, the flames higher. More warriors pranced on the monastery's battlements, bellowing, leaping, shaking their spears. The minutes continued to creep by.

A solitary figure emerged from the dark and addressed the contingent at the gate. He was highly agitated, gesticulating wildly as he pointed in the direction of the city. The entire group disappeared through the gates.

To the Adventurers' great relief, his arrival brought the pillaging of the monastery to a halt. A horn sounded, causing the raiders to immediately cease their whooping and prancing. They poured from the monastery's gates and loped off to the north.

Thurmond led the way through the now deserted gates. On the other side, he confronted a scene far worse than Malachai's heads in jars. Sprawled, gutted, mutilated bodies. Deep puddles of blood. Brains splattered on walls. The nauseating stench of death. Everything appallingly still and silent.

He stepped gingerly over gashed bodies of the woodsmen, fighting down an urge to retch. He heard Sarah's sharp intake of breath as she followed him through the gates and beheld the hideous destruction. She carried the instrument in its wooden chest. It was heavy enough to require both her hands. Roscoe and Torgul came next, fanning out slightly on both sides, weapons poised, alert for attack.

Malachai's instrument seemed to be growing heavier and heavier as she moved along. At one point, she had to pause and rest her arms. A few minutes later, she let it sag to the ground.

"Thurmond, could you carry this thing for a while. Something's making it get heavier and heavier, or maybe I'm growing weaker. I can't be sure."

With a word, the young man raised it to his shoulder.

"Not heavy at all, I think it's you."

"Then the damned thing is stealing my energy. It knows we're getting close."

They passed the still blazing stable. Though the stone walls remained, the interior burned as hot as a blacksmith's forge and filled the air with an obscene, oily smoke. Beyond that, more bodies, more blood. A man face-down in a watering trough. Another with neither hands nor feet. The dismembered remains of a dog. A shaggy human head impaled on a post.

They found the Black Stone on an earthen mound in the center of the monastery's grounds, a place of prominence where a statue of Allfather Charon had once stood. A dozen bodies lay stretched out before it, as if Ubo's doomed followers had fled to it, seeking its succor. The face carved on its surface seemed to bear a self-satisfied smirk.

By now, Sarah's head was reeling, her breath coming in short, hard gasps.

"I'm sorry to ask this, Thurmond, but would you stay and help me? I'm feeling so drained, I'm going to need you. I think you'll have to pull me away when the operation is over. Would you, please?"

"Of course, say no more about it."

Roscoe also stepped forward.

"Torgul and I are here, too. Just tell us what to do."

"You and Torgul must go out and wait by the gate. There's nothing more you can do. Just help us afterwards if you can. And Thurmond, don't get close to it, don't touch it. I can feel its power even if you can't. Just stand over there away from it unless I need you."

Torgul and Roscoe required no further urging—they left for the gate at once. Thurmond retreated until his back was against the wall of an adjacent building. This had, he knew, been Sarah's job all along. When Malachai gave them the instrument, he had touched her forehead, tasking her with this vital responsibility.

The young witch paused to remove her helmet. Casting spells was difficult enough without having one's head strapped into an iron bowl. She looked at the sky. The Drowned Cockerel was almost directly overhead, the Howling Basilisk just beginning to appear on the horizon. Its hour had come. It was time to begin.

With the tip of her sword, she traced a line in the sward until the Black Stone was enclosed in an unbroken circle. She added names of power and symbols of warding. She then knelt and unlocked the wooden chest. When opened, a powerful magic barrier would be removed, and she would be far less shielded from the baleful entity that lay within. She whispered a charm against evil and lifted the lid.

Inside, thick black velvet cushioned an oblong object wrapped in heavy woolen cloth. This she unwound, revealing a smoky gray crystal as long as her forearm and as big around as her fist. It had become so extraordinarily weighty that she could barely lift it from the box. Sarah was as ready as she would ever be. She took a deep breath and began the Incantation of Release.

As he waited against the wall, Thurmond kept his gaze riveted to the hell-stone. Suddenly he grew intensely cold, and all vision was blocked by a darkness so complete that it engulfed the light of the moon and stars, and even the furious glare of the burning stable. Through the gloom, he heard Sarah's voice raised in an inhuman shriek.

He stumbled forward, groping in the dark toward where she must be, not stopping until he tripped and fell over her recumbent form. She clutched at him with desperate, frantic fingers.

"You must finish…carry it…I can't…can't. Don't look into it…don't…."

Sarah lapsed into a swoon. He tried to rouse her, but failed.

What was he to do? He had no idea. She told him he had to carry it. She obviously meant the instrument—but to where? The only place he could think of was to the Black Stone, which was now becoming visible as light began to seep back into the monastery.

He took up the crystal from where Sarah had dropped it and walked carefully toward the Stone, stopping abruptly when he saw the lines cut in the sward. He knew better than to enter a magic circle. What now?

He looked down at the thing in his arms. What was the other thing Sarah had muttered just before passing out? *Don't look into it.*

Too late. A little face stared out from the depths of the crystal, a face so hideous that Thurmond's knees began to give way. His will oozed away like melting ice, and he felt himself being drawn irresistibly out of himself.

His body reacted without conscious thought. He hurled the crystal at the Black Stone with all his strength. He was vaguely aware of something shattering, a searing blast of heat, and a chthonic stench. Then he was running for the monastery's gate, sprinting as fast as he could while dragging Sarah by one arm.

He would have dashed straight through the gate, but Roscoe caught him by the arm. He spun about, eyes void of recognition, and jerked his arm in a desperate attempt to get loose. The old Adventurer then clasped him round the neck and held him tight. Even through their armor, Roscoe could feel his young friend's body quivering with fright. His nose was bleeding, red droplets fell from the end of his chin.

"God's fangs, laddie, what happened to you? Did you release the demon? Did the instrument work?"

Thurmond remained silent. With desperate fear in his eyes and blood oozing from his nose, he struggled free from his friend's grip and began once more to pull Sarah through the gates. Roscoe and Torgul could only follow.

The burning of the stable, as tragic as it was for the people trapped inside, was extremely fortuitous for the citizens of Gorgonholm. Alerted by the bright flames, they correctly assumed that the invasion was underway and immediately sounded the alarm. Throughout the city, the cry *bills and*

bows! bills and bows! sent men and women running to their positions on the battlements.

Bartos's engineers cocked their ballistae and cranked back the throwing arms of their mangonels. Fires were kindled beneath cauldrons of water and oil. Magicians prepared their spells.

Thus, when the Painted Men arrived at the city walls, they found the inhabitants quite ready to receive them. As they charged forward to heave their grapnels, they were struck by the devastating fire of the city's catapults— great scoops of fist-sized stones from the mangonels, heavy darts from the springalds, ballista bolts so powerful that they could pin one man to another.

As the attacking waves drew closer, archers and crossbowmen delivered a withering barrage from wall, gate, and tower. Illuminated by the bright moonlight, the Painted Men were easy targets, but they pressed forward, regardless of loss, to the edge of the moat.

The city's moat should have been a formidable barrier, but years of neglect had left it in sad condition. Its banks had broken down in many places, and the filthy green water was only as deep as a man's knees. Had there been more time, had the city not been so determined to destroy itself prior to the invasion, the civic leaders might have allocated funds for the needed repairs and had it filled with water diverted from the river.

These things, however, had not happened, and the savage invaders, accustomed to splashing through woodlands streams, crossed the barrier without so much as a pause. They reached the base of the wall where they were protected from the terrible arrow storm.

Now the city's women pelted them with everything they had—stones, heavy wooden timbers, brickbats, chamber pots. When these ran short, they yelled for their children to fetch more. The water and oil, to their dismay, was not yet hot enough to dump.

The Painted Men yowled, bled, and died, but they were many and fearless. Undeterred, they threw their grapnels and climbed up, hand over hand. The men and women atop the walls cut the ropes with axes and thrust spears into their tattooed faces as they appeared above the parapets.

It seemed for a while that the savages would be held off, that they must fail in the face of such determined opposition. But these wilderness-born men were fierce beyond all imagination. They despised death almost as much as they distained the laigi who opposed them. So they climbed on, heedless of their fallen comrades, their one desire being to see the blood of their enemy.

It soon became clear that there were not enough defenders to adequately cover every segment of wall. As soon as they rushed to repel one threat, they would be faced with an attack in a different sector. They fought as hard as they could, but they could not kill the attackers fast enough.

While the fighting raged along the south wall, an especially ferocious band of warriors surged around its end to assault the corner of the west wall. They were the Bad Eyes, a famed warrior society comprised of proven champions. Each sported an enchanted apron endowing the wearer with unparalleled virility and audacity.

The juncture of the southern and western walls was guarded by a mighty tower that gave archers within a clear field of fire along the base of both walls. But unfortunately, there were no archers within—they were all off with Sheriff Brandon and the Trained Bands. A handful of old men had been assigned to the tower, but these had left their posts to join in the defense of the South Gate, where the Keltin attack was centered. Thus, no arrows hindered the approach of the Bad-Eyes warriors.

The adjoining section of west wall was woefully undefended. When the first Bad-Eyes heaved themselves over the parapet, they were confronted by three elderly burghers too lame to do more than shuffle forward to their deaths.

Sadly, these blundering gaffers, in their excitement, neglected to lock the door to the tower, allowing the attackers to access the tower's interior and the spiral stairs leading to the ground below. Half of the attackers charged down the stairs to assail the South Gate from the inside. The remainder threw open the door to the southern wall walk and took the defenders in the rear.

CHAPTER 42

BATTLES ABOVE
AND BELOW

The Small Folk set out in their little boats at the same time the Painted Men were hammering at the city walls. They moved quickly across the underground stream, the splash of their tiny paddles hardly audible in the heavy, subterranean air. Their landing was as quiet as their crossing. Their unshod feet were silent in the Catacomb's stone passageways.

This was their natural element, for the Small Folk made the abode in underground deeps and could see in the dark as readily as any dwarf or goblin.

Small Folk feared and hated the larger humans, who they referred to as *erldogh-dbruh-aldkor*, meaning *giant-devil-freaks* in their unpronounceable tongue. Such feelings were well-founded, for their once flourishing culture had been almost exterminated by their full-sized foes. The surviving Small Folk had been driven into the most remote stretches of the western wilderness where even the Keltin tribes had not penetrated.

The shattered remains of their ancient forts and roads could be found scattered throughout the land. These were best avoided, for anyone encountering the Small Folk was likely to meet an unfortunate end.

Very few giant-devil-freaks had actually seen one of the Small Folk, but all had been raised on tales of their mischief and duplicity. They were notorious as thieves and tricksters. Their particular delight was the kidnapping of human children. Occasionally, they left one of their own runtish offspring in exchange.

Yet compelled by the call of the Stone, they had left from their hidden homes to join their traditional enemies in their attack on Gorgonholm.

They wore no armor, only simple tunics the color of leaves. Nor did they carry metal weapons, associating iron and bronze with the hated giant-devil-freaks. Their knives and axes were fashioned from flint, for the Small Folk were superlative workers of stone.

Their main weapon was the bow, quite small by normal measure, yet deadly in their skillful hands. Each of their tiny arrows, no larger than a common river reed, was tipped by a flinthead that had been knapped to a fantastic sharpness and then dipped in a most lethal poison.

The Small Folk were few in number, so they relied on stealth rather than strength, on agility rather than size, on cunning instead of ferocity. They now came slinking through the Catacombs, ready to emerge from the shadows and strike a deadly blow from behind. That, at least, was the plan as envisioned by Fergis when he sent them across the underground lake in little boats.

What actually occurred was altogether different.

The defenders of Old Shambles were by and large a crew of criminals, ne'er-do-wells, and degenerate reprobates, but they were intensely loyal to their decrepit neighborhoods. Though they slew one another for control of this particular corner or that stretch of street, all such enmity was forgotten when their turf was threatened by an external foe.

With invasion imminent, the leaders had gathered at the infamous Drowned Rat tavern for a conference of war. Corner boys and whoremasters, cutpurses and counterfeiters, forgers, and chiselers crowded into a narrow upper room to lay their plans. Two masked stranglers represented The Brethren. That group's mysterious leader, known only as The Patron, was not in attendance, though it was rumored he owned the Drowned Rat and was ensconced somewhere on the premises.

The most important attendees, however, were the smugglers, many of whom were intimately familiar with the secret windings of the Catacombs. Their smuggling route, they realized, was a weak point, an exposed rear entrance to the city—one of which their Keltin enemy was well aware.

It was agreed, therefore, that the Shamblers must take upon themselves the duty of guarding this open door. They had, in times of peace, been happy to supply the Keltins with weapons, but they would not allow those same weapons to be turned on their city. They had to protect their business interests.

Thus, as the Small Folk advanced though the dripping limestone passages, they found their way blocked by a stout barricade manned by corner boys and cutpurses. Superior archers, the Small Folk used their small, fast bows to shoot the Shamblers off this barrier. Within moments, they lay writhing on the floor, white froth bubbling from their slack mouths.

The Shamblers' sacrifice, however, was not in vain. Before he died, their leader, a pock-marked rapscallion known as Duckie, blew a whistle, warning his confederates to the presence of the foe. Thieves and murderers now came pouring from branching passages and adjacent chambers to meet the Small Folk hand to hand, steel daggers against flint knives, crossbow bolts versus poisoned arrows.

The fight quickly shifted into the network of smaller tunnels diverging from the main passageway. In such close confines, the Small Folk enjoyed a decided advantage over their larger opponents. The little men were tough, fast, and determined. They ran in close, slashing at throat, stomach, and groin, severing hamstrings, opening veins and arteries with nimble flicks of their wrists. Their small knives flensed meat from bone with remarkable ease. The slightest scratch of their diminutive arrows brought agonizing death.

The Small Folk pushed forward. One little warrior squared off with a huge Brethren enforcer. He ducked low and cut the tendon at the latter's heel. As the big man toppled forward, he grasped his diminutive opponent by the neck and dragged him down as well. The flint knife plunged again and again while the Shambler smashed the small warrior's skull on the tunnel's hard stone floor. This continued until both lay dead.

Corner boys, many no larger than their foes, were eager to prove their reckless courage. Leaping forward, they tackled the invaders and carried them to the ground. In a lethal variation of a boyhood tussle, the interlocked enemies rolled on the floor, biting, scratching, gouging at eyes.

The fighting grew even more confused as the passages became strewn with dead and wounded. Both sides tripped over the bodies of their comrades, slipped in pools of blood. Stone-tipped spears were thrust into bearded faces, iron swords clove child-sized skulls. Big and small screamed and died.

The Small Folk were relentless adversaries. Despite their terrible losses, they drove forward, stepping heedlessly over their own dead in their lust to slay the living, their archers sending a torrent of envenomed shafts into the close-packed ranks of the cityfolk. A renowned captain of thieves died on his feet, an arrow protruding from his throat. A veteran smuggler, hit in the arm, struggled briefly against the poison that set his blood aflame. Then he slumped, froth rolling from his lips.

The Shamblers were, by degrees, driven back. Merciless killers though they were, the urban criminals were unused to combat with an armed and resisting foe. To their credit, they did not rout, but neither could they stand against the warriors of the Small Folk. One step at a time, they were forced to retreat.

High in the sky above Gorgonholm, the obedient demons of the city's wizards did battle with the airy sprites of the Keltin shamans. The fighting was unwitnessed by human eyes, for it did not take place entirely on the mortal plane. If it had, the citizens would have seen a cascade of ungodly body parts falling from the heavens—torn fragments of leathery wings, arms sporting too many elbows, and a disturbing assortment of scales, talons, barbs, hooks, tentacles, and fangs.

The shamanistic spirits attacked in two separate formations. High above, the big, slow-moving elementals prepared to bombard the city with earthquake, hailstones, firestorm, and gale. Below them, the smaller, faster sprites swooped in—woodland nymphs, sloe-eyed sylphs, fire breathing salamanders, fairies, pixies, and nixies. These were to shield the vulnerable elementals from the counterattack of the city's infernal legions.

The Demon Corps of Gorgonholm did not fail to respond. They rose from their roosts in the attic of the spell-casters' guildhall, ready to intercept the attackers and send them spinning into the ethereal void. Count Borgo, an archfiend specializing in military science, led the mixed flock of chthonic entities. They spiraled upward, their wings pounding as they strove for altitude.

Borgo's demons were still flapping skyward when the sprites, attacking from out of the moonlight, stuck with the speed and fury of a lightning bolt. They tore through the infernal formation, sending imps cartwheeling through space, tearing the wings from black-beaked lampads, rending the soft flesh of succubi.

Count Borgo waxed wroth at this effrontery, executed a perfect turning roll, and ripped the guts from an unsuspecting pixie. He banked hard, climbed, reversed direction. Below him a kelpie was angling for attack position above a small devilkin in the shape of a flying toad. The kelpie never saw him coming. Borgo sliced through its graceful equine form just as a knife would cleave soft bread.

The archfiend laughed as only a demon can laugh while the kelpie's shredded remains fluttered earthward. His laughter ceased, however, when three sylphs suddenly appeared behind him. They were faster and more agile than the demon-lord, and their teeth were very sharp.

The Count dove hard and straight toward the ground, then pulled into a steep climb, using the momentum of the dive to bring himself to near vertical. He shot by the astonished sylphs, who were happy to pursue less formidable prey.

The higher altitude gave Borgo a better look at the battle. Below him, sprites and demons twisted, zig-zagged, and jinked. He saw a witch's familiar, a black rabbit named Sacke-and-Sugar, burned to ash by a pair of *thori*—tiny salamanders no doubt spawned by one of the huge fire elementals. A cacodemon pulled the legs from a nixie as if plucking fruit from a tree. An incubus, spinning out of control on one wing, smashed headlong into a brick chimney.

In fact, none of the sprites or demons destroyed in the fighting was actually dead, since such creatures were not exactly *alive*, at least not in the normal meaning of the word. Slain demons were returned to the bleak ethereal wasteland from which they had been summoned. Sprites might find themselves reborn as newly sprouted seeds, fledgling chickadees, or fingerling trout.

Borgo felt a familiar tingling in the row of long spikes projecting from his backbone—danger was approaching. He was aghast to discover, high above him, the heavy, slow-moving elementals silhouetted against the moonlit clouds. This was a distressing development, for Borgo and his minions were obligated by infernal pact to defend the city. The punishment would be agonizing if they failed to uphold their commitment.

Yet, there was nothing he could do. The battle had carried the demon host down to house-top level. There was no way to stop the attack.

The elementals reached their assigned targets and released the full fury of their powers. Cyclonic winds buffeted the tall towers so that they swayed like trees in a heavy breeze. The river rose from its banks as if intending to swallow the city's entire western wall. The ground began to shake so that the ancient houses and strong stone gates must crumble to dust. The cathedral was wrapped in a shroud of fire.

Certainly, this would have been the end of Gorgonholm had its wizards not employed all their skills to guard it against occult attack. Knowing they must face the earth magic of Keltin shamans, they had put in place the most astounding psychic shields to foil the elemental magic. Even sorcerers sometimes get it right.

So, the river lashed at the western wall, sweeping away most of the boats and docks, but the quayside buildings remained untouched. Winds howled like the souls of the damned, but no towers fell. The earth juddered, but the houses and gates, though hard shaken, were not destroyed. The cathedral was indeed wrapped in fire, yet it did not burn.

Count Borgo took stock. He was pleased with what he saw. His demons were fighting well, and the tide of battle was turning in his favor. He watched a pair of pit-fiends chase down and consume a hapless maenad. A nighthag clutched a wood nymph in her deadly embrace.

Borgo chortled as he watched an eight-legged bog-demon chase a swarm of fays through the buttresses of the cathedral. It seemed for a moment that they must escape, but then an ill-advised turn caused them to smash headlong into a stained-glass window, reducing the whole swarm to a smear of greasy goo.

The sprites were being driven from the sky.

But then, the demon-lord was once again filled with dread, for a second flight of elementals followed close behind the first. The power of the Gorgonholm's magicians, he knew, had its limits. Though they had successfully foiled the attack of the first flight, their magical shields must now be exhausted. The city lay completely open to this second wave.

Just as destruction seemed inevitable, a squadron of red-crested furies, flying in wedge formation, tore into the lumbering elementals from below. Armed with large, hooked beaks and flesh-rending talons, furies were among the most determined of non-corporeal entities. Once a fury latched on, it did not let go.

Yet the elementals were far from defenseless. Even as a trio of furies was ripping at its face, a great fire spirit spat an incandescent cloud that set their feathers aflame. A wind spirit puffed its flabby cheeks and sent more furies tumbling helplessly across the sky.

Count Borgo saw all this, and the anger grew huge within him. He summoned the surviving imps and night-hags, familiars and cacodemons, and sped to the attack. The slow-witted elementals, their attention focused on the furies, were taken unawares. Gashed and punctured, they deflated like ruptured wineskins and sank to the ground.

Mighty though he was, Borgo's powers were by now fully depleted. His fangs were blunt and his talons were dull. His tail-spike had snapped off in the body of a dyad. He would do no more fighting this day.

His force of infernal minions was woefully reduced and exhausted, but they had fulfilled their part of the bargain. The city had survived.

Great, then, was his distress when he saw a third flight of elementals approaching from the west.

CHAPTER 43

THE ARMIES ADVANCE

The river crossing went more smoothly than Fergis could have hoped. He stood atop the riverbank, watching the currachs scurry back and forth with load after load of lightly armed warriors. The rafts, too, were functioning perfectly, ferrying over larger groups of more heavily equipped men. Now, with dawn brimming in the eastern sky, the rafts could be lashed together to form a floating bridge, allowing for the rapid passage of more men, horses, and supply carts.

The lesser kings were marshalling the many clans into battle formation, a long dense line that grew in depth and length with the landing of each raft and currach. Some of the spirit of cooperation, Fergis noticed, had begun to dissipate, with the cantankerous clan chiefs taking exception to their placement in the line. He gave it no thought—one's place in the battleline was always a subject of dispute.

A contingent of Red Leg spearmen stepped from a raft and began hiking up the riverbank. Fergis decided to follow them. It was time for him to get out in front, to allow his warriors to see their leader and share his supreme confidence. He signaled a *gillie* to bring his horse, a shaggy garron. Keltin warriors traditionally fought on foot, but an Ard Righ was always more impressive when seen in the saddle.

The effect was greatly enhanced by his formal battle-dress, each item an ancient family heirloom. The shirt of fine woven links from the hands of

Goib, god of weapons and armor, the high helmet of polished bronze, the enchanted war-belt.

Mounting, he kicked his heels into the garron's flanks—Keltins distained the use of spurs—and rode forth to have a look at his army.

Fergis's enemies were also up and about as the sun rose above the horizon. Earl Ralf Mortimer was busily preparing his army for war. Setting up for a big battle took a lot of time. Enemy commanders would often arrange a truce to allow both sides the chance to get ready.

The earl's army was assembled on a grassy meadow a league or so south and east of the Gorgonholm. His scouts had reported the Keltin host to be across the river and preparing to advance on the city. He would interpose his army between Fergis and his objective.

During the night, there had been vague reports of fighting along the city walls. Ralf was too occupied with his main purpose to give such rumors much thought. The citizens, he assumed, would be capable of holding off whatever small force of raiders was annoying them.

The army of Avincraik was not appreciably different than that of its Keltin foe. Both were *ad hoc* amalgamations of many diverse, individual units. There was no permanent command structure. Unit commanders were appointed on the spot by Earl Ralf. Most often, such appointments were based on birth rather than aptitude or experience.

Ralf's senior commanders were all brave men and ardent warriors, but few were especially inventive or insightful. Intelligence and ingenuity were not respected as noble virtues. Still, most did their jobs to the best of their ability.

The nobles were, of course, all members of the chivalry, an elite society venerated in legend and song. Too many of them, unfortunately, had come to take such tales at face value, distaining the archers and spearmen that made up the bulk of the army. War, for most knights, was mostly an opportunity to achieve personal glory.

An armored knight on a trained warhorse was truly an awesome weapon, but Ralf had far too few of them to defeat so large an enemy host. He understood that a tight defensive formation of pikes, shields, and archers offered his best chance of victory. So there would be no thundering storm of heavy cavalry. The horses would be kept in the rear, used only for a final, decisive blow.

As a Mortimer, Ralf had been trained to fight Keltins since childhood. He knew them as profoundly vicious and fearless warriors that that would seek to swarm over his army in a single, tremendous onslaught. But they were also a highly agile force, capable of an abrupt swing to the right or left to envelop a flank. Or they might suddenly fall back in feigned defeat, a clever ploy to lure his men into a careless headlong charge that could be engulfed and annihilated. Keltins were supremely tricky.

Ralf's knights, of course, grumbled and griped when word came that they would be deprived of their chance to ride to fame and glory. What use was war if they could not use it to bolster their standing amongst their fellow nobles? Fighting alongside common pikemen would bring them little renown. But it was their duty to obey, so they shortened their lances and discarded the iron sabatons that made walking so difficult.

One young knight, Baron Henry Bone, was determined to secure some personal advantage from the day's events. Only two and twenty, he would soon become a baron, his aged father being on his deathbed. He felt, therefore, a burning need to demonstrate his prowess to the ranking men who must shortly acknowledge him as their peer.

As the sun rose in the sky, Sir Henry rode out of camp with a dozen men of his personal retinue. He cut a dashing figure. His bright surcoat bore the ancient and most noble arms of House Bone. These were repeated on the large banner held by the squire who rode at his side. Morning sunbeams twinkled on his mail, on his flat-topped helm, and on the sharp-ground point of his long lance.

His huge charger took high, prancing steps as it bore its youthful rider into the open expanse between the two armies. The Keltins, he knew, were out there somewhere, and he intended to distinguish himself by some deed of arms before returning to his own ranks.

Imagine his delight, therefore, when, coming over a small fold of ground, he discovered the enemy host advancing toward Gorgonholm. A trio of

warriors on shaggy ponies rode at some distance ahead of the front line—
obviously men of great import. One fellow was particularly impressive in his
gleaming mail and high bronze helmet.

Sir Henry could scarcely believe his good fortune. The slaying of a high-
ranking Keltin leader would bring him the distinction he craved so badly. He
quickly sent a man to the rear to warn Ralf of the approaching enemy. Then
he couched his lance and charged the man in the tall helmet.

Fergis saw him coming. He could, he knew, turn about and ride to the
safety of his army, for the knight was still some distance away. But that would
look cowardly, and Fergis, above everything, was no coward. So he pushed
forward, putting distance between himself and the two warriors that served
as his bodyguards.

He could by no means charge and meet the knight on an equal basis. His
garron could not stand against the massive warhorse. He had no spear, no
shield. The long lance of the knight must punch straight through his body.
And so, after a few deliberate steps, he reined in and waited.

Sir Henry's blood was up. His foe seemed to be asking for death, and the
knight intended to bring it to him. He began to shout the famous battle cry
of his family.

"A Bone! A Bone! A Bone!"

Drawing closer, he kicked his pointed spurs into his mount's flanks,
launching it toward the target with a speed that would have seemed impossible
from so large a beast.

All the while, Fergis sat impassive, unmoving. In his right hand, he
gripped his only weapon, a fine steel battleaxe provided by smugglers in
exchange for uisge.

Just before the lance point struck his chest, Fergis suddenly shifted to
the left, nimbly avoiding death by impalement. Then, as the knight's charger
carried him close alongside, the Keltin king rose in the stirrups and delivered
a crushing blow to the flat top of his opponent's helm. So great was its force
that it sheered right through the heavy iron plate, through the mail coif and
padded cap beneath it, and finally through Sir Henry's skull and into his
brain.

Fergis might despise most aspects of civilization, but he had to admit, he did love its steel weapons. Stirrups were another useful innovation.

Sir Henry's charger, aware that something was amiss, slowed to a stop, while the lifeless form of its rider slumped sideways and fell to the earth. The knight's men were filled with dismay. They had expected their lord to ride over the helpless Keltin as easily as he might ride over a child, but then the unthinkable had occurred.

What kind of men were these Keltins who so utterly disregarded the accepted conventions of combat? Didn't they realize that Sir Henry had had a right to prevail? How could they ride to battle against such men?

They turned and fled back to their own lines.

A tremendous cheer came from the Keltin host, who had, to a man, witnessed the encounter. Nothing could have aroused their fighting spirit more than this proof of the invincibility of their king. The danced, sang, screamed, shook their weapons, and laughed.

Fergis needed this morale boost more than he realized, for as the power of the Stone began to wane, dissent and disunity were beginning to spread through the ranks of his army. The clan chiefs, as always, were jealous of their position in the line of battle. But far worse, their commitment to the great cause—the utter destruction of the laigi—had begun to flag. Many, after all, had become wealthy through the trading of uisge. Why should they want to destroy this fine source of prosperity?

Others could see no personal gain in fighting a pitched battle against armored soldiers when there were so many isolated villages and farmsteads to raid. When opportunity presented, various small bands began to slip away to try their hands at softer targets.

Nonetheless, a mighty army remained, and at Fergis's signal, they continued their advance.

Earl Ralf's army was also on the move, so Sir Henry's companions had very little chance to spread their disheartening tale. Ralf was an able commander but by no means a military genius. He was wise enough to resist the temptation of a reckless charge, but he had little idea of what to do other than follow the concepts passed down to him by previous generations.

The bulk of his force was arranged in three great *battles*, the largest being the center under the command of Lord Drakar. Here Drakar's men, along with the city's Trained Bands and the clerical contingents, were bolstered by Hawkwood's mercenaries. It was expected that the main Keltin effort would fall on these men.

The left and right wings were commanded by Baron Phineas Hardbottle and Lord Pikadilly Fudg, respectively. These were composed of feudal levies of the various nobles who had responded to the call to arms. Earl Ralf stationed his reserve under Sir Marmaduke Twaddle behind Drakar's center. Lord Beaufort remained in charge of the camp, a league or so to the rear.

In all the commotion of getting the army into the field, it was inevitable that details would be overlooked. So it happened that Sir Lorenzo di Prativentosi, a young foreign knight come north in search of adventure, was left without a designated place in the line. He had been assigned to the left-hand battle under Sir Pikadilly, but when he had reported to that individual, he had received neither instruction nor command.

This, Sir Lorenzo realized, could be either a good thing or a bad one. Bad if the oversight led to the death of his men or himself. Good in that it allowed him a certain freedom of movement that he might use to his advantage.

With that in mind, he led his personal contingent of thirty-six mounted men-at-arms to the far end of the battle-line. They were the final unit of the army's right flank. Such a position, he reasoned, might allow for a quick ride around the enemy's opposite flank. Thus, he would keep his horses close at hand.

They formed up next to a levy of farmers and craftsmen from the shire of Groyne. Sir Lorenzo signaled his banner-bearer, a pug-nosed teenager he had acquired somewhere on his long road north.

"Unfurl the banner, Riley. Let 'em see who's standing next of 'em."

The lad did as bidden, revealing the Prativentosi family arms, a white rabbit rampant on a field of red and black. Lorenzo was aware that his arms would mean nothing to these northern lords. Strange as it was, some seemed to find the angry rabbit amusing.

Well, today he would show them just what that proud rabbit could do. He looked with pride at the men standing beside him. Most, like Riley, he had picked up during his journey, but a few were loyal family retainers who had been with him for the entire trek. They were rough men, battered, cursing, hard-drinking soldiers, but united by a singular bond of fellowship. The knight would trust any of them with his gold or his life.

Two, in particular, had been his boon companions since childhood. Federico was a tall, bear of a man with huge hands and hulking shoulders. In battle, he preferred to get close and smash his foe with a heavy flanged mace. Arturius was lean and fair-haired, as quick and cunning as Frederico was strong. Whenever possible, he chose to fight at a distance, slashing and stabbing with a long-shafted glaive.

But then, as the Keltin army hove into view, the brave young knight lost some of his confidence. He had always thought of Keltins as little more than rag-tag ruffians. What he saw coming was altogether different.

Sir Lorenzo had no firsthand knowledge of Keltins. His Etrusian ancestors had, centuries ago, driven the last of them from his southern homeland. His tutors—Lorenzo was well educated for a knight—had always stressed their utter barbarity, their paucity of civilized virtues, their complete lack of good taste.

The army moving against him now was anything but the wild mob he expected. The long lines were advancing in a slow, steady pace, shields overlapped in a solid, impenetrable wall that gently undulated with each forward step. Lorenzo glanced down Earl Ralf's battle-line—it was nowhere near as neatly ordered.

Worse yet, the Keltin force was so vast. The points of their spears resembled a moving forest. Dozens of battle standards proclaimed the presence of myriad tribes and clans. How could the savage king of a howling wilderness assemble so many warriors?

Perhaps, Lorenzo thought, he should have considered more carefully before committing himself to the earl's cause.

As the enemy host drew closer, the young knight took stock of the unit directly across the intervening space. These were the warriors that he would soon be facing. At least four times his number, arranged in a stout shieldwall backed by spearmen. Their leader, a huge man in a tall feather-crested helmet, looked to be some sort of great champion.

All this group had to do was advance. They had more than enough people to swarm over his own modest force. Once he and his men were down, the Keltins could sweep behind the earl's battleline and drive his entire army from the field.

Most definitely, Lorenzo thought, he should have given more thought before joining this fray.

CHAPTER 44

THE WORK OF SPEAR
AND SWORD

The Keltin line drew closer, and Ralf's archers loosed a volley of bolts and arrows that sent a great many of them to reside with their grim forest gods. Fergis's bowmen returned the fire, but their effect was slight. The short bows of the Keltins were no match for the deadly warbows of Ralf's archers.

Then with a chorus of trumpets and battle shouts, the Keltin host closed with its foe.

The air reverberated with the screams of the dying and the rolling clatter of swords striking shields. Spears darted in and out like the tongues of deadly serpents. Axe rose and fell, rose and fell. Blood squirted, brains splattered, heavy boots stomped the faces of the fallen.

Lorenzo braced himself for the worst as the enemy's powerful left flank grew closer and closer to his pitiful handful. Death was stalking across that field, aiming straight in their direction. They would be overrun in a moment.

But strangely, unexpectedly, the opposing unit ceased to advance. They simply halted and held their ground while the rest of their comrades moved to engage the enemy. They just stopped and stared, as if unaware that a battle was now raging along the rest of the line.

Lorenzo was puzzled. This being his first major battle, he did not really know what he should expect, but he was fairly certain that this was not a normal tactic, not at least when the enemy had such numerical superiority. Was it a trick to lure him into a misguided attack? Hardly likely—there were more than enough Keltins to fend off any assault he and his boys could offer.

What the hell was going on?

As the power of the Stone declined, the ardor of the Keltin soldiers, particularly the leaders, began to fade. The laigi, after all, were an unfailing source of wealth. The trading of uisge brought fine steel weapons to the hands of their warriors. Why would they want to end such an agreeable arrangement?

They began to recall the old grudges that had, for a while, seemed to slip from their minds. The ancient memories of murder and betrayal that had turned one tribe against the other for generations uncounted. The more they remembered, the more their anger grew.

None was angrier than Fergis's brother, Oengus mac Brude. Anger was, in sooth, his natural state, but today he was more given to wrath than ever before. He had, through some foolish notion of kinship, pledged his loyalty to his brother. Had actually bent his knee and, with his hands upon the sacred whetstone, made his unbreakable vow. What had driven him to such a disgraceful deed?

That memory was sour enough, but what had followed was far, far the worse. He had expected that Fergis would show his appreciation with an appropriate gesture, but his request to command the army's right wing—a prestigious position known as the king's right hand—had been refused.

Command of the right was traditionally awarded the most venerated of the Ard Righ's chiefs. Who was more entitled than his older brother? A brother who had been passed over for the very title Fergis now enjoyed. That great honor had gone to Coinneach mac Coinneach, while Oengus had been shunted off to the end of the left flank with scarcely a hundred spears at his command. This blistering disgrace had entirely erased the maudlin mood of family feeling that had previously plagued him.

He would have preferred to murder his brother at once, to stick a knife in his back during a council of chiefs and proclaim himself Ard Righ. He was, unfortunately, bound by the hideous oath he swore upon the whetstone. The consequences of breaking it were too terrible to consider.

He could not, therefore, directly betray his brother, but perhaps he could show his displeasure in other ways. He could refuse to attack with the paltry force allotted him. Or he could at least delay doing so—that ought to get Fergis's attention.

With this in mind, he called for his men to halt just short of the enemy battleline.

The battle continued to rage along the rest of the line. Heads flew from necks, arms from shoulders. Sharp points were shoved into yielding bellies. Heavy blades knocked eyes from sockets and teeth from jaws. Men shrieked and dropped into pools of muddy blood.

With their superior armor and weapons, the earl's soldiers inflicted far more casualties than they suffered. Apart from the ceremonial equipments of the leaders, few of the Keltin warriors wore armor. It was, in fact, regarded by many as unmanly to fight in protective gear. The bravest went to battle stark naked. Most Keltins carried swords and spears of bronze rather than iron or steel.

Avincraik's archers continued to do good service, shifting their fire wherever the threat seemed the greatest, shooting down the attackers as quickly as they could. But the Keltins, undaunted by their losses, kept coming. There were so many of them.

The main thrust came from the Keltin right, from bellicose Coinneach mac Coinneach and the spearmen of Ben Wyvern. Using their superior numbers, they kept reaching beyond the earl's left flank, forcing it to bend back in an effort to avoid being enveloped. The individual soldiers, instead of standing shoulder to shoulder, had to spread out to lengthen their line.

More Keltins kept coming, always pressing the earl's left, forcing it back step by step, until it must give way and allow the army of Avincraik to be destroyed from behind.

Seeing the danger, Earl Ralf dispatched Sir Marmaduke Twaddle and the reserve to bolster his wavering flank. Twaddle was heralded as one of the bravest and most chivalrous knights in all the land. He had always served his lord with acumen and aplomb. If anyone could secure the left, it would be him.

Unfortunately, Lady Fortune did not smile on Twaddle that day. As he was marshalling his troopers into position, he noticed a Keltin arrow arcing across the sky in his direction. There was little to fear—he carried a shield and was clad in the best of plate armor. The lightweight Keltin shafts could not penetrate such defenses. Many arrows came in his direction—there was nothing special about this one.

Here was Twaddle's mistake—in his arrogance, he forgot that even a lowly Keltin archer can sometimes bring down the most accomplished knight. That in spite of his proud warhorse, his fine armor, and his illustrious lineage, he could still be killed. Had he raised his shield just a little or perhaps turned his head the slightest bit, he might well have survived the day.

But he did not do these things, so the arrow slid cleanly through the narrow vision slot of his helm and entered his brain. The renowned Sir Marmaduke slumped in the saddle, all his nobility reduced to lifeless clay.

His men, luckily, did not witness the death of their leader, or they might have routed right then and there. They were at that moment far too occupied with the on-coming Keltins to pay attention to anything else. They did their level best to bolster the collapsing left flank, but the accursed Keltins kept surging against them like the waves of a raging sea.

Lorenzo knew he must act, that failing to decide was worse than a bad choice. On his immediate left, the men of Groyne were engaged in a continuous if somewhat desultory poking match with some Keltin spearmen. The unit to his front, however, remained stationary. So what should he be doing?

He studied their leader, the one in the high, feathered helmet who he had pegged as a great champion. Perhaps he was a champion, but there was something in the man's bearing that argued otherwise. He was too puffed up, too blustering. He seemed more like a man making a poor performance of being a champion rather than one truly possessing heroic qualities. A man greatly needing to prove himself yet lacking the courage to do so.

Such a man could be brought to ruin. Fearing his own weakness, he would search for a similar weakness in others. What Lorenzo needed to do, therefore, was create an irresistible perception of weakness.

Lorenzo's Etrusian forebears had been masters of strategy and tactics. They had refined military organization and maneuver to a fine science that allowed them to dominate the known world of their day. They had time and again defeated Keltin hosts every bit as huge and fearsome as this one, driven them from their ancestral lands, and enslaved their women and children. There must be a way.

A reckless scheme began to take shape. His idea could easily lead to his death—to the death of them all—but if that pompous buffoon across the way was stupid enough, arrogant enough, it could perhaps deliver them.

He signaled his men to draw further to the right, to put a twenty-foot gap between themselves and the men from Groyne. He pulled them backward another twenty feet, further widening the gap. Then he ordered the horses to be brought forward.

His scheme was about to be put to the test, for at that moment, the blustering fellow waved his sword and his warriors resumed their advance.

Fergis sat his horse on a small rise that afforded him a good view of his army's center and—much more importantly—its right wing. Most of the left was obscured by a small stand of trees, but it was the unimportant flank. The left, like the center, had only to pin the enemy line in place so that mac Coinneach on the right could do the main work.

All, as far as he could see, was working to perfection. Left and center were engaged but not pressing the attack in costly, sometimes suicidal charges, the right was progressing rapidly, pushing forward as the laigi flank curled in on itself. He saw the commitment of the enemy reserve and the early demise of its leader.

Fergis had received no recent news from the city, but the last messages had all been good. The Painted Men had sustained heavy causalities but had secured much of south wall and its massive gatehouse, so the way was open. From the Small Folk, he had heard nothing, but that was not unexpected— they were a strange, secretive people after all.

His brother Oengus had been given a very simple task. He had only to keep the enemy from circling around the left flank. Given the comparative sizes of the two armies, there was very little chance this would occur, but it gave the bumbling Oengus something to do. Fergis would never trust him with a more demanding task.

No word had come from that flank, so he assumed all must be going well.

Now he saw the enemy earl leading his small personal retinue in a vain attempt to strengthen his doomed flank. It was the time for the final stroke. Fergis burned to meet the opposing leader, this Earl Ralf, face to face and slay him with his own hand. He motioned to his own guard of picked warriors and rode to join the fight on the right.

The third flight of elementals unleashed nature's ire upon the city. Happily, this was the smallest of the three flights, composed of smaller, younger entities that lacked the awesome power of those that came before. Nonetheless, their destructive abilities were magnificent.

The stately Mad River, living up to its name, leapt from its banks, smashed down the workshops and warehouses that lined the quay, cascaded through the slaughterhouses and knackeries of New Shambles, and burst over the city's western wall. Dockside houses were battered to flinders, thick wooden pilings were sent spinning through the air like cornstalks in a tempest. A riverboat was torn from its mooring and flung into the city center, crashing down atop a pawnshop near Market Square.

Fearsome winds ripped through the streets, tearing the thatch from roofs, pulling the shutters from windows, bursting doors, and filling the squares with the scattered remains of household goods—blankets and clothing, torn bedding and splintered furniture. Defenders and attackers alike were swept from the city walls. The cathedral's great bronze bells were knocked from their tower and thrown to the ground with a hideous clang.

Fires erupted spontaneously in a score of places, consuming shops, homes, and churches. Survivors would later claim that their domestic hearths, normally so convivial and comforting, suddenly turned fierce, with red hot coals and blazing kindling inexplicably jumping from the grate to set the room ablaze. Fed by the high winds, the fires soon spread to adjacent structures.

Then the ground began to shake like a wet dog. Plates and goblets were sent plummeting from the sideboards of the wealthy. City Keep swayed and a long crack appeared in its east wall. The abbey of the Black Friars crumbled into a heap of beams, bricks, and roof tiles. Worst of all, the huge South Gate—already the scene of so much carnage—gave way without warning. Those inside were crushed in an avalanche of massive stones.

Their work done, the elementals then flew on to wherever they called home. As they did, the fury they had brought immediately began to slacken. The shaking stopped, and the wind eased its pitiless assault. The river calmed and returned to its bed.

But the Keltin shamans were not quite done. With the last of their power, they sent forth their spirit animals to drive the city's rat population into a frenzied attack. From cubbyhole and rafter room, cellar and garret, the rats gushed forth in a loathsome brown flood.

More and more joined in from sewer and storehouse, granary and stable. Beady eyes gleaming, incisors bared, they surged up from the tenements of Old Shambles and down from the opulent mansions of Hilltop, from the vaults beneath the Cathedral and the dungeons below City Keep. The streets and alleys became seething rivers of brown furry bodies.

The rats did not pause in this mad dash, did not turn aside for the tender meat of a homeless urchin cringing in a doorway nor for the stringy flesh of a blind vagabond cowering beside a public fountain. They bore straight on, ceaseless in their advance, until they reached, at the far end of Spellcaster's Wynd, the great meeting hall of Gorgonholm's magicians' guild.

The city's magicians, however, were prepared for this very circumstance.

Before the battle, they had sniffed the livers of birds, cast the bones of unborn goats, chewed vision-inducing berries, and licked the backs of brown toads, all well-known and approved methods of reading the future. They knew the rats would be coming.

The magicians took their places in the guildhall's most sacred chamber, the Hall of Conjuration. Cat-mint and valerian were burned in the immense bronze brazier standing in its center. Then they began to chant.

From back alleys and firesides, haylofts and kitchens, the cats of Gorgonholm rose up, stretched, and came running, eager to confront their natural prey. Toms and tabbies, brindles and blues, calicoes and kittens swarmed into Spellcaster's Wynd, snarling, spitting, hissing, backs arched, ears laid back.

They pounced on the foremost rodents, slashing with claws, sinking fangs into stubby necks, splattering the cobblestones with blood and fur and meat. Undeterred by their losses, the rats struck back, tearing at feline faces with their long teeth, scratching at soft bellies with short, burrowing claws.

Soon the street was filled with small furry bodies, rolling, jumping, yowling, squealing, biting, dying. Size and strength favored the cats as they ripped heads, legs, and tails from their smaller foes. Numbers favored the rats. Though ten of them died for every cat pulled down and eviscerated, the rodent horde continued to surge forward.

Striped tabbies were overborne and savaged. Kittens consumed. The gnawed remains of calicoes were stretched beside those of lop-eared, one-eyed toms. Torn and defeated, the surviving felines turned and fled. They leapt over fences, climbed trees, and jumped into the open windows of nearby houses. Anything to escape the terrible yellow teeth of the rats.

The magicians' guildhall lay undefended, the last guardians driven away. The rats paused only long enough to give an insidious squeal of victory. Then, through hidden cracks and secret holes, they poured inside.

CHAPTER 45

TWISTINGS AND TURNINGS

Sitting primly on her golden throne, Lady Fortune allowed herself a coy smile. Well, to be honest, no one really knew what her throne looked like, but considering she was a goddess, it must have been nice. The smile was more certain. She was often depicted wearing just such a smile as she twisted someone's fate in an entirely unexpected direction. Which was exactly what she was about to do.

The citizens of Gorgonholm, wallowing in their riches, gorging on exotic viands, lolling with plump courtesans, had seemingly forgotten the source of all their grand prosperity. They had grown arrogant and neglectful and therefore required a gentle reminder, which they were getting this very day. Their city was being destroyed by fire and flood, wind and quake. The citizens were facing certain death from painted savages atop their walls and subterranean pigmies beneath their streets. Their soldiers on the quivering edge of annihilation. Many of their leaders lay slain, while the left flank of their army was being driven back by the relentless Keltin assault.

Lady Fortune was by no means a cruel goddess, but she liked to maintain a sense of balance. When she saw mortals growing a bit too cocky, she brought them down a peg. When they were sufficiently crushed beneath the weight of her fateful wheel, it was her delight to raise them back up. She always preferred the astonishing and unforeseeable over the accustomed and predictable.

Satisfied that the citizens of Gorgonholm would be more mindful in the future, she smiled and spun her wheel.

Overhead, a single, immensely huge water elemental finally arrived over the city. It oozed slowly across the sky, so sodden and bloated that it had lagged far behind its fellows. With a sigh of great relief, it released its ponderous burden, launching a rainstorm of mythic ferocity.

The downpour, at first, seemed like a blessing from a kind and attentive god, for it extinguished the fires that had been consuming the city. But as it went on and on, the astonished citizens came to see that they must now be drowned.

The streets became raging torrents that flooded houses and sent the inhabitants scurrying for the safety of roofs and attics. The churning water carried all before it—the mangled carcasses of cats and rats, smashed carts, random bits of clothing, sundered baskets, a child's cradle.

Still the rain pelted down, washing the broken bodies of defenders and attackers from the fallen masonry of the South Gate. Courtyards became swirling eddies filled with drowned chickens, pigs, dogs, and humans.

Bound in by the city's stout walls and barred gates, the flood had no way to escape—it could only rise and rise. Desperate for egress, the water poured down every drain, filled every basement, poured into every crack and crevice, but these avenues were insufficient, and the water continued to mount.

Then, in the crypt of the Cathedral and the dungeons beneath City Keep, in the cellars of the Drowned Rat tavern and sundry other hidden locations, it found what it was seeking—the secret entrances to the city's Catacombs. Here, at last, was a way out.

In the Catacombs, the fighting was awkward, erratic, and bloody. In such confines, the Small Folk enjoyed significant advantages over their larger foes. They could negotiate the narrowest of crannies and wiggle through passages choked with dead bodies. And after so many generations in the dark, their eyes needed only the barest trace of light.

The Shamblers fought hard but were consistently forced to yield ground to the furious onslaught of their diminutive foes. Whenever they sought to make a firm stand, perhaps defending a sharp angle or blockading a steep incline, the Small Folk inevitably found some tiny fissure leading to their rear. Time and again, groups of Shamblers were cut off and killed.

On they pushed, those wee, merciless men, cutting down the giant-devil-freaks with their poisoned arrows and sharp flint knives. As they grew closer and closer to the surface, they could feel the subtle change in air pressure that signaled open sky. With their objective almost in sight, they slashed all the harder until the Shamblers were driven back in a forlorn and broken rout.

The Small Folk surged forward, guided by instinct toward fresh air and blue sky. They stormed into the chamber where Zeb, the crazed prophet, still huddled with his ragged followers. The old man raised his arms and began a chant of exorcism to banish this host of hell spawn. He never finished it. The little men slew him and his followers, scarcely pausing as they did so.

The Small Folk were about to climb the final set of stone steps leading to the upper world when the great flood, cascading from the streets above, swept them topsy-turvy back through the labyrinth of tunnels through which they had fought.

Their valor and skill at arms availed them not. Gaining momentum as it sought the lowest possible level, the ferocious torrent smashed them against stone walls, dragged them across rough stone floors. The narrow passages were clogged with their tangled corpses.

The surviving Shamblers were also caught, knocked from their feet, and washed away, so that invader and defender, living and dead, were carried inexorably downward.

Thus ended the assault of the Small Folk upon the city of Gorgonholm.

Fergis's heart sang as he strode through the field of slain that had been the laigi's left flank. He loved war! He rejoiced in the smell of fresh blood and the wide, astonished eyes of the dead.

Up ahead, the warriors of Coinneach mac Coinneach were now defeating the city-men's last reserves. He must hurry if he wanted to slay their earl with his own hand. Every Keltin warrior would be vying for the head of the enemy commander.

Then, to Fergis's dismay, a sinister black mist suddenly began to spread through the dense ranks of his soldiers. He had heard of the black mist. Every Keltin child knew the old stories of the filthy magical smoke that stole the breath from the lungs. The most valiant warrior, taking it in, must drop his weapons and stagger about—gagging, eyes bulging, tongue protruding—until taken by death.

Fergis's men began to choke and drop, one after another. Others turned and fled. Keltin warriors have no fear of sword or spear or axe, but this obscene death filled them with terror. Within moments, their triumphant flanking attack was reduced to chaotic ruin.

Fergis was aghast—this was no proper way for a man to fight! There could be no glory in strangling one's foe with black poison!

Lord Drakar de la Pole, commanding the center, watched in grim satisfaction as the attack on the left was broken. Caught by his black mist, the Keltins died in droves, and the survivors were driven back in confusion.

Drakar had, on this day, brought to the field several lightweight mangonels mounted on carts. These had originally been positioned behind the army's center, where he was in command. Seeing the decimation of the left flank and the imminent destruction of Earl Ralf's reserves, he had ordered his engines moved in their support. They had arrived just in time to prevent the utter annihilation of Ralf's army.

The typical mangonel was a siege weapon, too slow and cumbersome for open field battles. But Drakar's special engines were much lighter and more mobile than the typical heavy stone-casters. They were designed to hurl glass globes that shattered on impact to release a swirling cloud of black horror. The mist was his favorite weapon, one that he had employed time and again against his Keltin adversaries.

Drakar hated the Keltins with a deep, visceral loathing that bordered on madness. His sole passion was leading his men on devastating raids into Keltin territory—burning villages, slaughtering livestock, crushing men, women, and children beneath his horse's hooves. That such raids gleaned little profit mattered not at all. He loved their severed heads much more than gold.

When Fergis's army had first emerged from the morning mist, many of the earl's most esteemed soldiers had quailed at its immensity. Not Drakar. He had silently thanked his god for sending him so many Keltins to slay.

With the left stabilized, Drakar could now turn his attention to the battle that raged to his front where his men were heavily engaged.

The Trained Bands of Gorgonholm, the shopkeepers and craftsmen, had this day fought with skill and courage. They had sustained terrible losses, but they had held their ground tenaciously. The clerical units were no less valiant. Though the various sects had in the past spilled each other's blood, today they stood and died as one. But now, worn down by the long, ceaseless struggle with a relentless foe, the center was beginning to weaken.

Drakar had kept Hawkwood's mercenaries just behind the main battle-line. Whenever a section of line seemed about to give way, he would reinforce it with carefully rationed handfuls of these elite troops. But by now, this reserve force was fully committed in the main battle-line. If a break occurred, there was no one left to plug the hole.

The Keltin force seemed limitless. No sooner would one unit of Keltins be driven back, then another would advance to take its place. His supply of glass globes was expended. He had nothing left to stem the unremitting attacks that were wearing down his ranks. Soon now, his line would be broken, and his men massacred.

Drakar was not afraid to die. Indeed, he actually looked forward to death in battle as the only proper end for a warrior. But not today, damn it. Not today. Not when there were still so many Keltins to kill.

Fergis watched in disgust as the men of his right flank, the vaunted warriors of the legendary Coinneach mac Coinneach, were routed from the field by the black mist. He was well familiar with the character of his people—once defeated, they would not be quickly rallied. These warriors would fight no more that day. Luckily, the laigi's left and reserve was too depleted to mount a counter-attack.

He returned to his original position behind his center, but what he found there was far from reassuring. His men had battled long and well, with the largest and most illustrious clans—Hardshods, Fast-Shanks, Chewbones, and Hornfingers—bearing the brunt of the fighting. Their courage would be celebrated in song and legend for a thousand years. But the martial spirit of many other clans had now begun to flag.

The Keltin warrior was quite willing to face almost certain death in a headlong attack, but he was traditionally lacking in staying power. If the enemy was not overrun and slain in his initial assault, it became harder and harder for him to muster the energy to continue the fight.

Fergis saw his center starting to disintegrate as his men lost heart. They no longer pressed so eagerly forward, no longer shrieked their battle-cries with such maniacal fury. He watched a group of Long-Tooth clansmen draw apart from their brethren and squat discontentedly on the ground, no longer interested in the battle.

Others, consumed by petty jealousies and old-time rivalries, began to defy the commands of the warchiefs. When the Quickthrottles were ordered up in support of the exhausted Chewbones, their chief curtly refused because his grandfather's horse had once been slighted by a bumptious Chewbone warrior.

Worse yet, small groups of Red Legs and Cut Chin, notoriously unruly and factious clans, were beginning to desert the field. The countryside abounded in farmsteads and villages that promised far easier pickings. It was much smarter, they reasoned, to gather in the laigi's gold, cattle, and daughters than to spill their blood fighting the armored host of Gorgonholm.

All this was troubling, but there was worse to come. The sky grew dark as great, forbidding thunderheads suddenly appeared in the sky—a terrible omen of death. Given the mood of his army, Fergis was certain this must signal his defeat.

Actually, the boiling clouds were nothing more than the attack of his own shamans' elementals upon the city, whose streets were just then being deluged with rain. But in his arrogance, the Ard Righ naturally assumed that everything that happened had to be about himself.

Fergis knew nothing of the Black Stone, had always believed that the extraordinary unity of his clansmen stemmed from his own exceptional abilities as a leader. For their devotion to now fall away was nothing short of betrayal.

For the very first time, he began to doubt the certainty of his victory. Could he have been wrong about his destiny? Would he be laid low by the fickleness of his gods? Was such a thing possible? Was this to be the end of Fergis mac Brude?

His best chance was to reinforce his center with men from his left. He had heard nothing from that flank, but considering its strength, he anticipated no difficulty there. Regrettably, unwelcome news was about to arrive from that direction.

Oengus was puzzled. When the laigi facing him began to shift toward the rear, he assumed they were about to flee in fear. Instead, they had merely pulled back and away from the adjoining unit, creating a hole in their battleline.

In many Keltin legends, the battle-wise hero would prevail by thrusting a wedge of howling warriors through a careless gap in the opposing line. Then they would race down the rear of the line and kill their foes from behind. Such tales were specifically intended to instill an appreciation for tactics in young warriors.

Oengus, who fancied himself cut from the same glorious cloth as the heroes of yore, immediately determined to employ this stratagem. The laigi, he was certain, would be so dumbfounded by his unexpected maneuver that they would stand in helpless wonder as his men cut them down.

Convinced that his military acumen rivaled that of Cromlos, the Keltin god of war, he ordered his men to advance straight at the last unit in the enemy line where a red and black banner displayed a white rabbit. A rabbit, he thought, was a fitting symbol for the cowardly laigi. He would flay those weaklings as easily as one skins a rabbit.

When the two forces were no more than ten paces apart, Oengus gave a command and his trumpeter blew a special call. At once, his warriors turned, formed a wedge, and sprinted toward the opening so carefully crafted by Sir Lorenzo.

Lorenzo saw them coming, and the sight filled him with dread. He was sure his scheme had failed, that the Keltin leader was not as stupid as he appeared to be, that he was about to plow straight ahead and crush his modest contingent.

But then—miracle of miracles!—the Keltins swerved toward the opening he had left them, obviously intending to fall on the Groyne contingent from the rear. In doing so, however, they opened themselves to a flank attack from Lorenzo's men. He wasted not a moment but immediately ordered his men forward.

They hit the Keltins on the run, slashing into them from the side, cutting them down from the rear. Lorenzo was in the forefront, hewing left and right, striking down two men with his first two blows. His followers were on his heels—Frederico's mace smashing skulls and shoulders, Arturius's glaive stabbing furiously into faces and throats. Young Riley shouting at the top of his voice with Lorenzo's rabbit banner in one hand, a bloody sword in the other.

The Keltin unit seemed to dissolve. Where over a hundred determined warriors had stood only moments before, now there was but a scattered handful. Most were dead on the ground. A few were flying in unbridled panic. The remainder was trying frantically to form up around Oengus.

Sir Lorenzo knew nothing of the larger battle. Had no inkling that Drakar's black mist had saved his left flank from destruction, nor that the center was locked in a grueling melee with an overwhelming force. But he did recognize the wonderful opportunity that was his.

He called for the horses to be brought forward, for his men to mount. His steed jumped forward at the touch of his spurs, and with banner streaming, he led his small force around the shattered flank and straight into the enemy rear.

They rode over the pitiful remnant of Keltins attempting to rally around Oengus. These went down beneath the horses' hooves as if made of straw. The Keltin prince rose suddenly before Lorenzo—arms spread, mouth open, weaponless, confounded. Then he was gone, knocked backward by a passing blow from the horse's shoulder. The young knight caught a final glimpse of the hapless man landing upside down in a clump of brambles.

The men of Groyne had, up to this point, been exchanging spear thrusts in a stationary and rather uninspired fight with men of the Four Nose clan. Both sides had to this point been content to hold their positions while the main attack raged at the far end of the line. Now, however, all that suddenly changed.

Having dispensed with Oengus and his people, Sir Lorenzo's horsemen hit the Four Noses at a gallop, tearing right through them. The riders screamed like vengeful demons, cleaving skulls with long sweeping strokes of their swords. The Four Nose clan simply disintegrated.

Lorenzo spurred forward, smashing into the Mud Wallow and Split Tongues, driving them back in disarray. Misjudging the size of the tiny troop, the Keltins assumed a huge mounted force that had suddenly materialized behind them. Rather than be ridden down, they threw down their arms and fled.

With the Four Noses destroyed, the men of Groyne immediately plunged forward and followed Lorenzo into the enemy rear. As more and more enemy formations were broken, unit after unit of the earl's right wing swung behind Fergis's battle-line. Within minutes, the Keltin left flank was running in a blind panic.

Lorenzo now sped toward the rear of the huge Keltin center. Here the fighting was much more brutal, with both sides determined to tear the life out of the other. The enemy warriors were so fiercely absorbed in their work that few noticed the coming attack until swords and spears were driven into their exposed backs.

Taken by surprise, the center collapsed, with the Wolfjaw, Fire-Leaper, and Dancing-Snake clans in full retreat. These were joined by even the staunchest warriors of the Fast-Shank and Hornfinger.

Only minutes before, Drakar's men had been staring at their own deaths. Then without warning, the enemy turned their backs and ran. With a great roar of triumph, the defenders of Gorgonholm—the men of the Trained Bands, the clerics, Hawkwood's mercenaries—charged. This was the moment to avenge slain comrades, to strike terror into an ancestral foe, to show the Keltins the inevitable price for crossing the river.

More importantly, this was the chance to gain booty, to loot the dead for gold and silver torques and scoop up their elaborately embellished weapons. Keltin craftsmanship was superb, and their artifacts commanded high prices in the cities of the south.

This also was a dangerous moment, for in the past, the Keltins had sometimes fallen back in feigned retreat only to turn and slay their disorganized pursuers. This time, however, their defeat was both genuine and total.

Most of the Keltin host sprinted directly for the river, where they attempted to escape in the dozens of currachs that lined its banks. Others dove in and began to thrash their way back across, hands and feet flailing wildly. Many of these drowned, for few Keltins ever learned the art of swimming. When Drakar's men arrived on the riverbank, many hundreds more were trapped and slain.

By a little past noon, Fergis's grand army had been wiped out.

CHAPTER 46

BACK AT THE BAGGAGE CAMP

There were many ways to fortify a camp. While on the march, the ancient Etrusians would, each night, surround their encampments with a ditch-and-bank topped by sharpened palings. Caravaneers circled their wagons and piled their cargoes to create battlements. In a pinch, fallen trees could be used as a crude but effective abatis.

Lord Beaufort de Oinque had done none of these things, had done nothing, in fact, to guard Earl Ralf's war camp against a possible assault. It was not so much that Beaufort was disobedient or deliberately neglectful of his duty. Indeed, he conceived himself to be the most capable and reliable of Ralf's vassals.

The problem was—Beaufort was an idiot. Completely incapable of personal evaluation, he automatically assumed that his every decision was the correct one. Nobles, unfortunately, were often afflicted with the detrimental effects of inbreeding.

There were, of course, sensible soldiers in the camp who were horrified by Beaufort's failure to fortify the place. When they respectfully voiced their concerns, he waved them away. His lordship was far too occupied with wine and a bevy of servant girls to concern himself with such trivia. When they pressed their point, he grew wrathful and ordered them from his presence. When they protested loudly, he threatened to have them all hung.

Thus, this handful of competent soldiers was left to prepare the camp on its own. Its efforts were immediately frustrated by the obstinacy of the camp personnel.

When they attempted to move the wagons to form a barricade, the servants of Lord So-and-So and Sir This-and-That adamantly forbade them to touch their master's property. When they attempted to enlist them to construct a ditch-and-bank, they were flatly refused—house servants and teamsters would not do the work of unskilled laborers. Anyway, there was no time—the silver needed to be polished for the evening's victory feast.

In the end, very little got done. Some crates, a couple of dozen barrels, and a few logs were stacked to form a flimsy barrier around the earl's pavilion, but nothing more. The camp was left decidedly unprepared for self-defense.

With Malachai's demon released, the Adventurers had completed their primary mission, so they had nothing to do but return to the camp and resume their duties as guards. Thurmond assumed they were in for trouble for abandoning their posts, but when they got back, nothing was said about their absence. No one, apparently, had noticed they were gone.

Thurmond's nose continued to bleed, and Sarah remained shaky. When pressed to describe her experience, the young witch at first adamantly refused. But, little by little, she got her nerves under control. Then she called for a shot of uisge, which Roscoe naturally had close at hand.

Finally, she began to tell her tale.

"There wasn't much to see, at least not at first. Mostly I just felt things instead of seeing them. When I said the words that loosed the demon, the air grew very, very cold. I think it was drawing the heat from the air to add to its power. Then things went so dark that I really couldn't see anything."

She paused, as if the memory of these events was tearing at her soul.

"Then I got terribly sick, started puking and couldn't stop. Something that evil always makes people ill. But this was the worst I've ever felt, much,

much worse. My knees stated to shake so hard they couldn't hold me up. I fell down."

She paused again. When Thurmond began rubbing her shoulders, she calmed down and continued.

"I felt so sick I wanted to die. I fell to the ground and just lay there in a ball with my eyes squeezed shut. My stomach hurt so bad. My head felt like it was going to burst. Luckily, Thurmond was there to help me."

The young man waved his hand before his face as if trying to brush away an unpleasant sight.

"She warned me not to look, but I couldn't help it—I saw him."

Roscoe was puzzled.

"Saw who?"

"The demon we were carrying."

"What was it? What did you see that upset you so?"

"I saw its little face, and now I know what pure evil looks, but that wasn't the worst part. It was taking me, and I wanted to let him do it. It felt good somehow."

The old Adventurer wiped his brow with the back of his hand.

"God's great fearsome bowels, what a terrible thing to behold. But Sarah, you're pretty sure things was done right and proper? That your magic instrument did its job like it was supposed to?"

"I believe so. There was a gigantic release of psychic energy in that monastery, so something important happened. I'm not sure, but I think the demon somehow absorbed the Black Stone's evil energy. I think I helped the demon become infinitely more powerful than he was before. What bothers me is that if Malachai is controlling that demon, he can use that power for his own purposes."

Roscoe laid a comforting hand on the girl's shoulder.

"Well, Sarah darlin', we did what we had to do. Weren't nothin' else for it but to release that vile creature and knock down that cursed stone. Maybe Malachai will make us regret it and maybe he won't, but don't be frettin' about it 'cause there wasn't no other way."

Torgul reached out and, in a most uncharacteristic gesture, took her hand.

"What you and Thurmond done back there took a lot more courage than what I got. I thank you for it, whatever comes."

Though bone-weary from their exertions, Roscoe knew this was no time to rest. The camp's inadequate defenses caused him to shake his head in dismay. He gathered the other men-at-arms designated as camp guards. These were the same men who had tried and failed to rouse Lord Beaufort from his pleasures.

Roscoe could assume a commanding presence when required. He did so now, the torchlight glinting on his armor.

"Good evening, gentlemen. My name is Captain Roscoe Franklin of Grimsgard. We've got ourselves a serious problem here. If we wanna live to see tomorrow night, we gotta get this camp straightened out, so we do. Somebody's gonna have to take charge and get things organized. That somebody's gonna be me."

There was an awkward pause as the guards tried to determine Roscoe's true intentions. Where exactly was he going with this?

"You're all good lads, I can see that in your faces. Honest lads who ain't afraid of fightin' but none of you wanna die 'cause some damn-fool noble ain't doin' his job."

These words were met by a low rumble of agreement. The old Adventurer continued.

"All right then. It's gonna be up to us to fortify this place and give ourselves a fightin' chance. If old Beaufort wants to lie in his bed, I say we let him. Let him be lyin' there when the Keltins come to call, and they will be comin' soon, so they will. I seen 'em with my own two eyes, savage fellas all smeared with blue. They might be out there right now, watchin' us through the dark."

It did not take much of this kind of talk to convince the other guards to acclaim Roscoe as their leader. He was certainly a huge, imposing figure. Moreover, he was the only one who seemed to know what to do.

"So, I'll tell you what we're gonna do. We're gonna go drag them lackeys from their beds and set 'em to work. We can start nice, explainin' that the Keltins are crossin' the river and aimin' to eat their livers, but if that don't inspire 'em, we'll drive 'em out with the points of our swords."

This last was enthusiastically received by the other guards.

After much yelling and prodding, the laborers and servants began digging a shallow ditch around the slight hillock on which Ralf's massive pavilion was pitched. This was backed by a barricade of upended wagons, logs, crates, and barrels. It was, as field fortifications go, a feeble defense, but it at least offered a suggestion of security. By dawn, it was as ready as it was going to be.

Various grooms, wagon-drivers, launderers, and dog-boys were recruited into the guard force. These were joined by an assortment of cooks, bakers, and scullions. Even a number of the earl's personal servants were persuaded to abandon their household duties in favor of manning the barricade. As dire as their master's displeasure might be, it was preferable to being gutted by a Keltin swordsman.

But many, perhaps most, of the camp's inhabitants refused to come to the barricade. Unused to thinking for themselves, they elected to obey the last command they had been given before their lords rode off to war—to dutifully attend to their household tasks. Their duties most certainly did not include running off to join in some wild escapade with some crazy old Adventurer.

Roscoe hoped to use the earl's lavish pavilion as his headquarters and to avail himself of its well-stocked larder. Perhaps a soft bed. He approached a rotund little man, who stood in the doorway with his arms crossed.

"Good evenin' to you, milord, or perhaps I should make it good mornin', it bein' almost dawn and all. I am Captain Roscoe Franklin, and I am here to inform you that I'm requisitionin' this fine tent of yours for the duration of the battle, so I am."

The man was unimpressed by Roscoe's pretensions of authority.

"Well, let me inform you, milord, that this pavilion is the private quarters of Ralf, Earl of Avincraik. I am his personal chamberlain, Wynkyn Whoorm. If you so much as set one foot inside, I will inform the earl, and he will have your guts removed and hung around your neck. Do I make myself perfectly understood?"

Roscoe's face fell in disappointment—he had so looked forward to sampling the fine wines that must lie within. Then his countenance brightened.

"Well then, master Wynkyn, would you be so kind as to offer us some food and beverage? I'm wagerin' you've got an abundance of good victuals in there that would set right fine in our empty bellies. Could you see clear to bring my men somethin' to eat? They are, after all, laborin' to save you and this tent from destruction."

Wykyn made a dismissive gesture.

"It is your rightful duty to protect the earl's property. I am under no obligation to reward you for such a thing. The customs of feudal obligation are quite clear in matters like this. Anyway, I have no authority to dispense the earl's provender without his permission."

Roscoe growled and stalked off. God's buttocks, how he hated officious servants.

The guard force, however, did not go hungry. Slipping in and out of a side entrance, sympathetic serving girls provided clandestine flagons of ale, fresh bread, thick rashers of bacon, and joints of roasted meat. Thurmond cadged a chicken, which he shared with Sarah. Torgul received a string of pork sausages. Roscoe was rewarded with a haunch of mutton, which he consumed with great relish.

The defenders, most of whom were weaponless, drew swords and axes from a cart filled with arms and armor. Thurmond generally preferred broadsword and shield, but he wanted something longer for fighting over a barricade. He selected a halberd from a stack of polearms. It was a devastating weapon that could slice through mail like a knife through cheese.

Roscoe chose a stout, long-bladed sword with a two-handed grip, which he found much to his liking. The two-hander had been the favorite weapon of his youth.

When the main battle began in the early morning, the clash of the armies was too far off to be seen or heard from the camp. The Adventurers received only sporadic reports of the course of the battle. These came mostly from wounded men who had managed to drag themselves to the rear. The news all seemed bad.

A bloody sergeant brought word of the massive Keltin assault on the left wing. A young squire, the stump of his right arm bound in a filthy rag, told of the weakening center. A limping cleric claimed that Earl Ralf was dead and that he had personally witnessed his death.

Thurmond knew that battlefield rumors were notoriously unreliable, but such tidings were woefully distressing. Finally, he could stand it no longer.

"Roscoe, if things stand like they said and the earl is dead, then the day is lost. We can do nothing here except die. Wouldn't it be wiser to return home and try to defend our own people? At least we'd be in the tower."

The old Adventurer shook his head.

"Nay, boyo, that might be the wiser choice, but not a worthy one. The earl is my rightful lord, and he has to be able to count on me just as I count on you. How'd you feel if Torgul ran off just when things started lookin' grim?"

The dwarf shot his old friend a sour look, offended by the very suggestion of such a thing.

Sarah was less than convinced.

"But if the earl is dead—doesn't that release you from your oath of fealty?"

"Nay, lassie, such things is handed down. If Ralf is dead, then I'm in the service of his eldest son, whoever that might be."

Sarah was exasperated by this simplistic view of things.

"Whoever that might be? You don't know? You're willing to die to defend the baggage of someone whose name you don't know?"

"Not defendin' the baggage, nay, not that. I'd die to defend my honor. I swore an oath to be loyal to my liege lord, so I did. I'd be dishonored, we all would, if I did anything less."

Further discussion was interrupted by the arrival at the baggage camp of a large party of Black Tongue warriors.

CHAPTER 47

THE FIGHT AT THE BARRICADE

The Black Tongues earned their name by habitually chewing a certain root that turned their mouths the color of charcoal. It also provoked unsettling perceptions and unpredictable behaviors. For this reason, the Black Tongues were generally shunned by the Keltin brethren.

This particular group had abandoned the main battle early in favor of rampaging across the countryside in search of loot. They were known as a particularly bad bunch, and other clans had not been sorry to see them slip away.

They had intended to grab some quick loot by raiding a farmstead or two, but they were absolutely delighted to find Earl Ralf's baggage camp standing before them, for this was a rich prize indeed.

The Black Tongues attacked in true Keltin fashion, intending to overwhelm the camp guards in one spirited rush. So quick was their advance that many of the servants and camp-followers were caught outside of Roscoe's fortalice. The majority of these were slain out of hand. Men, children, old crones were given to the edge of the sword. Only young and comely women were spared.

The attack slowed as the warriors paused to loot the pavilions of the nobility, encumbering themselves with rich clothing, fine steel weapons, helmets and breastplates, saddles and bridles. Others raided the camp's kitchens, snatching jugs of wine, copper platters, and iron kettles.

Awakened by his female companions, Lord Beaufort was too befuddled to flee and could do no more than huddle beneath a feather mattress. Unfortunately, this very item caught the eye of a Black Tongue warrior who claimed it as his own. It was pulled away, leaving the old man revealed in all his scrawny nakedness.

Lord Beaufort suffered a hard death. The barbaric Keltins took one look at his pavilion's sumptuous furnishings and assumed that he was the Ard Righ, the high king, of the laigi. As such, his eyes, skin, and testicles carried profound magical properties and would be worth much gold. In their excitement, the raiders neglected to slay him before beginning to remove the desired parts. Beaufort's serving girls, thought to be his queens, were carried off to endow the next generation of Black Tongues with the puissance of their royal blood.

Coming to Earl Ralf's huge pavilion with its surrounding defenses, the Keltins immediately realized their mistake. Here was the real prize! The actual abode of the enemy high king! They gathered at the base of the small rise and took stock.

The raiders could see the head and shoulders of a very large man striding behind the barricade, giving orders, marshalling his soldiers. He wore an iron helmet and body armor made of small iron rings. He carried an immense sword.

He, they reasoned, had to be the genuine Ard Righ—not that skinny old man who had cried and begged like a frightened child. The warriors cast away the body parts they had so eagerly acquired. Who would want such useless trash when the parts of a real king, a real warrior, were ready for the taking?

The Black Tongues charged with an ungodly howl. The Adventurers and Gascar archers plied their bows with their usual vigor, but the Keltins did not slow. They sprang across the shallow ditch and began to scale the wall of boxes and barrels.

Holding his halberd at shoulder height, Thurmond stabbed again and again at the hideous blue-daubed faces appearing at the top of the barricade.

The weapon's long spearpoint penetrated eye socket and skull, slashed across cheek and throat. Man after man was sent tumbling lifeless into the ditch.

Beside him, Torgul was forced to stand upon a box, for the barricade was as high as his head. Bloodtroll rose and fell, sending still more Black Tongues to join their fearsome gods.

Yet all was not well, for most of the defenders were working men with no training in war. They were no match for the deadly warriors that came storming over the barricade. With the enemy upon them, many threw down their weapons and fled. Those who stood and fought were quickly cut down. The attackers were soon over the barrier and behind the defenders.

That would have been the end had it not been for Roscoe. He waded into the Keltins, swinging his big sword in great circles and half-circles around his head. One, two, three warriors were slain with so many strokes. A fourth, armed with a spear, launched himself from the top of the barricade, only to be struck down mid-flight like a swatted fly.

Roscoe's companions ran to his aid. Approaching from behind, Thurmond received a glancing blow on his helmet as Roscoe, unaware of his presence, delivered another great, circling stroke. The young man backed off—Roscoe did not need his help.

Stunned by the old Adventurer's ferocity, the surviving Keltins retreated back over the wall.

But the battle was not yet won, for a second group of Black Tongues had crossed the far side of the barricade and was in the process of massacring the defenders standing behind it. Sarah had, up to this point, held back from the fighting. Her skill with a sword was minimal, and she suspected that here, magic would be required at some decisive moment. This was the moment.

She began to throw sleep spells to send as many as possible into a deep, enchanted slumber. When her psychic energy ran low, she pulled a spell scroll from her pannier. It had been a spell from this scroll that invoked the locusts in Malachai's cellar. She knew that the spells on a scroll were often related in some way, so maybe she could summon another swarm of biting insects.

Two spells remained on the scroll—she read the first one.

A pair of gigantic figures immediately appeared—insect warriors at least seven feet tall, standing upright on the muscular legs of crickets. The other four limbs, more like human arms than insect legs, grasped two-handed swords with long, curved blades. These unlikely creatures bounded over the barricade, their weapons a red blur as they ripped into the astonished Black Tongues.

Encouraged, Sarah read the final spell.

An enormous insect materialized in the midst of the Keltin ranks. Its flat, green, shield-shaped body was as big as a pony. Unlike the cricket warriors, it stood passively as the raiders fell back in shock and horror.

One venturesome Black Tongue, approaching from the side, thrust his spear into the creature's abdomen. That was a mistake, for it caused the creature to spit a thick brown liquid so foul that fighters on both sides of the barricade had to stop and empty their stomachs.

The two scroll spells, like many spells, were of very brief duration. The cricket-men, the stinkbug, and, thankfully, the unendurable stench quickly dissolved into nothingness. Their appearance had been brief, but it was sufficient to turn the tide of the battle. The Black Tongues had had enough. They discarded their booty and sprinted back toward the river.

Seeing the enemy in retreat, the defenders gave a great whoop of victory. Those with bows fired their last arrows into their fleeing backs. Others began to loot the fallen bodies of friend and foe. Some simply slumped to the ground and stared off into space.

Grateful to be alive, Wynkyn lost all his former stuffiness. He ordered canvass sunscreens erected for the wounded, while his serving maids bound their injuries with clean linen bandages. Meat and bread were brought in abundance, and drink flowed freely.

The Adventurers had suffered only the most minor cuts and bruises. This was remarkable, for in close combat, everybody bleeds. Two of the Gascar archers were also relatively unscathed. Tuck had received a long, shallow gash on his upper thigh and a more serious cut to his left arm. Roscoe distracted him with banter while he sewed them closed.

"These'll give you nice scars, laddie, so they will. You'll be sittin in a tavern, with some buxom lass on your knee, and you'll strip back your sleeve and point to your left arm. *I got this*, you'll tell her, *standin' side by side with*

Captain Roscoe Franklin as we fought off a pack of howlin' Keltins. Musta been a thousand of 'em. Nay, more like ten thousand."

He put in the last stitch.

"That's what you'll say, and I guess you know what she'll be sayin'. She'll be sayin' *aye*."

Roscoe's untrained, unarmored tenants fared less well. They had stood behind the barricade as he told them, shooting their hunting bows at the oncoming Black Tongues. But once the Keltins were over the wall, they were defenseless. Three of the five were down dead. The two survivors—their names were Bung and Whump—had escaped only because they had had the good sense to run away as the Keltins were slaying their comrades.

The old Adventurer was filled with sadness. Three men were dead because they had followed him to battle. They had not been soldiers for whom a violent demise could be expected. Just simple farmers who wanted nothing more than a full belly and a warm cottage in the winter.

In sooth, Roscoe did not really know these men, was not even sure of their names, for he was not well acquainted with most of his tenants. But he knew their deaths would occasion great sorrow in Grimsgard. He would have to send a wagon to bring their bodies back for proper burial.

The exhausted, bloody defenders began to discuss the battle. Some boasted, some wept, but all agreed that it had been Roscoe who had saved them from certain death. Without his leadership, the barricade would have remained unfinished. Without his indomitable courage and skill at arms, the raiders would have slain them all.

Thurmond could only agree. They had all done their bit. The gore-spattered spearpoint of his halberd testified to his contribution. Sarah's spells and Torgul's axe had been deadly. But this day belonged to Roscoe. The old Adventurer had been truly magnificent.

Survivors now began to appear in the ruins of the ravaged camp. Some had managed to hide beneath the great piles of baggage. Others, struck down and left for dead, miraculously lived. Ravaged women. Men with terrible wounds. Lost, crying children. They wandered through the scattered remains of the camp, frightened, confused, broken in spirit. A few approached the barricade they had so recently spurned.

Just then, a boiling cloud of dust and the thunder of hoofbeats announced the approach of a body of horsemen. Were the Keltins coming back? Did the enemy army include cavalry? Thurmond had no idea. He shot Roscoe a questioning look, but his friend just shrugged his shoulders, equally uncertain.

The riders were, to everyone's great relief, not Keltins but a troop of armored soldiers. Seeing the ruined camp and the strewn bodies, they drew rein and approached cautiously. Roscoe climbed over the barricade and strode slowly toward them.

Thurmond started to follow, but Torgul grabbed his arm and held him back.

"Let him go by hisself, boy. Them are most likely friends, but everybody's wary. We don't wanna spook 'em."

Roscoe continued until he was within easy speaking distance. He raised his hand in a gesture of greeting.

"I'm Captain Roscoe Franklin, in command of the baggage camp. And who might you be?"

He was answered by a stocky man with a heavy black beard. One side of his face was smeared with dried blood.

"Sir Seymour Guff, knight of Earl Ralf's household. I seek Lord Beaufort. What of him?"

Roscoe smiled—he always endeavored to be friendly when confronting a delicate situation. He had, after all, no authority to name himself camp commander.

"Well as you can see, sir knight, we've had ourselves a bit of a tussle here. I expect you'll find whatever's left of Lord Beaufort in the wreckage of his pavilion over yonder. I was forced to assume command in his absence."

The bearded man scanned the welter of corpses and torn canvas that had once been the camp.

"It appears you've allowed the camp to be destroyed."

Roscoe was uncertain—would they try to blame the destruction on him? He hung his head in regret.

"We've had some hard fightin' here, and that's a fact. We was hit by a whole legion of them screamin' devils. But I'm happy to report that the earl's pavilion is all safe and sound, so it is."

The old Adventurer's face now assumed a most woeful cast.

"We've been told, sir, that the good earl is among the fallen. Is that true?"

The bearded rider spat and shook his head.

"Nay, not dead, but sore hurt. They're bringing him here in a cart as we speak. I was sent ahead to warn his people to get ready. Where's the one called Wynkyn? The earl will require his full attention."

Roscoe gave the knight his brightest smile.

"God's holy toes, that's jolly news indeed! And the battle, sir—how goes the battle?"

"The battle is won. The day is ours. The Keltin host is crushed, scattered, pushed into the river, and drowned."

Roscoe turned, spread his arms wide, and shouted loud enough for all to hear.

"The battle's over! We've won!"

The barricade erupted in jubilation. Teamsters, cooks, blacksmiths, and archers screamed for joy. Screamed and screamed until they could scream no more. All decorum forgotten, Wynkyn's serving wenches ran to embrace the men who had defended them so bravely. They hugged, kissed, and danced. Thurmond and Sarah naturally joined right in.

Roscoe commanded that the barricade be pulled down. Wynkyn scurried to make all necessary preparations. The intrepid defenders returned to their original stations in camp and began to sort out the living and the dead.

Soon after, the earl arrived in a mule-drawn cart. He came with a retinue of bickering surgeons, arrogant knights, and pompous attendants who thrust Roscoe aside as they carried the litter into the pavilion. No one was interested in anything he had to say.

CHAPTER 48

THE GLORY OF WAR

The wounded continued to arrive throughout the day—on horseback, on foot, carried in litters, dragged on sledges. Some with their skulls opened and brains exposed. Others struggling to hold their guts inside ripped bellies. Men with crushed ribs, shattered limbs, mashed faces. Men who must certainly die. Others who would live out their lives in crippled misery.

The savaged baggage camp could offer little solace to these suffers. Little was done in any army to prepare for the horrendous casualties of a major battle. Surgeons set bones and stitched gashes. Clerics laid their healing hands on those who had sufficient coin to pay for the service. Many wounded, however, received no aid, sometimes lying on a corpse-covered battlefield for days until their torn bodies rotted and their faces turned black with decay.

This day was even worse, for most of the baggage camp's provisions had been destroyed by the rampaging Black Tongues. Luckily, the camp survivors, in an extraordinary spirit of cooperation, pitched in to help. Sections of ruined pavilions were erected as sunscreens. Concubines and soldiers' wives tore their petticoats into bandages. Stable boys and wine stewards carried endless buckets of water to assuage the terrible thirst of the dying.

Roscoe's long experience as an Adventurer had lent him a certain grim skill, he could examine an arrow-pierced stomach or a depressed fracture of the skull and gauge with fair accuracy whether the sufferer was likely to live or to die. This became his painful function for the rest of the day as man after man was brought for his assessment.

Those beyond help were placed to one side, where, for most, the end came with merciful rapidity. Those judged capable of salvation were stitched, bandaged, and placed in such shade as the camp had to offer.

Thurmond, Torgul, and Sarah worked tirelessly, tending the wounded, offering whatever comfort was in their power. The uninjured Gascars, Wat and Cob, were enlisted as litter bearers and water carriers, as were Bung and Whump, the two surviving tenants.

Gradually, the story of the battle unfolded. They heard of the earl's grievous wounding as he fought to hold the collapsing left flank, and of the glorious ride of some minor knight who swept behind the Keltin line and broke the back of their mighty host.

Later in the day, help began to arrive from the city. Wains piled high with foodstuffs and drink. White Friar nuns, trained in the healing arts. Fishwives and harlots eager to comfort those who had so stoutly defended their city.

These brought the stories of the desperate fighting within the town walls—of the horrific assault on the South Gate, of the devastating onslaught of earth, air, fire, and water, of collapsed buildings and flooded streets.

They told of the brown river of rats that had surged through the city and invaded the magician's guildhall. This event was less consequential than anticipated, the only casualty being Mistress Commode, the sole female member of the order. Well into her nineties, she had been unable to follow the example of the other guild members who promptly climbed atop their high stools when the rats appeared. As a result, she lost a number of toes from both her feet.

Other tales told of greater gallantry. A score of black-hatted Adventurers had rallied near the charred remains of what had once been The Severed Head. This tiny group had successfully held off a much larger force of Painted Men who were advancing up Castle Wynd toward the city's very heart.

Other accounts were more spurious. There were those who claimed to have seen, at the final stages of the battle, a rotund figure in purple armor lashing a chariot drawn by coal-black horses. His scythed wheels, they said, slashed through the Keltins massing along the corner of the west wall. He was followed by a dozen skeleton warriors who quickly dispatched any who avoided his spinning blades. Such tales were, of course, highly unlikely and had to be disregarded by anyone of sound intelligence.

The story of the great battle, like that of all epic events, would always be filled with confusing elements and conflicting details, but at least this much is certain—the city of Gorgonholm was saved. Battered though they were, the high walls and tall buildings stood as proud and defiant as ever in the aftermath of the Keltin invasion.

As Earl Ralf lay in his pavilion, his body pierced by many serious wounds, his dead forbearers gathered in the great hereafter to see how things would go. Was he destined to join them this day, or would his soul cling tenaciously to his mangled flesh?

Although seldom given to strong passions, these ancient shades were filled with a tingling sensation they dimly recognized as pride, a feeling with which they had once been very well acquainted. They were gratified that their young descendent had fulfilled his purpose so manfully, that a Mortimer still defended the land over which they had held sway.

Surgeons and physicians clustered about the young nobleman, fussing and arguing. Some applied poultices of noxious herbs and the excretions of animals. Other claimed that in spite of his already substantial blood loss, he required further bleeding. They listened to the gurgle of his stomach, the rasp of his labored breathing. One gauged the color of his tongue while another judged the clarity of his urine.

A renowned physician consulted the hours and the stars and then prescribed cordials of gold leaf and quicksilver. A village healer—no one could quite explain his presence in the earl's pavilion—suggested a broth of hellebore and small, black mushrooms.

Amazingly, Ralf survived both his injuries and the fervent ministrations of those learned medical professionals. Near midnight, he opened his eyes and called for meat and mead. The Mortimers had always been blessed with stout constitutions.

The Adventurers put in a very long day. When food was available, they ate quick mouthfuls between cartloads of wounded soldiers. Dizzy with exhaustion, Thurmond sat down to catch his breath and promptly dozed off.

He slept, he could swear, for only the briefest moment, yet Sarah was suddenly shaking him by the shoulder.

"Come on—you've been sleeping for more than an hour. We need you."

Battles always attract carrion-eaters. A gathering of the raven, the wolf, and the eagle were known to be harbingers of slaughter. Battlefields were popular with human scavengers as well. Whole families now flocked from the city to plunder the slain.

Their enthusiasm was understandable, for a battlefield was a treasure trove of ownerless wealth. A good broadsword cost more than the average worker earned in six months of hard labor. A suit of plate armor was worth more than most peasants made in a lifetime.

Of course, few scavengers ever acquired an item of great value. Anything of real worth was almost always gathered up by soldiers while the battle was raging around them. Mailshirts were routinely stripped from fallen foes while their blood was still pumping from their veins. Fine weapons could be put to immediate use.

Nonetheless, simple commoners could acquire a plethora of lesser items that they could use, barter, or sell for hard coin—a fine hat, a belt with a knife in a sheath, warm clothing, new leather boots. So looting was well worth their while.

Most scavengers were ruthless in their foraging, stripping friend and foe alike. Helplessly wounded soldiers often received the quick thrust of a knife to hasten the taking of their things. Less mercy was often shown after a battle than during it.

Women, it was said, could be the cruelest scavengers of all, for the battlefield offered them their one chance to take revenge for the terrible pain and humiliation they had suffered at the hands of men. Not content to merely slay the wounded, they made them pay for all the years of abuse they had had to endure. Their victims were sometimes left alive, but with certain offending body parts removed.

When the battlefield was sufficiently picked over, many of the scavengers made their way to the camp where, they assumed, there would be people with money who might purchase their gleanings. Surprised by the devastation they found there, they immediately started to loot the already-pillaged baggage.

Caught in a frenzy of acquisition, the scavengers turned on each other, fighting over such spoils the camp had to offer. In the madness of the moment, the valueless became precious. Thurmond watched as two toothless crones wrestled over a strip of ripped tenting. A group of young boys pummeled a hunchback for some fragments of harness and pieces of broken furniture.

This continued until the scroungers were driven off by the camp survivors who were not about to lose their remaining belongings. The sight of such human degradation saddened the young Adventurer. There had been too many such sights that day.

He now stood beside a mound of severed arms and legs—the surgeons had been busy with their saws, cutting away limbs too badly damaged to save and cauterizing the oozing stumps. Many of their patients did not survive this procedure. Their stiffening bodies were stacked like firewood.

In his two years with Roscoe, Thurmond had seen much blood, but never anything on this scale. The very air stank of it. His gore-splattered hands disgusted him. His stomach turned over, and he thought he might vomit.

Sarah was suddenly at his side.

"You're looking a little queasy—what's the matter?"

The young man took a deep breath, but even the air tasted foul.

"You know, when I was a boy, I loved the old stories about great battles. But they never said anything about what goes on afterwards. There's not a lot of glory in a man trying to shove his guts back into his belly."

Sarah sighed.

"I know what you mean."

A blaring trumpet drew their attention to a large troop of horseman that came clattering into the camp. Thurmond recognized the black and silver banner of Lord Drakar. He despised the pompous noble, but at that moment, he was too tired and disillusioned to care. He turned again to Sarah.

"It's funny, instead of feeling proud of my deeds today, of the men I slew, I feel kind of ashamed. I had to do it—they'd have killed me if they could have—but it still seems wrong somehow. I've never felt this way before."

She nodded.

"I feel much the same. Maybe because there was just too much killing today. Maybe a person can only stand so much of this kind of horror."

Roscoe joined them. He appeared to be in good spirits, as if unfazed by the day's events.

"Good news, laddie, Lord Drakar released me from feudal service. We can leave as soon as we gather everybody up. Torgul's off lookin' for the others now."

Thurmond looked about him, at the shattered encampment and broken men.

"Roscoe—I was just talking to Sarah. This was our first big battle, and it's making us really doubt ourselves. How do you feel?"

"Well, boyo, this was my first big one as well, so it was. But my part in it wasn't much different than many little scraps I've been in, some of 'em with you beside me. Anyway, we didn't come across the river tryin' to kill our neighbors. Them Keltins did that, so we didn't have no choice but to try and stop em."

"Then why do I feel bad about killing them?"

"Maybe because you feel no hate for 'em. You could see that them and us fightin' each other didn't make a whole lot of sense."

"It does seem pretty stupid—all this killing for no real reason."

"Aye, maybe so. But that's the way things be, stupid or not."

When Torgul and the others arrived, Roscoe's face brightened.

"We're done here, so let's go home. I'd like to sleep in my own bed tonight."

PART 6

HOME AGAIN

CHAPTER 49

Roscoe Leads A Charge

Roscoe was wary. The countryside was rife with the scattered remains of the Keltin army, so it was best to be careful. Instead of riding directly to the towerhouse, they drew up on the far edge of the village common to assess the situation. Thurmond, Torgul, Sarah, the Gascars, and the two surviving tenants reined in behind him.

Something was amiss. The fields were deserted, no smoke rose from the village houses, but that was expected. Florio had brought man and beast into the tower to sit out the invasion. He would surely keep them there until certain that it was safe to venture out. The tower door was tightly closed, just as it should have been. Everything seemed to be well in hand.

What was it? Though he could find no reason for it, the old Adventurer knew something was not right.

"Somethin' ain't right here!"

That came from Torgul.

"We should've been spotted by the watchers on top of the tower. They should be wavin' to us and yellin' *hallo* by now. And Florio should've flung open the door and come runnin' out to welcome us home. I don't like it."

Roscoe suddenly realized what he had been missing.

Florio would have most certainly received word of the great victory—some rider must have brought the news. Therefore, he would have anticipated his master's return and prepared a fabulous celebratory banquet. The air should have been permeated by the aroma of his exquisite cookery, but nothing in that way was coming to his nostrils.

Something was definitely amiss.

He did not have to ponder this question for very long. Instead of a cheery greeting from the tower, a ballista bolt went zinging several feet over his head and struck an elm tree some distance away. This was followed by a stream of angry cursing and the metallic *clink* of the weapon's bow being drawn back.

A moment later, an unfamiliar mob came rolling out of the village, perhaps two score in number. Carrying weapons, but possessing no sense of order or discipline. Then another ballista bolt flashed from the tower and buried half its length in the soft sward eight feet in front of Thurmond's horse.

Roscoe cleared his throat.

"Let us move back a tad and take stock of things. I'd truly hate to see one of us struck down by my own dart-flinger, so I would."

As the Adventurers fell back, the mob, encouraged by this seeming retreat, advanced to the foot of the tower and began to form a battle-line.

The old Adventurer turned to the dwarf.

"You have sharp eyes, my brother, what do they tell you?"

Torgul growled under his breath, something about hairy bears.

"They're a right strange bunch. Not Keltins. I see some charcoal burners and what looks to be a mix of city folk and peasant farmers. Not people who'd normally ban together. They're all armed, but some of 'em only got farm tools for weapons. Only four or five got armor—hell!—they look like Royal Road Guards. They're the ones tryin' to push the other ones into line."

"So, not a formidable force, you would say?"

"I wouldn't think so."

Roscoe now looked at Sarah.

"Can you give us a nice little illusion to frighten those miscreants away? Perhaps a squadron of heavy cavalry?"

"Nay, Roscoe, I used up all my spells yesterday. My energy won't come back until I get some sleep, a lot of it."

"Any useful charms in your basket?"

"I've got another scroll with three spells. But you know, they're dangerous. I only use 'em when it seems like there's no other way."

Roscoe was unconcerned.

"Well now, that's just fine. Tuck it in your belt and keep it handy. We might need it yet."

He then raised his voice to address the entire group.

"Everybody spread out in one straight line. We're gonna charge 'em."

Leading a charge can be a tricky business. If the soldiers are slow to start, a leader will end up far in front, completely unaware that no one is close behind him. It is much preferable, therefore, for the leader to stand behind their soldiers, where he can propel them forward if need be.

Fortunately, Roscoe's charge came off to perfection, with the riders keeping together in a compact line, progressing from a walk, to a trot, to a canter, reaching a full gallop just seconds before impact.

As this thundering wall of man and beast bore down on them, the untrained, ill-armed mob made the wisest decision of their lives—they broke and ran. Had they stood their ground, half of them would have died within moments, trampled beneath the horses' iron-shod hooves.

Some dropped their weapons and sprinted toward the village. Others ducked behind whatever was at hand that might offer a modicum of cover—a bush, a woodpile, a manure cart. Recognizing the futility of their position, the Road Guards joined the rout.

Half a dozen were caught in the open and slain before Roscoe brought the attack to a halt. The survivors were allowed to flee through the fields to the safety of the woods on the far side. There was no fight left in them.

The sole casualty among Roscoe's followers was Whump. Neither he nor Bung were competent horsemen. Just as his mount began to gallop, the luckless plowman tumbled from his saddle. He landed on his head, breaking his neck and killing him instantly.

The riders regrouped between the village and the tower. Bung and the archers were dispatched to investigate the homes of the tenants, while the Adventurers planned their next move. Another ballista bolt sailed overhead, causing the old Adventurer to scowl.

"Whoever's up there firin' that thing has got a right poor eye, for which I am grateful. But it does peeve me that he's expendin' my darts so freely. I'm minded to go up there and put a stop to it."

Thurmond was using the tunic of a dead charcoal burner to wipe the blood from his sword.

"How will we manage that? You know how strong the door is."

But no sooner were those words out of his mouth when the door, for reasons nobody could guess, swung silently open.

Roscoe spread his arms in mock triumph.

"Now there you go—the master of the house has returned, and they're doin' the correct thing by openin' the door for him. Them darts they flung was all a misunderstandin', no doubt. Let us enter and receive their heartfelt apologies."

Thurmond was feeling less jovial.

"We best be mighty careful."

"Exceedin'ly so, boyo. Sarah, have that scroll ready. Torgul, would it please you to lead the way?"

This was an old tactic they used when an enemy was likely to be lurking around a corner or on the other side of a door. Expecting a human, the foe would most likely be watching a point somewhat above the dwarf's head. That split-second mistake was all Torgul would need to clear the way.

He glowered and drew his scramasax—there would be no room in the doorway for his two-handed axe.

"I'd be delighted."

Dwarves were, Thurmond knew, very territorial. Torgul would resent deeply the usurpation of his home. And woe to them if they had disturbed his bees.

At that moment, the Gascars returned with news of the village. Wat was downcast.

"It's bad, milord. Things thrown all about. Half dozen dead bodies in and around the huts. Bung went off to the woods, lookin' for the rest of the villagers."

This was terrible news, and it made Thurmond itch for revenge. Roscoe seemed deeply grieved, all the levity departed from his voice.

"You Gascars will remain outside and keep guard. The rest of us are going inside. Torgul—if you please."

The dwarf gave the tower door a resounding kick that sent it crashing back against the wall. Anyone behind it would have received a heavy blow. Then he was through the door, scramasax at the ready, the others right behind him.

The room was empty save for the piles of stored provisions.

Roscoe nodded toward the spiral stairs leading to the second level, and Torgul immediately began to ascend. At the top, he gave the door a push—it was open. That was unusual. A tower under attack kept every portal locked and barred. Everyone sensed a trap.

The room beyond, Roscoe's great hall, was dim with the only light coming from a scattering of candles. The Adventurers entered the room gingerly, expecting an attack. Instead, they were greeted by a tall, middle-aged, well-appointed gentleman standing with his back against the far wall. When he spoke, his voice was calm and surprisingly soft, yet somehow conveyed deadly menace.

"Well, hello."

Angry and indignant, Roscoe took a step toward the figure, but stopped when four crossbowmen emerged from the shadows and pointed their weapons directly at his chest. At such close range, they could scarcely miss. Three more men armed with swords and bucklers came down the stairs from the upper floors. They appeared to be Royal Road Guards.

The old Adventurer stopped and scowled.

"Who the hell are you? This is my tower, duly consigned to me by the Earl of Avincraik, whose man I am. So you can explain yourself to me or make your excuses to Earl Ralf."

The man gave him a sardonic smile.

"I am Ubo de Futz, Lord of Skut. And you are Roscoe Appleman. Aye, I know who you are. We shall see which one of us Earl Ralf cares most about, a proper nobleman or a jumped-up fruit monger. We shall see."

Roscoe was nonplussed. Was the man mad?

"Where is my steward—the elf? What have you done with him?"

Lord Ubo gestured toward the ceiling. There, hanging upside down from an exposed beam, was Florio. Motionless. Silent. Either unconscious or dead.

Roscoe was so tired that his usual eloquence failed him. A black rage filled his soul.

"What have you done to him? Does he live?"

Ubo's soft voice was suffused with evil glee.

"I really couldn't say. I do hope so because I still want to boil the meat from his bones in one of his own cooking pots. He inconvenienced me, don't you know? Still, the little fellow was so accommodating when I arrived here, bowing and apologizing for his former insolence. He even opened the door and invited us in."

Roscoe could barely contain himself.

"You killed six of my tenants."

"More than that, I'm afraid."

Ubo pointed toward the hearth, where Bodo lay face down in a pool of his own blood. The charred remains of his wooden leg lay smoldering in the ashes.

Roscoe's voice was so choked with emotion that he could barely speak.

"Others?"

"Probably. I meant to slay them all, but many ran away to the woods as soon as they got the chance. Things got a bit…mixed up…after most of my own people deserted me."

Roscoe had no idea what this meant. Ubo seemed to read the puzzlement in his face.

"Come, come—you know all about the power of the Black Stone, and I know you were out to destroy it. You must have done something because my people, most of them, suddenly lost the call and ran off. It must've left me, too, because I really don't care so much about such things any longer."

"What do you care about now?"

Ubo's smile was positively devilish. The Stone's influence might have waned, but he remained evil through and through.

"I care about enjoying myself, just as a noble should. I doubt if you've ever heard of Skut. Just a dreary, boring little fief far back in the woods. Not much excitement to be had. I haven't felt like a warrior for a long time, but this adventure has awakened my fighting spirit. Seizing this dreadful tower has made me feel rather like a conqueror."

Roscoe realized the man was utterly mad. He studied the men with the crossbows, calculated the odds. The only thing he could do was play for time.

"You've taken my home. What are you thinkin' to do with us?"

Ubo rubbed his chin as if weighing his options.

"That depends…."

Ubo paused, allowing the implied threat to become very evident.

"At the moment, I need you to share a secret. Your serfs told me that you're some kind of a famous monster killer and that you've amassed a huge treasure from this pastime. I want it. I found a bit of gold under your bed…"

Ubo gestured toward Roscoe's strongbox, which lay open beside the wall.

"…but I know you must have more, much more. I want it. Where is it?"

The small pile of gold in the box was indeed the totality of Roscoe's coin. He had won much treasure in the course of his career, but it always seemed to slide from between his fingers. He stared into Ubo's crazed eyes and decided to bluff it out and string him along.

"And if I won't tell you, what then?"

"Then you will give me the opportunity for some intense enjoyment."

Thurmond could stand this pointless bantering no longer. He knew that this vile noble meant to kill them all, had always meant to. If he could spring forward quickly enough, he might be able to slay this madman. Then, deprived of their leader, his men might well prove more congenial.

He began, ever so slowly, to move his hand toward the hilt of his sword. Preparing to leap, he shifted his weight to his toes. Unfortunately, this movement was seen by one of the crossbowmen, who brought his weapon to bear and squeezed the trigger.

CHAPTER 50

THE WRATH OF CHANTICLEER

Far overhead, Pozi lay stretched at full length along one of the massive open beams that braced the tower's heavy stone walls. She had often used this hiding place, where the thickness of the wood concealed her skinny body from anyone below. She liked to lurk up there and eavesdrop on the gossip of the scullery maids and the more serious talk of the Adventurers. Pozi always liked to know what was going on.

But this time, her life depended on remaining absolutely silent and invisible. If this horrid man, this Ubo, learned of her presence, he would slay her as readily as he had slain her step-father, Bodo. Maybe worse—she had heard the things he had promised to do to poor Florio.

The elf had allowed them into the tower. He had thought they were soldiers sent to protect them from the Keltins, the same soldiers he had once shot at with that big crossbow on the roof. That had been a terrible mistake. Once inside, Ubo had thrown him to the floor and kicked him until he no longer moved. When her step-father tried to stop him, one of the soldiers had cut him down with his sword.

Then they had all laughed, as if someone had made a great jest.

Pozi had instantly known what was likely in store for her. She had grabbed Florio's long toasting fork and scurried hand over hand up the edge of a tapestry until she could reach an iron bracket set into the stone wall. It had once held the stuffed head of a wild boar.

At that height, the old mortar had crumbled from between many of the stones, leaving ledges and crevices just the right size for her clever little toes and fingers. With the fork in her teeth, she shot up the wall as easily as a cat climbs a tree. Sixteen feet from the floor, she clambered onto the beam.

She had now lain up there for a night and a day—cramped, hungry, afraid to do anything but stay entirely motionless. Her heart had leapt for joy when Roscoe and the others returned, but then those disgusting men had taken them by surprise. Now one of them was raising his crossbow, about to shoot Thurmond.

At the far end of the beam, just within reach of the toasting fork, sat old Chanticleer, the biggest, meanest rooster in the village. All the children lived in fear of this ill-tempered bird, for he was quick to attack with spur and beak while lashing their faces with his muscular wings. He, like all the village poultry, had been brought into the tower when a siege was anticipated.

Chanticleer and his seven wives now slept peacefully with their heads under their wings. Many of Roscoe's birds had been butchered to sate the appetites of the intruders, but they had avoided this tough old cock while there were younger, more tender fowls to be plucked and eaten.

Pozi's arm moved without conscious thought, as if the limb itself knew what must be done. The sharp prongs of the toasting fork jabbed smartly into the rooster's tail, sending him flying from the beam with a loud *yawp*. He came down fast, in a flurry of wings, and, as luck would have it, landed squarely atop the crossbowman just as he fired his weapon.

The man flinched under the impact, spoiling his aim. The bolt flew high and rebounded off the stone wall. Pleased with this outcome, Pozi next applied the fork to each of seven hens, filling the room with squawking, outraged poultry.

Everyone below instinctively looked up as the chickens landed among them. Everyone, that is, except Sarah, who seized the moment to read one of the scroll spells. The room was immediately plunged into a magical fog so thick that every person in the room was as good as blind.

This did not, of course, stop them from pitching forward to where they believed the foe to be. Ancient legends tell of heroes fighting blindfolded, using some uncanny warrior sense to intuit the presence of their enemies. The next few confusing moments proved such tales to be utter nonsense.

No one could see or sense anything, and because every person in the room was shifting about, it soon became apparent that a random slash would hit friend as easily as foe. They slashed nonetheless at every passing sound. Several loud grunts and a shrill scream told of blows finding living targets. Then a loud thump, as if something heavy and soft had fallen from a substantial height.

The spell expired quickly, and the room cleared. Two chickens were dead, as was one of the Road Guards. Torgul's face was spattered with the man's blood. Roscoe had received a hard blow to the head that had dented his helmet and left him dazed and bleeding.

Most of the fighters had, after the initial episode of wild swinging, stepped rearward and placed their backs to the walls. They were now more or less evenly spaced around the room. The exception was Ubo, who stood in the chamber's center, his foot resting on Florio's recumbent form, his sword point pressed to his breast.

His voice was as calm and cold as ever.

"Well, wasn't that enjoyable. I imagine it was rather like some game peasants play, fighting in the dark with knives. I never stoop to such low antics, so I cut the rope that was keeping this goblin aloft. Now then, if you value his life, you will...."

Ubo never finished the sentence, for at that moment, one of the Road Guards, a scraggly, one-eyed brute, stepped behind him and thrust his dagger into his back. The nobleman gasped and dropped his sword. Three more times the dagger plunged. Lord Ubo Futz fell on his face and died.

One-Eye addressed the Adventurers.

"My name's Pons. I was Ubo's sergeant-at-arms before all his plans fell apart. Me and my boys, we been lookin' for a way to get clear of him after we saw he was some kinda mooncalf, but we couldn't figure how. Stabbin' him seemed like a better plan than fightin' you.

"We could go on killin' each other, but I don't see no profit in that.

Now I just saved all your hides, so maybe you'll let us walk out of here. Call everythin' square."

The Road Guards drew together in a clump. They were a dangerous lot—ruthless, armored, and skilled with weapons. They outnumbered the Adventurers. Fighting them would be a risky proposition.

Thurmond was undaunted. He wanted to kill them all.

"You come here and slay our friends, and now you think you can just leave? I'm gonna drink your blood!"

He started forward, intent on carrying out his threat, but Torgul grabbed him by the arm.

"Hold on, boy—this is Roscoe's call. He's the one in charge here."

The young man was so angry that he scarcely heard the dwarf's words. When he tried to shake off the restraining hand, Torgul spoke again, more harshly this time.

"Hold on, I say!"

Roscoe was plainly hurting from the blow to the head. Strong as he was, his voice was slow and shaky.

"You'll leave at once, takin' only what you came with. Anything of mine you'll leave behind. Don't ever come back here. If you do, it'll be the last place you ever come to. Don't say a word—just go."

The old Adventurer gestured for his comrades to step back from the door to allow the intruders a clear path. As they moved down the stairs, he shouted out the window to the Gascars below.

"There's a group of men comin' down. Let 'em go in peace, but keep an eye on 'em. Keep your bows strung."

And with that, the battle ended.

Florio, they were happy to discover, was unconscious but still alive. Though badly beaten, he had, as far as they could tell, sustained no serious injuries. They stripped off his bloody garments and began to bath and bandage his hurts. Quite unexpectedly, the elf opened his eyes. He began to stammer.

"I…I knew you'd come back…I knew you'd save us from…from this mess I've made. Oh, Roscoe…you trusted me, and I failed you. I'm so sorry. I…."

The old Adventurer's voice was gentle but firm, though still weak from the blow to his head.

"You hush up, boyo, with that kind of talk. I don't want to hear it. Whatever it was you did, you had your reasons, so I don't want no apologizin'."

But Florio was not to be stopped.

"Would that my hand had withered before I used it to unbar the door."

Sarah laid a cool, wet cloth on the elf's head.

"Florio, Torgul and Thurmond are going to carry you down to bed. You're not badly injured, but you need to rest. But before you go, it would useful to know what went on here."

"I don't know much, really. I assumed the men were soldiers sent to protect us from the Keltins. When they came before, I fired the ballista at them. I was afraid they wanted revenge, so I went out to try to make amends. When I brought them inside, one of them struck me on the head. I spent most of the last day hanging from a beam."

At that point, Pozi finally came down from above. Even with Ubo dead and his men departed, she was reluctant to leave her hiding place. To the startled Adventurers, she seemed to materialize out of thin air.

Thurmond grabbed her in a bear-hug, delighted to see the girl alive.

"Where did you come from?"

"I've been hiding up on one of those beams. I saw everything that happened.

She spoke as if the words were bursting from her lips.

"That one-eyed man struck Florio from behind, then the tall one, that dead one over there..."

She stopped to point at Ubo's remains.

"...he started kicking him. That's when Bodo—I mean my father—he tried to stop him, but one of them killed him. Then they all laughed. Another one took off his wooden leg and threw it in the hearth like it was just a piece of kindling. They thought it was a jest."

Sarah wiped a wisp of hair out of the girl's eyes.

"What happened then, Pozi?"

"The tall one told his men to take the tenants out to the barn, told them they could have as much fun as they wanted. I was pretty sure I knew what he meant. Anyway, I could see a little bit of the yard through the window.

There was a whole army out there, scores and scores of men. I still don't know who they were."

"But after dark, something weird happened. All of a sudden, the men in the yard started arguing, and pretty soon a lot of them were leaving. That tall guy got really mad and said he'd chop off all their heads, but he couldn't stop them from going."

Sarah took the girl's hand.

"You've been up on that beam all this time?"

"Aye, except when they were all up on the roof shooting that crossbow thing. I slipped down for a minute and unbarred the doors. I gave the bottom one a little push, so you'd know it was open."

Thurmond was astounded.

"That was you? You did that? You're not only brave, you're right smart."

The girl rolled her eyes.

"Of course I'm smart. Did you just notice? And it was me who pushed Chanticleer off his perch with a toasting fork."

Thurmond laid his hand on Pozi's shoulder.

"You saved my life then. That crossbowman was going to kill me for certain except the rooster landed on his head. You pushed the rest of the chickens, too?"

"I did."

"Then I think maybe you saved all of our lives."

"Maybe I did, but I can't talk any more right now. I've been up on that beam forever, and I really need to go pee."

They put Florio to bed and carried Bodo's body to his own little house. His children and his wife Bess were absent, no doubt hiding in the forest. The Gascars hauled Ubo and the slain guardsman from the tower and dumped them with the other bodies in the yard—they would keep until morning.

They were all too worn out to do more.

CHAPTER 51
PICKING UP THE PIECES

The people of Gorgonholm were up early the next morning, collecting the wounded and pilfering the dead. Wives, parents, and sweethearts swarmed to the battlefield in search of missing husbands, sons, or lovers.

The bodies of fallen nobles were naturally treated with the utmost respect. Wrapped in fine linen shrouds, they were transported by wagon to the tombs of their venerated ancestors. Lesser folk did the best they could, sometimes carrying their dead back to local churchyards, but more often settling for a battlefield burial. Unclaimed bodies were tossed into mass graves.

The slain Keltins were left to rot where they fell. The carrion beasts would feast well in the days ahead.

The streets of the city were jammed with citizens assessing the damage, checking on their neighbors, swapping rumors. Bishop Boniface, it was reported, had been struck by a Keltin spear and had instituted a new tithe to pay for the necessary treatments.

Some maintained the earl had been killed while leading a glorious charge around the Keltin flank. Others said *nay*—he had indeed led the charge but was only wounded. Still others claimed he had slain the Keltin king in single combat.

Sheriff Brandon was also lauded. His trained bands, it was told, had smashed straight through the Keltin center and driven their army into the river. He had slain, they said, seven enemy chieftains in the course of the day, then sat down to a lunch of seven eggs.

Another tale was more cautionary. In the battle's aftermath, a group of vengeful townsmen had seized a number of abandoned currachs and pursued their beaten foe across the river. When they stumbled upon an empty Keltin war-camp, their lust for loot had overwhelmed their passion for revenge. When they stopped to pillage, they were surrounded and slain by a contingent of Chewbone warriors that had rallied in the forest just beyond the camp.

An entertaining encounter near Market Square drew a large group on onlookers. The skipper of a small riverboat was engaged in vociferous argument with the owner of a demolished pawnshop, the exasperated pawnbroker demanding compensation for his shop and stock, the skipper accusing him of stealing his boat and insisting that he return it at once to its rightful place on the dock.

Father Egrigius, abbot of the Black Friars, was quite calm when confronted with the ruins of his abbey. He knew that war was expensive and that in the coming weeks, many of the nobles would be forced to borrow large sums from his order. Their interest payments would be more than adequate to cover the cost of rebuilding.

But why merely rebuild? Why not commission an edifice worthy of his order? He envisioned sweeping buttresses, leering gargoyles, and a bell tower tall enough to block the view from Bishop Boniface's private apartment. That would surely stick in that old fool's craw.

Remarkably, the city streets were cleaner than anyone could remember, for the great flood had swept away the accumulated filth of generations, leaving a clean, crisp smell that many found annoying. For days thereafter, tiny sodden men, the surviving remnants of the Small Folk, were seen crawling from flooded basements or squeezing up through sewer drains. These were quickly hunted down and slain by vengeful citizens.

Far more Shamblers survived than might be expected. Like roaches, they were notoriously hard to kill. Those who managed to escape the knives of the Small Folk and then live through the horrendous deluge were amazingly philosophical about their experience, acknowledging that a good purging every five or ten years was useful of ridding their quarter of the bad blood.

Besides, there would now be new opportunities, for the Brethren would be forced to open their books and admit new members.

In Grimsgard, the morning began like any other. The summer sun awoke eventually and spread its warmth over the countryside. Torgul's bees buzzed and set out to fetch their daily quota of pollen. Chanticleer crowed mightily and strutted through the village, searching for new wives. Cocks are not sentimental creatures.

Roscoe's tenants emerged from the sheltering woods and crept back to their village. Word had gone out that the master had returned and killed the bad lord who had attacked their homes. He had, it was said, also slain the Keltin king in single combat and sent his army running back across the river. There was nothing Lord Roscoe could not do.

It was a day for both grieving and rejoicing. Grieving because there were friends and neighbors to put in the grave. Grieving for wives and daughters violated by the soldiers of the bad lord. Grieving for their goods and livestock stolen or destroyed. Yet rejoicing for the fact that they lived still! The bad lord was gone, the Keltins were gone, and the villagers' hearts continued to pump blood through their veins. That was indeed a thing to be happy about.

Grimsgard boasted no church or chapel, so there was no cleric to officiate at the burials. Various tenants had, from time to time, asked Roscoe to fetch one from the city, but the old Adventurer was adamant in his refusal. He would not allow the church to gain a foothold in his estate. Once established in the village, the holy fathers would waste no time asserting their authority over every aspect of their lives. Roscoe would never allow that.

The dead were laid to rest in the patch of ground that served as the village cemetery. It was, by force of habit, referred to as *the churchyard*, although the closest building was a cowshed. Ubo and his henchmen were dragged into a field and burned on a pyre of logs.

With the dead attended to, Roscoe turned his attention to the restoration of his fief. Several tenants were sent to remove the blood and filth from the towerhouse. Having held the fief's livestock during the anticipated siege, it needed a thorough cleaning. Roscoe had assumed that Sarah would take over Florio's kitchen duties while the elf recovered, but she only gave him a disappointed look and went out to the village to tend the injured tenants.

Left to his own devices, the old Adventurer wandered into the kitchen, looking for some breakfast.

"God's great naked pate! Thurmond! Torgul! Come and help me! This is a terrible thing to behold!"

Thurmond was only too glad to abandon his current task. He and the dwarf had been shifting heavy furniture so the cleaners could proceed with their work. They found their friend with his arms hanging limply at his sides, his eyes filled with dismay.

"Alack! Our kitchen has been ravished. Have you ever seen such wanton disregard for basic decency? There's not a thing left that's fit to eat."

His words were sadly true. Ubo's boys had run riot though Florio's marvelous kitchen. The flagstones were cluttered with pots, pans, and utensils knocked from their hooks. Jars of sauces and preserved fruit had been opened, tasted, and smashed. Large crocks had been tipped sideways, spilling a medley of pickled meats, marinated vegetables, and stewed herbs. Dried onions rolled underfoot. And over everything was spread a thick coating of finely ground flour.

Roscoe was beside himself.

"This is just plain wrong, so it is! It's bad enough that those poxy buggers broke into my home and abused my people, but this is too much! It's utterly heartless, keepin' a man from his breakfast!"

Thurmond saw things a bit differently.

"We've got to get this place cleaned up. If Florio sees it like this, in his weakened state, the shock could bring on a brain fever. It could kill him."

Before the old Adventurer could reply, a dismal cry came from behind them.

"God in a great bronze bowl! Why? Why?"

The elf stood in the doorway, clutching the frame with one hand, his lips quivering, a fat tear rolling down his bruised cheek.

By late afternoon, things in the tower had been more or less set to right. The animal dung had been scraped up and hauled away, the broken crockery had been removed from the kitchen, and the blood had been mopped from the floors. Florio did not come down with a lethal brain fever. In fact, he steadfastly refused to return to his bed until he had seen the kitchen floor swept and the counters wiped clean.

Fortunately, Ubo's men had been less than thorough in their rapine. A bit of searching revealed sufficient foodstuffs for a morning repast—a pot of snails boiled in dark ale, a number of day-old loaves with a small tub of rendered mutton fat for a topping, and a jar of what was thought to be some sort of dried fruit.

Breakfast was served on a long table beneath the ancient linden tree on the common. It was simple fare compared to Florio's usual exotic cookery, but Roscoe insisted that the elf return to his bed and recover before assuming his station at the stove. By the time they sat down, the old Adventurer was so famished that he could, he proclaimed, eat a live baby goblin.

Things were just returning to normal when their meal was interrupted by a large, dark shadow that suddenly fell across the table. Looking up, they recognized Asmodeus on his demon-steed circling overhead. He spiraled toward the ground and landed a dozen yards away. Sliding from the saddle, he fed his mount with something from his saddlebag. There was a pitiful squeal as the hell-creature closed its jaws.

Asmodeus was decked out in full military finery. His thigh-high boots and boiled leather cuirass were dyed a rich plum. Gorget, bracers, and open-faced casque were enameled a dark burgundy. Over all was thrown a thick cloak of maroon wool. His helmet sported a tall lavender plume.

The wizard strode to their table, sat down, poured himself a mug of ale from the pitcher on the table. He offered the Adventurers a self-satisfied grin.

"I just wanted to look in on my minions. You're all still alive, I see—or at least you appear to be."

Roscoe was growing increasingly weary of the wizard's condescension.

"I am no man's minion. I am master of this freehold by the grace of...."

Asmodeus waved away his objections with a smirk.

"Please pardon me, *Your Majesty*, I had quite forgotten your elevated position. Now if *Your Exaltedness* will kindly allow me to finish, I'd like to inform you that the Black Stone has been completely overthrown. Its powers sent…elsewhere. I have arranged for it to be dumped into the river. Some fish will certainly die, but with any luck the thing will not rise for another thousand years."

This caught Sarah's attention.

"We were successful then? We used Malachai's instrument correctly? It worked as it was supposed to?"

The wizard allowed her a bland smile.

"Eminently so."

"And that contributed to our winning the battle?"

"Indeed, it did. Breaking the power of the Stone was more important than all the swords and spears combined. It brought immediate disunity to the Keltin host, so that it crumbled more and more as the day progressed."

He stared intensely into the young witch's eyes.

"You are woefully untrained, but your natural abilities are great. Be very careful—you might easily summon entities beyond your control. The result would be worse than death."

None of the Adventurers knew how to respond to these words, so they sat in an awkward silence until Thurmond remembered an item he had stashed in a leather bag at his feet. He extracted it and placed it before Asmodeus.

"I stole this book from Malachai's workshop. Is it valuable?"

The wizard's eyes narrowed slightly. He extended his hands as if to pick it up, paused, then pulled them back as if afraid to touch it. He considered a moment, then finally reached out, opened the volume, and began to thumb through the pages.

"This might be of some small interest to the right person, but it is of no considerable value."

Thurmond raised a doubtful eyebrow.

"It gives detailed instructions for imbuing dead flesh with artificial life. I would think it to be of great interest."

Asmodeus tossed it down contemptuously.

"As I said, it is an item of slight worth."

Thurmond returned it to the leather bag.

"Very well—I offered it to you as a courtesy, but perhaps Master Jarvis will prove more eager."

The wizard puffed out his chubby cheeks.

"Jarvis! That common merchant! What would he do with such a book? He'd sell it to some bumbler who would send a legion of undead to plague our city. Nay, we can't have that. Give it to me. I'll give you a thousand golden sovereigns for it."

This was certainly a princely sum, but Thurmond had recognized the covetous gleam in Asmodeus eyes when first presented with the volume. And he knew a thousand sovereigns was a paltry amount to the wealthy wizard.

"Not nearly enough! Besides, I want something beyond gold."

Asmodeus grew cautious.

"Beyond gold? What do you have in mind?"

"I want your sworn oath that you will shield us from Malachai. He may mean us harm. You must do whatever is necessary to protect us."

This was a serious demand. For all his childish whimsy, Asmodeus adhered to a strict code of honor. Such a pledge might embroil him in a deadly feud with an opponent of awesome power. But Thurmond was not yet finished.

"And I would need no less than five thousand sovereigns to even consider the transaction."

This was less of an issue. The wizard possessed almost limitless wealth. Still, he did not like being dictated to by this upstart whelp.

And that whelp was still not done.

"And lastly, I want that."

Thurmond pointed to the curved dagger hanging on Asmodeus's girdle.

"You want my dagger? It's an ensorcelled blade, my boy. You would have no use for it."

"Makes no difference. You have heard my terms. They are not negotiable."

Asmodeus considered having his demon eat the accursed boy, perhaps eat them all. Then he could just take the book. But was the price really that high? The book possessed great power. He could feel the energy bursting from it.

Personal items absorbed the psychic signatures of their owners, and this one was brimming with Malachai's essence. As such, it could be used against him, much as hair and nail cuttings could be used to empower a curse.

Formidable though he was, Malachai would not be eager to offend anyone possessing the item.

Meeting the boy's demand for protection would not be difficult. The gold was inconsequential. He could always send spirits to fetch more from a distant land where that mineral was as common as iron. The dagger rankled, but why should he allow such a small point to complicate an otherwise satisfactory arrangement?

"I agree to your terms. I solemnly swear that I will protect you and yours from any attack by Malachai, even at the cost of my life. I will send my steed to fetch your gold, he will return with it shortly. Here is your dagger."

He unhooked the weapon from his belt and pushed it across the table. Then he refilled his mug with ale.

The demon returned with the gold much quicker than any mortal creature could have done. Asmodeus dumped it on the table for the Adventurers' inspection. Fearing an illusion, Thurmond disbelieved with all his might, but the sovereigns remained solid and real. Then he handed over the book.

Their business concluded, the wizard mounted his fiend and flew off.

CHAPTER 52

THE DIVISION OF
THE SPOILS

Thurmond slid the dagger over to Sarah.

"This is for you. I don't know what it does, but I'm guessing it's powerful. Anyway, you deserve it."

"Why me?"

"You heard him. Defeating the Black Stone was what really defeated the Keltins. You did that, and you saved us all."

"I did not! Don't forget, you finished the operation after I passed out. We all played a part—even Bart—even Drax. I do fancy the dagger, though. Thank you for it."

Roscoe poured the last of the ale into his mug.

"She's right, boyo. Us Adventurers always share the credit just like we share the blame. And look at this fine pile of gold your cagey thinkin' brought us. You done right fine, laddie, so you did."

Then Roscoe rose and donned his big, black Adventurer's hat, which he had previously hung on a branch of the linden tree. He cleared his throat like he always did before making an official proclamation. He kept his tone stiff and formal.

"As your captain, I declare our latest Adventure officially at an end. It is now, as custom dictates, time to proceed with the ritual of division. Brother Torgul, do you have what's left of the wizard's original payment?"

"I do."

"Place it upon the table, if you please."

The dwarf produced the leather wallet given to them by Asmodeus at their initial meeting. Though their journey had been costly, a considerable amount remained.

Roscoe spoke again.

"Now let us add these old coins to the new ones on the table, and sort them into even piles so that each Adventurer may recognize their quantity and worth."

These words were part of the traditional ritual by which Adventurers insured a fair distribution of spoils. Only the strictest adherence to custom could keep such dangerous men from quarreling over the loot, and Roscoe was determined to follow the process to the letter. Following his instructions, the others immediately began stacking the sovereigns.

"Now, Brother Sarah...uh...I mean...."

Roscoe always stumbled when speaking to Sarah in formal proceedings. She was the first and only female Adventurer, and he had not yet arrived at a suitable form of address. She smiled.

"It's all right, Roscoe—get on with it."

The old Adventurer was a bit flustered by the interruption of the ritual. He needed to get it back on track.

"Well, anyway, that dagger Thurmond gave you was rightfully part of the spoils, so it wasn't his to give away, properly speakin'. But I have no personal objection to him doin' so. How about you, Brother Torgul?"

"No objection."

"Fine then. I declare the dagger to be exempt from the division."

The coin count complete, Roscoe called for a final tally. The amount was entirely pleasing to each of them. They now moved to the next step of the process.

Roscoe again cleared his throat.

"We will now begin the division of the spoils. Brother Torgul, as second in rank, you will please move the appropriate coinage to the correct places on the table. I, as Adventure Captain, am entitled to my customary share of three eighths."

A large pile of sovereigns was pushed before the Old Adventurer.

"And you, Brother Torgul, as my lieutenant, are entitled by custom to a share of two eighths."

The dwarf raked in a somewhat reduced pile for himself. Roscoe continued.

"Brother Thurmond and…hmmm…."

Sarah held up her hands in mock surrender.

"You can call me Brother Sarah if it makes things easier. It really doesn't matter."

Roscoe was uncomfortable with that idea. It seemed to somehow detract from the solemnity of the ritual, and Sarah, he suspected, found its inappropriateness slightly amusing. But he could think of nothing better.

"Alrighty then, Brother Sarah, back to business. You and Brother Thurmond, as Adventurers in good standing, are each entitled to a share of one eighth. Brother Torgul, do your duty."

Smaller piles were placed before the two fledgling Adventurers. Roscoe again cleared his throat has he prepared to bring the proceeding to its final stage.

"Does anyone present dispute the fairness of the division?"

Sarah cautiously raised her hand. Roscoe gave her a stern look.

"You dispute the fairness of the division, Brother Sarah?"

"Nay, I dispute nothing, but I have a question."

"Questions are not a customary part of the proceedin'. But, oh well, go ahead. You may ask it."

"What becomes of the other eighth?"

"That will be used to cover any outstanding expenses associated with the Adventure. I intend to reward the Gascars with a weighty bonus. They are stout fighters and true-hearted men, as they proved during the fracas at The Blind Pig."

Sarah was not yet satisfied.

"But even with all that, there will surely be some gold left over. What will you do with that?"

Roscoe now grew a bit indignant, his voice terse. The girl's interruptions were not part of the ritual. This was a clear deviation from custom.

"I will follow accepted custom, of course. It will be divided by the same ratio of three, two, one, and one. Do you have any more questions, Brother Sarah, or may I now proceed?"

Sarah appeared unaware of his growing annoyance.

"Nay, no more questions, but I have a suggestion. Why not put that money away to fund our next adventure. We seem to be having a lot of them."

The old Adventurer wrinkled his brow in frustration. He did not want to like Sarah's suggestion, but he was forced to admit it was a good one. He once more cleared his throat.

"Brother Sarah's suggestion will be given all due consideration. Now, I hereby declare this proceeding...."

Sarah raised her hand again, but did not wait to be recognized.

"Wait! One more thing! I just remembered Pozi. We need to give her something, you know, for the chickens."

Roscoe finally gave up trying to adhere strictly to the ritual. He allowed his voice to lapse into its usual, friendly lilt.

"That's a fine idea, lassie. I'll see to it. And I'll sock some coin away to pay for our next adventure, so I will. Therefore, I declare this proceeding closed so I can go fetch myself another pot of ale. All this talkin' has left me with a ragin' thirst."

Within a week, life at Grimsgard had returned to what passed for normal. Death was a frequent visitor to rural hamlets, so the inhabitants were well used to the loss of family members. Periods of mourning were of blessedly short duration.

Roscoe was quite generous with his tenants. He gave large indemnities to those who had lost loved ones, particularly to Bess, for her husband Bodo had been a good and loyal man. He also provided funds for the repair of their homes and the replacement of their possessions. The villagers were profoundly grateful for his bounty, for a landlord was under no obligation to provide for his serfs in this way.

The exception was Bess. She blamed Roscoe for the death of her husband, and announced her intention to leave the village to live with her brother's family in the city. Roscoe's generosity did nothing to soften her bitterness.

In truth, everyone was happy to see her go. Never a pleasant woman, she had shamelessly browbeaten poor Bodo, and she was regularly embroiled in nasty confrontations with her neighbors. Even the village dogs seemed to dislike her.

But her departure created a problem—what to do with Pozi? Neither the girl nor Bess wanted to continue their association, Pozi called her step-mother an ill-tempered dragon. Bess referred to the girl as a back-talking little turd.

After presenting Pozi with a reward of ten golden sovereigns, an utterly astounding sum, Roscoe broached the subject of her future.

"So child, with Bess leavin', you'll be needin' someone to look after you. Is there a family in the village you're fond of? Name 'em, and I'll arrange for them to take you in."

Pozi crossed her arms and shot the old Adventurer a look of utter distain.

"I am not a child, so don't call me one! I turned thirteen while you were away on your old adventure, the one you wouldn't let me go on. I'm a woman now, and I don't need anyone looking after me. Thank you very much."

Sarah endeavored to calm her down.

"You're quite right, Pozi, of course. Roscoe is just trying to find out what you want to do, now that you're of age."

Pozi remained querulous. She was at times entirely a slave to her emotions.

"Well then, he should've just asked me that instead of talking to me like I was a baby."

Roscoe could be remarkably patient when the situation called for it.

"Sorry, Pozi. I meant no insult. Let me rephrase my question. Now that you're all grown up, what are your plans?"

The girl finally began to calm down.

"I would think that's pretty obvious. I want Sarah to become my mentor."

Sarah was shocked.

"What? Me? Do you mean you want to learn the magical arts?"

"Nay, don't be silly. I've no head for such as that. But I'm quick and clever. I can climb and pick locks and creep on my tippy-toes as quiet as a phantom in the night."

This left Sarah even more confused.

"I don't understand. Why do you want me as your mentor if you don't want to learn magic? What do you want to do?"

Pozi was triumphant.

"I want to become an Adventurer. To wear a black big hat like yours and travel to faraway lands to fight monsters and win treasure—just like you do."

Sarah pursed her lips in disapproval.

"You can't be serious. The life of an Adventurer is fraught with dire peril. It's no life for...."

She was interrupted by Roscoe and Thurmond bursting into laughter. Even Torgul allowed himself a slight guffaw.

Sarah never liked to be laughed at. She turned on them, her eyes blazing. "What?"

The old Adventurer was unrepentant.

"You was about to tell Pozi that adventurin' ain't no kinda life for an innocent young girl—that's all."

CHAPTER 53
THE FIELD OF SPEARS

Each new day crowded out the old one until three weeks had passed. The rubble of the collapsed South Gate was cleared away, and a conclave of master masons came to blows while debating how best to replace it. Construction on the new Black Friars abbey progressed more rapidly—no one wanted to feel the ire of Father Egrigius.

A new Severed Head tavern rose from the ashes of the old. Half-timbered buildings went up quickly, and only a severe shortage of thatch delayed its reopening. After the terrible windstorm, half the city's houses needed new roofs.

Market Square regained its former liveliness. Farmers brought in beets and onions, bakers offered bread and pies, and rivermen hawked the freshness of their catch. A strolling minstrel strummed his gittern and sang a love song, much to the delight of nearby shopgirls. A bagpiper struggled to squeeze a tune from his reluctant instrument. Hucksters offered worthless charms. Harlots cast seductive glances.

One muggy afternoon, a contingent of armored riders clattered into the square. They wore the livery and carried the banner of Earl Ralf Mortimer. One blew a loud call upon a trumpet to summon the attention of the populace. This was completely unnecessary because all eyes were already upon them. Then a herald in a fantastically embroidered tabard stood in his stirrups and made known their earl's desires.

"Know all and sundry that Ralf, Earl of Avincraik, has decreed a grand tournament of arms to be held in celebration of our glorious victory over the foul Keltin invaders. Said event to be held in the month of the Dancing Crone on the very ground where said victory was won. All and sundry are invited to attend, make merry, and benefit from the good earl's largesse."

A similar, written notice was posted on the cathedral doors.

Thurmond was excited. He had always wanted to attend a tournament. Ever since childhood, he had relished stories of knights jousting for the favor of beautiful maidens. He did not exactly know what was meant by *favor*, but it sounded promising. His namesake, the Thurmond of legend, was a superlative jouster.

And now here he was, after so many years, jostling his way through a dense crowd, thoroughly thrilled by all the mad pageantry—the colorful pennants streaming on long lances, the bright armor and huge warhorses of the knights, the shouts of the heralds, the cheering of the spectators, the mingled aromas of cooking meats, wet hay, and horse dung.

Jousting, he knew, was a sport, an exhibition of manly prowess. The swords and spearpoints would be blunted, not intended to kill. But it was still a rough game. Broken bones were common and deaths were not unknown. The sharp end of a broken lance might enter the eyeslot of a helmet, and an unhorsed rider could easily land on his head and break his neck. The unfortunate Whump came to mind.

Thurmond, of course, would not be fighting this day. Jousting was the pastime of the nobility. A village boy such as himself might live through a score of battles, but he would never be allowed on the tourney field. Even if he somehow acquired the enormously pricey warhorse and plate armor, even if he learned to use the twelve-foot lance, his humble birth would still be an insurmountable barrier. So today he came just to watch.

This particular tournament had been christened The Field of Spears in reference to its location on the former battlefield. A gang of serfs had been sent first to clear the grounds of bones and bodies. Trees had been cut, bushes cleared, boulders removed.

A large area had been leveled for the many semi-permanent pavilions the nobles would occupy during the month-long event. These were now arranged in a large half-oval around the jousting field. On the other side, big wooden stands allowed the Quality to view the jousting in comfort and privacy. All intervening spaces were taken by the smaller pavilions of the lesser gentry. Above all flew the banners of the great noble families.

Beyond this inner circle, a temporary city had sprung up. Wine merchants, ale mongers, and food venders competed for the most advantageous locations. Armorers and horse-breeders offered their wares to the knights and nobles, while jewelers and clothiers pitched to their ladies.

Cooks cooked, servants served, and grooms groomed. Pages ran errands while squires pursued their lady-loves. Armor was polished, and songs were sung.

Tournaments were not common in this part of the kingdom, so few of the attendees had ever witnessed spectacle so lavish. They streamed in from the city, from nearby villages, and from distant towns and settlements. All were in best of spirits and determined to enjoy themselves to the utmost.

The Adventurers had dressed for the occasion in fine new garb. Torgul all in black leather with bronze accents. Sarah in a sideless surcoat divided vertically in her father's colors of scarlet and gold. The gown beneath was of snow-white linen. Thurmond's dark green doublet was cut shockingly short, and his hood boasted a long, liripipe tail with a small silver bell at the tip.

Roscoe's attire was the most extravagant of all. His crushed velvet doublet was as short as Thurmond's—a most unlikely choice for a man of mature years—with edges wonderfully dagged and enlivened with gold thread. His hose were naturally crossed-gartered.

Pozi came with them. She wore a new sky-blue dress and had ribbons braided into her long, dark hair. Before meeting the Adventurers a few months ago, the girl had spent her entire life in a tiny, squalid mountain village far to the east. She had fled with them to escape a dismal marriage to a much older man to whom her father had sold her for ten goats and an iron kettle. Although Pozi was a decidedly precocious, cocky child, she was intimidated by all the lavishness and ebullience of the tournament and walked nervously behind Sarah.

Thurmond was eager to see some fighting, but Roscoe inevitably guided them to an ale stand, where they edged their way through the boisterous throng until reaching the plank trestle that served as a bar. Four young men, each wearing the white belt and golden chain of knighthood shouldered up beside them. When the Adventurers' beverages arrived, the knights immediately seized them for themselves.

One of the four, a strapping youth scarcely older than Thurmond, gave Roscoe a challenging look. When the old Adventurer said nothing, he went a step further.

"What are you waiting for, grandpa? Pay the man for the ale."

Roscoe refused to be provoked.

"I see you're wearin' the badge of Baron Horatio Durt—a right noble warrior who fought with us in the war. I'd be right pleased to buy you laddies a round of ale."

Roscoe blundered here. He had hoped to appease the young bullies by praising their liege lord, but as it turned out, the baron had not participated in the battle. He had feigned illness in order to dodge the call to arms, and sent far fewer soldiers than required by his feudal obligation.

None of these knights had been in the group sent to war, and they felt quite uncomfortable whenever confronted by those who had been in the fighting. So instead of taking Roscoe's words at face value and allowing their enormous egos to be pleasingly stroked, they heard a subtle insinuation.

The knight's eyes narrowed,

"Don't call me *laddie*, old man. And I don't give a dead man's arse what pleases you and what don't."

Roscoe recognized the look in the young man's eyes. He was looking for an excuse to draw his weapon.

"My apologies, sir knight. I meant no offense."

He placed a coin on the bar and backed away, putting the crowd between himself and his antagonist. He kept moving until lost from view. Pleased with themselves, the four knights erupted in laughter and toasted themselves with the stolen ale.

Sarah looked at Thurmond. His face was frozen in an expression she knew well. It meant death. She whispered sharply in his ear.

"Nay! nay! Do not even think it! You'll cause Roscoe no end of trouble."

She looked to Torgul for support, but he had disappeared. Then she spotted him standing behind the knights, his hand gripping the hilt of his scramasax. They were entirely unaware of his presence. Pozi had drifted to one side, obviously intending to jump into the middle of whatever was about to happen.

Sarah grabbed Thurmond's sword arm and held it tight.

"You'll get us all killed. They're nobles. The law is always on their side. That's why Roscoe walked away—he understands."

Somewhere deep inside his brain, Thurmond knew she was right. Knights were almost never held accountable for slaying commoners. If he and his companions slew these four, even in self-defense, they would most likely be hung. Although his soul screamed to kill these supercilious bastards, he was gradually learning to let his brain rule his passions. Without a word, he turned and strode away from the bar, Torgul, Sarah, and Pozi close behind.

Roscoe was relieved when he saw his companions leaving the ale stand. He had positioned himself behind a wagon loaded with wooden casks where he would be sure to see them if they exited, but still be able to rush in if they lacked the good sense to walk away from the four idiots inside.

The old Adventurer had good reason to be extra cautious this day. A messenger had brought him a summons to the earl's afternoon court. He was nervous about it. On one hand, he was optimistic. He had, after all, successfully defended Earl Ralf's pavilion against a determined assault. On the other hand, it was never wise to come to the attention of nobles. They were too self-centered, too unpredictable. Too many things could go wrong.

At the baggage camp, he had told the earl's knight—Sir Seymour?—that he was in charge. That had been an exaggeration, of course, but it might be enough to blame him for its pillaging. No one would really care if he was really at fault.

There was also Lord Ubo. It might make no difference that the madman had invaded his home and killed his tenants. He had been a noble, and the earl might not forgive his death under any circumstance.

And then there were the gems, the ancestral family gems that Roscoe had rescued and returned to Earl Ralf. Jarvis had concocted an ingenious lie that had led to the old Adventurer receiving Grimsgard as a reward. But what if Ralf had found out the truth of the matter? That would bring a death sentence, surely.

In any case, Roscoe knew he was on dangerous ground, so it was no time to involve himself in a brawl, especially with members of the chivalry. He was entirely grateful that his companions, especially the hot-headed Thurmond, had sufficient intelligence to follow his lead and walk away.

Reunited with Roscoe, the group now made their way to the tourney field, but so dense was the mass of spectators that very little could be seen. Torgul solved the problem by pulling a handful of copper farthings from his purse and tossing them into the air so that they rained down on people's heads. As the crowd began scrambling for the coins, the Adventurers moved forward into the newly opened spaces. The dwarf repeated this trick twice more before they reached the wooden barrier separating the spectators from the combatants.

A melee was underway at the moment. Having already broken and discarded their lances, a score of knights in two groups were pounding away at each other with swords and maces. This was followed by a series of smaller encounters with groups of three. After this came a long series of jousts in which single knights strove to unhorse their opponent.

Growing bored of the fighting, Pozi offered to fetch the party a round of ale. Roscoe gave her a handful of coins and off she went. She had scarcely returned when she was sent off to bring another round. Then another. Then another.

Sarah, too, began to grow restless. She found the fighting interesting to a point, but how much head-knocking did she really want to stand and watch? She excused herself and went to explore the rest of the event. She could hear music playing—some old song about *summer ycumin' in*—and had caught a glimpse of a man leading a trained bear.

The jousting was followed by foot combats. Pairs of knights squared off, first with poleaxes, then with huge two-handed swords, then with halberds.

Though the edges and points had been dulled, the impact of such heavy weapons left several fighters stretched unconscious on the ground.

The day wore on. Knights with swords and shields now exchanged blows. Torgul departed—tournament combat was too dandified for his taste. And after so much ale, he needed a nap.

Thurmond was seriously disappointed. In the old stories, tournaments offered knights an opportunity to display not only their fighting skills, but also their honor and courtesy. It was unchivalrous to strike an opponent from behind. If a weapon was dropped or broken, the fighting paused while it was replaced.

What he saw today was altogether different. Those knights—men holding the highest titles—the realm's most venerated lords and barons—the supposed epitome of the chivalry—took every cheap shot they could manage. Opponents were struck after they had yielded and lowered their weapons. Groins were a favored target. One great baron, having unhorsed his young challenger, deliberately rode his huge warhorse across his fallen foe.

He saw how young warriors would show great skill when jousting with one another but would deliberately miss their mark when contending with their social betters. One fellow actually rolled from his saddle as if unhorsed, though his opponent's lance point had plainly missed him by several inches. Such was the true nature of knightly honor.

The young Adventurer recalled the arrogance of the knights at the ale stand. Their behavior was mirrored by other knights as they forced their way through the mass of spectators, shoving aside both men and women in complete distain. When an unfortunate child failed to clear the path, he was knocked from his feet by a backhanded blow.

All the while, Roscoe stood silent, his hands gripping the railing of the wooden barrier. He had been watching as the sun traversed the sky, and knew it was time to see the earl. He had told his comrades nothing about the summons. If they knew, they would insist on accompanying him, but the old Adventurer was determined that they would not share his fate.

He looked over at Thurmond.

"I gotta go unload some of this ale. I'll see you back here in a little bit."

CHAPTER 54

STANDING BEFORE EARL RALF

Earl Ralf's pavilion was surrounded by a tall wooden palisade. Obviously, he had been giving more thought to his personal security since the raid on the baggage camp. Two sentries stopped Roscoe at the gated entry and demanded to know his business. He gave his name and was told to wait while one of the guards went for instructions.

Wynkyn Whoorm, the earl's chamberlain, appeared. He recognized Roscoe from the battle and ushered him inside. The old Adventurer was sorely tempted to ask Wynkyn the reason for his summons, but in the end held his tongue. He would find out shortly.

This pavilion was even larger and more elaborately furnished than the previous one. A long central chamber served as the earl's audience hall. Curtained doorways led off to small side rooms.

The chamber was packed with people—servants and guards in livery, barons and lords in bright heraldic surcoats, high-ranking clerics in the elaborate robes of their orders. Attendants and messengers came and went. Noble ladies paraded their elegant gowns. Petitioners sought redress from injuries, while merchants came in search of promised payments.

Ralf sat at the far end in a high-backed chair on a raised platform. From this vantage point, he conducted the business of his earldom. The tournament was no mere celebration, it was also an important opportunity for the earl to meet with his vassals, dispense justice, and settle old feuds. A given amount of time was set aside each day for such purposes.

When Roscoe entered, the earl was addressing a rotund man with a bald head who knelt at his feet. He could not hear the words, but the earl's stern bearing suggested anger, while the portly man's cringing demeanor revealed his terror. The earl made an abrupt gesture. Two guards sprang forward, seized the man's arms, and dragged him out through a side entrance to whatever fate awaited. Perhaps it was Ralf's day for doling out punishments.

That business done, a herald now stepped forward and raised his voice for all to hear.

"Sir Lorenzo di Prativentosi will approach His Excellency."

A young knight strode up the long central aisle and knelt before the earl. The old Adventurer did not recognize the arms on the knight's surcoat. It looked to be a rabbit—a most unlikely choice for a heraldic charge. He must be some kind of foreigner.

The earl's grim expression once more suggested displeasure. It looked like the knight was in trouble. Perhaps he had run away during the battle or committed an outrage upon a noble lady.

This time, however, there was no call for guards. As the knight got to his feet and faced the assembly, the herald again spoke to the crowd.

"Let it be known to all that this worthy knight, having served with great gallantry in the recent war, has, in recognition of said service, been invested with the title Lord of Skut and granted feudal tenure over the lands, resources, castle, village, structures, livestock, and peasantry of the demesne of Skut. Let there be joyous noise in acknowledgment of his deeds and elevation!"

The crowd, as instructed, boomed out a tremendous *hurrah!* Though, in sooth, few had been paying much attention up to that point. Once again, the herald spoke.

"Let Sir Lorenzo now speak the words of homage to Earl Ralf, his liege lord."

The young knight turned and once more knelt before the earl. He began to recite the oath of homage, repeating the herald's words line by line.

Then it struck Roscoe like a blow from a mailed fist—*Lord of Skut*. That is how the madman Ubo had styled himself just before being murdered by his own man. The earl was wasting no time in replacing his slain nobleman.

Just how much did Ralf really know about Ubo's death? Did the perfidious Road Guards place the blame on him? Is that why he was summoned here today? Would he be questioned about his demise? Tortured? Roscoe could feel beads of sweat running down his sides beneath his fancy new tunic.

Wynkyn stepped beside him.

"You are next, so prepare yourself. Approach only to the edge of the carpet. When signaled by the herald, advance and kneel before the earl. Speak only when spoken to. Answer the earl's questions clearly, but be brief. Do not ramble on. And speak up—the earl hates mumblers. One last thing, you must always address the earl as *Your Excellency.*"

His oath finished, Sir Lorenzo rose, as did the earl. The two men grasped each other's wrists and exchanged quiet words. Both were smiling now. As the young knight strode from the pavilion, the crowd once more erupted in cheers.

The herald again came forward, and old Adventurer then heard the words he dreaded above all others.

"Roscoe of Grimsgard will approach His Excellency."

In his career as an Adventurer, Roscoe had fought ogres, goblins, trolls, kobolds, bandits, raiders, Keltins, and ravenous beasts. He had faced spears, swords, poisoned darts, spiked clubs, hurled stones, stingers, claws, and venomous fangs. He had been assailed by ghosts, wraiths, and night-bumping fiends. But never could he recall being as frightened as during his long, long walk up the aisle to where Earl Ralf waited.

Helpless and alone, he felt like a man walking to his own execution. Against a monster or another warrior, he at least had a chance. But here he was completely at the mercy of a powerful and perhaps cruel nobleman, a man who would no more care for the life of a commoner than a fisherman cares for the life of his worm.

He paused at the edge of a carpet spread before the dais, and then, at the herald's gesture, knelt before his liege lord. Earl Ralf stared down at the old Adventurer for several seconds, his face unreadable. Finally, he spoke.

"So, you are Appleman. Or I hear you style yourself Franklin now. You've had a rough go of it. Your holding has been attacked twice in the last six months. Both times you were absent."

Since the earl had asked no question, Roscoe did not reply. He could have said that on both occasions he had arrived home in time to save his holding from destruction, but he was afraid to contradict the earl's words.

Then to his amazement, Earl Ralf seemed to read his thoughts.

"But both times, you managed to return and drive off the attackers."

Still no question, so Roscoe remained silent. The earl, however, desired a response.

"Tell me what happened."

Roscoe tried to moisten his lips with his tongue, but his mouth was bone dry. If ever he needed a mug of ale, it was now.

"Well…Your Excellency, it's like this, so it was—both times we was raided by men who had clean lost their wits. First time, it was a man who called himself Gavin. He brought a score of hired swords with him and tried to batter down my door, but my reeve and my tenants held out until I got back. Second time it was some tall fella with a bunch of wood-cutters and charcoal burners. That was an easy fight 'cause most of 'em ran off before I got there."

The earl raised a knowing eyebrow.

"That tall fellow—that would be Lord Ubo, wouldn't it?"

"Aye, Your Excellency. He said his name was Ubo, that he did."

"And he was slain in the subsequent fighting, is that not correct?"

The earl's expression was inscrutable. Roscoe wanted to lie, but he sensed a trap and felt he had no choice to but tell the truth.

"Aye, that is correct."

"Did you slay him yourself?"

"Nay…Your Excellency. I did not."

"Who did, then?"

It dawned on Roscoe that the earl knew all about the incident, that somebody had already given him the details. His questions were a test of his veracity, so his only chance was to be completely honest.

"He was slain by one of his own men, a rogue names Pons. He and his men had been Royal Road Guards, but they abandoned their duties and joined with Ubo."

Earl Ralf frowned.

"Are you aware that Lord Ubo had previously attacked the Gray Friars' monastery and slaughtered the good brothers inside?"

This was indeed news to Roscoe. When he entered the monastery, it had been in the hands of the Keltins. The earl's tone, when he continued, was deadly serious.

"Nay, Your Highness, I mean Your Excellency, I heard nothin'..."

Ralf cut him off.

"These have been trying times, Roscoe. Friend has turned against friend, father against son, wife against husband. Commoners have risen against their rightful lords and the citizens of Gorgonholm have almost destroyed their own city.

"Lord Ubo, one of my own nobles, invaded holy ground and slew the reverend brothers within. Then he attacked my personal property, the fief of Grimsgard, which you hold in my behalf. I wish to congratulate you, Roscoe, for a job well done."

The old Adventurer was astonished. He was being praised, not condemned, and the earl was not yet finished.

"Furthermore, it has recently come to my attention that it was you who rallied the defenders of the baggage camp after the death of Lord Beaufort. Through your efforts, my personal pavilion and household staff escaped despoliation at the hands of the Keltins. This has been corroborated by my chamberlain, Wynkyn Whoorm, and by a knight of my household, Sir Seymour Guff."

Could it be? It sounded to Roscoe as if he might be rewarded instead of punished, but before he could consider further, the earl continued.

"I am, therefore, minded to make you a knight in recognition of your valiant service. Are you prepared to accept this honor and take the oath of fealty to me, the County of Avincraik, and the Kingdom of Poitiers?'

Roscoe's mind was reeling as if he had been struck in the head with a mace. There were, he knew, times when commoners had been raised to the ranks of the nobility, but such occurrences were extremely rare. He had never considered that such a thing could happen to him.

He finally managed to blurt out an answer.

"I am prepared do to so, Your Excellency."

The earl reached back and drew his sword from where it hung in its scabbard on the corner of his chair. He extended it to Roscoe horizontally with the naked blade across the palms of his hands.

"Place your hands on the blade between mine."

Roscoe did as he was told, and the herald began to recite the ceremony of knighting. Roscoe repeated it as best he could. He pledged his loyalty from that moment until the end of the world. He swore by the sun, moon, and stars, by the thunder and the lightening, by the night and by the day, by the wind in the trees, the rocks in the hills, the fire in the hearth, and the fish in the sea. He swore on the spirits of his dead ancestors and on the souls of his children's children's children. He swore on his own heart, liver, kidneys, lungs, bowels, and spleen. He swore by things he did not understand nor even knew existed.

The pledging done, he was girded round with a swordbelt of white leather, and a heavy golden chain was placed around his neck. The herald explained their symbolic significance.

"Let the whiteness of the belt remind you of your duty to stay pure to the ideals of chivalry and remain clean in word and deed."

Roscoe remembered the young knights in the ale stand. They seemed to have forgotten the meaning of their belts.

The herald went on.

"Let the chain remind you of the weighty pledges you have made this day and of the unbreakable bond that links you to your lord."

Earl Ralf stood and sheathed his sword.

"Let this be the last blow that you receive without seeking proper vengeance."

With those words, he punched Roscoe hard in the side of the head, causing him to see comets and stars. When his ears ceased to ring, he could once more heard the earl speaking.

"...the fief of Grimsgard will be yours to hold in your own right to support you in a style appropriate to your station. I therefore endow you with the title Lord Grimsgard, along with all attending rights, privileges, and responsibilities."

The old Adventurer was now bidden to kneel once again and take the same oath of homage sworn by Sir Lorenzo. He vowed to faithfully support his liege lord in times of war and in times of peace, to put his lord's interests before his own, to harm his lord's enemies and succor his friends. To protect his lord's castles, villages, fields, forests, and rivers against deprivations great and small. To treat honestly and faithfully with his fellow nobles, coveting not their lands or possessions. To appear, when summoned, with the requisite number of armed retainers for service in his lord's army. To dispense justice in his lord's name when so required.

The list went on and on until Roscoe lost track of all the things he had sworn to. Then the herald once more shouted to the crowd.

"Let it be known to all that Roscoe Appleman, having proven himself through worthy deeds, has been elevated to rank of knight, and has, in recognition of his loyal service, been invested with the title of Lord Grimsgard and granted feudal tenure over the lands, resources, castle, village, structures, livestock, and peasantry of the demesne of Grimsgard. Let there be joyous noise in honor of the new lord!"

The crowd, which up to this point had been gossiping, arguing, and in some cases sleeping, burst out in a tremendous cheer. The herald silenced them with a raised hand and continued.

"I have been commanded by His Excellency to contrive suitable and unique arms for the new lord. They are as follows—*per pale Or and Sable, a wyvern erect gripping a pole-ax counterchanged.* Let there be joyous noise!"

Again, there came a surprisingly rousing cheer before the assembly relapsed into the more pressing business of bitching, back-biting, and minding other people's business.

When it was over, he found himself escorted into a side room with chamberlain Wynkyn, who explained the real meaning of what had just befallen.

CHAPTER 55

FINDING ROSCOE

Thurmond grew concerned when Roscoe failed to return from the privy. He assumed at first that his friend had stopped off for more ale, but as time went by, he knew something was wrong. Perhaps he had run afoul of the four obnoxious young knights.

He was just about to start searching when Sarah returned with Pozi in tow. The three set off together and soon came across Torgul snoozing in the shade of a blacksmith's wagon, oblivious to the unholy clanging of hammer on anvil.

Thurmond kicked the bottom of the sleeper's boot.

"Torgul, wake up! Roscoe's missing. I think he's in trouble. We gotta find him."

The dwarf sprang to his feet as if launched from a springald.

"Let's go."

They hunted high and low. They tried searching singly, in pairs, and as a group. They inquired, pleaded, threatened, and bribed. They investigated the privies and peeked through the flaps of pavilions. Nobody they spoke to had seen him, though many could not be bothered to reply. Roscoe was not to be found.

It was Pozi who finally solved the mystery. She sized up the two men standing guard at the entrance to the earl's compound. The one was young and pimply, no more than fifteen summers. Good! He would be the easier of the two. The second was older and had a long, angry scar running down his cheek. He would be more challenging.

Stealing an onion from a nearby food stand, she cut it in two with her belt knife then held it under her nose until she began to cry. She slapped her own face a couple of times to bring some color to her cheeks. Then she approached the younger guard.

"Good soldier, will you help a young girl in distress? I've lost my papa, and there are some horrible men who are bothering me. I don't know who else to turn to—won't you help me?"

Before the young guard could stammer out a response, Scar-Face replied in a deep, gruff voice.

"Be off, you little tart. Our job's to watch the earl's gate. We say who goes in and who goes out, see? We can't be botherin' with the likes of you. Now git!"

She had expected this—guards were never nice. There must be something about just standing around all day, the job was so boring that it made people mean.

"I beg your forgiveness, milord. I never meant that you should leave your post and help me look for him. It's just that guardsmen are always so bright and alert. I thought maybe you'd seen him. I'd be so grateful. Papa gave me a silver penny, and I'd be happy to give it to anyone who helps me find him."

She was now talking the older man's language. A silver penny was his daily wage.

"Let's see this penny your daddy give you."

Pozi held it up for his inspection, being careful to keep it back where he would not be tempted to try to snatch it from her hand. He would never be able to do so—she was as quick as a striking adder. But if he tried and failed, he would be angry, and she needed his cooperation at the moment.

Scar-Face was now all smiles.

"Well, now, little missy, you just give me that penny, and I'll tell you where he is."

"I'm ever so grateful for your help, good sir. But shouldn't I at least tell you what Papa looks like?"

He gave her a lascivious wink.

"If that's what you want, missy. What's Papa look like?"

The girl described Roscoe right down to his cross-gartered hose. The Scar-Face opened his mouth to speak, but before he could, the younger, pimple-faced guard jumped in.

"Why, we know him, his name's Roscoe something. He come through here answerin' the earl's summons, he was. He's still inside, been in there a while now."

Pozi was puzzled.

"A summons from the earl? Why?"

Pimple-Face only shrugged.

"Dunno, they don't tell us stuff like that."

Scar-Face stuck out his hand.

"That'll be one penny for takin' up our valuable time."

Pozi laughed.

"Only if you can catch me, you fat old lump of horse dung!"

She stuck out her tongue, clicked her heels, and disappeared into the crowd.

Pozi found the others gathered a short distance away, arguing about their best course of action. While she told them of her conversation, she pulled them to a point where they could see the two guards for themselves.

"There they are—the nice one and the mean one, just like I said."

Thurmond was dubious.

"It doesn't sound right. Why would the earl summon Roscoe? Nay, that guard was making it all up. He only wanted your penny."

Pozi rolled her eyes in frustration.

"You weren't even there, so you didn't hear him. The old one was a liar and a lecher, but the young one was nice. He really wanted to help me."

Sarah was less skeptical.

"I believe her, Thurmond. Maybe Roscoe was summoned."

"But he would have told us. I would have gone with him."

Torgul grumbled.

"If he thought he was in for trouble, he wouldn't want us along. Wouldn't want to drag us into it."

Thurmond hoped the dwarf was wrong, hoped that Roscoe had gotten drunk and fallen asleep somewhere. But if he had been summoned by the earl, that was probably bad. Why else would the old Adventurer have kept it a secret? Not wanting to alarm his friends unduly, he struggled to keep his voice calm.

"Here's what we'll do. Pozi, you'll watch this gate while the rest of us keep searching. Can you do that with those guards spotting you?"

She gave him a bored look.

"Obviously."

But before they could put their plan into action, Roscoe emerged from the earl's gate, a white belt cinched around his hips, a golden chain hanging from his neck. In his hand, he held a rolled parchment scroll.

Thurmond was so excited to see him that he failed to notice the belt and chain. A stream of words burst from his lips

"Roscoe, we've been looking all over. What were you doing in there? Why didn't you tell me where you were off to?"

The old Adventurer did not answer, he only stood, smiling, and looking a bit sheepish.

It was Sarah who first drew attention to his new accouterments.

"It looks like you've got quite a story to tell us. I think it's going to be a long one. Maybe we should head for an ale stand before you start."

Quite unexpectedly, Roscoe shook his head.

"Now that's a fine idea, Sarah, so it is. But to tell you true, I think I'd rather be headin' home. Somebody might start askin' me questions, and I ain't yet ready to start explain' these new fripperies—not yet. But I'll tell you all about it as we ride along."

They crowded their mounts around Roscoe, squirming with anticipation, but the old Adventurer, usually so loquacious, remained unspeaking. Finally, it was Torgul who could endure the silence no longer.

"God's hot breath, Roscoe, you promised us a tale, and I mean to have it. Either you start speakin' up or I'm gonna make up my own story about you.

You won't like it, but it'll get around, and people will start believin' it. Then what really happened won't matter no more."

This brought Roscoe out of his reverie.

"Spare us that, Brother Torgul. I don't know what would be worse, havin' lies spread about me or listenin' to another of your endless dwarven poems. I'll tell you my tale."

That morning, he had risen at dawn and had been sitting in the yard gnawing a chicken leg to hold him over until breakfast. No one else was up and about when the messenger arrived with the summons. Fearing the worse, he had told no one.

He described meeting Wynkyn at the gate of the earl's compound, of the lavish pavilion and opulent nobles. Of the bald man who was dragged away and the young knight who was named Lord of Skut.

Lastly, he revealed the details of his knighting—the lengthy oath, the unexpected blow to the head, the chain and belt. He was now a bona fide member of the chivalry. They had endowed him with his own coat of arms, which was depicted on his parchment scroll.

"Looky here, that's a wyvern with a halberd, just like my Adventurer's tattoo. Wynkyn said he saw my ink after the battle at the baggage camp and told the heralds. See how it's divided down the middle, yellow and black, with the color of the wyvern switched opposite on the two sides? That dividin' line is symbolizin' the barricade we held around the earl's pavilion. At least that's what Wynkyn told me."

"But that ain't all, these arms are mine forever, and I can pass 'em down if I ever have me a son. I can display 'em on a banner or on my clothes, on anything I please. I can even ride in tournaments now. I'm officially a nobleman, so I am. What do you think about that?"

Thurmond said the words that were on everyone's lips.

"I'm not sure I like it at all. All the nobles I've met have been just alike— right bloody bastards, they've always seemed to me. Prideful and hardhearted and not caring a snap for anybody but themselves. Are they going to be your friends now?"

Roscoe was taken aback.

"Why would you say such a thing to me, boyo?"

"Because it seems like there's something in a white belt that sucks all the heart out of people. Look at Bart, or those bullies in the ale stand, or how those knights cheated in the tournament. Are you going to become like them?"

Everyone held their breaths. These were very bold words, and no one was sure how Roscoe would react. Once before, Thurmond had used strong words that pushed his friend to the point of drawing his sword.

The old Adventurer was uncertain how to respond. He wiped the sweat from his brow, giving himself a chance to consider.

"I'll say this, Thurmond, the first time any of you catch me actin' like Bart or any of them others you mentioned, I want you grab me by the neck and stuff my head into a chamber pot. Got that?"

He laughed loudly, but the others did not join in. They were still uncertain of their friend. If he was now, in fact, a noble as he claimed to be, would he not feel and act differently than before?

Roscoe looked at their cautious faces. His companions were plainly afraid of him. He huffed.

"This won't do at all. Stop frettin' about me—I'm the same jolly Roscoe I've always been, and I always will be. Just wait and see, things is gonna work out fine, so they are."

Torgul smirked.

"Maybe so, but I'm gonna keep a chamber pot ready, just in case."

This broke tension, and they all began to laugh. Roscoe, however, was not yet finished with his tale.

"If you folks would kindly stop laughin' at me and just listen for a few moments more, I've got somethin' important to tell you. Wynkyn told me what was really goin' on. I thought bein' knighted was a reward for savin' the earl's pavilion and all. But that wasn't the real reason, and when he was explainin' what the earl was really thinkin', I suddenly got this idea. It's a truly grand design."

CHAPTER 56

ROSCOE'S GRAND DESIGN

"It's like this, see...."

The Adventurers had dismounted and took their ease in the shade of a great elm tree.

"...I didn't have no say in the matter. I wasn't asked *do you want to be a knight*? I was just called up and made one. What should I have done—refused? You don't say nay to a man like Earl Ralf."

"Then after I was all proper knighted, the earl says that I can have Grimsgard as my own estate. That didn't mean too much at the time, seein' as how I already got it, but it got a lot clearer when Wynkyn was tellin' about it afterwards."

"It's all different from what I thought. No matter what was said during the ceremony, I wasn't knighted and given land for my worthy deeds. Same with that young knight who was made Lord Skut. It was all part of the earl's scheme to raise money."

"In war, people get killed. Most of 'em are just common foot soldiers or poor peasants armed with a rake or a hoe, but there' always a few nobles that go down. This means the earl gets to appoint new nobles to take their places. But it costs 'em money—they gotta pay for their titles."

Sarah broke in with a question.

"Why would Wynkyn tell you this?"

"I think he's grateful for us savin' his hide from the Keltins. Anyway, it ain't no secret, lassie. Everybody knows about it except us poor dumb Adventurers. Wynkyn says there was a bunch of people from town wantin' to buy their way in."

Thurmond spoke.

"Why did he pick you?"

"Just a guess, but I think he knows I can fight like a mama troll, and part of the deal is that we gotta give him so many days of soldierin' every year. Also, he knows I'm too simple-minded to be treacherous. But mostly, he knows we got money."

Now Torgul joined in.

"How much do you gotta pay?"

When Roscoe named the sum, their mouths dropped open in disbelief. Roscoe, however, remained undisturbed.

"I know it's a considerable amount, and its more than I've got on hand. But I've got a year and a day to pay it off. So I'll give him what I can right now, and I thought you three might be willin' to make me a wee loan. You know I'm good for it, and it's the adventurin' way, don't you know, helpin' a brother out."

Torgul was not taken in by his friend's glib tongue.

"And where will the rest come from?"

Roscoe smiled broadly.

"No problem at all—we'll have plenty of time for an adventure or two. I'll start sniffin' around. There's bound to be a vampyre in need of a stake, or maybe some nasty troll's been molesting a village. I'll find us somethin', don't you worry."

Thurmond recognized Roscoe's smile, he always used it when making something dangerous or unpleasant seem appealing. Winning so much gold would be far more perilous than the old Adventurer was painting it, far more challenging than facing a difficult troll or hungry vampyre. They would have to take huge risks. Some or all of them might die. This was something to consider carefully.

"All right, Roscoe, I'll loan you as much coin as I can. I just hope we can find an adventure that'll pay enough to make all this worthwhile."

Torgul nodded.

"Been kinda quiet around here lately. I'm ready for some excitement."

Sarah, as usual, had her doubts, but she knew she could not hold back.

"I'm in."

Pozi was hopping up and down with glee.

"Me, too! Me, too! Me, too!"

The old Adventurer's eyes twinkled as they always did when his glib tongue was victorious.

"Well fine, if that's settled, perhaps it's time to reveal my grand design."

His companions shouted out as one.

"Tell us! Tell us!"

"As I recall, Thurmond, you never really knew who your proper daddy was. Is that correct?"

"Aye, my mother always said it was Beaufort, that worthless nobleman who was killed at the baggage camp, but I always suspected the village carpenter. It's hard to say, my mother knew a great many men."

"So nobody could ever say for sure."

"That's right, why do you want to know?"

"All in good time, boyo. Now, what was the name of that village you grew up in?"

"I never knew its name. It must have had one, but we all just called it *the village*."

"Hmmm, we might want to find that out, might could make a difference. You said it was somewhere east of here?"

"Several days walk. What difference does it make?"

"It's all part of the design, laddie, so just be patient. You're how old now?"

"Someplace around nineteen. I never knew my exact birthday, but it was sometime in the summer."

"That's fine. Nineteen years ago I was adventurin' from one end of this county to the other, slayin' monsters and takin' their gold. Things was lots wilder back in them days, and I was a regular hellhound. Great days, so much fun."

"Can't even remember all the places I went or things I done. Met a lot of folks, some was nice, and some wasn't so nice. Met a lot of lovely ladies, so I did. Lots of village women was real eager to keep company with a dashin' young Adventurer, especially one with a purse full of gold sovereigns."

Thurmond was getting more and more uncomfortable with Roscoe's questions and cryptic comments.

"What's your point? Where are you going with all this?"

"Just part of the design, so just hold your piss. Now who's to say that a dashin' young Adventurer didn't come through your village, whatever it's called, and chanced to meet a sweet lass by the name of…what did you say your mother's name is?"

"Marge. Her name is Marge."

"Well, let's just suppose that the lovely Marge took a shine to this Adventurer, and the result was—you!"

"You're saying you're my father?"

"I'm sayin' it's possible, laddie, and so it is."

"But you never really came to my village or met my mother."

"Who can tell, boyo. There was lots of villages and pretty young girls."

"God's holy britches! Why would you even think such a thing?"

"Remember your conversation with Sarah's daddy? He signed a paper recognizin' her as his daughter, even if she was from the wrong side of the blanket, so to speak."

Sarah now joined the conversation.

"My mother was a chambermaid. That document you mentioned—without it, I'm just another nameless bastard, but with it, I'm officially his child and could be in line to inherit his estate and maybe even his titles."

"That's the very paper I had in mind, so it is. You thought for while it might make you into a grand lady, as I recall."

Sarah was embarrassed by this remark. She had, for a brief time, fallen afoul of her own vanity.

"Aye, I suppose that's true. It pains me to recall those days. But it matters not. Everything must go to Bart. He's older, and he's legitimate. Most of all, he's male."

Thurmond smirked.

"Don't give up hope, Sarah. I figure they hanged him and his crew for trying to kill us back at The Blind Pig. If they did, you still might find yourself Lady Sarah Staynes."

He was teasing her, and she did not like it. Before she could reply, Roscoe intervened.

"Let's not get sidetracked. I was speakin' of my grand design, you may recall. Now then, boyo, supposin' I was to draw up a paper like Sarah's, namin' you as my natural son, and conveyin' all my worldly goods to you after my time is come. Then my title, Lord Grimsgard, might could come down to you."

Thurmond was flabbergasted.

"You could do that? It's possible?"

"I do believe it is. Wynkyn told me that bein' a lord is lots different than bein' a franklin. Before, I was just kinda the earl's caretaker. Now the land and everythin' are mine, to do with as I choose. And my title is what's called *heritable*, meanin' I can pass it down to my firstborn son, which, boyo, is your very own self. How's that sound?"

"Why me?"

"Well, Torgul can't do it. If you haven't noticed, he's a dwarf and would have a hard time passin' for a little Roscoe. Besides, nobody in these parts would stand for a dwarf bein' a lord. And Sarah? She's already got a daddy. So that leaves you."

"Anyway, laddie, I like you and think you'd make a fine lord. All that stuff you was sayin' about knights and nobles? You weren't wrong."

"If I don't have an heir, Grimsgard will go to somebody else, and I wouldn't wanna it hand down to just anybody, like maybe to one of them fellas we met at the ale stand. Nay, it's gotta be you. Just don't be in a hurry to replace me."

Sarah understood the wisdom of Roscoe's design, but she remained uncertain about the likelihood of its success.

"Do you think the earl would allow such a thing?"

The old Adventurer threw her a knowing look.

"I think Earl Ralf would agree to about anythin' if enough money was involved. We'll need to hire a man-of-law to get the words just right, then a scrivener to write it out on fine white parchment and fancy up the borders with all kinda flourishes and curlicues. Finally, we gotta get a notary to witness the signin' of the document and affix his seal. And when all is attended to in right legal and proper fashion, I'll lay it before Earl Ralf with a big bag of gold. Why would he say no?"

Thurmond felt like he had been hit in the head with a hammer.

"When I was growing up in my village, a priest would come to it two or three times a year, and they would always tell us the same thing, that we were supposed to be happy about being hungry and living in shit. They said that Allfather Charon put us where he wants us and that to want anything different was to defy his will. That's what they were always preaching."

Sarah snorted, amused.

"I guess you weren't paying much attention to the holy fathers' teachings then."

"Not much, I ran off as soon as I could."

"As did we all, Thurmond. None of us were satisfied with the lives handed to us."

"I know that, Sarah, but it's been hard. We've had to take terrible risks just to live our own lives in our own way. Runaway apprentices are whipped, branded, sometimes mutilated. I was just a young boy—I didn't even know a place to run to. I was just real lucky."

Roscoe grunted in agreement.

"None of the nobles want the commoners bustin' loose. That would be the end of all their special privileges, so it would."

"I should've remained a carpenter's apprentice just so Lord Beaufort could live in a castle? Is that what you're telling me?"

Roscoe smirked.

"Somethin' like that, laddie. We can't have you disturbin' the proper way of the world."

Both laughed, but there was a degree of bitterness beneath the humor. Finally, Thurmond spoke.

"I'm having a hard time believing all this is real. You're the son of a fruit monger—not a real noble. Maybe the earl was just making it all up."

That made Roscoe chuckle.

"All this stuff about knights and nobles—it's all just something they made up."

EPILOGUE

Contrary to Thurmond's fondest wishes, neither Bart nor his men were hung. After the incident in the Blind Pig, they were hauled before the local baron for judgment. The baron, a light-minded individual, took one look at Bart's white belt and decided in his favor. Why should he care what a fellow knight did to peasants?

Noble visitors were rare in these parts, and the baron was eager for worthy company. Bart was invited to his castle, where they feasted and hunted together in grand style. When the baron returned their horses, arms, and equipment, Bart and company rode north and therefore missed the great Battle of Gorgonholm.

Drax was not so fortunate. His fight with Thurmond left him with a fractured spine that deprived him the use of his legs. Lying in agony, he figured it would not be long before the Adventurers returned to finish him off. With a supreme effort he dragged himself from the bath house with his hands. He crossed a plowed field, and hid in a grove of trees.

In his pouch, he carried the final healing potion he had stolen from Sarah's pannier. If it could heal his broken back, he might still have a chance. Lady Fortune, however, was not smiling on Drax that day, for that potion was the one Malachai had identified as a deadly poison. Within moments of consuming it, he was seized by sharp, wrenching cramps, as if a ferret was clawing its way from his stomach. He died in writhing agony just before dawn.

Many villages and farmsteads were devastated during the dark period known as The Troubles, the time of the Black Stone's mephitic influence, but no group suffered such catastrophic losses as the Gray Friars. The monastic brothers were mostly annihilated. Many fell in the battle between the cellarer and the choir master, more were slain by the rabble that followed Lord Ubo.

The few Grays who had managed to run away and hide now came slinking back, hoping to rebuild their shattered monastery. Unfortunately, a new menace threatened their good intentions. Their powerful rival, the Blue Friars, always alert for opportunities to increase their wealth and influence, saw the weakness of the Grays and sought to claim the monastery with its lucrative grist mill for themselves.

Desperate, the Grays sent word of their plight to other Gray Friar monasteries, begging for reinforcement. They also began to recruit from among the many men left broken and wandering by the recent turmoil. Cob answered their call.

Roscoe was keen to have the Gascar archers remain at Grimsgard as his men-at-arms. Wat and Tuck were eager to do so, but Cob required a more spiritual environment. He found it at the monastery and insisted that his two companions join him there. Reluctantly, they tagged along.

The Grays were naturally eager to employ three stalwart archers to man their walls. In time, Cob realized that his true calling was among this clerical brotherhood. He took the required vows and donned the gray robe. Wat and Tuck remained as his side, but were never as driven by religious fervor and refused to take the cowl.

Fortunately, the dispute between the Blues and the Grays was settled without bloodshed when the earl declared that the latter would retain its property.

Sheriff Brandon survived the battle unscathed, though he did not kill seven Keltin chieftains nor eat seven eggs. He continued his efforts to re-establish order in the city of Gorgonholm. One of his early tasks was to rebuild his constabulary, many of whom had disappeared during the troubles or had been slain in the war. He was especially pleased to hire nine tough, weapon-trained men who had, until recently, served as Royal Road Guards.

The sheriff was, of course, legally obligated to arrest the Road Guards, who had, after all, deserted their posts. But he really needed men, so their transgressions were overlooked.

Pons and his followers were, in turn, delighted to swap the king's badge for a surcoat emblazoned with the arms of the city. There would be no more long, painful days on horseback or nights on the cold, wet ground. There would be good food, strong drink, and the company of willing ladies.

Most importantly, there would be abundant opportunity to extort gold from vulnerable citizens.

The corner boy Cheese escaped the great deluge in the Catacombs that swept so many Shamblers to their deaths. He and his crew, at the moment of the flood, had been on the surface, seeking a hidden passage by which he might descend behind the ranks of the Small Folk. This tactic, the sudden attack from behind, had served him well in his previous battle between Greens and Blues. Indeed, it became his preferred method throughout his criminal career. Gaining a reputation as a deft murderer, he was initiated into the Brethren, who needed to restore a membership depleted by wartime losses. He rose rapidly through the ranks, becoming in short order one of their most dreaded assassins. His lustrous career was brought to an abrupt halt by someone even more vicious and conniving than himself.

Some of the Small Folk survived the flood as well. A few made their way to the surface, where they were chased down and killed by the citizenry. A larger group took shelter in an isolated air pocket and somehow escaped the cascading water. Lost and confused, they wandered deeper and deeper into the Catacombs' inky depths, where they eventually established their own tiny kingdom. Creeping forth under cover of night, they stole food, tools, and needed supplies from the houses far above. They also abducted women to serve as their wives.

The Small Folk quickly adapted to life in their subterranean world, consuming mushrooms, molds, tiny white lizards, and blind fish, so that after a while, they no longer required the resources of the *erldogh-dbruh-aldkor*, the giant-devil-freaks, and stopped coming to the surface altogether. Their eyes grew dim, and their skin became almost translucent. They stopped wearing clothes, and, after many generations, lost the use of tools. Some took to the many underground lakes and rivers and became fish-like in shape and appearence.

Zeb the Prophet and his followers were slaughtered when the Small Folk stormed into their subterraean hideout. Unarmed and panic-stricken, the starving Shamblers could do nothing but huddle together and die. Those few surviving the poisoned arrows and flint knives were carried into oblivion by the great flood of water that came surging down from the streets above.

The woman called Ellen and her two children were the only survivors of the horrendous onslaught. Having climbed on a rocky shelf above the eye-level of the little men, they remained unseen while their comrades were butchered. They were also slightly above the water level of the flood.

Her health shattered by both starvation and shock, poor Ellen did not live long after her ordeal. Her children, however, displaying the resiliance of youth, survived. Thoroughly inculcated with Zeb's teachings, they returned to the surface where they proclaimed his beliefs to whomever would listen.

Zeb's philosophies proved remarkably popular with the city's poor, and siblings soon found themselves the leaders of a devoted following. The older of the two, a boy named Glitch, succumbed within the year, following a dinner of rancid eels. His sister Warla continued to lead an ever increasing group of true believers until she was arrested by the church, convicted of heresy, and hanged on the gallows at City Keep.

Fergis mac Brude, High King of the Keltins, made good on his resolution to do away with his brother Oengus, and lucky for him he did, for Oengus had a plot of his own. Fergis beat him to it by only one day.

Following the defeat of the Keltin host, Fergis's tenure as Ard Righ had become extremely tenuous. The clans had suffered terrible losses, and the lesser kings were looking for someone to blame. It was not difficult for Oengus to draw several of them into a compact to remove his troublesome younger brother and appoint himself High King. Hamish Wolf-Eye, the notoriously treacherous chief of the Quiet Belly clan, had been especially willing.

Hamish had a shaman with unparalleled skill in bone magic. He could blast someone's luck by playing a flute made from the shin bone of a twelve-year-old virgin. He could render a warrior invulnerable to injury by beating him senseless with the rib bone of a gigantic cave bear. Most dramatically, he could send inevitable and irreversible death by merely pointing at his victim with a long, narrow bone, the exact origin of which was a closely guarded secret.

Fergis, of course, had his own personal shamans. Those who had predicted a great victory over the laigi were sewn into the skins of cows and flung into a lake. The more reliable ones were allowed to live. These now informed him of his brother's plot, though their information came mostly from human rather than occult sources.

The Ard Righ wasted no time. Hamish Wolf-Eye was slain by Fergis's spearmen early in the morning as he squatted in a privy. Oengus was caught asleep and dragged from his bed. Forced to kneel before his brother, he refused to beg for his life. This suited Fergis, who had him beheaded on the spot.

The deaths of these enemies did not, however, solve Fergis's problems.

Many clan chiefs remained hostile. More pressing, Oengus's bone-shooter was still at large, eager to avenge the murder of his clan chief.

Malachai fully intended to wreak vengeance on the hapless Adventurers for the burning of his workshop, but he became so involved with the enjoyment of his newly enhanced powers that it kept slipping his mind. Even the best among us, alas, can be given to procrastination.

With the power of the Black Stone checked, Asmodeus was once again able to devote himself to his favorite pastime—enjoying himself. He decided on a whole new wardrobe, so skeletal fingers were kept busy measuring, cutting, and sewing. His demonic minions were sent to scour ethereal worlds for new and exotic shades of purple. He also spent time wandering in his garden, exploring the subtle flavors of the fruits and pungent fragrances of the flowers.

One of his chief pleasures was spending time with his new pet. The troll hand proved to be quite affectionate, rubbing against his legs as they strolled among the flowers, climbing into his lap for a cuddle. At other times it could be quite a rascal, climbing the curtains and jumping out to grab the bony ankles of the servants. It spent its days romping about the mansion and its nights curled upon a velvet cushion.

ACKNOWLEDGMENTS

I am profoundly grateful to the people who helped me during the writing of this story. Thank you, Crissy, for forty-seven years of love and support, and also for your vigilant proofreading. Thank you, Dr. Kate MacKenzie, my incredible daughter, for your proofreading, and thank you Andrew MacKenzie, my sword-fightin' son, for your thoughts and suggestions. Thank you, Loren Preuss for your proofreading and good ideas—I expanded the Blue Horse chapters at your suggestion. And thank you, Mad River Boys, for many years of rollicking good fun. Mad River, Forever!

Coming Soon!

Isle of Tangled Dreams

Robert John MacKenzie

from Chapter 12: In the Hands of the White Inquisition

The cage floor was painful, and the snoring of his elderly cellmates was annoying, but Thurmond finally managed to fall asleep. So deep was his slumber that he was not awakened by the *clop* of horses' hooves on the cobblestones, nor the jangle of the heavy keys, nor even the loud screeching of the cage door's rusty hinges.

He did not wake up until roused by angry shouts in some incomprehensible tongue. Then someone seized his arm and pulled him to his feet. It was Zadar.

"Better get up, guy. You don't want to make these fellows mad."

Five soldiers in leather armor stood at the cage door, all bearing the flaming mace badge of the powerful Bishop of Toldo. Behind them a tonsured cleric sat on a palfrey. His white surcoat, worn over a long-sleeved mail hauberk, carried the arms of the White Inquisition. His sharp nose reminded Thurmond of a raptor's beak.

The only light came from a torch stuck into a sconce on a nearby wall. Two of the soldiers drew their swords and stood by as the others pulled the prisoners from the cage one by one and fixed them to a very long chain.

When Zadar's turn came, Thurmond tried to follow close behind him so that they would be together on the chain, but a tiny white-haired woman wanted to be next. She jumped forward, and squeezed into the doorway with him.

When Thurmond refused to give way, she lashed out with her boney elbow, striking him in the ribs and stomach. Then, in a display of remarkable strength for one so small and frail, she wedged herself against the doorframe and pushed him back into the cage.

Thus it was that Zadar became the sixth prisoner on the chain, the old woman the seventh, and Thurmond the eighth. A heavy iron collar was closed around each of their necks and secured by a heavy barrel-shaped lock.

With all the prisoners locked together, the soldier-guards sheathed their swords, mounted horses, and produced heavy, braided knouts. The mere sight of these fearsome implements was enough to inspire instant obedience from even the most demented of the prisoners. The cleric gave a nod, and the procession set off down the street.

They had taken his gold, belt, pouch, and dagger while he was unconscious, but they had at least left him his boots, so Thurmond had no problem walking as he made his way through the darkened city. That was also true for Zadar.

Most of the oldsters were barefoot. Many were stooped with age or suffered from twisted limbs and enflamed joints. Encouraged by the knouts, they staggered along as best they were able, but they could manage no better pace than a lurching shuffle.

They eventually arrived at a pair of iron-bound city gates, which were opened with alacrity when the sharp-featured cleric made a gesture to the sentries who manned them. So far, the man had not deigned to utter a single word.

The procession passed through the gates and emerged into open countryside. Thurmond was not particularly skilled at reading the stars, but he thought they were heading south. This would be correct if they were, in fact, as Zadar had suggested, bound for Cadz, which lay in that direction.

He did not know the distance to Cadz, but it was certainly not close by. Many days walk for sure, especially at this dragging pace. The young man suddenly realized that he was chained to a line of the walking dead. Few if any of the old, sick, and crippled men and women would survive the trek.

He started to call out to his new companion.

"Hey, Zadar, how far…"

He never finished the sentence. The guard riding just behind him struck him across the shoulders with his knout.

"*Sin hablar!*"

Thurmond might not speak the language, but he understood those words with perfect clarity. He trudged along in silence, his back feeling as if it had been set on fire. He hated the knout-wielder intensely. His soul screamed to pull him from the saddle and strangle him with a section of chain.

The white-haired crone chained between Thurmond and Zadar continued to give trouble. She deliberately kicked up dust that blew back into the young Adventurer's face. For no apparent reason, she would give the chain a hard yank, hurting his neck and causing him to stumble forward. He decided to name her Ogiera after a mean-spirited crone in his home village who had been the bane of his childhood.

The sun rose in the eastern sky, and the day began to grow warm. As hours wore on, warm gave way to hot. The prisoners were without water, and their pace slowed to a crawl as their bodies dried out. The guards all carried water bags on their saddles, but they would not have dreamed of sharing with a pack of miserable heretics.

They passed through numerous roadside villages, for this section of Piquara was densely populated. None of the villagers—neither the washerwomen, nor the plowmen, nor the goatherders—would even glance in their direction. The mere sight of condemned heretics was bad luck.

Just before noon, they arrived at a roadside tavern where the prisoners were finally permitted to stop and rest. The cleric disappeared into the building's interior while the five guards sprawled beneath a thatched awning. Serving girls brought them platters of meat, loaves of bread, and pitchers of beer.

Two men came from the stables dragging a large wooden tub of water. They set it down some distance from the prisoners and departed at once. Every aged, rheumy eye was on the tub, but none dared to rise and move to it until a guard motioned toward it with his knout. The bent-backed oldsters then surged toward the water with a vigor that would have seemed inconceivable only minutes before.

The first to reach it simply stuck their faces in the water and began to slurp. They were nearly drowned when the others, throwing themselves of top of them, pushed their heads under. Thurmond and Zadar were unwilling to join this melee. When they were finally able to slake their thirst, there was only a greasy residue left in the bottom of the tub. They drank it anyway.

They waited several hours at the tavern while the guards relaxed in the shade of the awning. There was no shade for the prisoners. They dozed as best they could in the ever-increasing heat of the afternoon. When the cleric finally emerged from the tavern, his men immediately jumped to their feet and brandished their knouts. That was all it took to get the prisoners on their feet and moving.

Late that afternoon, the first prisoner died. An old man fell and did not get up, did not flinch when struck repeatedly with the knout. The guard did not check to see if he breathed or if his heart still beat. He simply drew a key from a cord around his neck, unlocked the iron collar, and signaled for the march to proceed. The withered body was left beside the road.

They walked until sunset. The cleric turned his horse from the road, dismounted, and watched without speaking as the guards prepared a crude camp. The horses were unsaddled and picketed, and a fire was kindled. A small kettle was unpacked, and a stew set to boil. The prisoners were thrown some scraps of stale bread.

Piquara was an arid, rocky land. The summer days were hot, but the nights could grow cold. In their thin clothes, without cloaks or blankets, the prisoners could only huddle together to keep warm. Thus, Thurmond, Zadar, and the white-haired hag snuggled up against the chill night air. Her body reeked of insanity and was crawling with lice.

The two young men could at least converse in careful whispers.

"Zadar, tell me more about this great burning we're headed for. What is it?"

"They're called *Rituales Doloroso*. It means Rituals of Pain, or something like that. All the cities take turns hosting them. The White Brothers gather up as many heretics as they can, maybe a couple hundred, and make a big show of burning them to appease God."

Thurmond was aghast.

"And people come to watch this?"

"They're amazing spectacles, guy. Thousands of people come from all over. It's like a great festival with acrobats and fire jugglers and merchants selling goods from faraway lands. On the last day, there's a grand procession with all the clerics in their white robes. Then the heretics are driven through in chains so the crowd can spit and throw things."

The young Adventurer did not like hearing any of this.

"Sounds like you've been to one of these shows."

"Certes, when I was a little boy. My father brought me down here to visit family."

"And you liked what you saw?"

"I loved it! Guy, it was like nothing I'd ever seen, with big bright banners everywhere. There was bear-baiting, and I saw a stilt-walker that must have been ten feet tall."

"Did you watch the actual burning?"

"Aye, my father lifted me up on his shoulders so I wouldn't miss anything."

Thurmond was beginning to have doubts about his new companion.

"Did you enjoy it?"

Catching Thurmond's tone, Zadar grew defensive.

"Hey, I was just a little kid. I just took things like I saw everyone else taking 'em. They were all having fun, so I didn't question it. Everybody loved the *Rituale*."

"Where we come from, back in Poitiers, the people would rise up and put a stop to such goings on."

"Maybe so, but the folks down here are different. They have real faith, and they trust the church to know what's best for 'em. They call Archbishop Odius—he's the Inquisitor General—the Light of Truth and the Hammer of Sin."

"So, how do you feel about these things now that you're the one destined for burning? Do you really think the Inquisitor General knows what's best for people? How about that hawk-faced cleric who's leading this party—does he care what's best for you and me?"

Zadar sighed.

"I'm not a violent man, Thurmond. But you are, and I'd sincerely love to see you stick a dagger between two of his ribs. That's what I think, guy."

www.ingramcontent.com/pod-product-compliance
Lightning Source LLC
Chambersburg PA
CBHW020229110726
47898CB00004B/1205